PRAISE FOR AMY ROSE BENNETT'S DISREPUTABLE DEBUTANTES SERIES

"Amy Rose Bennett's *How to Catch a Wicked Viscount* is a delightful Regency romance infused with heat, energy, and glamour. Bennett effortlessly captures the ingredients that make Regency romance so compelling to readers: sparkling dialogue, passion, and the elegant ballroom manners that mask the danger and risks that lie just beneath the surface."
    —*New York Times* bestselling author Amanda Quick

"A sweet and spicy read, full of sly wit and rich with delicious details that pull the reader into the scene. A delightful confection of ballroom banter and bedroom seduction."
    —*USA Today* bestseller Sally MacKenzie

"Amy Rose Bennett is a fresh new voice in historical romance with a flair for historical atmosphere. In *How to Catch a Wicked Viscount* she introduces us to a set of lively characters embarking on a fun, lighthearted, tried-and-true reader-favorite romp."
    —Anne Gracie

"Sexy, sweet, romantic, and funny, *How to Catch a Wicked Viscount* will steal your heart away. Amy Rose Bennett is a charming new voice in historical romance."
    —Anna Campbell

"The first book in Bennett's new Disreputable Debutantes series sets up and delivers on an appealing premise: clever Regency heroines willing to sacrifice their reputations for disreputable love matches."
    —*Kirkus Reviews*

Titles by Amy Rose Bennett

HOW TO CATCH A WICKED VISCOUNT
HOW TO CATCH AN ERRANT EARL

How
to Catch
an
Errant Earl

Amy Rose Bennett

JOVE
New York

A JOVE BOOK
Published by Berkley
An imprint of Penguin Random House LLC
penguinrandomhouse.com

Copyright © 2020 by Amy Rose Bennett
Excerpt from *How to Catch a Sinful Marquess* © 2020 by Amy Rose Bennett
Penguin Random House supports copyright. Copyright fuels creativity, encourages
diverse voices, promotes free speech, and creates a vibrant culture. Thank you for buying
an authorized edition of this book and for complying with copyright laws by not
reproducing, scanning, or distributing any part of it in any form without permission.
You are supporting writers and allowing Penguin Random House to continue to
publish books for every reader.

A JOVE BOOK, BERKLEY, and the BERKLEY & B colophon
are registered trademarks of Penguin Random House LLC.

ISBN: 9781984803948

First Edition: April 2020

Printed in the United States of America
1   3   5   7   9   10   8   6   4   2

Cover art by Aleta Rafton
Cover design by Judith Lagerman
Book design by George Towne

To my darling Richard,
your support means the world to me.
I love you, always.

ACKNOWLEDGMENTS

To my amazing editor, Kristine Swartz, thank you so very much for helping me to make this book of my heart the best it could be! Your insight is invaluable. Many thanks must also go to the talented team at Berkley Romance for all your hard work. It's truly appreciated.

As always, I must extend a huge thank-you to Jessica Alvarez, my fabulous agent. I am so deeply grateful for your sage advice and support.

To Sue, Phil, Ben, and Danny, this book—indeed, this entire series—would not have come about if it weren't for you. I'll never forget our trip to Switzerland and the wonderful hospitality you extended to our family. We can't wait to visit again.

To Cindy and Leigh, likewise! Thanks for the fabulous digs in London and for putting up with my incessant book talk!

And of course, I want to thank my husband for all the big and little things you do every single day. From bringing me coffee to whisking me away for much-needed breaks, I'm truly spoiled and blessed. And to Caitlin and Claire, thank you for your understanding, patience, and love when I'm in "the zone." And for all the hugs and giggles, too. I love you both to the moon and back.

CHAPTER 1

It's oft quoted "charity begins at home." But any well-bred lady or gentleman with a truly benevolent disposition must devote some time and energy to worthy causes, especially those philanthropic endeavors which better the lot of the deserving poor.

This Season, do consider attending a ball, public assembly, or perhaps even a *musicale* in aid of charity. Visit our Society Advertisements section to find a comprehensive list of upcoming events.

The Beau Monde Mirror: The Society Page

Gunter's Tea Shop, Berkeley Square, Mayfair, London

April 2, 1818

Thank goodness it is raining.

At least that's what Miss Arabella Jardine told herself as she stepped over the puddles beneath the portico of Gunter's and caught the attention of a jarvey on the other side of Berkeley Square. As the hackney coach splashed its way toward the tea shop, she could pretend she was only dashing away raindrops, not tears, from beneath her spectacles as she turned back to face her three dearest friends in the entire world. Friends she'd bonded with three years ago at Mrs. Rathbone's Academy for Young Ladies of Good

Character before they were all unceremoniously expelled amid a cloud of scandal for "conduct unbecoming."

Friends she'd only just been reunited with at Gunter's. As they'd taken tea and indulged in all manner of gastronomic delights, they also shared their hopes and dreams. Made plans for the future. Just as they'd done at Mrs. Rathbone's when they formed the Society for Enlightened Young Women. But now, due to circumstances beyond her control, Arabella was obliged to farewell her friends yet again.

Blast her family and their inconvenient plans to embark on a frivolous Grand Tour. Arabella endeavored to suppress a scowl as she fiddled with the buttons on her fawn kid gloves. She wanted to stay here in London with Charlie, Sophie, and dear Olivia. Being dragged across Europe to gawk at endless musty cathedrals and crumbling castle ruins was surely a waste of time and money. Money she could put to good use elsewhere given half the chance . . .

Lady Charlotte Hastings—or Charlie to her friends—pulled Arabella away from her disgruntled thoughts by enveloping her in a warm hug. "My darling Arabella, you must hold to your promise to write to us while you are gadding about the Continent." Charlie's unruly auburn curls tickled Arabella's cheek. "I don't care where you are—even if you're atop Mont Blanc or exploring the depths of the Black Forest—I will pay for the postage."

"Aye, as long as you all write back to me too." Arabella adjusted the shoulder strap of her leather satchel as Charlie released her. The hack had drawn up beside them. "I want to hear all about how your husband hunting goes this Season." Her gaze met each of her friends in turn. "Each and every one of you."

"Of course," said Sophie with a shy smile. A bright blush suffused her cheeks, and Arabella rather suspected she was thinking about Charlie's very dashing, very eligible brother, Nathaniel, Lord Malverne. He'd joined them at Gunter's for a little while, and Arabella was certain she'd detected a spark of interest in the wicked viscount's eyes as he'd conversed with Sophie. Even though Sophie's reputation was tarnished by the academy scandal—and her family was most decidedly "lower gentry"—why wouldn't he be interested? Shy yet sweet Sophie, with her glossy black hair and enormous blue eyes, was breathtakingly beautiful. Indeed, all Arabella's friends were fair of face and disposition, and accomplished in all the ways that mattered in the eyes of society.

Unlike herself. Arabella swallowed a sigh. Not only was she a Scottish orphan with dubious parentage and "unnatural bluestocking tendencies"—at least according to her aunt Flora—she possessed a gap-toothed smile and was so long-sighted, she had to wear glasses most of the time. Even if she did make a debut this Season alongside her friends, she was certain she'd never receive anything more than a passing glance from most gentlemen of the ton. It was a good thing she had other plans for her future. *Secret plans.* As soon as she bid her friends goodbye, she was going to put them in motion this afternoon. All going well.

Her resolve to succeed in her mission reaffirmed, Arabella pushed her spectacles firmly back into place upon the bridge of her nose; Charlie's exuberant hug had dislodged them a little. "Are you ready to leave, too, Olivia?" The jarvey was scowling at them from beneath the hood of his dripping oilskin. They really should go.

Olivia sighed heavily. "Y-y-yes," she replied, gathering up the skirts of her fashionable gown and matching pelisse so the fine fabric wouldn't trail through the muddy puddle directly in front of her. Her mouth twisted—Olivia's stammer always got worse when she was anxious—before her next words emerged in a bumpy rush. "As m-much as I hate to bid you all adieu as well, I m-must. Aunt Edith will undoubtedly be w-watching the clock."

Final hugs were exchanged, and once Arabella and Olivia were safely installed in the damp and dim interior of the hackney, it pulled away, barreling across the sodden square.

Olivia de Vere currently resided in a rented Grosvenor Square town house with her horribly strict guardians. Even though her home was only a relatively short distance from Berkeley Square, Arabella had made arrangements to share a hack with her friend not only to avoid a soaking in the rain but also to help Olivia escape her gilded cage for the outing to Gunter's.

A wee bit of subterfuge had been involved; Olivia's termagant of an aunt believed Arabella's aunt Flora had accompanied them on their excursion—which wasn't the case at all. Even though Gunter's was a respectable establishment, there would be hell to pay if Olivia's aunt learned her niece had visited the tea shop without a suitable chaperone.

"I really w-won't see you again before you depart for the Continent, will I?" The expression in Olivia's dark brown eyes was so forlorn, Arabella's heart cramped with sadness. She suspected Olivia was often as lonely as she was.

"I'm afraid not," she replied softly. "Bertie, my cousin's husband, has booked us all on the Dover packet, and we're due to set sail for France in three days' time."

Olivia's mouth twitched with a smile. "I'm rather tempted to stow myself away in your trunk. I won't take up much room."

Arabella laughed, pleased to see her friend's spirits returning. "Believe me, I would take you if I could. Aunt Flora and my cousin Lilias are sure to be exacting in the extreme during the journey. Your company would be most welcome."

Olivia reached out and squeezed her hand. Despite the sheeting rain and the traffic snarls, they were fast approaching Grosvenor Square. "I have a feeling you are going to have a m-marvelous time, despite your misgivings. And who knows, perhaps you might meet a charming Italian prince or handsome Swiss nobleman who'll sweep you off your feet." Olivia's eyes glowed. "Just imagine it."

Arabella very much doubted that would be the case. And unlike Olivia, Charlie, and Sophie, she didn't possess a romantic bone in her body; love matches weren't for plain, practical women like her. However, she dredged up a smile in an effort to appear lighthearted. "Well, unless his name is on the list of eligible gentlemen we just devised at Gunter's, I don't see how I can seriously consider his suit." She lowered her voice even though no one else was in earshot and rain was drumming on the roof of the hackney. "I mean, with no one of our acquaintance to vouch for him, what if he's really a dastardly rogue with a skeleton or two in the closet—literally—like a murdered first wife? Or as Charlie mentioned earlier today, what if he's afflicted with the pox?"

Olivia giggled and gave a theatrical shudder. "Perish the thought."

"At least your broodingly handsome neighbor, Lord Sleat, is on the list." Charlie had mentioned the Scottish marquess was a friend of her brother's and a highly suitable candidate for a husband. Even though he'd been terribly wounded at Waterloo and now sported an eye patch, apparently he was quite the gentleman beneath his rugged exterior. And *very* popular with the ladies of the ton.

"Yes." Olivia sighed and tucked a lock of dark brown hair back into the confines of her fine straw bonnet. The hackney coach had stopped before her town house, and she threw a wistful glance at the adjacent residence with its ornate pillars and shiny black double doors. "But I don't see how I shall ever cross paths with him. He very much keeps to himself." Her mouth curved into a wry smile. "I think I shall secretly dub him the mysterious marquess."

The front door to her own house cracked open, and Olivia grimaced. Gathering up her reticule, she hugged Arabella one last time. "Take care, my lovely friend. I must go before my aunt sends one of her horrid footmen out to haul me inside. Have a wonderful trip."

After waving Olivia off and issuing new instructions to the taciturn jarvey, Arabella hastily closed the hack's door against a sudden squall of icy rain that snatched at her sage green skirts and her leghorn bonnet. Settling into the battered leather seat once more, she removed her glasses to wipe off the rain spots with a lawn handkerchief, then checked her hem and brown kid boots for splashes of mud. For the most part, she wasn't fussy about her appearance, but she wanted to make a good impression at her next appointment. The matron at London's Foundling Hospital was expecting her . . . and Dr. Graham Radcliff.

She hadn't added the physician's name to the Society for

Enlightened Young Women's list of eligible gentlemen. Her association with this particular man was her very own closely guarded secret, one she didn't feel ready to share with her friends quite yet.

Arabella's stomach tumbled oddly, and she frowned at her reflection in the hack's rain-lashed window. She was nervous, and she did not want to be. Was the rising feeling of anticipation and trepidation in her heart related to the fact that she was about to tour an establishment sure to bring back certain memories she'd rather not revisit? Or was it because she was going to meet the clever and engaging Dr. Radcliff once again? He'd suggested her visit coincide with the meeting of the hospital's board today. As well as providing medical expertise to the institution, the physician was one of its directors.

She fiddled with the worn pewter buckle of her grandfather's old leather satchel. The good doctor's letter of introduction to the Foundling Hospital's matron, Helen Reid, lay safely within. It had been just over a year since she last encountered the gentleman—a former medical colleague of her dearly departed grandfather, Dr. Iain Burnett. Arabella sometimes suspected her grandfather had been not so subtly trying to play matchmaker when he first introduced her to the widowed physician at a charity *musicale* in London in aid of the Foundling Hospital.

A smile trembled about Arabella's lips at the bittersweet memory. That had been in the autumn before her grandfather passed away. And a year and a half after the academy scandal erupted and Arabella's name had become mud in polite society—both in London and Edinburgh, where she now lived with Aunt Flora, Lilias, and her husband Albert Arbuthnott. There was one unpalatable truth Arabella had already learned in life: the stain of scandal was not easily removed, tending to cling to one's person wherever one went.

If tonnish society—here or in Edinburgh—ever learned of the real scandal attached to her past, she'd surely be banished forevermore.

At least Dr. Radcliff didn't know anything about *that*. What he did know of her—that she was a bluestocking who'd rather attend a public lecture on vaccination than an assembly or ton ball—hadn't shocked him in the slightest. Indeed, on the two occasions they'd met, Dr. Radcliff always treated her with the utmost respect. And over the past year, they'd corresponded regularly about all manner of medical and social welfare topics—from the latest recommendations in treating infant colic, to the pressing need to expand access to free medical dispensaries for the poor, to the case for improving nutrition for the inmates of charity poorhouses.

It seemed Dr. Radcliff truly understood her desire to advocate for public health programs, just as her grandfather had done. In her opinion, improving the well-being of infants and children in institutionalized care was of paramount importance. Hence her visit to the Foundling Hospital. She wanted to learn as much as she could about the famous institution's practices, because one day—if she ever had the means and social connections—she dreamed of opening a similar hospital or orphanage in Edinburgh.

An impossible dream perhaps, but Arabella was committed to making it a reality. One thing she didn't lack was determination.

The Foundling Hospital, Guilford Street, Bloomsbury, London

"I'm afraid the matron cannot see you this afternoon, Miss . . ." The plump, middle-aged housekeeper of the Foundling Hospital squinted down at Dr. Radcliff's letter. The hospital's entry hall was not only chilly and damp but also poorly lit, and it took her a moment to find Arabella's name again. "Miss Jardine, is it?"

"Aye, that's right." Beneath her disheveled blond curls, Arabella's forehead knit into a frown. This wouldn't do at all. Out of the corner of her eye, she noticed the hall porter reaching for the handle of the front door. A large-boned, heavily browed man, he looked as though he wouldn't hesitate to eject her at a moment's notice. Turning her attention back to the housekeeper, Arabella decided to argue her case. "But I have an appointment. Dr. Radcliff arranged it. He's on the hospital board, I believe."

The woman sniffed haughtily as her gaze flicked over Arabella. She clearly wasn't impressed by Arabella's person. Given her plain attire and the fact she was unchaperoned, it was obvious she wasn't well connected or from a family of means. It didn't appear to matter that she knew the physician either. "Yes, I know Dr. Radcliff," she said, handing back the letter. "Fine gentleman he is. And ordinarily Matron would be happy to show you about. But not today. Perhaps you could come back next week when we run our public tour."

A knot of frustration tightened inside Arabella's chest. "Unfortunately that won't suit as I'm leaving town the day after tomorrow for an extended period of time. Is there anyone else who might be amenable to showing me around? One of the other staff members perhaps? A nurse or teacher? Dr. Radcliff mentioned he would be attending a board meeting this afternoon. Is there somewhere I could wait for him?" It suddenly occurred to her that she was more disappointed about the prospect of not seeing Dr. Radcliff than missing out on a guided tour. And she hadn't expected that.

The housekeeper sighed heavily, her ample bosom straining the seams of her plain black gown and white cotton pinafore. "I really don't think so, Miss Jardine," she said in a clipped tone. "Besides, I'm sure the good doctor has better things to do with his time. Just like our matron. With a number of children falling ill overnight—" The woman clamped her lips together as if she'd said the wrong thing. "Everyone is just too busy."

Alarm spiked through Arabella. "Oh, dear. I hope whatever it is, isn't too serious." No wonder the matron was busy. Illness could spread like wildfire through a place like this, with devastating consequences. She'd once witnessed a measles outbreak in Edinburgh's North Bridge Orphan Hospital, an institution she'd visited with her grandfather on many occasions. "Is there anything I can do to help? I've a good deal of nursing experience myself."

The housekeeper arched a thin eyebrow, clearly unconvinced by Arabella's claim. "I don't think so. Matron has everything well in hand, miss." Her gaze skipped to the porter's, and Arabella felt a cold draft wash over her back and eddy about her ankles as he opened the door.

Taking a step closer to the housekeeper, Arabella slipped her hand through the slit in her gown's woolen skirts and pulled her coin purse from her pocket. The woman's eyes gleamed when she heard the coins chink together. "Miss . . ."

"Mrs. Bradley."

"Mrs. Bradley." Arabella opened her purse and removed one of her precious sovereigns. She'd intended to purchase a few bits and pieces on Bond Street before she returned to the Arbuthnotts' rented town house on Half Moon Street. But she was willing to make a small sacrifice if it meant she could stay. "Would it help if I offered you a wee donation as a token of my appreciation for your trouble?" she said in a low voice. "If you could spare a little time to take me through the girls' wing. And then as I suggested, I could wait somewhere for Dr. Radcliff. I hear there's a picture gallery . . ."

Mrs. Bradley snatched up the proffered coin and tucked it into the pocket of her pinafore faster than an alley cat pouncing on a rat. She gestured at the porter to shut the door. "Very well, Miss Jardine." Turning on her heel, she strode across the hall toward another door. "Follow me."

As soon as Arabella entered the girls' dormitory in the hospital's east wing, with its endless rows of narrow beds covered in stiff white sheets and rough, dun woolen blankets, an icy shiver skated down her spine and her stomach clenched. Her breath caught and her pulse fluttered wildly like a trapped moth beneath her skin. She had to curl her gloved hands into fists to hide her trembling fingers.

It was always the way. It didn't matter that she'd visited similar places countless times with her grandfather. No amount of rational thought could overcome her body's visceral response, the immediate instinct to turn and run, run, run out the door and back into the street into the fresh air and light.

Perhaps it was the absence of curtains at the high, barred windows, or the echo of footsteps on cold, bare floorboards that caused such a reaction. Then again, it could have been the sharp scent of laundry starch and lye soap that transported her back to another time and place. Another orphanage she'd rather not remember with its mean-spirited nurses and their harsh orders. Their hard eyes and even harder hands that pushed and slapped and pinched.

But it was those very memories that drove her ambition. Her desire to make things better for other abandoned or orphaned children. Fifteen years may have passed since she was last an inmate of Glasgow's Great Clyde Hospital and Poorhouse, but she would never, ever forget how it felt to be a small, desperate child rendered mute with crushing fear and despair. The terrible, smothering sense of being completely alone and unloved.

Unwanted.

If Mrs. Bradley noticed Arabella's odd demeanor, she didn't remark upon it. She simply delivered what appeared to be a well-practiced speech about the children's routine: when they rose and when they slept, how a cleanliness inspection was always conducted after morning prayers, the nature of the children's personal chores and domestic "employments" based upon age, and the amount of time allocated to academic studies such as arithmetic and literacy lessons.

All the while, Arabella strove to listen and make mental notes of details such as how many children were accommodated within the hospital, the budget allocated for uniforms, and the number of teaching and nursing staff employed by the board. This was what she needed to know in order to begin making her own plans to establish a foundling home and orphanage.

But right now, she couldn't seem to focus, even when she endeavored to jot down pertinent information in a notebook she retrieved from her satchel. It seemed she would have to come back another time to gain a better understanding of the running costs that would be involved.

Unless Dr. Radcliff would be willing to share such details. He was on the board after all. But that would require Arabella to summon the courage to tell him about her ambitious plans. And she didn't know him well enough for that. Well, not yet . . .

By the time Mrs. Bradley had shown Arabella through the refectory, one of the classrooms, and the laundry, she was feeling almost like herself again. Seeing the children—who all appeared to be sufficiently nourished and adequately clothed in gowns of brown serge, crisp white pinafores, and matching bonnets—had helped to reassure her that the Foundling Hospital took better care of its inmates than the Great Clyde Hospital had. Some of the younger girls had even traded shy smiles with her.

Mrs. Bradley gave the hospital's sick ward a wide berth—as was to be expected given an outbreak of illness—so the last port of call was the kitchen.

The familiar smells of boiled beef and baking bread hit Arabella as soon as she and Mrs. Bradley crossed the threshold into a cavernous room. Like the laundry, the kitchen was abuzz with activity. Older girls who appeared to be aged between nine and perhaps fourteen diligently peeled and chopped potatoes, kneaded bread, or stood by the fireside tending to whatever bubbled in the enormous cast-iron pots. Arabella also spied a much younger child who couldn't have been more than five huddled on a low stool by the fireside, half-heartedly working a small pair of bellows—a totally unnecessary activity in Arabella's opinion, considering the fire was already burning brightly.

Indeed, the kitchen was a good deal warmer than any of the other rooms she'd visited so far. Condensation clung to the windows, and it wasn't long before Arabella felt sweat prickling down her back and along her hairline.

The fearsome cook—Mrs. Humbert—was a stout, florid-faced woman with work-roughened hands, a caustic tone, and a scalding glare. When her gaze scoured Arabella, she tried not to flinch. She'd just mustered the courage to ask Mrs. Humbert if the children were ever provided with any other type of vegetable besides potatoes, when all hell broke loose.

The young girl by the fire tumbled off her stool onto the flagged hearth, her body jerking oddly. The other girls who stood nearby screamed and jumped back. Ladles and spoons went flying, and a pot of rice pudding overturned.

"What the 'ell is goin' on?" screeched Mrs. Humbert, advancing toward the commotion.

"Sally's choking." A tall redheaded girl pointed at the little one on the floor. "She must've nicked a piece of carrot out of the boiled beef pot again."

"Li'l toad. Serves 'er right." Mrs. Humbert elbowed several gawking girls out of the way. "After I've finished fumping 'er on the back, I'll box 'er ears."

Arabella rushed to the fireside too; the little girl's eyes had rolled back in her head, and her mouth had twisted. Her body was rigid and her muscles twitched.

"She's not choking. And you'll do no such thing, Mrs. Humbert." Arabella dropped to her knees beside the child and glared back at the fuming cook. "She's having a seizure."

Planting her fisted hands on her ample hips, Mrs. Humbert towered over Arabella. "An' 'ow would you know, Miss 'igh-and-Mighty?" she demanded.

Arabella narrowed her gaze as she tugged off her gloves. "I know." Ignoring the cook's thunderous scowl and Mrs. Bradley's protests, she turned the girl, Sally, gently onto her side and placed a hand on her forehead. The child's skin was burning hot and her cheeks were bright red, but Arabella didn't think the heat of the fire was to blame. "Does Sally have a history of epilepsy?" The cook and housekeeper stared at her blankly. "You know, the falling sickness?"

"'Ow would I know?" huffed Mrs. Humbert.

Mrs. Bradley shook her head. "Not that I know of, Miss Jardine."

"She has a fever. A high one. It can trigger fits in babies and young children." Arabella began loosening the child's pinafore and gown. "We need to cool her down. Can someone please fetch a cloth soaked in cold water? The seizure will soon pass."

Sure enough, within a minute, Sally regained consciousness. She moaned and blinked a few times before tears welled in her large, pansy brown eyes. Eyes that seemed too large for her small, flushed face. "My head hurts," she whispered.

"You had a wee fall," said Arabella gently, stroking her hot cheek. "Do you think you can sit?"

Sally nodded and Arabella helped her up. The child whimpered and buried her face in Arabella's shoulder. "She needs to be taken to the sick ward and assessed by a doctor."

Mrs. Bradley nodded. There seemed to be a newfound respect in her eyes. "Of course. We have an infirmary. Up you get, Sally."

But little Sally was still shaking and crying. Standing up seemed quite beyond her, so Arabella picked her up. Her body was so slight, she barely weighed a thing. "I'll carry her."

"Very well." For the second time that afternoon, the housekeeper bade Arabella to follow her.

A short time later, Sally had been installed in a cot in the infirmary, and the hospital's matron was thanking Arabella for her quick thinking and care.

"Dr. Radcliff mentioned you were coming today, Miss Jardine," she said, ushering Arabella outside and down the corridor. They paused by a large window that overlooked a sodden garden featuring a bed of drooping daffodils. A slender, attractive woman who was perhaps in her thirties, the matron had a calm yet efficient manner about her. "I apologize for not being able to show you around the hospital myself."

"I understand completely," said Arabella. "I can see how busy you are." There were half a dozen other children occupying beds in the infirmary, and Arabella suspected they were all suffering from the same ailment. "Measles is terribly contagious, so I truly hope you can contain the outbreak." Because she hadn't contracted the disease when she helped treat children at the North Bridge Orphan Hospital, her grandfather had surmised she'd already had the illness as a child.

Beneath her starched white cap, the matron's brow plunged into a deep frown. "How did you know?" she asked in hushed tones. "Did Mrs. Bradley say anything? I asked her not to. We don't want to alarm the public unnecessarily. Or the board, especially when the children have yet to be seen by a doctor. I hope I can count on your discretion."

"Yes, of course," replied Arabella. "And to answer your question, no, Mrs. Bradley didn't mention it was measles. But when I loosened little Sally's uniform, I noticed the rash on her neck and shoulders. And on her face. It's quite distinctive."

"Yes . . ." The matron gave her a considering look. "You've either encountered measles before, or had medical training. Or both."

Arabella smiled. "Both. My grandfather was a physician. I used to assist him in his practice."

"Ah." The matron nodded. "And you know Dr. Radcliff as well, I hear."

Arabella felt her own cheeks grow hot. "Yes."

"Did someone mention my name?"

Arabella turned at the sound of a pleasantly deep male voice behind her. It was indeed Dr. Radcliff. Arabella's blush deepened as her gaze met the doctor's, and she nervously adjusted her glasses, hoping the action would help hide the fact that her face was so red.

The doctor was just as amiable as she recalled. A trim gentleman of middling height and age—his brown hair was shot with silver at the temples—he wasn't particularly handsome, but he possessed a charming manner and kind brown eyes. Eyes that held hers for a moment longer than was perhaps necessary before he bowed over her hand.

"Miss Jardine," he said, a genuine smile playing about his lips. While his gaze held a warm light, his long fingers were cool against her skin. "It has been far too long."

"Yes, it has," Arabella replied, dismayed that she sounded a little breathless. "It's lovely to see you again." The doctor released her hand and she curled her fingers into her palm;

she fancied she still felt his touch. Giving herself a mental shake for being such a wigeon, she added, "And before I forget, I must thank you for arranging a tour for me. It's been most enlightening."

"I'm pleased to hear it. And you're most welcome, Miss Jardine. I know you have a passionate interest in facilities such as this one." The doctor turned his attention back to the matron, who was observing them both with a quizzical expression. "Good afternoon, Matron. I understand you have need of me."

"Yes." The young woman gave a succinct recount of the situation, even describing Arabella's intervention when Sally had taken ill. "So, unfortunately, it seems we might have a measles outbreak on our hands," she concluded gravely.

Concern shadowed Dr. Radcliff's eyes. "Would that you and Miss Jardine were wrong, Matron. But I rather suspect you're not."

He caught Arabella's gaze again. "If circumstances were different, I'd suggest we take a turn about the picture gallery and then ask Mrs. Bradley to arrange tea for us all"— he nodded at the matron—"in one of the parlors. But I'm afraid it will have to be another time. I hope you understand, Miss Jardine."

"Yes of course." Even though disappointment tugged at her heart, Arabella summoned a smile. "I look forward to it."

"Perhaps when you return from the Continent?" Dr. Radcliff was following the matron toward the infirmary. "How long will you be away? I don't recall your mentioning that in your last letter."

"Four months at this stage."

The doctor paused on the threshold. "Be sure to send me your direction. I want to tell you all about my plans for a new clinic for the poor at Seven Dials. I'm modeling it on Dr. John Bunnell Davis's Universal Dispensary for Children. Oh, and be sure to squeeze in a visit to L'Hôpital Necker, L'Hôpital des Enfants-Trouvés, and L'Hôpital des Enfants-Malades in Paris if you have the chance. They're all wonderful hospitals."

Arabella inclined her head. "I will. Goodbye, Dr. Radcliff. Matron." But Matron was asking the doctor if he had any Godfrey's Cordial on hand as he stepped into the room. And then the door closed behind him.

Arabella sighed as she retraced her steps along the corridor, heading toward the hospital's main entrance. It was such a shame that fate had conspired against her this afternoon. She'd been so looking forward to spending a little more time with Dr. Radcliff. Of course, their encounter had been so brief, she couldn't be sure if he looked upon her as anything more than a friend. They were certainly like-minded individuals. And from what she'd seen of him on the three occasions they'd met, he was a most congenial, even-tempered man. He would make some lucky woman a lovely husband. If he wished to marry again, of course . . .

Arabella had no idea what his wishes were in that regard. But after today, it had become abundantly clear to her that she wouldn't mind at all if Dr. Graham Radcliff began to view her as a prospective spouse. As a doctor's wife—particularly someone with Dr. Radcliff's social connections—it would be much easier for her to realize her goal. To make a real difference to all those children who were forced to endure inferior conditions in poorly funded and managed institutions up north.

For now, though, she could at least take heart in the fact that Dr. Radcliff wanted to continue corresponding with her. And dare she believe he wanted to see her again when she returned to London? Why else would he ask how long she would be away?

It might still be raining, but Arabella's spirits weren't the least bit dampened as she hailed another hackney coach. Hopefully this Grand Tour she was about to embark upon would be over with before she knew it. And then she could get on with the life she truly wanted.

CHAPTER 2

It seems scandalous scoundrels and wanton women
galore were present at a certain address in C. Square
last night.

Find out what really happened at that ball . . .

One wonders if the ton's most Errant Earl will
ever learn his lesson?

The Beau Monde Mirror: The Society Page

Langdale House, St. James's Square, London

April 19, 1818

Gabriel Holmes-Fitzgerald, the Earl of Langdale, gave a
huff of disgust as he threw the *Beau Monde Mirror*
onto the walnut occasional table beside his wing-back chair.
It was a wide-held view that the so-called newspaper was
little more than a gossip rag meant to titillate rather than
illuminate.

Yet the article he'd just read was very close to the truth.
Too close, in fact.

Gabriel sighed heavily as he poured himself a cup of
coffee from the silver pot his valet had just brought to his
sitting room, hoping the bitter brew would ease the pounding in his head—a megrim brought on by poor sleep rather
than the aftereffects of alcohol—and to mask the taste of
stale tobacco in his mouth from smoking a cheroot last
night. He didn't doubt the "Errant Earl" in question was

him, not Lord Astley, the earl he'd been openly cuckolding for several months.

Indeed, the nobleman had confronted Gabriel about the adulterous affair in the middle of his very own ballroom at Astley House, right in front of the who's who of the ton, including Camilla, his very beautiful and—unfortunately for the Earl of Astley—very accommodating wife. No wonder the incident had been recounted in the *Beau Monde Mirror*. It was probably even mentioned in the *Times*.

It served him right, he supposed, that he should be so roundly and publicly chastised. Gabriel scrubbed at the stubble on his face and winced. Lord Astley might be fast approaching middle age, but he could still plant a decent facer. But then, a split lip and bruised jaw were but a small price to pay considering Lord Astley had been on the brink of calling him out last night. And Gabriel had not wanted to meet the irate earl on the dueling field. Because that would mean he'd have to shoot the man, and frankly, he couldn't be bothered. For the most part, he'd enjoyed his time between the sheets with Lady Astley, but as he was a superb shot—his reputation as an excellent marksman in Wellington's army was well earned—he'd rather not kill a man over something as trifling as a casual affair.

Well, it had been casual for Gabriel, at any rate. Unfortunately, he was only just beginning to realize it had meant rather more to Lady Astley.

He'd already thrown the tearstained, heavily perfumed note Camilla had sent early that morning into the fire. He skimmed the contents—full of overwrought declarations of undying love and the mad suggestion that they should run away together. The woman should be making amends with her husband, not pursuing him. Even though it would hurt her, it was for the best if he severed all ties with her cleanly and immediately.

And that would be relatively easy to do now that he'd decided to quit town.

Rising from his seat, Gabriel moved to the window and, after flicking the claret velvet curtains aside, looked down onto the square below. It was a dismal rainy day, but that hadn't stopped a small mob of jeering protesters from congregating in front of his town house. No doubt they believed hurling insults at the door of "Langdale the filthy libertine" would help him to "learn his lesson." Gabriel's mouth tilted into a wry smile over the rim of his coffee cup. He might not be quite as infamous as Lord Byron, but he was, in effect, charting a similar course to avoid having to deal with the consequences of such a public scandal.

Aside from that, he needed a change of scenery. He was sick of London and tonnish society. Bored with frequenting the same clubs and gaming hells, the same brothels, tupping the same society women. Doing the same meaningless things over and over again. While he'd never tire of the company of his old comrades-in-arms—Lord Malverne, Lord Sleat, and the Duke of Exmoor—he'd recently been overwhelmed by an oppressive, suffocating sense of ennui. And when he was so afflicted, he knew from past experience that he was in danger of doing something wild. Of venturing so close to the edge of disaster—just for the thrill of it—that he might actually regret it.

As he'd said to Nate, Lord Malverne, after the altercation with Astley—it was always too much or too little with him, even if it led him to self-destruction. There was never any middle ground. For his own well-being—and that of Lord Astley and his lady wife—it was better that he leave London. As soon as his valet had finished packing his trunks and Gabriel dressed for the day, he would depart for the Continent posthaste.

Of course, given that his decision to leave had been made on the spur of the moment, he hadn't quite decided on his destination or how long he would stay away. He'd travel to Dover and at that point choose whether to sail for Calais or Ostend. Last night, when he first discussed his plan with Nate, he mentioned he might spend some time in Switzerland and rent a villa by Lake Geneva. Gabriel smirked. Now, that really would be following in Byron's footsteps.

However, as he regarded the leaden gray skies and the swathe of heavy rain sweeping across the square—the downpour had at last sent the mob at his door scurrying for cover faster than a pack of rats abandoning a sinking ship—Gabriel decided the warmer, sunnier climes of southern France or Italy, or even Greece, had more appeal. Basking on a sun-flooded terrace by the bright blue Mediterranean Sea, supping on plump figs, creamy goat's cheese, and rich red wine would surely refresh his mind and spirit even if there was no hope for his benighted soul.

Ryecroft, his valet, tapped on the door and announced his bath was ready. "Also, Jervis wishes to inform you that your cousin, Captain Timothy Holmes-Fitzgerald, has made an unscheduled call. He's been installed in the front parlor for the time being as Jervis wasn't certain you'd want to receive him . . ."

Jervis, his butler, was right. Gabriel wasn't sure he wished to see his bloody penny-scrounging, self-serving, profligate cousin at all. For a man who had once served in His Majesty's cavalry, Timothy didn't appear to possess an honorable bone in his body. Indeed, Gabriel suspected his own little finger contained more integrity.

Sighing heavily, he set aside his coffee cup. "Fetch my green silk banyan, Ryecroft. And have one of the footmen show him to the library. Tell Captain Holmes-Fitzgerald I'll be down directly."

Ryecroft's forehead wrinkled with a frown that bordered on disapproving. Clearly his master's current state of dishabille—unshaven and unwashed with a rumpled cambric shirt, loose trousers, and leather slippers—affronted him. "It won't take long to shave you, my lord. And I've already put out the clothes you request—"

Gabriel waved a dismissive hand. While it was tempting to make Timothy wait, he'd rather be rid of him. "If my cousin dares to arrive on my doorstep without an invitation at an indecent hour, he'll have to take me as he finds me. I've no desire to make an effort for the sorry sod."

Ryecroft bowed. "Very good, my lord."

A short time later, Gabriel entered the library to find Captain Timothy Holmes-Fitzgerald sprawled across a silk-upholstered settee at the fireside with his muddy hessians propped on the marble-topped table and a glass of brandy in hand. "I hope you don't mind that I helped myself, cuz," he drawled, lifting his drink in the air.

By the look of him—his slightly glassy gaze and ruffled appearance—Gabriel suspected Timothy had arrived in an inebriated state. And it was only midday.

Ignoring his cousin's greeting—such as it was—Gabriel stalked over to his desk and flopped into the leather chair behind it. His headache had already kicked up a notch. Hopefully this meeting wouldn't take long. In fact, he already knew how it would go.

Timothy would declare his father's latest business venture was failing—again—and he therefore needed a ridiculous sum to shore up the investment. It was complete balderdash.

Gabriel's uncle, Stephen Holmes-Fitzgerald, had always been astute when it came to managing his family's finances. But Gabriel also knew that his uncle's health had begun to fail over the past year and since that time, he suspected Timothy had been dipping into the dwindling family coffers— when his father wasn't looking—to hide his ever-increasing gambling and drinking debts. But those debts had to be repaid at some point lest his father find out. Hence Timothy's periodic visits to Gabriel to try to cadge money from him. Timothy might claim he'd been discreetly taking care of the family's business interests to ensure his father wasn't exposed to any undue stress. But Gabriel knew the truth of the matter.

He glanced at the Boulle mantel clock above his cousin's dark curly head. He'd give Timothy five minutes to haggle with him and not a second more. As much as Gabriel would dearly love to send Timothy away with nothing but a flea in his ear, he also didn't wish to cause his ailing uncle unnecessary pain. Stephen Holmes-Fitzgerald, his own father's younger brother, was a man of great integrity, and Gabriel had always admired him. So in the end, even though it irked him, he would write Timothy a banknote for a few thousand pounds. And then he'd kick him out.

"How much do you want this time, Timothy?" he asked, not bothering to disguise the note of boredom in his voice. He began to toy with a charcoal pencil within his reach.

"Now, now. Don't you want to know how I am?" Timothy sat up straighter, placing his soiled boots on the fine Turkish rug. "Or how my father is?" The smile twisting his mouth in the moment before he took a sip of brandy was more of a sneer.

Alarm jangled through Gabriel. "I hope he hasn't taken a turn for the worse." During Timothy's last visit about a month ago, he mentioned his father had been diagnosed with a canker in the belly.

His cousin sighed. "I'm afraid he has, old chap. The doctor says it might only be a matter of weeks—two or three months at the most—before he goes to meet his maker."

Gabriel raked a hand through his hair. How could he in all good conscience leave for the Continent now? "Is the physician certain?"

Timothy shrugged. "As certain as anyone of his profession can be. Everyone knows most of them are quacks." He rose to his feet and, after topping up his glass from the crystal decanter on the sideboard, sauntered over to Gabriel's desk.

Gabriel watched him all the while; his knuckles cracked as his hands fisted on his thighs. He sometimes wondered if Timothy was actually a devotee of opium. It would explain why his pupils were often no bigger than black pinpricks in his pale gray eyes. And why he was always so short of funds. "You know that when your father passes, you'll not get another penny from me," he bit out through clenched teeth.

Timothy settled himself in the bergère before the desk with a studied nonchalance that increased Gabriel's unease tenfold. His cousin had always been an arrogant man, but there was something else about him today—a calculating, almost cutthroat gleam in his cold gray eyes—that made Gabriel's nerves prickle with awareness, rather like a hare waiting for the hawk to swoop. It was an unfamiliar feeling and Gabriel didn't like it. Not one little bit.

Another smirk. "I wouldn't count on that, cuz."

What the devil is Timothy playing at? Gabriel forced himself to yawn and lean back in his chair, feigning an indifference he in no way felt. "I really wish you would speak plainly," he said as he picked up the pencil and began to absently sketch a hawk's wing on a blank piece of parchment left out on the blotter. "I have better things to do with my time."

Swirling his brandy, Timothy studied the whirlpool he'd created in his glass for one long moment. He was deliberately taunting Gabriel. Making him wait. When he at last raised his gaze, his pale eyes glinted with a feral light. "As soon as my father dies, I'm going to take your title and everything else you own."

Gabriel paused in his sketching and arched a sardonic brow. "What, you're going to murder me in cold blood? Because the only way you'll become the next Earl of Langdale is over my dead body."

Timothy made a scoffing sound in his throat. "Good God. There's no need to be so dramatic, cuz."

"Well, you've clearly lost your mind then. You won't get a damned thing unless I die. There's no other possible way."

"Isn't there?" Timothy watched him over the edge of his glass as he took another sizable sip.

Gabriel returned his stare without flinching. "No."

"I wouldn't be so sure." Timothy put down his glass and made a show of brushing a speck of dirt off his pantaloon-clad thigh. "You see, Father's developed a habit of quaffing laudanum like it's small beer to ease his pain"—he gave a snort of laughter as though that were the funniest thing in the world—"and not that long ago, he let something slip. Something about your parents' marriage." Timothy's arctic-ice gaze returned to Gabriel's. "Or lack thereof . . ."

Gabriel's blood ran cold. "What do you mean?"

There'd been a huge scandal almost thirty years ago when his father, Michael, Lord Langdale, had eloped to Scotland with the beautiful and not-quite-of-age heiress Caroline Standish. An only child of the abominably wealthy Walter Standish, Caroline—or Caro, as Gabriel's father had once called her—had wed the wicked Lord Langdale "over the anvil" in a small toll-side alehouse in Springfield, just outside of Gretna Green. Caro's irate father, who'd made his fortune mining lead in Yorkshire, had chased them over the border but was too late to stop the marriage.

Apparently the notorious "Priest of Hymen," Joseph Paisley, had conducted the wedding ceremony. At least, that was the name Gabriel had been able to make out on the stained and crumpled marriage lines he'd presented as evidence of his parents' union when he'd submitted his petition for a writ of summons to the House of Lords—as he was required to do—in order to claim the earldom of Langdale following the death of his father two years before.

"Surely you understand, cuz." Timothy gave an exaggerated sigh as if he were about to deliver a complicated explanation to a simpleton and his forbearance was rapidly running out. "But just in case you don't, as soon as my father croaks, I'm going to mount a challenge for the title."

Gabriel's eye twitched. "On what basis?"

"Well, obviously that you're a bastard," replied Timothy in a tone that was so patronizing, Gabriel had to grip the arms of his chair to stop himself from throttling the dog. "Because your parents' marriage was never legal according to the laws of *this* land. Surely you're familiar with the Hardwicke Act. Even under Scots law it's likely it won't stand up to scrutiny. And once you're declared illegitimate"—Timothy made an expansive gesture encompassing the room—"all this will be mine."

Fuck. What had his uncle said to Timothy? "You're wrong. My parents' marriage was valid. The House of Lords has already accepted my right to inherit." Gabriel's father wasn't the first English peer to have eloped to Scotland with his sweetheart, and he certainly wouldn't be the last. Indeed, the *Beau Monde Mirror* regularly reported such scandalous goings-on.

"Yes, but no one has contested your claim. Until now." Timothy paused, no doubt for dramatic effect. "You mark my words, cuz, the Committee for Privileges and Conduct will hold a hearing when I demand one. And as the so-called priest who officiated at your parents' so-called marriage died four years ago, he can't be subpoenaed to testify.

Oh, and let's not forget your mother is missing, so she won't be able to attest their irregular marriage was valid either."

Timothy leaned back and steepled his fingers beneath his shadow-stubbled chin. He was clearly relishing this encounter far too much. "How long has it been since she deserted your father for another man? Fifteen years and counting? Even if you could find her, I doubt she'd make a credible witness given her shameful past. And do you have any idea who the witnesses were or where they can be found? My inquiry agent certainly hasn't been able to locate a record of the marriage in Scotland. You might possess some sort of certificate—and I use that word in the loosest possible sense—but without another verified copy in existence, no record in a civil marriage register, and no witnesses to speak of, you're really not going to have a cat in hell's chance, old boy. I'd say you're about to get well and truly rogered."

"Get out." Gabriel's command emerged as a low, thunderous growl.

Timothy raised his hands in a placatory gesture. "Now, there's no need to be rude, cuz. I mean—"

"You heard me." Gabriel stood so quickly, his chair toppled backward and crashed into the bookcase behind him. "Get out this instant before there *is* a dead body in this room. And it won't be mine."

Timothy must have registered the murderous rage in Gabriel's eyes, as he immediately leapt to his feet and retreated across the room. However, conceited cock that he was, he couldn't resist a parting shot when he reached the door. "You're a bastard and a disgrace to the family name just like your father was. I can't wait for the day you're stripped of your title."

As soon as the door slammed shut, Gabriel wiped a shaking hand down his face. *Bloody fucking hell.* What in the devil's name was he going to do? He stood to lose a great deal—not just his title and social standing, but his country estate Hawksfell Hall and Langdale House here in St. James's Square. While he was exceedingly wealthy, a great slab of his fortune was also linked to the entail.

A short time ago, he was lamenting the fact that he was bored out of his thumping skull. Now that he hovered on the brink of disaster, he couldn't claim he was bored anymore.

Gabriel crossed to the sideboard and sloshed a large measure of cognac into a glass. The alcohol seared his throat as he tossed it back. And then he poured himself another larger nip.

Would the Committee for Privileges and Conduct really deem his parents' marriage invalid and thus declare him a bastard? Gabriel couldn't be sure.

One thing was certain: Timothy wouldn't be swayed from this course of action. Not when the earldom of Langdale and all the privilege and wealth that went along with it could be his. Especially when he had a taste for opium and needed the funds to continue living in the lap of luxury. An addiction to dissipation could make a man do desperate, even dangerous things. And Gabriel knew what that felt like all too well.

He had to do something to save what was rightfully his. But what?

Too agitated to sit, Gabriel stood by the fire, sipping his cognac as he stared into the wavering flames. He might have to delay his journey or put it off altogether. Engaging his own inquiry agent to locate the whereabouts of the missing marriage register, any witnesses, and perhaps another copy of his parents' marriage certificate was essential. Timothy could have lied when he claimed they no longer existed. Yes, he'd send word to his man of affairs and get him to hire someone reputable this afternoon.

And what of his mother?

Gabriel threw back the rest of his cognac. Unfortunately, everything Timothy had said about her was close to the truth as far as Gabriel knew anyway. She had indeed run off fifteen years ago—but whether she had done so with a lover, Gabriel wasn't sure. There certainly had been enough rumors flying about to suggest that she had.

Even as a young child, Gabriel sensed the tension between his parents. Memories of their tempestuous arguments and his mother's tears still haunted him to this day.

At the age of thirteen when his mother left, he understood her reasons to some extent. And he could forgive her for that and all the scandal she left in her wake.

But he'd never forgive her for abandoning him. For leaving him alone with a man who didn't understand him and despised him throughout his childhood because he was a "weak milksop" and a "namby-pamby." A ruthless man who, Gabriel quickly learned, had an appetite for debauchery. A man who ridiculed him, goaded him, even beat him on occasion, forcing Gabriel's adolescent self to become a "man" in his father's own image. A rakehell of the worst kind.

A filthy libertine.

Gabriel's gaze slid to the enormous oak desk that dominated one side of the room. After his father died, he was shocked to discover that his mother had actually written to him, Gabriel, every single year. And for some unfathomable reason, his father had kept the letters. They'd been secreted in a sandalwood casket in one of the desk's locked drawers, a small bundle tied up neatly with a thin scarlet ribbon.

Gabriel hadn't read them and for reasons he'd put off examining, had never been tempted to, even when another letter arrived last year. He'd simply added it to the pile, then locked the drawer again.

After replenishing his glass of cognac, Gabriel returned to the desk, righted the chair, then took a seat. There was no avoiding it, he had to open the letters. Or the most recent one at the very least. It was the only real hope he had of finding his mother. Once he did, he'd bring her back to London so she could attest her marriage to Michael, the sixth Earl of Langdale, had been valid. Hopefully she would also be able to provide the names of the witnesses who'd been present at the ceremony.

Gabriel might be catching at straws, but he had to try to save his inheritance. He *wouldn't* give up.

With hands that were noticeably unsteady, Gabriel removed the casket from its hiding place. The scent of sandalwood and another more delicate, feminine fragrance—perhaps it was orange blossom—greeted him as he lifted the lid and tugged the ribbon loose. Drawing a steadying breath, he then cracked open the red wax seal on the topmost letter and slowly unfolded the parchment.

My darling Gabriel, it began.

Gabriel swallowed around a hard lump in his throat. His vision blurred.

Christ. Was he actually crying? He dashed at his stinging eyes with the heel of one hand and made himself scan his mother's flowing script with a dispassionate gaze. Names of towns leapt out at him. Geneva, Nyon, Montreux, Villeneuve . . .

Gabriel tipped his head back as relief flooded through him, more potent than the cognac flowing through his veins. Less than a year ago his mother had been in Switzerland. And thank God, she'd also mentioned several places she'd stayed—a particular villa at Villeneuve and a château at Nyon. She'd also expressed a desire to move on to Venice and then to another villa in Tuscany. There would be a lot of ground to cover, but at least Gabriel had an idea of where to begin his search. He had to make an effort—take a chance—otherwise he risked losing everything he held dear.

It looked as though he was going to visit the Continent after all.

CHAPTER 3

On my return, after breakfast, we sailed for Clarens,
determining first to see the three mouths of the
Rhone, and then the castle of Chillon; the day was
fine, and the water calm.

Mary Shelley, *History of a Six Weeks' Tour*

Maison du Lac, Clarens, Switzerland

July 2, 1818

Oh, Bertie darling, please don't be cross with me." Lilias
Arbuthnott's spun-sugar voice floated down the stairs
to the entry hall of Maison du Lac, where Arabella and her
cousin's husband, Albert "Bertie" Arbuthnott, waited. "I'll
be down shortly. I just have to find my parasol. You don't
want me to get freckles, do you?"

Beneath copper red brows, Bertie rolled his eyes. It appeared neither his wife's dulcet tones nor her concerns
about her complexion had moved him. "Well, don't blame
me if the gendarme at Château de Chillon refuses to take
us on the tour because we're so late," he called back up the
stairs. "Dr. and Mrs. Kerr drove off with your mother over
twenty minutes ago. And Arabella and I will leave, too, if
you don't hurry. You have one more minute." He pulled his
silver watch from the pocket of his navy blue tailcoat and
flipped it open. "Starting from now."

"Oh, Bertie. Why must you always be so impatient? I'm going as fast as I can."

"You've just wasted five seconds."

"That's not fair."

"And another three."

"Bertie!"

Arabella released a sigh of exasperation as she finished tying the spring green ribbons on her straw bonnet. After putting up with Lilias and Bertie's constant squabbling for three months, she was ready to throttle both of them. For a married couple who wanted for nothing in a material sense—Bertie was the second son of a very wealthy Scots merchant banker—Arabella didn't understand how they could always be so discontented.

She wandered through the front door of the villa onto the gravel forecourt into the bright summer morning, and her pique began to ebb away almost immediately. The vista of Lake Geneva and the towering Alps with their snow-dusted peaks beyond was simply breathtaking. A bad mood couldn't possibly last long in a setting as enchanting as this. Not when the sunlight danced upon the deep blue waters and a light breeze caressed her face.

They had originally planned to stay at the Hôtel d'Angleterre in Montreux. But then a Scots couple they'd become acquainted with in Lausanne—Dr. Kerr, a middle-aged minister in the Presbyterian Church and his wife Eleanor, the sister of the Countess of Cheviot—had extended an invitation to share their well-appointed villa in the village of Clarens, just outside Montreux.

Skirting the dogcart that had been readied to take them to Chillon Castle, Arabella took up a position beneath a large chestnut tree on the edge of the drive and glanced up at the house. Maison du Lac was quite a grand affair with an even grander backdrop of the Savoy mountains. A whitewashed stone house, it consisted of three stories with large airy rooms and sumptuous furnishings within. There was even a small conservatory attached to the morning room in the east-facing wing. After sharing a bedchamber with her aunt Flora for weeks on end, Arabella was more than happy to have her very own bedroom complete with a marvelous view. Every morning when she awoke, it was like glimpsing heaven when she pulled back the floral chintz curtains from the wide sash window.

Of all the places they'd visited so far during the last three months, Switzerland was by far her favorite. They'd sojourned in Paris for a month, traveled at a leisurely pace to Geneva, and had then made their way about the lake in the same relatively desultory fashion. If Charlie, Sophie, and Olivia could have shared this journey with her instead of her irksome family, it would have been perfect. Oh, how she missed them.

Or dare she think it, Dr. Radcliff? She'd sent a letter to Charlie and one to the doctor just before she left Paris eight weeks ago, informing them of all her news. She'd also provided them both with the Hôtel d'Angleterre's address if they wished to reply. She'd been in the area a week now, and the proprietor of the hotel had kindly agreed to forward any correspondence that arrived for her to the Maison du Lac, but so far, nothing had been sent on. Arabella yearned to hear how Charlie, Sophie, and Olivia's husband hunting was progressing given the Season was drawing to a close. And if Dr. Radcliff had opened his dispensary at Seven Dials. If at all possible, she'd love to pay a visit to the clinic on her return to London at the end of the month. And before she headed north to Edinburgh once more. Away from everyone she held so near and dear.

Arabella sighed. She really shouldn't be so maudlin. Not on such a glorious day. Perhaps she could borrow the Kerrs' hired dogcart later today and make a trip to the Hôtel d'Angleterre to check if there was any mail waiting for her. The two gray ponies strapped into the traces looked docile enough to handle.

Lilias appeared in the villa's open doorway in a flurry of white muslin, her pale blond curls bouncing about flushed cheeks, Bertie following in her wake. She pouted as she pushed open her matching silk and lace-edged parasol.

"Oh, Mama and the Kerrs took our landau, Bertie? That is most unsatisfactory. I don't like the dogcart. It's not sprung properly."

Bertie took her arm. "If you'd been ready sooner, you could have gone with them," he muttered as he handed her into the cart. Picking up her sprigged muslin skirts, Arabella climbed in on her own, then took a seat beside her cousin, who was now complaining about the grubbiness of the cart floor. Ignoring his wife, Bertie leapt with ease into the driver's seat in front, and with a flick of the reins, they were off at a spanking pace.

Praying her glasses or her bonnet wouldn't fly off—or that she wouldn't get poked in the eye by Lilias's parasol—Arabella clutched her buttercup yellow silk shawl to her chest with one hand and gripped the side of the dogcart with the other. Lilias had been right—the cart was poorly sprung, and Arabella felt every bump and rut in the winding dirt road as they barreled along, following the curves of the lake. But she really couldn't complain when around every corner appeared another eye-dazzling vista.

Sitting on a rocky islet on the very edge of Lake Geneva, the medieval fortress of Château de Chillon was apparently a perennial favorite with tourists. Indeed, Arabella had read all about Mary Shelley's visit to the picturesque castle in her book detailing her tour through Europe with her husband, Percy, in 1814 and 1816. Of course, Arabella had also read Lord Byron's haunting poem "The Prisoner of Chillon," which detailed the trials of a monk, François Bonivard, who had been chained to one of the pillars in Chillon's dungeon for six long years in the sixteenth century. The poem had certainly brought a tear to her eye—she couldn't even conceive of such suffering. It appeared darkness could lurk in the hearts of men, driving them to do cruel and unspeakable things, even when the world about them was so beautiful.

Arabella was also dying to know if the rumors were true—that the very wicked Byron had carved his name into one of the dungeon's pillars. She hoped a visit to the infamous chamber was part of the tour.

By the time they reached Chillon, Lilias was as sullen

as a storm cloud because her arm was bruised from being bumped against the side of the cart, there was dirt on her hem, and her curls were windblown. To escape the scolding she was presently giving Bertie, Arabella slipped from the dogcart and followed a tree-lined path leading to the entrance of the castle. Pausing by a low stone wall, she took a moment to admire the château's gray squat stone towers and circular turrets. All was peaceful save for the sound of the lake gently lapping at the ancient castle's foundations and the soft rustle of the oak canopy above her head . . . And then Lilias and Bertie caught up. Only now it was Bertie who was nagging Lilias to quicken her pace while Lilias complained her slippers were pinching her toes.

As she'd done on many other occasions during this holiday, Arabella decided she would steal away at the first opportunity. Aunt Flora frequently berated Arabella that she would get lost one day—and then she'd be sorry for being so foolish and irresponsible—but Arabella never paid heed. Even in a crowd, she could pick out the sound of Lilias's piping voice. And as Bertie was so tall, his coppery head stood out like a bright beacon. It was well-nigh impossible to lose track of her family.

She fell into step behind the Arbuthnotts and within a minute they'd reached the castle's front entrance, where a uniformed gendarme waited with the Kerrs and a prune-mouthed Aunt Flora. After Bertie had finished apologizing to Dr. and Mrs. Kerr and his mother-in-law for being so tardy, they all crossed the small moat via a covered bridge into a cobbled courtyard.

Aunt Flora accosted Arabella as soon as they were out of the Kerrs' earshot. Laying a silk-gloved hand on Arabella's arm, she tugged her into the shade of the arched gateway. "What were you doing this time, Arabella, to make Bertie and Lilias so late?" her aunt demanded in a harsh whisper. The frost in her pale blue glare could turn Lake Geneva to ice in midsummer. "Did you wander off as you so often do, or did you have your nose stuck in some wholly inappropriate book? We were left to swelter in the hot sun for nearly half an hour. What will the Kerrs think?"

"I'm guilty of both charges I'm afraid," replied Arabella. As much as it rankled, she'd learned it was easier to just agree with her aunt. Lilias could do no wrong in her mother's eyes, so there was no point in arguing that it was her fault. "And I'm sorry the Kerrs were inconvenienced."

"As well you should be, Arabella. I won't have you upsetting such an esteemed and well-connected Scots minister and his wife. What if Mrs. Kerr tells her sister, Lady Cheviot, that we're nothing but inconsiderate and uncultivated bumpkins? Because of the academy scandal—and your thoroughly unhealthy interest in all things medical—your reputation is already sullied, my lass. Surely you don't wish the rest of the family to suffer because of your thoughtlessness bordering on recklessness. I pray daily you will not follow in your mother's footsteps and bring us all to the brink of social ruin."

Arabella bit her tongue to stop herself from flinging a retort after her aunt as she sailed over to Lilias, Bertie, and the Kerrs, head held high with a false smile plastered on her face. How dare Aunt Flora bring up her mother's past? While Arabella fully acknowledged her own transgression three years ago, it wasn't fair her aunt should castigate her own sister—a woman who'd disappeared twenty years ago in tragic circumstances and was now presumed dead. At least, that was the heartbreaking conclusion Arabella's grandfather had been forced to draw after his search for his missing daughter Mary proved fruitless.

Arabella dipped her head and closed her eyes against the prick of hot, angry tears. It seemed all the frustration and resentment she'd been tamping down for so long was bubbling to the surface, ready to boil over. She needed to be alone. Away from her aunt.

If she had brought one of her "wholly inappropriate books," she would turn on her heel and walk out of the courtyard, across the castle's bridge, and find a shady spot on the soft grassy bank of the lake. But she didn't have a book with her. And she *had* been looking forward to the at least until her aunt had unfairly rebuked her and slighted her poor mother. As usual, she'd just have to make the best of it.

At the first opportunity, she would slip away and explore the castle by herself as she had planned.

Arabella began to slowly skirt the edge of the courtyard. The gendarme was presently sharing shocking facts and figures about the fate of some of Chillon's prisoners in centuries past—how heretics and women accused of witchcraft had been gruesomely tortured and burned at the stake in this very courtyard. Even children had been murdered. Dr. Kerr nodded gravely, whereas Mrs. Kerr, Aunt Flora, and Lilias were all gaping in abject horror.

Bertie's red brows bristled with anger. When Lilias put a hand to her forehead and swooned against her husband's side, he interrupted the gendarme with a wave of his hand. "Excuse me, monsieur. I think you should choose another topic. Something that won't offend the ladies of the party."

Despite the fact that she had a strong stomach, Arabella was inclined to agree.

The Swiss guard gave a puzzled frown and pulled at the curled end of his oiled mustache. "But, Monsieur Arbuthnott," he said, clearly mystified by the appalled expressions of those surrounding him. "This is what we tell everyone who visits Château de Chillon for a private tour. But if you prefer, perhaps we can move down to the dungeon." Waggling his eyebrows, he gestured toward an open doorway at Arabella's left. "The ladies might like to see the signature your naughty Lord Byron etched into a pillar, *non*?"

Aunt Flora shook her head emphatically. "I, for one, do not wish to see or hear anything about that dreadful man or his ghastly poem about the prison."

Lilias shuddered. "Neither do I."

Mrs. Kerr concurred. "That man is too wicked for words," she declared with a haughty sniff. "My sister, the Countess of Cheviot, met him once, and she believes he's a sinful scoundrel beyond salvation. I have no interest in *anything* Byron has written. In print or carved in stone."

"I am more than happy to go along with whatever the

ladies decree," observed Dr. Kerr. He took his wife's arm. "Come, Eleanor. I hear there is a fine banqueting hall and a chapel somewhere about."

"*Oui, oui.* There is indeed, my good monsieur." The gendarme beckoned them toward another archway on the other side of the cobbled courtyard. "This way, *s'il vous plaît.*"

After Bertie offered one arm to Lilias and the other to Aunt Flora, the trio followed the gendarme and the Kerrs.

Arabella breathed a sigh of relief. Her aunt hadn't bothered to look back and she wouldn't follow. For the moment she was free to do as she liked. The others might not want to explore the prison, but she certainly did.

As Arabella stepped through the doorway the gendarme had pointed out, the entrance to the dungeon yawned before her, a dark gray mouth flanked by iron-hinged doors of thick latticed wood. Her belly fluttered with a combination of excitement and trepidation as she carefully picked her way down the worn stone steps into a chamber that appeared to be a wine cellar, of all things; the vaulted ceiling was supported by slender stone columns, and large wooden barrels were stacked neatly against rough brick walls. A narrow gash of a window on the far wall provided sufficient light for her to discern another arched doorway leading to a larger, cavernous chamber.

The dungeon.

It was much cooler down here in the dank shadows, and Arabella gathered her shawl about her shoulders as a shiver slid down her spine. Standing on the prison's threshold, she took in the seven massive pillars supporting the high vaulted ceiling that brought to mind a Gothic cathedral, not a dungeon. A series of tall, arched windows on the lake side spilled enough sunlight into the vast chamber for her to see it had been carved from the very bedrock upon which Chillon sat. The wall to her right was little more than roughly hewn stone, and in some places, the floor was littered with jagged rocks and piles of dark gray boulders.

The opening of Byron's poem "Sonnet on Chillon" wandered through Arabella's mind as she slowly traversed the chamber.

Eternal Spirit of the chainless Mind!
Brightest in dungeons, Liberty! thou art,
For there thy habitation is the heart—
The heart which love of thee alone can bind . . .

She might have felt imprisoned when she was but a child, alone and afraid in the orphanage without any hope of love or light in her life, but at least the institution had more creature comforts than this godforsaken place. She counted the pillars until she reached the fifth one; this was where the monk Bonivard, the prisoner immortalized in Byron's poem, had been chained to an iron ring.

After removing her silk gloves and tucking them into her reticule, Arabella reached out and splayed her bare hand against the cold stone. Poor man. Her heart wept for him and everyone else who had suffered within these castle walls: men, women, and children alike. And that's when she heard something, a soft rustle followed by a quiet scuffing sound like a footstep on stone.

She wasn't alone. There was someone down here with her, perhaps in the next chamber. Arabella's pulse pounded in her ears and a frisson of unease slid over her skin, raising gooseflesh. She wasn't prone to flights of fancy, but for one mad moment, she wondered if the dungeon might be haunted.

There was only one way to find out. Inhaling a bracing breath, Arabella called out, "*Qui est là?* Who's there?" and stepped around the pillar.

And then she gasped. The tall, masculine figure standing before her, stealing her breath clean away with his fallen-angel smile, wasn't an apparition. Far from it.

He was simply the handsomest man she'd ever seen.

CHAPTER 4

We passed on to the Castle of Chillon, and visited
its dungeons and towers.
            Mary Shelley, *History of a Six Weeks' Tour*

The handsome stranger folded his tall, muscular frame
into an elegant bow; clad in the attire of a gentleman
rusticating in the country—a simple neckcloth, hunter green
riding coat, snug buckskin breeches, and top boots—he was
a perfect specimen of a young, athletic male in his prime.
"My apologies, fair lady," he said, his wide mouth tipping
into another enigmatic smile. "I did not mean to startle you."

Yes, Arabella was startled, by the man's physical beauty
more than anything else, and it took her a moment to actually register that he was English. And very well-spoken.
His cultured accent brought to mind ton ballrooms, whereas
his voice was rich and deep with an appealing rasp—a
rough, smoky edge that reminded Arabella of the whisky
her grandfather used to drink.

As the man straightened, a stray beam of sunlight illuminated his sun-bronzed countenance, revealing moss green
eyes beneath slashing black brows and a riot of ebon curls.
An aristocratic blade of a nose, carved cheekbones, and a
sharply cut jaw. His unabashed gaze roamed over her face,
and Arabella's cheeks grew hot beneath his curious regard.

Amusement sparked in the man's eyes, and Arabella realized that she was not only blushing but openly gaping at

him. And she hadn't uttered a single word. He must think her bird-witted.

"I . . . I will confess I am a wee bit startled," she said at last, annoyed with herself for being so rattled. "Are you . . . are you here for a private tour?" She glanced past him, into the chamber he must have come from, but she couldn't see or hear anyone else.

Another smile, this time a little wider. Arabella became transfixed by a dimple in the man's lean cheek. "Not exactly," he said in his whisky-warm voice. "One could say I'm simply here for the scenery." He removed a large book that had been tucked beneath his arm and showed it to her—it appeared to be an artist's sketchbook.

"You've been drawing down here?" Arabella frowned. "Surely you'd have a better view from outside."

"Ah, but you see, I sometimes like to sketch the outside from the inside. To capture the essence of something just out of reach. And to show the light beyond the darkness." He arched a brow. "I'm a little peculiar that way."

"But the windows are too high." Arabella tilted her head up and squinted over the top of her glasses; she needed them for reading more than anything else. "One can only see the sky from here."

"There's a larger window in the next chamber with a view of the lake," he said. "Come and see."

Before Arabella could argue that she really shouldn't be lingering in a deserted dungeon with a strange Englishman, he was walking through to the next room as if he expected her to follow without question; he had the air of someone who was accustomed to being obeyed. A natural authority. Ordinarily, Arabella would exercise caution in a situation like this—it wouldn't do to get caught alone with a gentleman she didn't know—but she hadn't been down here long, and she calculated that she still had a little time until Aunt Flora came looking for her.

So she followed.

The man's description of the chamber had been accurate. Four stone steps led down to a barred window as large as a doorway. The wooden shutters were open, and one

could see across the expanse of bright, turquoise blue water
to the mountains on the far side of the lake.

Arabella descended the stairs to better take in the view,
and after a moment, the gentleman joined her. Proffering
his sketchbook, he asked, "What do you think?"

In the narrow space before the window, he was obliged
to stand quite close to her. His upper arm touched hers and
his scent drifted around her—sandalwood soap, leather,
and the musk of clean male. Decorum decreed that Arabella should move away, but it seemed her body had other
ideas; her feet were rooted as firmly to the stone floor as the
dungeon's ancient pillars as she took the book. When the
man's bare fingers brushed against hers, her nerves tingled
with a strange awareness, and the hot rush of her blood
made her pulse quicken and her face burn.

How odd. Disconcerted at her physical reactions to this
man—and yet flattered that he would ask her opinion—
Arabella dropped her gaze to the page, hoping her bonnet
would hide her flush of pleasure. The sketch of the scene
through the window was rendered in charcoal and cleverly
done. In fact, the detail was quite astonishing, the interplay
of light and shade masterful. The texture of the lightly ruffled water and the bold lines of the jagged mountains were
captured perfectly behind the grill of dark, latticed iron bars.

"I think you're quite the artist," she said, lifting her gaze
to the man's face. As she'd studied his drawing, she sensed
he'd been watching her. And she was right.

As their eyes met, he smiled. "Thank you."

"Do you paint too?"

"Sometimes. But it's only a hobby. Something to while
away the time as I wait—" He broke off, then laughed. "It's
a good thing I don't need to make a living from it."

Arabella handed the sketchbook back to him. "I think
you could if you needed to."

"Perhaps." He closed the book, tucked it under his arm
again, and then flashed a dazzling smile that revealed perfect teeth. "Have you seen Lord Byron's signature yet?"

"No. I wasn't sure where to look."

"It's back in the main chamber. I'll show you if you like."

"Aye, I would. Very much."

After retracing their steps, they paused at the third pillar. Sure enough, Byron's name was carved into the gray stone.

"I've heard that some dispute the authenticity of the autograph," Arabella said softly. But the quiet awe in her voice had nothing to do with Byron and everything to do with the man beside her. To her dismay, she found she was captivated by the sight of the stranger's long, decidedly masculine fingers as his hand rested on the column beside the poet's name. There was a smudge of charcoal on one of his knuckles, and for the first time she noted that he wore several silver rings. Sunlight glancing off the largest signet ring revealed a hawk's head with flashing emerald chips for eyes.

She really should ask this man's name. But before she could voice her question, he responded to her remark.

"I think it's real," he said. "It's something Byron would do."

"You know him?"

"I've met him on the odd occasion," he said after a momentary pause. "In London. But it was a few years ago now."

Arabella nodded. So her initial assumption had been correct. This man was well connected and probably a member of the ton. "I hope you don't mind, but I really should ask you . . ."

She trailed off. The gentleman was watching her face again and she wasn't used to such scrutiny. He was making her flustered, putting her to the blush like a silly, infatuated debutante. *Again*. It was a feeling she really didn't like. "Why do you keep looking at me in that way?" she asked, unable to mask the slight note of indignation in her voice. Her Scots burr was also more pronounced, making her sound a little harsher than she'd intended.

The man didn't seem put out though. A spark of curiosity lit his green eyes as he cocked his head. "In what way?"

"Like you're studying me."

"Well, perhaps I am. A little," he conceded. "But in my defense, I rather enjoy looking at beautiful things I'd like to draw. Or paint. Blame it on my artist's eye."

Arabella arched an eyebrow. "You were right. You are peculiar. Or you need to borrow my spectacles."

To her astonishment, the roguish gentleman threw back his head and laughed. The deep throaty rasp of it echoed about the chamber. "You certainly don't mince your words," he said at last, propping a wide shoulder negligently against the pillar. "But perhaps you'll forgive me when I tell you I've been in Switzerland a month and despite the beauty of the countryside, I'm a trifle tired of sketching and painting the same scenery."

"And you really want to draw me instead?" Arabella didn't believe him. With her glasses, willow-thin frame, and less-than-perfect teeth, she was as plain as could be.

"Yes I do. In fact, I'd love for you to sit for me. There's a castle garden, did you know? If you would allow me to escort you outside, I'm sure we could find a nice shady spot right by the lake."

Arabella frowned. She suddenly didn't trust this charming stranger's pretty words and smooth-as-silk manner. It was about time she went upstairs. Aloud she said, "I hardly think that's appropriate. I don't know you."

"Then allow me to introduce myself." The gentleman stepped back and affected another courtly bow. "I'm Gabriel Holmes-Fitzgerald, Lord Langdale."

Lord Langdale? Arabella knew that name. "You're on the list," she murmured without thinking.

The gentleman—an earl no less—gave her a quizzical look. "List?"

Arabella blushed. She couldn't very well admit the Society for Enlightened Young Women had put together a list of prospective husbands—many of whom were rakehells—before she'd quit London. So she said, "I mean . . . you're a friend of Lord Malverne's, are you not? I'm a very good friend of the viscount's sister, Lady Charlotte Hastings. We attended—" Arabella broke off but then lifted her chin. She was tired of being ashamed about that particular aspect of her past. Besides, why should she care about Lord Langdale's opinion? It wasn't as though she looked upon him as a prospective suitor, let alone a husband. "Charlie and I attended the same young ladies' academy. Until we were expelled. I'm Arabella Jardine."

"Ah . . ." Understanding dawned in the earl's eyes. "I do recall something about that. What a deuced nuisance that business must have been for you."

Arabella blinked, taken aback by Lord Langdale's unexpected reaction. Was that a glimmer of sympathy in his eyes? Most people tended to look aghast when they heard about the unladylike things she and her friends had done. How they'd smuggled alcohol, *cigarrillos*, lewd pictures, and erotic reading material into the dormitory for a late-night party. "Aye. It was." *And still is, considering Aunt Flora can't seem to forget about it.*

Which reminded Arabella, she'd been gone awhile now and she really *must* find her family, lest they discover her down here alone with the very rakish Lord Langdale. The furor that would ensue didn't bear thinking about. Stepping away from the pillar and the earl, she glanced toward the door of the wine cellar and the stairs leading up to the courtyard. "I'm afraid it's time for me to go. My family is probably looking for me."

Lord Langdale inclined his head. "Of course. But before you leave, I must ask you for your direction."

"I beg your pardon?"

Lord Langdale's perfectly cut lips lifted in a smile. "For noble not nefarious reasons, I assure you, Miss Jardine. I have a letter for you. From Lady Charlotte."

"Oh, how wonderful." Arabella's heart leapt with such joy, she clapped her hands together like a child who'd just received a box of sweetmeats at Christmas. "But I must ask you, how has that come about?" She began to head toward the stairs, and Lord Langdale fell into step with her.

"Some correspondence recently arrived from England. Lord Malverne arranged a private courier to deliver mail to my villa in Villeneuve," he explained, offering his arm as they encountered an uneven section of the dungeon floor. "Do you know the town?" he asked as he tucked her hand into the crook of his arm. "It's only three miles from here."

When Arabella nodded, Lord Langdale continued. "But I

digress. The note from Charlie, which accompanied your letter, mentioned you were currently staying at the Hôtel d'Angleterre in Montreux. But when I visited the hotel a few days ago to deliver your letter, the proprietor informed me that Miss Arabella Jardine was not, and had never been, a guest there." The earl smiled down at her as they paused at the bottom of the stairs. "So it seems we are well met indeed."

Ah, so that's why she hadn't received any correspondence. What a perfidious hotel manager. Tamping down her annoyance, Arabella smiled back at Lord Langdale. "Yes. It would seem that we are. However, I must leave you here, my lord. For the sake of appearances, you understand. But I will quite happily share my address with you. It is the Maison du Lac in Clarens."

Lord Langdale relinquished his hold on her arm. "Excellent. I will make sure your letter from Lady Charlotte is delivered later today."

"Thank you." Arabella dipped a quick curtsy. She supposed she should have done so earlier when the earl had introduced himself by name. But she'd been so surprised by his disclosure, she didn't think to adhere to the usual proprieties. "It's been a pleasure meeting you, Lord Langdale."

He bowed and offered a lopsided smile—a rakish smile if ever she'd seen one. "Believe me, the pleasure has been all mine, Miss Jardine."

Arabella had almost reached the top of the stairs when he called after her, "You know, I would be most honored if you *would* agree to be my muse sometime?"

"And you, my lord, should definitely have your eyes checked," she called back over her shoulder. "Farewell."

Lord Langdale's rich laughter followed her out into the sunshine. What a lovely, unexpected adventure she'd just had. And she had a letter from Charlie to look forward to.

When Arabella caught up to Aunt Flora and the rest of the party in the arsenal, she was still smiling, even when her aunt quietly harangued her for disappearing. Nothing could dampen her spirits today. Nothing at all.

CHAPTER 5

Sky, mountains, river, winds, lake, lightnings!
Lord Byron, "Childe Harold's Pilgrimage"

Storm clouds were gathering over the Savoy Alps in great towering piles of bruised purple and gunmetal gray, casting the forested slopes and the castle of Chillon below into dark shadow.

Gabriel cursed beneath his breath as he urged his mount into a brisk canter; he doubted he'd make it to Maison du Lac before the tempest hit. He was about to get soaked.

When he set out from his villa just outside of Villeneuve for the six-mile journey to Clarens, it was true there had been an ominous mass of snowy white cumulus clouds in the brilliant blue sky, as was to be expected on such a sultry afternoon, but impulsive numbskull that he was, he ignored them. Of course, just as he'd expected, within the space of fifteen minutes, the weather had taken a turn for the worse. But he'd promised Miss Arabella Jardine she would have her letter from Lady Charlotte Hastings, and he was—if nothing else—a man of his word. Storm or no, she would receive it.

Thunder growled, and a brisk wind whipped at his hair and riding coat as he bent low over his horse—a fine bay gelding—and urged it into a gallop as they cleared the outskirts of Montreux and continued to follow the meandering lakeside road. Despite the fact that he was about to get caught in a storm, it felt good to be doing something useful for once. Bestowing a small act of kindness upon a relative stranger. And an intriguing one at that.

When Arabella Jardine had wandered across the cold stony floor of Chillon's dungeon, Gabriel had been quite inexplicably transfixed by the sight of her. He'd waited in the shadows, torn between the desire to reveal his presence, as a gentleman should, and to observe her progress. Mired in frustration about the complete lack of progress he'd made in trying to find his mother over the past few months, he'd decided—on a whim—to visit Chillon and sketch its famous dungeon. The chill, dank, desolate setting seemed to fit his mood perfectly.

And then he'd seen her. A breath of summer and sunshine in the cool gloom. A vision in shades of yellow and spring green with her guinea gold curls spilling from the confines of pins and bonnet. As she'd passed by one of the dungeon's windows and the light had illuminated her simple splendor, a line from "The Prisoner of Chillon" had sprung into his mind. With her slender form, gilded by sunlight, she was like "a sunbeam which hath lost its way, / And through the crevice and the cleft / Of the thick wall is fallen and left, / Creeping o'er the floor so damp, / Like a marsh's meteor lamp."

Yet that description didn't capture her fearlessness—for how many young women would venture into a dungeon alone?—or the tender heart lurking beneath. When she removed her gloves and touched Bonivard's pillar with her bare hand, the bereft expression washing over her face had made the breath catch in Gabriel's chest. *Who is this intriguing young woman?* he'd burned to know.

So he stepped out of the dark shadows and made her acquaintance. And he hadn't been disappointed. While Miss Arabella Jardine blushed at his mild attempts at flirtation, she hadn't been afraid to speak her mind; he was certain no one in recent memory had dared to assert he was peculiar. With her blond curls, fair countenance, and wide hazel eyes—a veritable kaleidoscope of brown and green and gold—she clearly had no idea how attractive she was. True, she wasn't a conventional beauty, considering she wore spectacles and possessed a tiny gap between her two front teeth, but to his practiced eye—as both a libertine and aspiring artist—she was quite visually captivating. Guileless, even fierce in her honesty, she was the most refreshing, fascinating female he'd encountered in a long time.

So perhaps it wasn't only honor—a quality he would freely admit he didn't possess a great deal of at times—that had driven him to make this ill-advised dash to her door . . .

Miss Arabella Jardine certainly wasn't the sort of woman he usually pursued. When he'd learned her name, and the fact that she was good friends with Nate's sister, Charlie, he knew he most definitely shouldn't make a conquest of her even though the base male in him would very much like to. Yes, he'd have to keep a tight rein on his control when he saw Miss Jardine again. His reckless urges had landed him in dire trouble on more than one occasion in his life. He wasn't about to make the same mistake this afternoon.

Once Gabriel entered the picturesque village of Clarens, the first heavy raindrops had begun to fall. By the time he paused to seek directions to the Maison du Lac at a small lakeside inn, the shower had turned into a downpour. But Gabriel's destination was less than a mile away, and he reasoned that getting drenched had never killed anyone. While he could wait out the storm at the inn, drinking cider and supping on meltingly soft cheese and fresh bread, there was no guarantee it would be over anytime soon—at least according to the innkeeper. And at the moment, it seemed to be more of a rainstorm than a violent cataclysm of the elements.

However, as Gabriel continued along the narrow country lane that would lead him to Arabella's villa, conditions rapidly deteriorated, and he realized much too late that his hubris had turned him into a king-sized fool. He seemed to be in the center of a wild maelstrom of wind and water and crashing thunder. White-hot flashes of lightning blinded him while driving rain slapped at him, and it took all his concentration and strength to stay in the saddle and safely steer his terrified mount. To his left, the lake itself—usually so calm and serene—had been whipped into a frenzy by the cruel, stinging lash of the wind. The oak and chestnut trees lining the lane to his right bowed and tossed in the face of the bullying onslaught.

Thank God he could see wrought iron gates up ahead. And the glimmer of lamp-lit windows beyond.

As he approached the open gates, he was obliged to slow down. One of the gates swung wildly back and forth in the wind, the shriek of its protesting hinges making his horse shy, and his booted foot slid from a stirrup. Cursing profusely, Gabriel somehow maintained his seat, but then disaster struck. Deafening thunder boomed like a cannon, reverberating through him, and an oak tree beside the gate seemed to explode in a volley of violent sparks.

His mount reared, front hooves flailing, and Gabriel plummeted onto the gravel drive.

Fucking hell.

He landed heavily on his side, and searing pain shot through his body, momentarily robbing him of breath and thought and sight. When he managed to crack open an eye, he saw, through a haze of agony and sheeting rain, his horse dashing toward the house. It wasn't that far to shelter and help. If he could just get up . . .

Sucking in a shuddering breath, Gabriel tried to lever himself upward, but another wave of excruciating pain crashed through him. *Bloody, blazing hell, I've buggered my shoulder*, was the last thought that flashed through his mind, right before darkness crowded his vision and blessed oblivion claimed him.

Arabella sat in the window seat of Maison du Lac's spacious drawing room, riveted by the spectacle of the wild summer storm as it swept down from the mountains and across the lake, turning the sunny afternoon into the darkest night. She'd never witnessed such a stunning display; the flickering sheet lightning and jagged thunderbolts slashing across the sky took her breath away.

Behind her, Aunt Flora lay moaning upon a chaise

longue, a lavender-scented towel draped across her eyes as Lilias held her hand.

"Draw the curtains, Arabella, and light the lamps instead," her cousin bid in a beseeching tone after a particularly bright flash of lightning lit the room. "The storm is making Mama's megrim worse."

Arabella sighed. She knew from experience that Aunt Flora didn't have a megrim at all; although she'd never admit it, she was afraid of storms. But Arabella didn't wish to make her aunt's attack of nerves worse, so she did as she was asked.

"Are you sure she can't have any more laudanum?" Lilias added as Arabella drew close. "Mama's bottle of Kendal's Black Drop is empty, but I know you have plenty in that frightful medical bag of yours."

"I'm afraid not," said Arabella. It secretly amused her that Aunt Flora and Lilias loathed the fact that she insisted on taking Grandfather's old leather physician's bag wherever she went. But whenever they needed something to treat any sort of ailment—from a megrim to an aching tooth to a bout of indigestion—they had no trouble asking her for it whatsoever. "It isn't a good idea to have too much."

"And who told you that?" Aunt Flora pulled the towel from her forehead. Her pale blue eyes were hard and accusing as she looked up at Arabella from the pile of silk cushions behind her head. "Just because you spent years gallivanting about with my father, pretending to be a doctor, doesn't mean that you are one. My physician says I may have as much as I need."

Arabella shook her head as she took in her aunt's constricted pupils and her generally agitated state. She already relied on the strong drug too much for Arabella's liking. Laudanum was certainly a useful drug for reducing significant pain and fever, but her grandfather had always warned his patients about the dangers of overuse. And it seemed that, of late, her aunt had come to rely on it more and more.

"Why don't I ring for some nice herbal tea?" she suggested. "Chamomile always helps megrims. Or would you like some of Mrs. Kerr's orgeat cordial? I'm sure she'd be more than amenable to sharing it if I said it was for you." As far as Arabella knew, the minister's wife was napping upstairs—or hiding from Aunt Flora, who'd been nothing but querulous since their return from Chillon in the early afternoon. Dr. Kerr and Bertie were hiding in Maison du Lac's small library at the back of the house. "If you prefer something a little stronger, I think there might be a nice sweet sherry on the tray in the dining room too."

Aunt Flora sniffed. "I know one shouldn't drink before dinner, but a sherry might help."

Arabella nodded. "Of course." She crossed the carpeted room and pushed through the elegant silk-paneled doors into the dining room. There was enough ambient light filtering in from the drawing room for her to see by as she poured a small measure of the sherry into a twist-stemmed crystal glass.

Lilias's sweet fluting voice was almost drowned out by the furious drumming of the rain and the pummeling wind. "Might I have one—"

An earsplitting crack of thunder shook the house at the very same moment lightning illuminated the room in a blinding flash. Lilias and Aunt Flora screamed and Arabella jumped, dropping the sherry all over the floor.

Good heavens, that was close. Her heart crashing against her ribs, Arabella peered through the leaded panes of the dining room window and the veils of scudding rain beyond. Had the lightning struck something? A tree? Out of the corner of her eye, she was certain she'd seen a flare of light, a shower of glowing sparks. It was difficult to see, but as she pressed her nose to the window, something else caught her eye—a dark shape bolting straight for the house. Was that a horse?

Oh, God. It was. A riderless horse. Before the panicked beast disappeared from view around the side of the house, Arabella caught a fleeting glimpse of an empty saddle.

So where is the rider? On the drive or somewhere farther down the lane or even on the road? There was only one way to find out.

Picking up her skirts, Arabella dashed from the room,

ignoring Aunt Flora's demand to explain where she was going. In the entry hall, she almost collided with Bertie.

"What's wrong?" he asked, gripping her by the shoulders. "Is Lilias all right?"

"Yes. But there's a riderless horse outside," she said, slipping away from him. "I'm worried someone has taken a fall."

Bertie's mouth was agape as she grabbed a random coat off a hook by the door—a garrick—and threw it about her shoulders. "Are you mad? You're not seriously going out in that, are you? It's far too dangerous."

But Arabella was already hauling the heavy wooden door open. A squall of stinging, icy rain flung itself across the threshold, making her gasp. "Well, somebody has to," she called over her shoulder as she stepped onto the portico. Pulling in a bracing breath, she bent her head and plunged into the storm.

Blinded by the driving rain and cutting lash of the wind, Arabella ran pell-mell down the drive, slowing her pace as she drew closer to the gate. An ancient oak had been struck; one of its enormous branches had been ripped away from the trunk and then was tossed upon the gravel like a severed limb.

Then something else shifted just beyond the felled branch. A dense black form like a hunched-over figure.

A man.

Thank heavens she'd trusted her instincts.

Dropping to her knees when she reached the man's side, Arabella prayed he was only unconscious. She reached out to touch his shoulder, to turn him over as he was facedown on the drive, but when he shifted and moaned, she stopped herself. What if he'd injured his back or his neck? If that were the case, she must be very careful when moving him. She didn't want to make his injuries worse.

She might need to summon Bertie, Dr. Kerr, and one of Maison du Lac's manservants to help. If only Bertie had followed—

The man gave a great shuddering moan and lurched upward into a sitting position.

Thank God he was all right. Well, relatively all right

considering the most indecent profanity Arabella had ever heard suddenly burst from his lips.

"Fucking hell."

Arabella blinked in surprise. "Lord Langdale?"

The earl turned to look at her; even though the rain had plastered his black curls against his forehead, and mud was smeared across one cheek, Arabella immediately recognized his too-handsome face. And then there was that distinctive, deeply rasping voice of his.

"Miss Jardine." Lord Langdale's mouth twisted into a rictus of pain as he attempted to smile. "This is not what I had in mind for our next encounter."

"I should hope not." Arabella touched the arm he was leaning on. "You're injured. Tell me what I can do to help you up and get you inside."

"I rather think I've dislocated my shoulder," he said. "The left one."

Arabella ran her gaze over him. It was difficult to tell if that was the case given the earl wore a riding coat, and in the pouring rain, visibility was poor. However, he was certainly favoring his left arm. "Well, you have got yourself into a wee pickle then, haven't you?" she said.

He gave a snort of laughter then grimaced. "Yes indeed."

"Do you think you can stand? You can lean on me if you need to."

"Yes . . ." He sat up straighter and even that small movement made him gasp. "I'll try very hard not to swear, but I hope you can forgive me if I do."

"I assure you, I won't think any less of you, my lord."

By the time they reached the villa's portico, Arabella had learned quite a few more colorful curses. Some had put her to the blush. One or two she thought she might file away in her head for future reference.

Bertie at last stepped forward to lend his assistance as they struggled up the short flight of stairs. Lord Langdale had leaned on her shoulder the whole way, and she was grateful for the reprieve. She was more than a tad out of breath.

"Be careful," she warned as Bertie took her place beside the earl. "Lord Langdale may have dislocated his shoulder."

Bertie's eyebrows shot up to meet his coppery hairline. "Lord Langdale? *The* Earl of Langdale?"

"I'm afraid so, old chap." In the light of the entry hall, Arabella could see how pale Lord Langdale was beneath his tanned face, and deep grooves of strain bracketed his wide mouth. "So sorry to darken your doorway like this. But needs must when the devil drives, as they say."

"This is Bertie Arbuthnott, my lord," offered Arabella, shrugging off the sodden greatcoat and tossing it onto a wooden bench by the door. "My cousin-in-law, so to speak."

Lord Langdale gave a quick nod. "Pleased to make your acquaintance, Arbuthnott. Is there somewhere I could sit—"

"Bertie. What on earth is going on?" Lilias appeared in the vestibule, followed by a grave-looking Dr. Kerr and an astonished Mrs. Kerr. "Goodness." Her mouth dropped open when she took in the sight of the sopping wet earl leaning on her husband and then Arabella, who was equally soaked to the skin. She threw her an accusing look. "What have you done now, Arabella?"

Ignoring Lilias, Arabella addressed Bertie. "Let's get Lord Langdale somewhere quiet and warm. The library perhaps? And I'd like some towels." To the minister she said, "Would you mind fetching my medical bag, Dr. Kerr? Or ask one of the servants to? It's the large brown leather bag in my room. On the chest of drawers by the door."

To her surprise, Lilias jumped in. "I'll get it," she said and rushed from the room, heading up the stairs.

Arabella frowned. Lilias was *never* helpful.

Before she could think on it further, Mrs. Kerr pinned Arabella with a disapproving glare and said in a clipped tone, "If someone is injured, don't you think we should send for a real physician? And how do we know this man actually *is* Lord Langdale? I'm assuming you mean *the* Earl of Langdale from Cumberland. He's never set foot in Almack's to my knowledge, so I wouldn't know if it is him or not. And neither would you, Miss Jardine, because your aunt tells me you've never set foot in Almack's either. This stranger you've just brought into the house could be anyone."

Arabella glanced after Bertie and Lord Langdale. They

were already making their way to the library at the back of the villa. Had the earl overheard? She supposed it didn't matter if he had. She was certain he wouldn't give a brass farthing if Eleanor Kerr doubted his identity. As to her other charge, that she, Arabella, wasn't really qualified to treat anyone who was injured, Arabella would clearly explain to Lord Langdale what she could or couldn't do for him after she'd made an assessment, and then he could decide if he wanted her help or not.

She was about to tell Mrs. Kerr exactly that when Dr. Kerr said, "Eleanor, the nearest physician is probably in Montreux or Villeneuve. And who in their right mind would venture out in this weather to summon one? You only have to look at Lord Langdale to see how foolhardy an enterprise it would be. Let Miss Jardine see what she can do for the earl first. And yes, it is *the* Lord Langdale," he added when his wife opened her mouth to protest. "I once saw him giving a speech in the House of Lords."

Arabella thanked Dr. Kerr. She had not expected his support and she was grateful.

He inclined his gray head. "If you need any further assistance, do call. I would be more than happy to help."

"Perhaps you could ask someone from the stables to track down Lord Langdale's horse? I saw it bolting round the side of the house earlier. I'd hate to think it would get injured too."

The tempest was still raging outside. Indeed, the front door rattled ominously as Dr. Kerr said, "A very sensible idea, Miss Jardine. I will."

As Arabella exited the hall, she was sure she heard Mrs. Kerr mutter that she had no idea how Flora could tolerate her niece's "utterly disgraceful bluestocking nonsense." And it was right about then that Arabella thought one of Lord Langdale's expletives would do quite nicely.

Thank goodness Mrs. Kerr couldn't read her mind.

CHAPTER 6

One night we enjoyed a finer storm than I had ever
before beheld. The lake was lit up—the pines on
Jura made visible, and all the scene illuminated for
an instant, when a pitchy blackness succeeded, and
the thunder came in frightful bursts over our heads
amid the darkness.

Mary Shelley, *History of a Six Weeks' Tour*

When Arabella entered the library, it was to find Lord
Langdale sitting upon a leather wing-back chair by
the hearth, nursing his injured shoulder with his good arm.
The fire and several branches of candles had already been
lit; shadows flickered over the book-lined walls and the earl's
drawn face.

Bertie must have helped him to remove his riding coat,
as he was currently in his shirtsleeves and waistcoat. It was
abundantly clear his left shoulder was dislocated; even beneath the damp cambric of his shirt, it was easy to see his
upper arm was set at an unnatural angle.

One of the villa's maids, a middle-aged matron, was
casting curious looks and fleeting smiles at the earl from
beneath her cap as she placed a pile of linen towels and
washcloths on a low table before the fire. Heavens, even
older women weren't immune to Lord Langdale's physical
charms. But the poor man, given his state, didn't need to be
ogled in such a way, so Arabella promptly dismissed her.

"I've just been explaining to Lord Langdale that Dr. Kerr is not really a physician but rather a doctor of theology," said Bertie as she approached the fireside. "But that you *might* be able to help . . ." Judging by the skeptical look in his eyes, he wasn't so sure she could.

"Thank you." Arabella offered the earl a towel to at least dry his face—his sodden black curls still dripped into his eyes. She then removed her spectacles and wiped away the rain spots with one of the washcloths. She must look a fright and nothing like the cool, calm, and collected medical practitioner she aspired to be; her sprigged muslin skirts were muddy and plastered to her legs, and the wind and rain had turned her hair into a damp, matted bird's nest. Under different circumstances, she would have changed into dry clothes, but Lord Langdale was in so much pain, she was loath to waste time attending to what amounted to a frivolous need.

She also wanted to help the earl before she lost her nerve.

"Now, Lord Langdale, before I take a look at your shoulder, I must be quite frank with you," she said as she replaced her glasses and took a seat on a leather ottoman in front of the earl. She had no idea what he would make of her, but she would be remiss *not* to offer assistance. "While it's true I'm not a doctor by virtue of my sex, I have several years of nursing experience, courtesy of my dearly departed grandfather, a well-regarded physician in Edinburgh, at least. I haven't reset a dislocated shoulder on my own before, but I did assist my grandfather to do so on a number of occasions. One particular technique he taught me is a little unconventional but most effective. So in light of all that, are you still happy for me to take a look? I'll be perfectly honest and tell you straightaway if I don't think I can manage the business."

Lord Langdale's green eyes were glazed with pain as he peered at her from beneath hooded lids. "I trust you. If you say you can do it, I'll take you at your word."

Arabella nodded. "Good."

Bertie, who was hovering by the fire, still didn't look convinced. "Are you sure about this, Arabella? I mean, it's highly irregular . . ."

His remark died in the air when Arabella arched a disdainful brow. "And have you ever pushed a dislocated limb back into place before? Did you know there are particular techniques that are more effective than others depending on the nature of the dislocation?" When Bertie shook his head, Arabella said, "Well, it seems as though Lord Langdale is stuck with me then." She softened her tone as she added, "Can you find me a pair of scissors, Bertie? In the desk perhaps? I had thought Lilias would be here with my medical bag by now—"

At that moment, Lilias burst in. Her cheeks were a bright shade of pink as she cast a timid look at Lord Langdale on her way to the fireside—whether her cousin was flushed from rushing, being in the handsome earl's presence, or feeling flustered about something else altogether, Arabella couldn't be sure.

"Thank you, Lilias," she said, taking the large bag. Sitting it on the hearthrug at her feet, she then undid the metal clasps. "I trust you've returned the bottle of laudanum . . ."

Lilias's face turned bright red. "You know how persistent Mama can be," she said. "She only wanted a wee b—"

A resounding crash split the air, making Lilias squeal and clutch at her husband's arm. Arabella's heart had kicked with fright too.

"I don't think that was thunder," observed Lord Langdale drily.

"No." Bertie's fiery brows had plunged into a frown. "I agree."

"Do you think a tree has toppled onto the house?" asked Arabella. The sound of things splintering and shattering had accompanied the crash. Aside from the massive chestnut tree beside the drive, there were a number of very tall firs and elms close to the villa.

"Yes. I suspect something's hit the conservatory." Bertie headed for the door. "Sorry to leave you, but I'd best check the extent of the damage. With any luck, the rest of the house has been spared."

Lilias scurried after him. "I'll go and check on Mama."

As the door closed behind them, Arabella caught Lord

Langdale's eye. "It looks as though it's just you and me now."

"Yes . . ." His face was as white as the linen towel draped across his uninjured shoulder, his mouth a rigid line. "I'd offer to help your cousin-in-law, but it seems I'm not fit for anything at the moment."

"I'm sure Bertie will manage. Let's concentrate on sorting your shoulder out first." Arabella delved into her grandfather's bag and removed the bottle of laudanum. "I think it would help if you took some of this, my lord. The procedure will be easier to perform if you are not in so much pain. The more relaxed you are, the better."

Lord Langdale shook his head. "No. Thank you." His tone was suddenly cold.

"But—"

"I said no!"

He snapped at her with such vehemence, Arabella flinched. Confusion mingled with hurt and a dose of pique as she murmured, "I . . . I apologize if I have offended you . . ."

"No, let me offer a sincere apology to you, Miss Jardine," Lord Langdale said gravely. The emerald fire in his eyes had died to be replaced by an expression of bleak remorse. "I should not have spoken to you like that. I . . . I'm not myself. Suffice it to say, laudanum does not agree with me."

"All right, my lord. And your apology is accepted." Arabella placed the dark bottle of laudanum back in the bag and dug out her own pair of scissors. The steel blades winked in the firelight.

The earl cocked a brow. "After my very rude outburst, I can trust you with those, can't I?"

Arabella recognized he was trying to ease the tension in the air by injecting a little levity into the conversation. "At this point in time, I'd say you don't have much choice, my lord. But don't worry, I'm only going to use them to cut off your clothes. Well, at least the garments covering your top half."

Lord Langdale's mouth twitched with the ghost of a smile. "If I weren't in so much pain, I'd probably suggest you don't need to confine yourself to my top half, just for the pleasure of seeing you blush, Miss Jardine. But I'd rather not provoke you any further."

"Aye, that would be wise, my lord." Arabella's gaze transferred to the back of the wing-chair, where the earl's coat lay. "At the risk of provoking *you* further, I'm afraid I'm going to have to ask you to move to the chaise longue. The back of your seat is too high, and I won't be able to see what I'm doing if I need to manipulate your shoulder from behind. Aside from that, it will be easier to remove your shirt and waistcoat if you're on the other lounge."

"If it means you'll be able to fix me, I'll sit anywhere, or get into any position you want, Miss Jardine. Within reason, of course. I'm not sure if I'm capable of standing on my head at the present moment."

The earl blew out a sigh and eyed the chaise longue on the other side of the hearthrug.

"Do you need a hand?" Arabella asked.

He shook his head. "No, I think I can manage. I'm just taking a moment to summon the courage to move." His gaze lit upon a silver tray atop an oak cabinet near the desk. "Is that a bottle of brandy or cognac I spy over there? It would be for medicinal purposes only, I assure you."

Considering he'd rejected the laudanum, Arabella didn't see any harm in it. She brought over the bottle and a crystal tumbler. "It's cognac."

"Excellent." Lord Langdale took the bottle and waved away the glass. After pulling the cork out with his teeth, he then took a large swig. Then another. "It's very good," he said after he'd swallowed down a third large mouthful. "Right." He handed the bottle back to Arabella, and she placed it on the side table along with her scissors. "Here we go."

Clenching his jaw, Lord Langdale surged to his feet. For one heart-stopping moment, he swayed to one side and Arabella gripped his good arm. Sliding her arm about his lean waist, she murmured, "Here, let me help you."

"Thank you."

By the time he was safely seated on the chaise, he was

breathing hard and trembling, and there was a sheen of sweat on his face.

Arabella offered him the cognac again, and he gulped down a bit more. Goodness, she imagined the earl would be well and truly foxed if he had too much more. But he had rejected the laudanum, so she couldn't very well judge him for doing whatever he could to ease his agony.

All going well, his shoulder would be back in place very shortly.

Arabella retrieved her scissors and knelt on the floor in front of Lord Langdale. Trying to ignore the quickening of her pulse and the wild fluttering in her belly, Arabella forced herself to concentrate on the task at hand. "Right, let's get on with it, shall we? We'll need to deal with your cravat and waistcoat first."

He gave a short nod, then loosened his neckcloth, collar, and the fastenings at the top of his shirt with a shaking hand while Arabella applied herself to undoing the buttons of his sodden silk waistcoat. When the garment sagged open, she tried very hard not to notice his long, lean torso or how the soaked, almost sheer cambric of his shirt clung to the hard swells of his well-developed pectoral muscles.

She frowned and worried at her lower lip when her gaze traveled lower to the waistband of his buckskin breeches. "Shall I tug your shirt out, or would you prefer to? I don't want to hurt you . . . at least any more than necessary."

"I'll do it." Drawing a shallow breath, he gingerly tugged the fabric free at the very front. "Will that do?"

"Aye." She held on to the hem and picked up her scissors from where she'd deposited them on the silk-covered seat of the chaise longue. Lord Langdale's clothing was drenched through and the chair's fabric would probably be ruined, but there wasn't much she could do about it.

She was about to make the first cut when Lord Langdale murmured, "I think this is one of the most novel ways I've ever been undressed."

"*One* of the most novel? Heavens." Arabella made a series of careful snips up the middle of the earl's shirt, stopping just below his sternum. "The mind boggles."

"Well, if you're curious, I could tell you about the time—"

"No." Arabella made a smooth slice up to the shirt's gaping neckline. With a quick snick, the garment was completely cut in two. Glancing up into the earl's face, she continued, "I'm not the slightest bit curious . . ." But then her voice trailed away.

Lord Langdale was looking down at her through half-closed lids, and Arabella suddenly found herself trapped as though entranced by a mesmerist. Her pulse raced faster than quicksilver, and she suddenly felt giddy as though she'd been drinking cognac too. Goodness, this beautiful man was dangerous. Even though he was in a seriously injured, disheveled state, his rakish charm was in no way diminished.

But she had a job to do. And swooning at the earl's feet like a silly miss who'd never seen a bare male chest before was not conducive to getting it done. Arabella swallowed and pushed herself up. "Now that I think on it, I probably should have cut through the back of your shirt instead of the front," she said, moving behind him.

"But where would the fun have been in that?"

Arabella frowned at the back of his head. Was he implying he enjoyed seeing her on her knees between his legs? She was sure he was making a joke of a sexual nature at her expense. "You have a wicked tongue, Lord Langdale," she said as she efficiently snipped down the back of his waistcoat.

"I'll take that as a compliment."

"And you're incorrigible too." She started on the back of his shirt.

"I won't disagree."

"Good."

Very soon, Lord Langdale's shirt and waistcoat were in tatters. "I'm sorry I've ruined your clothes," she said as she helped to gently peel the garments off his right side. Her eyes widened when she observed a tattoo adorning the earl's substantial biceps—a heraldic crest featuring a hawk's head—but now was not the time to remark upon it.

He grunted. "It's no matter."

She could hear the strain in his voice. Lord Langdale's muscles and ligaments would have well and truly seized up by now, so she said, "I'll cut through the shoulder seams here on the left so everything else falls away. The less you move the better."

"Again, I won't disagree. Removing my coat was an ordeal in and of itself."

As soon as Lord Langdale's left shoulder and arm were bare, it was evident he'd suffered an anterior dislocation, just as Arabella had suspected. Because the humerus bone had been partially forced out of its socket, Lord Langdale's shoulder had an unnaturally square rather than rounded appearance.

Arabella rubbed her hands together to warm them. Her heart was skittering crazily, but she had to ignore how nervous she felt. She knew how to carry out this procedure, and the earl was relying on her. This was not the time to be fainthearted. "Are you ready, Lord Langdale? I'm afraid what I'm going to do next will hurt—quite a lot—but it must be done."

"I know. I'm ready."

"All right." Arabella drew up the leather ottoman and sat directly in front of him. "You need to sit up as straight as possible, but try to relax your shoulders. Easier said than done, I know." Leaning close, she grasped the earl's left arm and carefully positioned it in such a way that his elbow was tucked into his side and his forearm was at a ninety-degree angle to his upper arm.

"Taking some deep breaths might help," she added as she began to gently but firmly knead the hard mound of muscle at the top of his wide shoulder with her other hand. "I'm using a wee bit of massage to help reduce the stiffness." She transferred her attention to his clearly defined deltoid muscle, then the firm bulk of his biceps, noting how the earl was biting down on his lower lip as though to suppress a moan. His eyes were closed, and the skin was pulled tight over the crests of his cheekbones. "It will be over soon."

He gave a jerky nod, then drew a shaky breath. Then another.

"That's it, breathe deeply. And arch your back a bit if you can. Well done." Arabella began to flex Lord Langdale's elbow as she continued to work his muscles. She wasn't comfortable inflicting more pain upon her patient, but her grandfather had taught her that sometimes one needed to be cruel to be kind. "Very soon, I'm going to bend your forearm up just a little more so your hand rests upon my shoulder. All going well, everything will pop back into its rightful place."

Again he nodded. "Believe me, the sooner the better, Miss Jardine."

"Good." Arabella adjusted her grip at Lord Langdale's elbow. "Take another deep breath and relax those shoulders. Here we go." As she continued to massage the earl's deltoid, she began to move his forearm up, and in the next instant, the humerus slid smoothly back into the joint.

"By God," the earl exclaimed, his eyes popping open. "That was brilliant, Miss Jardine. The pain is all but gone."

Arabella couldn't hide her flush of pleasure as she folded the earl's forearm across his lean torso and encouraged him to support it at the elbow with his other arm. "My grandfather was a very clever man."

"And you're equally as clever."

Buoyed by a sense of profound relief that her treatment had succeeded, as well as being flattered by the earl's heartfelt compliment, a smile tugged at the corners of Arabella's mouth. "Thank you, my lord." She got up from the ottoman and retrieved one of the towels. "I'm going to fashion a sling, as it's best to keep your arm as immobile as possible," she explained as she sliced the linen into a triangular piece with her scissors. "You'll need to wear it for at least a week, perhaps even two, to reduce the risk of another dislocation. Are you able to stand?"

"Of course." Lord Langdale rose smoothly and smiled down at Arabella as she positioned the linen to support his arm. "Are you sure you're not a doctor?"

Arabella laughed. "I wish I were, but alas, society will not permit it." She secured the sling with knots behind Lord Langdale's neck and at his elbow. "I like to do what I can though."

"Forgive me for saying so, but you do seem rather young

to possess such medical skill." Lord Langdale watched her as she put her scissors away and closed her physician's bag. "How long did you work alongside your grandfather?"

"Five years, more or less. From the age of fifteen until I turned eighteen and was sent to Mrs. Rathbone's young ladies' academy in London. And then for another two years after I was expelled." A soft smile curved her mouth as she secured the bag's buckles. "When my grandfather discovered I'd been stealing his medical texts from his study and reading them, he began inviting me along to his practice to observe. Much to the horror of my aunt Flora. That's Lilias's mother. She was the one who insisted I attend the academy to curb my 'unhealthy interests.'"

When she looked up, Lord Langdale was studying her so intently, she blushed. Suddenly, she was acutely aware of the fact that she was entirely alone with a rakehell. And a half-naked one at that.

Such a situation was entirely justified when she'd been working on the earl's shoulder. But not now. She lingered here with this wicked, shirtless, fallen angel of a man, at her own peril. Bertie and Dr. Kerr were probably dealing with the issue of the toppled tree and the damaged conservatory. However, her aunt, Lilias, or even the very proper Mrs. Kerr might walk in at any moment . . . Arabella shivered inwardly. That would surely be a disaster of monumental proportions.

"I . . . I imagine you'd like something else to wear, my lord. A banyan perhaps? Would that do until Bertie is free to find you other clothes that would suit?" Picking up her bag, she edged toward the door. "And then I'd best check if I'm needed elsewhere . . ."

"Wait . . ." Lord Langdale snagged his discarded coat from the back of the wing chair. "I have something for you, Miss Jardine. It's the reason I came here this afternoon."

When he withdrew a damp bundle of folded parchment paper sealed with wax, Arabella's pulse leapt. She dropped her bag. "Is that the letter from Charlie?"

He smiled as he crossed the carpet with long, sure strides and presented it to her with a neat flourish. "It is indeed."

Arabella took it with shaking hands and hugged it to her chest. "Thank you so, so much," she murmured as warm delight spread through her heart. "This means the world to me. Although, when you mentioned you had a letter for me this morning, I certainly didn't expect you to deliver it personally. And straightaway."

"Call me impetuous, but it seemed the easiest and fastest way to get it to you. In hindsight, it wasn't such a good idea." Thunder grumbled in the distance as if it agreed with the earl.

"No, it wasn't." Arabella looked up into Lord Langdale's face. Lightning flickered through the room, momentarily illuminating the sharp cut of his jaw, the perfectly sculpted bow in his upper lip. The glimmer of his deep green eyes.

The sweep of his long, sooty lashes when his gaze fell to her lips.

Arabella's breath caught, yet her heart raced so wildly, it seemed to drown out the sound of the rain drumming against the library windows. Why was he staring at her like that? Examining her mouth as though . . .

No. A man like Lord Langdale might deign to flirt with her, but he couldn't possibly be interested in *kissing* someone like her. Not plain, practical, bespectacled Arabella Jardine with all of her peculiar tendencies and unladylike ways.

Arabella swallowed in an attempt to loosen her tongue. There must be something she could say to dispel the strange electric tension crackling between them. "However, I'm very glad you did take the trouble to deliver it," she said at last, pushing her glasses farther up her nose. "And so very grateful. It's been such a long time since I had any news from my friends. And I . . . I really can't thank you enough." Oh, dear God. A blush scalded Arabella's cheeks. She sounded like a daft, babbling idiot. How many times had she thanked the earl now? She didn't want to know.

Laughter danced in Lord Langdale's eyes, curse him. He knew she was flustered, and he found it amusing. "You're very welcome, Miss Jardine," he said. His decidedly distracting dimple flashed as his mouth curved in a slow, lazy smile. "But it is I who should be thanking you after all you've done for me."

"'Twas no trouble at all." Arabella bent down to push her letter into her bag, but to her dismay, found she was all thumbs when she tried to undo one of the buckles. When she eventually straightened, she feared her entire face was as red as a beet. "I really should go."

"Yes . . . only . . . if you'll indulge me, there's just one more thing." Arabella's breath caught as Lord Langdale's right hand slowly rose to her face. With gentle fingers he adjusted her glasses upon her nose. "They were crooked," he murmured as his fingertips feathered across her hot cheek.

Oh. Confusion reigned. Why was he doing this? Flirting with her as though he wanted to seduce her? Indeed, the earl was so close, she could feel the heat of his body, penetrating her cold, damp clothes. His masculine scent drifted around her—warm and musky yet clean like the rain—and she couldn't move away. Didn't want to move away. Burning curiosity and a strange yearning—a secret stirring deep inside her—impelled her to stay, even though a rational part of her brain told her no good could come of this. That she must go. At once.

Clearing her throat, she summoned her voice. "Thank you."

Lord Langdale's gaze captured hers. Held. "It was my pleasure." He dropped his hand but didn't move away. "I must warn you, Miss Jardine," he said in a voice that was almost a purr. "I'm a man prone to acting on impulse, and I'm sorely tempted to kiss you right now."

"You are?" she whispered. Incredulity stole her breath.

"Yes."

"Why?"

His green eyes grew darker. "Because we're here. And alone. And you have the prettiest mouth." He reached up and ran his thumb over her bottom lip, making her shiver. "In fact, I've been thinking about kissing you all afternoon." He leaned closer, and his breath coasted along her ear. "Can't you feel it? This irresistible urge, this magnetic pull between us? This overwhelming compulsion? Aren't you curious to know what it would feel like to have my lips upon yours? Teasing you? Tasting you?"

Arabella closed her eyes and placed her hand against the hot, hard wall of his chest. She could feel the strong, slow thud of his heart. "We shouldn't . . ." she breathed. But oh, she so wanted to. Because she could feel that pull too. The sharp tug of doing something rash and forbidden.

Aside from her night of indiscretion three years ago—and her inconsequential acts of rebellion like sneaking away from her family in a crowd—Arabella never did anything wrong. Never strayed from the narrow, boring path of decorum. But here was Lord Langdale, the most handsome man she'd ever seen—offering to kiss her. He was a beautiful devil, temptation personified, and heaven help her, it seemed she couldn't resist his invitation to sin.

"I've often found that it's the things we shouldn't do that give us the most pleasure," he murmured against her cheek. "Just one kiss is all I ask for, Miss Jardine. No one will ever know."

How clever and cruel of him to use reason to undermine her defenses. Aunt Flora was indisposed, Lilias was attending to her, Bertie and Dr. Kerr were dealing with the fallen tree, and Mrs. Kerr, well, she barely noted her existence anyway.

Yes, no one will ever know . . .

Scraping together the last remnants of her self-control, Arabella parted her lips and her chest rose as she drew breath to bid Lord Langdale a firm adieu, to tell him goodbye. But instead, she curled her hand around his naked bicep, and all that escaped her was an incoherent whimper of surrender.

In the very next instant, Lord Langdale's mouth found hers.

The warm velvet press of his lips was such a novel sensation, Arabella instantly froze, stunned into immobility. Not because she'd been taken by surprise. He couldn't have made his intentions any clearer. No, she stayed perfectly still, not breathing, not moving a muscle, simply because she'd never been kissed before and had no idea of the mechanics involved. What to do. How to respond.

Clearly not put off by her inexperience, Lord Langdale drew back, then brushed his lips over hers again, a coaxing, gentle nudge. Then once again he applied that wonderfully lush yet firm pressure that was clearly an invitation to something more. Something deeper and sensual and irresistibly decadent. Something she'd never known she'd wanted until right now.

Pushing her up against a glass-fronted bookcase, he held her there with his hard, lean body, kissing her softly, patiently showing her what to do. His injured arm in its sling pressed against her torso while his free hand cupped her face, tilting it upward, angling it just so. When she at last moved her lips beneath his, following his lead and mimicking his actions, he gave a soft groan of appreciation.

And then she felt his thumb gently dragging on her lower lip, encouraging her to open her mouth. To yield. As soon as she did, his wicked tongue pushed inside, and she gasped at how shockingly intimate the incursion felt. But she didn't pull away. She let him slide deeper, to taste her. To explore her mouth with slow, silken, deliberate strokes.

Her knees trembling, her heart pounding, she curled her arms about Lord Langdale's neck lest she fall. Her fingers threaded through the damp, silky curls at his nape, and she summoned the courage to slip her tongue into his mouth to taste him back. The earl groaned again and his hand slid behind her head, spearing into the tangled mass of heavy, damp curls. His kisses became hungrier, harder as she gained confidence and kissed him back with equal enthusiasm, if not skill.

She'd never known the act of kissing could be so wonderful. So all-consuming, like being caught up in a powerful yet utterly pleasurable storm. A strange liquid warmth that could only be desire licked through her body, gathering low in her belly and feeding a growing restlessness deep inside her. She did indeed want something else. Something more. And she sensed Lord Langdale was the only one who could give it to her.

He shifted his position slightly, his large hand skimming over her shoulder and bare arm before settling on her torso, spanning her rib cage. His thumb caressed the underside of her breast, and she gasped with surprise as much as pleasure. When she didn't pull away, he stroked her again, and his hot mouth brushed across her jaw.

"This is madness." The gust of his warm breath, his lust-roughened voice against the shell of her ear, made her shiver. "You were right, we shouldn't be doing this. And I lied . . . one kiss isn't nearly enough."

"No . . ." Neither of them moved. Lord Langdale's hand crept higher and cupped her entire breast, and she instinctively pushed her tight, aching nipple into his palm. "No, it isn't enough," she conceded. "But we should stop. Before things go too far."

"Yes . . ." Still he lingered, his hand on her breast, and so did she.

This couldn't be real; she must be dreaming. Arabella Jardine was in the arms of a sinfully handsome rakehell. An *aroused* rakehell. She could feel the insistent jut of his manhood against the softness of her belly. By rights, she should push him away, rebuke him, rush from the room, before things really *did* go too far.

Before they were caught.

But she didn't. It seemed she was gripped by madness too. And confusion. "I still don't understand." Drawing back a little, she sought Lord Langdale's lust-glazed gaze. "How could someone like you want someone like me?" She really wanted to know before she ended this entirely ill-advised yet completely enthralling encounter.

He couldn't want her. Not really.

Perhaps he'd sustained a blow to the head. Now *that* would make sense.

"Because . . ." began the earl unsteadily, "there's just something about you. I can't explain it." He nuzzled her earlobe, then tugged on it with his teeth. "And God help me, you taste so very good. Feel so very good." He gave her breast another gentle squeeze. "Just one more kiss and then we'll stop," he rasped against her hair, his tone rough yet somehow soft as velvet. "I promise."

Just one more kiss . . . Yes, she could agree to that. Because she knew she'd never have this chance again.

Arabella turned her head seeking Lord Langdale's mouth, and he claimed her again without hesitation. He kissed her slowly, deeply, his tongue caressing hers in long, languorous strokes, exploring her mouth with a thoroughness that made her head spin.

She reached out and splayed her hand against Lord Langdale's muscular chest where his heart now raced in a thunderous gallop beneath her palm. The pulsing ache in her lower belly had intensified, and without thinking, she pushed herself against his lean hips. She wanted to be closer to that intriguing male hardness more than she wanted air to breathe—

"Arabella Mary Jardine! What, in the name of God, do you think you are doing?"

*O**h, hell, bloody hell.*
       Gabriel ripped his mouth from Arabella's and when he turned his head, he cursed again.

Devil take me. Two middle-aged women and Arabella's cousin, Lilias, all stood in the library doorway staring at him and Arabella with wide-eyed, openmouthed horror.

Immediately releasing Arabella, he took a step back, then realized he really shouldn't have when one of the older women—a thin, waspish-eyed matron with graying fair hair—shrieked. Her gaze was fixated on the front of his buckskin breeches where his raging cockstand was clear to see.

Damn it. He moved closer to Arabella again.

"Ladies, I'm so terribly sorry to have startled you—"

"Startled?" cried the ashen-haired matron. "I'm more than startled, young man. I'm absolutely horrified and disgusted. In all my forty-nine years, I've never encountered such a flagrant spectacle. Such appalling indecency. You haven't just compromised my niece. You've corrupted her." She turned her ire-filled gaze on Arabella, who stood pressed against him, trembling. "Arabella. Step away from *that* man this instant."

"Aunt Flora, this gentleman is the Earl of Langdale. He was delivering a letter sent by a mutual friend, Lady Charlotte—"

"The purpose of his visit is immaterial, and I don't care if he's the king of Persia. And as far as I can see"—her gaze flitted to Gabriel's shirtless torso before returning to Arabella—"he's definitely *not* a gentleman. And you, my lass, are no lady."

Gabriel curled his hand around Arabella's upper arm, staying her—for his own sake as much as hers. Aside from her cruel words, there was something about the manner in which Aunt Flora was looking at her niece that he didn't like—the woman's hostility was a force to be reckoned with. The way her frost-blue eyes had narrowed when she'd transferred her gaze to Arabella, it was clear she thought her niece a detestable creature too.

"I'm so sorry about all this, Lord Langdale." Arabella's voice was low, her tone defeated. Mortification weighed every word and every gesture as she tried to free herself and push past him. "I really should go."

"No. No you don't need to go. Because I . . ." Gabriel swallowed, his throat suddenly as dry as the Sahara. "I will do the honorable—"

She shook her head. "No. You don't need to do anything. I haven't a reputation to save to begin with so there's little point—"

"Wait. What were you going to say, Lord Langdale? Before my niece so rudely interrupted you?" Aunt Flora's eyes were suddenly alive with razor-sharp interest.

Gabriel frowned down at the young woman trapped between him and the bookcase. Was he really going to do this? Offer for Arabella's hand to save her from certain ruin? It was his fault entirely that he'd landed her in proverbial hot water, all because he lost control, acted impulsively, and taken what he'd wanted, just like he always did. But for once in his life he would behave as a gentleman ought to.

Drawing a steadying breath, he caught Arabella's gaze. "Miss Jardine, there's only one course of action to take here. You've been well and truly compromised and therefore, I am obliged to offer for your hand."

"No." Arabella shook her head. Her mouth was a hard, flat line. "No, you don't need to do that. I don't want—"

"Arabella Jardine, don't be ridiculous—" her aunt began, but Arabella would hear none of it.

"Aunt Flora, I refuse to marry Lord Langdale over something as trivial as . . . as a kiss."

Gabriel settled a hand on her shoulder. "Miss Jardine, we both know it was more than that."

"Why are you doing this?" she demanded hotly, the gold in her hazel eyes sparking. "You can't want this. I'm nothing. No one."

Her vehement anger stunned Gabriel into momentary silence. When he next spoke, his words were measured, his voice cool, despite the heavy sense of dread thudding through his veins and the wild churning in his gut. "I thought I made it clear, I want to do what is right and honorable."

The young woman, Lilias, piped up. "You could do worse, Arabella."

Aunt Flora spoke again. "Arabella, actions—such as those we all just witnessed—have consequences."

"I don't care." Arabella's voice caught on the last word, and tears welled in her eyes. She looked up at Lord Langdale. "Please let me go, my lord. I beseech you."

The stricken look on Arabella's face tugged at Gabriel's heart in the oddest, most unexpected way. He dropped his hand and stepped back.

"Thank you," she whispered, and then she was roughly pushing past her aunt, cousin, and the other woman, who'd remained disconcertingly grim-faced and tight-lipped throughout the whole fraught exchange.

Gabriel ran a hand down his face before he returned his attention to Arabella's bristling aunt. "Madam, forgive me.

I'm not sure how to address you as we have not been properly introduced."

"Cranstoun," she said with a huff as she stepped forward. "Mrs. Flora Cranstoun." She gestured at the older woman still hovering in the doorway. "And this is Mrs. Eleanor Kerr. Her husband is *Dr.* Kerr, the resident minister of the Crown Court Church in London, and her sister is the Countess of Cheviot. And this is my *married* daughter"—she nodded at the pretty young blonde who looked only a few years older than Arabella—"Mrs. Lilias Arbuthnott. Her husband, Albert, is the son of the merchant banker Walter Arbuthnott. I trust you've heard of the firm Arbuthnott and Allan? There are branches in Edinburgh, Glasgow, and London."

Well played, Flora Cranstoun, Gabriel thought. They might be on the outskirts of a tiny Swiss village, but it seemed the eyes and the ears of the ton were everywhere and there would be no escaping scandal's net.

Aloud, Gabriel said, "I have indeed heard of the firm, Mrs. Cranstoun. Ladies." He nodded in turn to Mrs. Kerr and Arabella's cousin. "I apologize for my state of dishabille. But unfortunately, I suffered a dislocated shoulder after falling from my horse, and the only way to put it to rights was to remove . . ." He shrugged his good shoulder. "Well, I think it's fairly evident."

Flora Cranstoun sniffed. "Yes. Well. Be that as it may, I think the sooner we fetch you something to wear, the better, Lord Langdale. And then"—she pinned him with a frosty stare—"you shall secure the hand of my niece. Otherwise your name will be dragged through the mud when we return home. You mark my words."

If Gabriel hadn't been in so much discomfort—his shoulder was growing more stiff and sore by the moment—he would have laughed. The woman clearly had no idea his name was already well and truly smeared with stinking mud. And about to become mired in it if his cousin Timothy publicly asserted that he was a bastard with no claim to the earldom.

"You have my word, Mrs. Cranstoun. As soon as is practicable, I will approach Miss Jardine again. My offer to marry her is most sincere."

"I should hope so."

Arrangements were made for Bertie Arbuthnott's valet to secure dry clothes for Gabriel, and then the women departed in a flurry of righteous indignation. No doubt Flora Cranstoun was about to read Arabella the riot act. He winced in sympathy as he poured himself a glass of cognac. It really was a very good drop.

But no matter how much alcohol he downed to try to blunt his emotions, he couldn't hide from the fact that his life was now an even bigger shambles than it had been a few hours ago. This time, he only had himself to blame.

Chapter 7

A rainbow spanned the lake, or rather rested one
extremity of its arch upon the water, and the other
at the foot of the mountains of Savoy.
    Mary Shelley, *History of a Six Weeks' Tour*

Arabella slammed her bedroom door shut, then proceeded to pull out the pins from her damp, tangled
hair as she paced the Aubusson rug.

Stupid, stupid, stupid. Why, oh why had she become so
enthralled by Lord Langdale's indecent good looks and
practiced charm that all her sense had flown straight out the
window?

She'd known it was dangerous to be alone with him after
she'd fixed his shoulder. Yet she stayed, courting disaster
all because she'd been silly enough to fall under his rakish
spell.

And now her aunt would do her damnedest to make sure
Arabella accepted Lord Langdale's unenthusiastic proposal. Not that she could blame the man for being reluctant.
He'd obviously thought it would be a bit of fun to toy with
someone like her. To turn a blushing bluestocking around
his little finger. The flaw in his plan had been he'd underestimated the nosiness of her relatives.

What rankled the most was that she, Arabella, should
have known better.

What a monumental mess she'd landed herself in.

Glancing in the looking glass, she almost shrieked. Good Lord, she looked as if she'd been dragged through a hedge and then dumped in a mud puddle the size of Lake Geneva. She picked up her silver-backed brush from the dressing table and began attacking her hair with rough, jerky strokes. When she'd finished repairing her appearance, she would seek out Lord Langdale and tell him again, in no uncertain terms, that his proposal was not needed or welcome. Dr. Graham Radcliff would make a far better husband for someone like her.

But the doctor hasn't written to you, Arabella. Not once since you left London . . .

Arabella pushed the inconvenient thought away. There were probably a myriad of reasons why she might not have received a letter from Dr. Radcliff. At any rate, in the face of her flat-out refusal to marry him, surely Lord Langdale would give up and go. Aunt Flora would wail and complain, but Arabella wouldn't be swayed.

Lord Langdale did not fit into her plans for the future, and she refused to give up on her dreams.

Once her hair was tightly braided and constrained by pins at the back of her head, Arabella threw on dry undergarments and the first gown that came to hand—a plain cotton gown of olive green. She was just seeking a pair of slippers—her green silk ones had been ruined by the rain—when her aunt invaded her room.

"Arabella," she began without preamble as she shut the door firmly behind her. "You cannot refuse Lord Langdale. I forbid it."

Arabella pulled a plain pair of brown kid slippers from her traveling trunk. "I can and I will," she said as she slid them onto her stockinged feet.

Aunt Flora crossed the room in a flash and slapped her across the cheek with such force, Arabella's glasses flew off.

"You filthy little slut," she hissed as Arabella reeled backward, coming up hard against the oak footboard of the bed. "I always knew you were cut from the same soiled cloth as your mother. You *will* marry Lord Langdale. I'll not have you bringing shame upon this family all over again, do you hear me?"

Arabella blinked as tears of pain, shock, and fury stung her eyes. She brought a trembling hand up to her smarting cheek. "But . . . but how can that be?" she flung back. "If no one finds out, nothing untoward will happen—"

"Don't be so naive," snapped Aunt Flora, her ice-blue eyes darting fire. Courtesy of the laudanum, her irises were as tiny as pinpricks, her manner agitated. "Of course people are going to find out about your loose moral character. Eleanor Kerr is absolutely horrified, and justifiably so. Do you think she would stay quiet about something as shocking as this? Indeed, I'm surprised the Kerrs aren't demanding that we pack our bags and leave tonight. When Mrs. Kerr's sister, Lady Cheviot, hears about your disgusting display of wanton behavior, the scandal is sure to spread like wildfire back home. And here, too—Eleanor Kerr seems to know everybody who's holidaying in the vicinity."

Aunt Flora paced over to the window then back again. "Just think how the gossip will affect my poor Lilias and Bertie. Bertie's father is a wealthy, powerful man. I'm eternally grateful he overlooked the disgrace tainting our family after the academy incident and gave his blessing to Bertie and Lilias's marriage. But this time, you've gone too far." She jabbed a finger at Arabella's chest. "I won't have you destroying my Lilias's standing in the eyes of polite society. I just won't."

Arabella retrieved her glasses from where they'd landed on the cream silk counterpane covering her bed, and slid them onto her nose with unsteady fingers. "It was only a kiss," she said faintly.

"It was far more than that, lassie. Don't think I didn't notice the state Lord Langdale was in when Mrs. Kerr, Lilias, and I walked in. Aside from that, he was half-naked."

"But there's a perfectly legitimate reason for that."

"I don't care, Arabella." Aunt Flora crossed her arms across her narrow chest. Her cheeks were flagged with bright color while the rest of her countenance was as pale as the white fichu about her neck. "You were caught and now you must pay the price. Your grandfather might have indulged your whims, but I will not. Behave as you ought to for once in your sorry, wicked life."

Arabella drew a shaky breath. "I'll think on it." It was with a sinking heart that she grudgingly acknowledged Eleanor Kerr might very well blab to her sister and everyone else she knew back home and abroad. And, of course, Arabella didn't want to hurt Lilias.

But more than that, she certainly didn't want or need another scandal about her less-than-perfect behavior splashed across the newspapers and gossip rags at home. If that happened, her plans to court the support of wealthy patrons for her own charitable programs and institutions would surely come to naught.

And what would Dr. Radcliff make of it all? She was publicly labeled an immoral hussy three years ago after she was expelled from Mrs. Rathbone's young ladies' academy. He surely wouldn't be able to overlook such a thing a second time. She couldn't bear it if he thought less of her.

Of course, if she married Lord Langdale, her hope of working alongside a like-minded man to improve the lot of the less fortunate would be irrevocably dashed to pieces too.

Whichever way she looked at it, she was trapped.

"You'll do more than think on it, Arabella." Aunt Flora's tone was as hard as flint. "I expect to hear Lord Langdale announce you've accepted his proposal within the next hour or two."

Arabella placed a hand on her churning stomach. "I can't believe he's willing to go along with this."

"Neither can I. According to Dr. Kerr and Bertie, he is a well-known rakehell, but at least he appears to have a modicum of decency. Which is lucky for you. Lord knows, you are *not* a catch by any stretch of the imagination."

With that, Aunt Flora stalked to the door, her lavender gray silk skirts whipping about her ankles with each determined step. "I'm going to sit with Mrs. Kerr and Lilias in the drawing room. Dr. Kerr and Bertie are still assessing the damage to the conservatory and the morning room. In case you didn't know, one of the wych elms has come down. It seems this afternoon has been a disaster in more ways than one. Nevertheless"—she opened the door with a decided yank—"dinner will be served at the usual time. I expect to see you there with your *fiancé*."

"Where . . . where is Lord Langdale?"

"Getting dressed, I expect. I imagine he will be joining us all for dinner. Mrs. Kerr has kindly decreed that he might stay, *if* he does the right thing by you."

As the door shut, the cynical part of Arabella couldn't help but think Aunt Flora really meant the "right thing" by the family. If she wed Lord Langdale, she would no longer be a thorn in her aunt's side. Not only that, Lilias's cousin wouldn't be a besmirched bluestocking anymore, she'd be a countess; apparently being married to a rakish nobleman—no matter how wicked his reputation—*was* socially acceptable.

The irony of the whole situation was not lost on Arabella.

Left alone, she crossed to the window and drew back the chintz curtain to stare out at the sodden, branch-and-leaf-strewn lawn and the lake and mountains beyond. The storm had abated somewhat—the dark clouds were dispersing, and there was only a light, gauzy drift of rain now.

Arabella's chest rose and then fell as she let out a shaky sigh. There was no avoiding it. She had to seek out Lord Langdale. But before she did, she'd retrieve Charlie's letter from the library. A kind word from a dear friend was exactly what she needed before she threw herself headlong into the great yawning abyss of the unknown.

She couldn't quite believe it. Sophie was married. Charlie's letter in hand, Arabella quit the library and, without a clear destination in mind, wandered down the main hallway of Maison du Lac until she reached the morning room. Several servants were still dealing with the aftermath of the fallen wych elm; one of the tree's enormous branches had smashed through a wide sash window, sending glass and water and fractured twigs and leaves all over the silk-upholstered window seat and the polished parquetry floor. Even though the adjacent conservatory appeared to be ruined beyond repair, at least the main house had suffered minimal damage.

Arabella claimed a spot near a set of French doors that looked out onto a small flagged terrace, and perused Charlie's letter again. The idea that her sweet, shy friend Sophie Brightwell had fallen head over heels in love with Charlie's devil-may-care older brother, Viscount Malverne, and he with her, was, in a word, astonishing.

Of course, she'd noticed the spark of attraction between the pair when they all shared tea at Gunter's that rainy day in April. At the time, Charlie was most adamant that her brother Nate wasn't the marrying kind. But it seemed she'd been wrong. Sophie and Nate were a love match, and when Charlie had penned this letter, they were engaged, due to wed at Lord Malverne's Gloucestershire estate on the twentieth of June.

Which meant Sophie was already Lady Malverne. Even though Arabella could scarcely fathom it, she was nothing but thrilled for her friend. She deserved every ounce of happiness life gave her.

The porcelain clock on the mantelpiece chimed five o'clock, and Arabella folded up Charlie's letter. After pushing it into her pocket through the side slit in her skirt, she opened the French doors. The rain had ceased, and through the gaps in the retreating clouds, a pearlescent pale blue sky peeked through. The faint arc of a rainbow glimmered at one end of the lake, which was now a soft pewter gray and quite serene.

A light, cool breeze lifted her damp curls off her cheeks, and she closed her eyes as she leaned against the doorframe. Behind her, she could hear the tinkle of glass as it was swept up and the wet slap of the mop on the wooden floor. The quiet humming of one of the housemaids. She needed to find Lord Langdale and tidy up her own mess. But at the moment, she just couldn't dredge up the will to move.

"Miss Jardine. I've been looking for you."

Arabella's breath caught at the sound of that deep, gravelly voice. "Yes. I half expected you would," she said as she turned to face the earl. He'd donned fresh clothes—a pair of black breeches, a fine cambric shirt, and a striped silk banyan. She was pleased to see he still wore the sling to support his injured shoulder.

"Only half?" he asked with a small smile.

"We both know you don't really want to marry me, so we don't need to pretend otherwise," she said, aiming for a light tone so the trepidation tripping through her heart wouldn't show. "And while it's very noble of you to want to save me from ruin, I think you've already gathered that I'm not pleased about the situation either."

Lord Langdale studied her face for a long moment, then offered her his good arm. "Will you take a turn about the garden with me, Miss Jardine?"

She inclined her head. "Of course."

After she'd tucked her hand into the crook of Lord Langdale's elbow, they crossed the flagged terrace, then descended three shallow stone steps onto the debris-strewn lawn. The shattered conservatory lay to their left, the wrought iron frame jutting up around the uprooted elm and the remains of battered hothouse plants like the twisted bones of a giant beast's broken rib cage.

"I've been thinking about our encounter, Miss Jardine, and it struck me that you were the one who apologized to me after we were discovered in flagrante delicto. However, I do believe I'm the one who owes you an apology. I shouldn't have kissed you. My behavior was quite despicable, all things considered. You provide me with expert medical attention, and then I repay you by compromising you."

"I don't agree. We are both equally to blame," Arabella said firmly. "It's not as though I wasn't an enthusiastic participant. Nevertheless, your apology is accepted, my lord."

"Thank you." They skirted the ruined conservatory, surveying the damage in silence for a good minute before Lord Langdale said, "You also asked me *why* I kissed you, and for the life of me, I'm still not sure. There is something about you that fascinates me, Miss Jardine. And I do believe we might rub along quite well as husband and wife."

Arabella stopped and faced him. A troubled frown knit her brow. "How can you say that when we hardly know each other?"

He shrugged his good shoulder. "It's just a feeling I have. And I'm rarely wrong about these sorts of things."

She narrowed her eyes, entirely skeptical of his claim. "I wish I possessed that sort of confidence, my lord. But alas, at this point in time, I'm not sure about anything other than we are both in a rather large pickle with no hope of escape."

They mounted the steps of a small, white-pillared belvedere with an uninterrupted view of the lake. The stone bench lining the rear wall was damp, so they leaned against the marble balustrade instead.

The rainbow had faded a little and the wind had picked up, skipping across the lake and ruffling the surface into tiny, white-capped wavelets. It stirred the black curls framing Lord Langdale's beautiful face as he turned to regard her. "I also recall you asserting that you are nothing and no one," he said in a soft, low voice. His deep green gaze searched hers as though he was trying to solve a particularly perplexing puzzle. "I do not believe that for one moment. From what I've seen of you so far, nothing could be further from the truth."

"Thank you." Arabella found herself blushing and she looked away, examining the view as though she'd never seen it before. "You're clearly easy to please."

He laughed, the chuckle a rich, warm vibration that tugged her attention back to him. "I'm really not." His expression changed. A shadow flickered in his eyes. "However, there are some things you should know about me, Arabella. A long time ago, someone who was very dear to me betrayed my trust, and so from that day on, I decided that honesty was a personal quality I valued above all others. For that reason, I want you to know that I will *always* be honest with you, no matter what. Which leads me to my next disclosure . . ." His frown deepened. "I must warn you that I am not the prize catch your family probably thinks I am."

"What do you mean?" She wasn't a prize catch, either, given her background. Aunt Flora certainly thought so.

He sighed and leaned his weight upon his good arm. "It's a complicated story," he began, his tone uncharacteristically somber. "But suffice it to say, I have a relative—a first cousin by the name of Timothy—who has told me point-blank that he is about to challenge my claim to the earldom of Langdale."

Arabella frowned. "How terrible for you," she said softly. "I . . . I honestly had no idea that such a thing was even possible."

Gabriel grimaced. "I'm afraid it is. Timothy is convinced my parents' marriage wasn't valid, and if that is the case, I'm illegitimate."

Oh. Arabella swallowed, her mouth suddenly dry. She feared she might be regarded as illegitimate too. But before she could summon the courage to tell Lord Langdale, he began to speak again.

"Actually, the reason I'm here in Switzerland is that I'm looking for my mother. She and my father parted ways when I was thirteen, and she's been living on the Continent ever since. I'm hoping she can provide evidence to refute Timothy's claim. I have good reason to believe she's been residing in Italy, and a year ago, she was in the village of Nyon and then Villeneuve. But so far, my search has proved fruitless. I'm hoping the local inquiry agent I have employed will be able to provide me with some useful intelligence in the next week or so."

Arabella's heart cramped with sadness. "Oh my goodness. I can't even imagine how difficult this all must be for you. And now you are faced with the unpleasant prospect of being caught in the parson's mousetrap. All because of one silly kiss."

Gabriel's gaze trapped hers. "It wasn't a single kiss, Arabella. And what we did was far from silly."

Arabella blinked at him. He'd used her first name. The intimacy of such a thing, combined with the way he was looking at her so intently, set her heart capering and tied her tongue into tight knots.

"At any rate," the earl continued, seemingly oblivious to the fact that she'd just been struck dumb. "I thought you should know about my circumstances before you agreed to accept my proposal. Even if I lose the title, I assure you I have substantial funds set aside that are not linked to the entail. You would want for nothing in a material sense, but the name you take as my wife might bear the ignoble stain of bastardy. And that would have consequences for any children we might have. I would understand completely if you did not want to marry me for that reason."

Children. Arabella swallowed and her belly did an odd flip-flop. "I must confess, I hadn't even thought that far ahead." Which was foolish of her. Of course a man like Lord Langdale would want children.

"I would expect you, as my wife, to provide me with an heir. But only if I'm able to retain my title." He paused, letting the import of what he'd just said sink in. "There's little point otherwise. I'm reluctant to bring a child into this world if I'm officially declared a bastard by the church courts and the Committee for Privileges."

Arabella frowned. "So let me see if I've understood you correctly. What you're telling me is we won't have marital relations unless and until you can successfully refute your cousin's challenge."

Lord Langdale tilted his head and examined her face. "Not exactly," he said carefully.

"What do you mean by that? I'm confused. If we . . ." Arabella blushed to the roots of her hair. "If we do consummate our union, there's a risk I might fall pregnant. I know how these things work."

"Even though our marriage will be in name only for the most part, it will be consummated so its legality can never be questioned. But there are certain measures I can take on our wedding night that will ensure I don't get you with child."

Oh. Arabella knew about the technical aspects of sexual congress and conception—in theory. She thought she understood the particular "measures" Lord Langdale was alluding to . . .

He suddenly reached out and covered her hand with his. "I know I'm asking a lot of you, Arabella." His deep voice was laced with a softer, almost nervous edge. "I should also tell you—in the spirit of being open and honest—that I'm not sure if I'm capable of fidelity. I've always been a man with a great appetite for life's carnal delights, and I'm not confident that I can control that aspect of my character."

Arabella's heart sank. She hadn't anticipated the earl would be so forthcoming about that particular topic. She focused her attention back on the lake, her eyes smarting with the effort to hold back tears. To hear Lord Langdale admit he wouldn't remain faithful to her—before she'd even agreed to marry him—stung her pride more than just a little. She knew she was plain—her aunt had told her often enough—and not the sort of woman who turned men's heads. Especially not someone as divinely attractive as Lord Langdale.

When her wave of self-pity had passed, she said, "I appreciate your candor, my lord. At least I won't be entering marriage with the wool pulled over my eyes. Indeed, your disclosure shouldn't really surprise me in the slightest." Arabella recalled the conversation she'd had with Charlie, Sophie, and Olivia in Gunter's when they were compiling a list of prospective husbands. Charlie had insisted they all consider her brother's rakish friends; Lord Langdale's name had been near the top of the list. "I've heard you are quite the rakehell, so it would be naive of me to think you would change your ways. I hope you can forgive me for being indelicate—I'm afraid it's my practical, medical mind that makes me so—but as you wish to consummate our union, I trust that you are physically well. Despite your great appetite, as you put it."

Lord Langdale laughed. "Even though my pedigree is being contested, I assure you I am healthy as a horse. I've always taken measures to prevent contracting anything unpleasant, shall we say?" He waggled his eyebrows. "I'm more than happy to submit to a thorough inspection if required."

Arabella arched an eyebrow. "That won't be necessary, my lord. I'll take you at your word."

The earl's expression sobered. "After I have my heir, I

am not opposed to the idea of you taking a lover, Arabella—if that's what you want, and as long as you are discreet about it. Which reminds me, I've been quite remiss not to ask you: What do *you* actually want? You're a capable, clever young woman. Do *you* want a husband and family of your own? What are your aspirations in life? What are you passionate about?"

Arabella blinked in astonishment. No one had ever asked her such a thing before in such a direct fashion. Not even her grandfather, who'd loved her dearly. And Lord Langdale had posed the question as though she had a choice in the matter; it was a most novel experience to be treated thus. "Even though I cannot be a doctor, I still want to make a difference in this world. I want to help people less fortunate than myself. Especially infants and children who've lost their parents and have limited prospects; perhaps because I, too, am an orphan. I'd especially like to advocate for improved conditions in Edinburgh's and Glasgow's orphanages; the ones I'm familiar with are in an appalling state. And I'd also like to see an increase in the number of medical dispensaries, not just in London but in other large towns. As for marriage, I've never been sure that I'd actually meet someone who would want me as a wife. I am a rather opinionated bluestocking after all. But I always imagined that if I did marry, that I would like to have children one day."

Gabriel nodded. "Of course. The House of Lords accepted my parents' marriage was valid when I claimed the title after my father's death, so I'm confident my cousin's challenge will ultimately fail. But even if the worst should happen and I did lose the earldom, just know that as your husband, I would do my very best to accommodate and support your philanthropic endeavors if nothing else."

"That's reassuring to know. And very kind of you." Arabella's gaze dropped to the balustrade where Lord Langdale's large hand lay alongside hers. The hawk's head signet ring winked at her. This mercurial man was offering her the chance to fulfill her long-held dream. If she didn't marry him, it was highly likely she would be socially ruined anyway—Aunt Flora had made that abundantly clear—and then she'd never achieve her goals. Even though she didn't really understand why Lord Langdale wanted to marry her—other than out of a sense of obligation—she realized she would be foolish to refuse him.

"I must confess, it's a lot to consider," she said at last. "I never expected to marry for love, so a practical arrangement suits me well." She'd been willing to consider Dr. Radcliff as a prospective spouse for the very same reason after all. "And I agree that it would be a sensible idea to delay the begetting of a child until your title is secure."

Lord Langdale leaned negligently against the balustrade. His mouth tipped into a beguiling smile. "So, Miss Arabella Jardine, are you telling me that you will at last consent to my offer of marriage?"

Arabella drew a bracing breath. Was she really going to do this? It seemed she was. "Yes, Lord Langdale. I will accept your proposal."

He grinned. "Well, that's a relief. I was worried your aunt Flora would call me out."

Arabella laughed. It was refreshing to know the earl had a sense of humor even in less-than-ideal circumstances. She decided it was one of the things she liked about him. "Honestly, I don't think any of them—my aunt, Bertie, or Lilias—think I'm worth the effort."

Lord Langdale's brow furrowed, and concern filled his gaze. "I've only known you a short time, but it's evident that there's no love lost between you and your family."

"No . . ." Arabella sighed. "There's not. My aunt and I have always had a prickly relationship. I have no doubt at all that she'll be glad to see the back of me."

Sympathy lit the earl's eyes as he offered his uninjured arm. "Shall we return to the house to share our felicitous news anyway?"

"Aye." Arabella placed her hand on his muscular forearm and they descended the stairs of the belvedere. "Did you know Aunt Flora has invited you to dinner?"

Lord Langdale nodded. "Yes . . ." He cast her a sideways glance. "Actually, Dr. Kerr has also invited me to spend the night."

"Oh . . ." Arabella's pulse leapt, and she dropped her gaze to the wet grass. Just thinking about Lord Langdale sleeping under the same roof as her made her quiver with an emotion she suspected might be nervous anticipation. After they were married, they'd be sharing a bed. And to think she'd only just met the earl this morning. This was a strange day indeed.

When she didn't say anything else, Lord Langdale added, "Although I'm sure the Kerrs' hospitality is contingent upon the announcement of our betrothal."

"I expect so." Arabella gathered her wits and decided to focus on the practical. "But I'm glad you're staying, because it will save you the trouble of trying to return to Villeneuve before it grows dark. Given the ferocity of the storm, the roads might be treacherous, and you're in no fit state to ride. My goodness—" Arabella halted. "Your horse! I do hope it's all right. Dr. Kerr sent someone to look for it."

Lord Langdale smiled. "It is indeed, thanks to you. Dr. Kerr informed me that you were the one who saw the poor beast bolt behind the house. Aside from a bruised hoof, he's quite fine."

"Good." Arabella smiled back. "I'm quite relieved."

They'd almost gained the villa's rear terrace when Lord Langdale said quietly, "I expect we'll be married by the end of next week. If you agree."

Arabella stopped so abruptly, she almost stumbled. "In a week?" she said faintly. "Why . . . why so soon?" In her mind they would perhaps get married when they returned to London. Clearly she'd been mistaken.

Lord Langdale's brow creased with concern as he studied her face. "I do believe you're more reluctant than I am to wed. But I don't see any point in delaying the inevitable. Do you?"

Arabella sighed. "I suppose you're right. Forgive me if I sound a trifle unenthusiastic, my lord. But I'm still becoming accustomed to the whole idea of being your wife."

"That's only natural. I'm going to ask Dr. Kerr to officiate at the ceremony here, but to ensure our marriage is also recognized in England, we will also be wed by an Anglican clergyman when we return home. I'll not have anyone questioning the validity of our marriage."

"I understand. And I agree, that sounds eminently sensible to me too."

"Good. There's just one more thing . . ." Lord Langdale glanced into the now deserted morning room before turning back to face her directly. "Two actually."

Arabella frowned up into his handsome face. His deep green eyes were partly shielded by the sweep of his black lashes, so she couldn't quite ascertain his mood or intent. "Yes?"

"Firstly, I would like it very much if you called me Gabriel rather than Lord Langdale, or my lord."

"Oh, of course, my . . . I mean, Gabriel." His name felt strange on her lips. Though she couldn't deny it suited him very well.

"And secondly," he continued in a low, dark-velvet voice as he moved closer. "I'm bedeviled by a burning need to kiss you. To seal the plighting of our troth. If you consent . . ."

Arabella swallowed. Temptation too strong to resist thrummed in her veins. "I . . . very well," she murmured huskily. "To plight our troth."

Her breath hitched as Lord Langdale—Gabriel—cupped her face ever so gently. His thumb caressed her cheekbone, and his heated gaze dipped to her lips. Slowly but surely, he bent down and claimed her mouth in a soft, bone-melting, languid kiss. The satiny glide of his lips and the warm, silken dance of his tongue made her toes curl in her slippers. Her knees grew so weak, she had to clutch at the lapels of his borrowed banyan.

"I really wish this cursed arm of mine wasn't in a sling," he whispered against her mouth when they broke apart. "I want to lash you against me. Sweep you up and carry you away somewhere. Somewhere private."

A reluctant smile pulled at Arabella's lips. She was bemused that he seemed to want her so much. But then she was a warm, willing female and he was a rake. She shouldn't put too much stock in his professed desire. "You did warn me about your appetite," she murmured.

"Yes, and right at this very moment, I'm simply ravenous." Gabriel kissed her again, and by the time they came up for air, Arabella was certain she was developing an appetite for all things carnal too.

"We should go inside," she said, forcing herself to step away from his lean, hard body. She'd been nervous about the prospect of being bedded by Gabriel on their wedding night, but if his kisses were anything to go by, she had no doubt she would be in expert hands.

Gabriel nodded. "Yes, we should. Though I think I need a moment. I'm a bit hot and flustered and I don't want to shock the ladies again."

Arabella laughed. "I could always throw a bucket of cold water over you. I think one of the housemaids left one in the morning room."

"And here I was thinking you were kindness personified."

"I have little sympathy if your pain is self-inflicted. You were only going to kiss me once, if I recall. To plight our troth."

"Yes." He sighed and adjusted his banyan to hide the front of his borrowed breeches. "But the problem is, Arabella, once I start kissing you, I can't seem to stop."

She cast him a wry smile. "I've noticed."

"I haven't heard you complain," he countered as he offered his arm.

"No . . ." And that was a problem. Arabella's contented mood faded as her *fiancé* escorted her into the villa. She'd only just met Gabriel, and given the way her pulse capered when he smiled and her head spun when he kissed her, she suddenly realized she might be in serious danger of losing her heart to this man. A man who'd just professed he could never be faithful. A man who was unlikely to fall in love with a plain, bookish, bespectacled bluestocking.

This marriage wouldn't be a love match like Sophie and Lord Malverne's. It was a business transaction. Gabriel—if he retained his title—wanted an heir one day. And she hoped to secure funds to support the charities dear to her heart.

It was as simple as that. And it was something she would do well to remember in the coming days and months. And years.

At least she would no longer be beholden to her aunt and the rest of her family.

Now that was something she could smile about.

CHAPTER 8

❧❧

Clarens! sweet Clarens! birthplace of deep Love!
    Thine air is the young breath of passionate
thought . . .

              Lord Byron, "Childe Harold's Pilgrimage"

Clarens, Lake Geneva, Switzerland

July 9, 1818

The next week passed in a series of odd fits and starts.
There were quiet, dragging hours in which Arabella,
left to her own devices, couldn't wait to be wed to Lord
Langdale one minute, only to be assailed by a bout of
stomach-churning nerves in the next. And then there were
times when she was caught up in a whirl of frenzied activity as preparations were made for the upcoming nuptials.

All her clothes were freshly laundered and packed into
her trunk; most of her things would be sent off to Gabriel's
villa in Villeneuve the day before the wedding. Mrs. Kerr
and Aunt Flora fussed about the fare that would be served
at the small wedding breakfast at Maison du Lac: Would
they have a buffet of cold collations, vegetable dishes, jel-
lies, flummeries, and Italian ice creams, or serve a hot meal
à la russe at table? Flowers—an assortment of lilies and
roses—were chosen for her bouquet and the small Gothic
church, Église Saint-Vincent, situated on the side of a steep
hill just above Montreux; the protestant minister had kindly

acquiesced to Dr. Kerr's request to use his church to conduct the ceremony.

The Kerrs also seemed to have an inordinate number of tonnish acquaintances in and around Montreux, Vevey, and Villeneuve; indeed, the number of English and Scots tourists who liked to visit Switzerland during the summer truly astonished Arabella. Clearly at Eleanor Kerr's behest, a parade of these busybodies descended on Maison du Lac each day for "morning calls." They might offer congratulations to Arabella, but she suspected they probably just wanted to take a look at the veritable nobody who'd recently become engaged to the notorious Earl of Langdale.

And Gabriel . . . she saw her husband-to-be only once in the days before their wedding, which was both a disappointment and a relief—she wanted to get to know him better, but at the same time, when she did see him, her equilibrium was well and truly shaken, especially when he kissed her. She was in danger of turning into a lovestruck mooncalf, and that wouldn't do at all. Falling in love with Lord Langdale would be foolish in the extreme. After their marriage was consummated, at least Gabriel was likely to keep his distance. At least until his title was secure . . .

Aside from making wedding arrangements, Arabella gathered that Gabriel had been busily trying to determine the whereabouts of his mother. She sincerely hoped Lady Langdale could help Gabriel to refute his cousin's claim that her marriage to Gabriel's father hadn't been valid. For Gabriel's sake and her own—she really did want to have a child one day, if at all possible.

Even though Gabriel was largely absent from Maison du Lac, he was certainly attentive in other ways. He sent Arabella flowers every day—huge bouquets of fragrant roses, lilies, and honeysuckle—and a sweet little note with each one. *Counting the days until you are mine. I saw these lilies and immediately thought of you.* All were signed *G*, the single letter rendered with a great flourish. And on the day before they were due to wed, he arranged for a modiste from Villeneuve to deliver the most exquisite wedding gown Arabella had ever seen—a confection of delicate ivory silk, rich cream satin, and the finest gold tissue. It fit perfectly, and Arabella felt very spoiled indeed.

And then at last, her wedding day dawned, bright and beautiful. The sky was a clear azure blue, the waters of Lake Geneva a deep indigo as Bertie drove the Kerrs' landau along the road leading to Montreux and then up the steep hill to Église Saint-Vincent. The magnificent view helped subdue the storm of nervous fluttering inside Arabella's belly.

However, when she stepped into the cool, dimly lit interior of the church on Bertie's arm, and saw her handsome bridegroom waiting for her by the simple wooden alter at the end of the aisle, her heart somersaulted in her chest. She was immediately transported back to the dungeon of Château de Chillon. Had it really only been a week since she'd first encountered this beautiful, charismatic man? If she'd had an inkling of what would transpire between them, would she have turned and fled from the dungeon, or would she still have blithely followed him regardless?

Speculating about what-ifs and what-might-have-beens was pointless now. In less than a half hour, she would no longer be Miss Arabella Jardine but Arabella Holmes-Fitzgerald, the Countess of Langdale.

For better or for worse, her life was about to change forever.

Gabriel handed his lovely young bride up into his phaeton before leaping up beside her. The young tiger handed him the reins, and then with a flick, they were off, barreling away from Église Saint-Vincent, following the winding road down the terraced slope, between low stone walls and verdant hedges.

"Hold on, my fair Lady Langdale," he said as he negotiated a particularly tight turn halfway down the hill.

"Don't worry, I am," Arabella replied. Her bonnet had slipped off the back of her head, and her golden curls were flying. "I don't doubt you are skilled at driving a phaeton, but I fear my heart might give out before we reach the bottom. Which would be a shame for you, my lord, if I don't survive long enough for you to enjoy our wedding night."

Gabriel immediately slowed the pace of the matched grays strapped into the phaeton's traces. "It's my sincere hope that you will enjoy it too," he said in a soft, low voice he knew would make her blush. "And I apologize for driving too fast. Blame it on my selfish eagerness to have you all to myself at long last." He leaned closer and added, "It's been far too long between kisses."

Was that an unladylike snort he heard? Gabriel slid his new wife a quick glance before he fixed his attention back on the road. She hadn't blushed at all. His seductive wiles clearly weren't working on her. At least not yet. "You doubt me already, Arabella? I know I've been largely absent and I'm sorry for that."

"No, you don't need to apologize, Gabriel," she said, her slender shoulders lifting and falling with a small resigned sigh. "It's quite all right. My reaction was thoughtless. I know you have other pressing business to attend to."

Guilt shredded Gabriel's gut. He'd neglected Arabella. Hurt her feelings. And he didn't want her to feel that way before they'd even begun. He wasn't a total cad. He needed to clear the air. "No, I'm the one who's been thoughtless. But I thank you for your forbearance. Now that we're wed, I've been possessed with a renewed urgency to find my mother. I fear time is running out and it won't be long before Timothy begins proceedings to stake his claim." The inquiry agent Gabriel had employed in London before he quit town had recently sent word that his uncle Stephen was still hanging on by a thread. But that had been two weeks ago . . .

"I do understand. Truly," Arabella said, her lips twitching with a timid smile. She reached out and gave his forearm a tentative squeeze.

Gabriel smiled back and this time she did blush, a bright shade of pink. Her shyness and total lack of artifice touched him. Gone was the brave young woman who charged out into the storm like Minerva, the goddess of wisdom, medicine, and war; who tended to his injured shoulder with the skill of a practiced physician. She hadn't been hesitant about touching him then . . .

He was impatient for her clever touch now.

Transferring the reins to one hand, he tugged off one of his riding gloves with his teeth, then covered Arabella's small bare hand on the seat beside him. And a genuine smile of pleasure broke across her lovely face.

That was better.

Truth to tell, part of the reason Gabriel hadn't visited Arabella was he hadn't wanted to frighten her with the strength of his ardor. For reasons he still couldn't fathom, he desired her with an intensity that astonished him. She wasn't attractive in a conventional sense, but she drew his eye as no woman had in some time. And while she might be young—she'd recently shared with him that she was one-and-twenty—there was no doubt she was wise beyond her years. Not only that, he *liked* her.

Even though he'd done the honorable thing for once in his life, Gabriel knew deep down he wasn't a saint. If they didn't have mutual friends—Charlotte and Nate Hastings—he supposed he might've set about simply seducing Arabella to satisfy his curiosity as well as his lust. Indeed, perhaps the only real reason he hadn't cried off marrying her in the end was that he feared Charlie and Nate's new wife, Sophie, might harangue Nate to call him out—and that would not turn out well for either of them.

Yes, this devilish attraction he had for Arabella was damned inconvenient. Especially when his place in society was far from secure. Come what may, he would endeavor to be a good husband to Arabella, but earl or not, he would never be her, or indeed any woman's, chivalrous knight in shining armor; he wasn't entirely heartless, but he didn't want to deal with an emotion as troublesome as love. He had to bite his cheek to suppress a wry smile. Given his reckless nature and wandering eye, he was more of a knight-errant. Or as London's *Beau Monde Mirror* had oftentimes dubbed him, the Errant Earl.

If Timothy succeeded in his quest, perhaps Gabriel would soon be known as the Errant Bastard.

At least he had been honest with Arabella about his shortcomings. He'd never been in love, and he truly doubted he could remain faithful to any woman. Once he'd had his fill of Arabella and his ravenous need faded, she wouldn't be taken by surprise when he sought satisfaction elsewhere.

When they reached the bottom of the hill, Gabriel steered the phaeton eastward toward Villeneuve.

"Oh . . . I think you missed the turn to Clarens," said Arabella, turning in her seat to glance back down the road.

"No. I didn't."

"But the wedding breakfast—"

"Your family and the Kerrs can enjoy it on their own. I told Bertie we wouldn't be attending after all." Gabriel didn't feel the slightest bit guilty about spiriting her away. As far as he was concerned, her ungrateful aunt Flora and the judgmental Kerrs could go hang. "You're all mine now, my sweet Arabella. We shall dine at Villa Belle Rive."

Gabriel swore he heard his wife mutter the word *incorrigible* beneath her breath. But when he stole a glance at her face, she was smiling.

Just outside of Montreux, not far from Chillon Castle, they hit a bump in the dirt road and he couldn't suppress a groan as his shoulder protested. Arabella noticed immediately.

"You really should still be wearing your sling," she said with a frown. "I don't wish to nag you on today of all days, but you're clearly flouting my medical advice."

"Call me vain," he said with a grin. "I didn't want to spoil the lines of my beautifully tailored superfine coat on my wedding day. My shoulder is much improved though. The liniment oil you gave me has worked wonders."

Arabella nodded. "Good."

"You can rub some in later if you like."

A bright red blush flooded Arabella's smooth-as-ivory cheeks. "If you behave yourself."

He laughed and kissed her hand. "My dear Lady Langdale, we both know that's never going to happen."

*   *   *

Gabriel's rented villa was beautiful. A mansion really. Arabella gasped as Gabriel drove his phaeton up the gravel drive to the grand set of double doors.

The three-story château was situated on the very edge of the lake on its own tiny peninsula. Its walls were tinted a pale shell pink while the gabled roof was a soft blue-gray. Elegant poplars lined the drive, and banks of white roses flanked each side of the villa's front terrace.

When Gabriel helped her to alight from her seat, Arabella found she was pressed between the carriage and her new husband.

"Welcome to Villa Belle Rive, my lovely wife." Pulling the already dislodged straw bonnet from her head, Gabriel swooped down to steal a tender kiss. "I hope you'll be able to forgive me for not carrying you over the threshold."

"If you tried, I'd have to scold you severely."

Gabriel threaded his fingers through hers and led her toward the front door. "Only a scolding? Now, if you were to offer a spanking to go along with it, I *would* be sorely tempted to whisk you off your feet."

Arabella couldn't be certain, but judging by the mischievous twinkle in his eyes, she suspected Gabriel's jest contained an innuendo of a sexual nature, but for the life of her, she could make neither head nor tail of it.

She was only just beginning to understand how wicked her new husband might actually be.

Gabriel introduced her to the villa's small contingent of staff who stood lined up in the airy vestibule. The butler, housekeeper, cook, and half a dozen servants were Swiss. A pair of liveried English footmen and Gabriel's valet, Ryecroft, were also present.

The trim, middle-aged man bowed deferentially. "My lady, welcome to Villa Belle Rive. Your trunk has already been installed in your chambers, and Colette"—he gestured toward one of the young Swiss housemaids—"is at your disposal. She speaks a little English."

"Thank you, Ryecroft." Arabella smiled at the girl; she

couldn't have been more than fifteen or sixteen. "Bonjour, Colette." She'd never had a maid to attend to her personal needs before, and the whole idea was quite novel. The maid blushed prettily as she bobbed a curtsy.

The formalities over, Gabriel offered Arabella his arm and escorted her up a sweeping marble staircase. The walls above the walnut paneling featured frescoes of near-naked water nymphs and other fantastical creatures cavorting by a pond in a wooded glade. "Your chamber is adjacent to mine," he said as they traversed the gallery at the top of the stairs. "And after you've freshened up, I wondered if you might like to join me for our own private wedding breakfast. Our suites share a balcony, which overlooks the lake."

"Of course. I would love that." Arabella was grateful that Gabriel didn't seem to be in a hurry to rush her off to claim his husbandly rights *just* yet. They paused by a set of white wooden doors with brass handles, and Gabriel pushed them open.

"I shall join you shortly," she said.

Gabriel's gaze caught hers. "I'll be counting the minutes," he replied in a low voice as smooth and rich as aged whisky.

Arabella's toes curled in her gold slippers. *Heavens above.* Her new husband might not be smitten with her, but if he continued to employ his rakish charms, she didn't think she would mind at all if he rushed her off to bed. The door closed behind her and she released a wistful sigh. *If only we really were in love, then everything would be perfect . . .*

Left alone, Arabella inspected her bedchamber and the adjacent dressing room with wide-eyed amazement. Like the rest of Villa Belle Rive, her suite was lavishly appointed.

A set of wide French doors opened onto a stone balcony that overlooked Lake Geneva, with its impressive backdrop of towering snow-capped mountains and brilliant blue sky. The doors and windows were festooned with ivory lace and pale blue damask curtains trimmed with antique gold. The velvet bed hangings and silk counterpane adorning the enormous four-poster bed had obviously been chosen to match. Each piece of satinwood furniture featured gilt trimmings, and sitting atop every table was an enormous arrangement of fragrant white roses, lilies, and honeysuckle.

To the left of the gray marble fireplace was another door, which Arabella supposed led to Gabriel's chambers. When she padded across the thick Aubusson rug—also in shades of pale blue, gold, and ivory—to the dressing room, she discovered all her clothes had been neatly arranged in the armoire and her grandfather's medical bag sat on a wooden chest. In lieu of a chamber pot or a necessary cabinet, there was a water closet.

Never, in all her life, had she stayed in such opulent apartments. She'd known Gabriel was wealthy, but it seemed she'd grossly underestimated the extent of his fortune. Apparently her husband was as rich as Solomon.

After tending to her disheveled curls in the looking glass—the wind had played havoc with her hair during the open-air carriage ride to Villa Belle Rive—Arabella stepped onto the wide balcony. Large ornamental pots of lavender had been placed at regular intervals around the pretty space, and a small arbor of climbing roses stood near a wrought iron dining setting.

Skirting the table that contained an array of domed silver platters, silver cutlery, and fine china plates, Arabella removed her glasses and took up a position by the stone railing to drink in the breathtaking view. The delicate scent of the roses drifted by on a gentle breeze, and a feeling akin to contentment flooded her. Villa Belle Rive was aptly named indeed.

At the soft snick of a latch, Arabella turned to find Gabriel emerging from his suite.

Her heart skipped a beat as he prowled toward her with the grace of a sleek black panther. "I forgot to give you something," he said, reaching into the pocket of his superfine jacket. "Our marriage lines, my lady wife," he added, presenting them with a flourish. "They are yours to keep."

"Thank you, my lord." Arabella took the folded piece of parchment. As was customary, Dr. Kerr had given her their marriage certificate at the church. However, because she hadn't wanted to stuff the all-important document into her small reticule, thereby crushing it, she'd entrusted it to Gabriel. "I'll put it away."

Gabriel arched a winged brow. "And then we shall dine?"

"Yes. I would like that."

When Arabella returned, it was to find Gabriel pouring French champagne into delicate crystal glasses. He pulled out a chair for her and she sat carefully; she didn't want to snag the delicate silk and gold tissue gown on the wrought iron. She placed her glasses beside her linen napkin in case she needed them again.

"To us," Gabriel said, touching his glass to hers. His gaze burned hotter than the summer sun shining above. "To bright and happy days and the fulfillment of all our mutual desires."

Oh my. Arabella could do nothing but tilt her head in agreement. Closing her eyes, she took a sip of the fine wine, savoring the flavor and the feel of the bubbles on her tongue. "This is lovely," she murmured.

When she looked up at Gabriel, he flashed his rake's smile. "More than lovely," he returned. "The word 'breathtaking' springs to mind. You have the most beautiful hazel eyes."

A blush crept over Arabella's cheeks, and she dropped her gaze to the white lace tablecloth.

She'd hardly ever been without her glasses in front of Gabriel, and no doubt his kind remark was intended to reassure her that he desired her. Nevertheless, she didn't think she'd ever get used to receiving compliments from this man. A piece of her—a small, wholly feminine part—wished he was sincere. That these romantic gestures were genuine displays of affection and not simply a means to an end. "I don't always need to wear my spectacles," she explained in a manner she hoped was matter-of-fact rather than self-conscious. "Well, I need them to read, and to sew, and to do anything up close. But if I'm regarding anything a foot or more away, I can see quite clearly. It's just easier to keep them on most of the time."

He nodded in apparent understanding. "You might wish to put them on again," he said, reaching into his jacket a second time. "At least for a moment."

Arabella blinked in surprise when he placed a slim case covered in dark green velvet in front of her. "What's this?" she asked as she slid her glasses back into place.

Gabriel grinned at her over his glass of champagne. "Open it and you'll see."

Arabella lifted the tiny gold latch and opened the lid. And gasped. Inside on a bed of white satin lay the most beautiful necklace she'd ever seen. Set in gold and surrounded by diamonds, the heart-shaped emerald pendant sparkled and winked at her in the bright afternoon light.

"Gabriel," she breathed. "You . . . you shouldn't have."

"Yes. I most definitely should. It's my wedding gift to you."

"Thank you."

"May I help you to put it on?"

"Aye. Of course."

Arabella lifted up the ringlets at the back of her head, exposing her nape so Gabriel could fasten the necklace's clasp. His fingers were warm, his touch light on her skin, but even so, Arabella shivered with awareness. Very soon he would be touching her in far more intimate places than her neck . . .

"Let me see you." Gabriel reclaimed his seat and studied her décolletage. "Beautiful," he said softly. "The colors suit you well."

"Thank you," she said again. Guilt pinched, and she blinked rapidly to suppress the unexpected prickle of tears. "I feel terrible. I'm afraid I didn't get you anything."

"Your delightful smile is the only gift I want, Arabella," he said gently. "And as your husband, I declare that no tears are allowed on our wedding day. Now"—he lifted one of the silver domes to reveal an array of tiny savory pastries featuring tender pieces of crayfish, steamed asparagus tips, and something else, which Arabella suspected might be foie gras paté. "I don't know about you, but I'm famished. Let's eat."

Gabriel played servant, offering Arabella the platter of pastries and another plate overflowing with soft golden cheeses, luscious figs, fat purple grapes, and fresh bread, and it wasn't long before her plate was full. She tasted everything, but after her third crayfish pastry, she paused.

"You're full already?" Gabriel asked as he tore off a chunk of bread and topped it with a slab of washed-rind cheese. "Or are you saving room for dessert?" He nodded at a pair of crystal bowls brimming with strawberries and cream.

Arabella sipped her champagne. "I . . . I have to tell you something. Something I probably should have told you before now." It was difficult to continue eating when her conscience kept pricking at her.

"Oh, yes?" Gabriel put down his bread and cheese and gave her his full attention.

Arabella forced herself to hold her husband's gaze as she said, "You've been so forthright about your history. But I'm afraid I haven't been as forthcoming about my past. And I want to be as honest and open as you have with me."

Gabriel's lips quirked. "What, you're going to tell me you're already secretly married?"

She smiled, appreciating his attempt at levity. "No. It's about my parents. And their marriage. Or lack thereof . . ." Her voice quivered.

"Hey, now." A line appeared between Gabriel's black brows, and he covered her hand with his. "Whatever you tell me, I'm sure it won't shock me. Or change my opinion of you."

Arabella really hoped so. Drawing a steadying breath, she made her confession before she lost her nerve. "My mother—her name was Mary—passed away when I was but a babe. When she was eighteen, she eloped with a man named William Jardine against my grandfather's wishes," she said quietly. Unable to meet her husband's eyes, she pushed her plate away, and then toyed with the stem of her champagne glass. "I've been told they married over the anvil. But my family never knew where the hand-fasting occurred or who the witnesses were . . . or if indeed there were any witnesses. There are no marriage lines, or any sort of certificate to speak of." Arabella looked up from the table. "So I'm afraid . . ." She swallowed and her face heated with a flush of shame. "I'm not sure if I was born in or out of wedlock. The foundling hospital and orphanage where I was placed after my mother gave me away had no record of my parents' marriage or my birth either. It's something my aunt Flora has never let me forget," she added bitterly. "She believes marriage should only occur within the church. That irregular marriage is sinful and isn't valid in the eyes of God." She hadn't told him the worst of it though.

"Oh, Arabella. I'm so sorry. What a tragic start you had in life." Gabriel gave her hand a gentle squeeze. "But let me reassure you, my opinion of you—no, my *regard* for you— hasn't changed. At all."

"Thank you." Arabella offered him a tremulous smile. "I wanted to tell you sooner. Honestly I did. But when you told me about the trouble you were having with your cousin Timothy, it didn't seem like the right time. And we'd only just become engaged. And then when you visited Maison du Lac again, we barely had a moment's privacy. So that's why I'm only telling you now. I hope you can forgive me."

Gabriel smiled. "Arabella, there's nothing to forgive. Who am I to pass judgment when my parents have done more or less the same thing? My father and mother eloped to a small hamlet just outside of Gretna Green. It's true I have a marriage certificate of sorts, but it is of dubious quality. Not only that, the register cannot be found, and the fellow who officiated passed away several years ago. That's why I desperately need to find my mother. She may have a copy of the certificate. And she might be able to help me locate the witnesses present at the ceremony."

Arabella nodded. "I hope you can find what you need."

"So do I. And thank you for sharing such a confidence with me." Gabriel removed his hand and reached for the champagne bottle. His silver rings flashed. "Now, that's enough of being maudlin on this wonderful summer's day. Our wedding day no less. Let's enjoy ourselves."

Arabella smiled. She was grateful that Gabriel hadn't wanted her to elaborate upon the scant history she'd shared—

whether she knew the fate of her parents or how long she'd remained in the Great Clyde Hospital and Poorhouse in Glasgow before her grandfather had come to claim her. That story was for another time.

As Arabella reached for her topped-up champagne, her simple gold wedding band glinted in the sunlight, reminding her that she now belonged to Lord Langdale and the course of her life was irrevocably changed.

For better or for worse. It was comforting to know there would be no secrets between her and Gabriel. And that Gabriel accepted her for who she was. This might not be a love match, but that didn't mean there couldn't be mutual respect and kindness and fond regard.

At long last, Arabella felt some of her apprehension about the future drain away. Until Gabriel said, "Arabella, I have one small request . . . May I draw you?"

Gabriel watched Arabella tense—her fingers tightened around the stem of her champagne flute, and her lips thinned. Her gaze slid away from his to where she'd placed her glasses on the table. "I'm . . . I'm not sure," she said before sipping her wine. A rose-tinted blush washed over her cheeks.

Damn, he hadn't wanted to make her feel uncomfortable, not when he'd just begun to sense that she was relaxing. He was usually so adept at wielding his charms to seduce a woman. However, Arabella was quite different from his usual conquests and he sensed he needed to tread carefully. To employ an approach that was far subtler than his typical modus operandi. The only problem was, he was also inexplicably possessed by the need to do quite the opposite. To simultaneously impress, flatter, and spoil her with an enthusiasm that was far from subtle. God damn it, he was acting like a peacock at the height of mating season.

No doubt Arabella was feeling jittery about consummating the marriage. And of course he would endeavor to make the process as pleasurable as possible when the time came.

Indeed, if he were honest with himself, he couldn't wait to tumble her. But he would show suitable restraint. He didn't want to hurt or frighten her. Not that Arabella seemed the sort to be easily daunted. From what he'd seen of her, she wasn't a skittish young miss by any means. The word *fearless* sprang to mind when he recalled the way she explored the dungeon at Chillon on her own and how she rushed headlong into the storm to help him when no one else in her family had.

He was also beginning to sense she lacked a true sense of her own worth.

I'm nothing. No one.

It bothered Gabriel that she doubted herself. That she thought herself odd and not worthy of attention. In Chillon's dungeon, she quipped that he needed his eyes checked when he'd been transfixed by the sight of her. And in Maison du Lac's library, she questioned his reason for kissing her, frowning up at him as though he was mad for wanting to do so.

He didn't want Arabella to feel like that. He wanted her to know she was attractive in so many ways.

And eminently desirable.

He sipped his champagne, turning over different approaches in his mind. There must be something he could say to persuade her to sit for him. Then inspiration struck. "I've wanted to capture your likeness since we first met at Chillon Castle. Perhaps you could consider it your wedding gift to me . . ." He knew he was being a manipulative bastard, but it was for a worthy cause.

"Well, how could I say no then?" Arabella pushed away her glass and at last met his gaze. "Tell me what to do. How would you like me to sit for you?"

Naked but for that necklace. Gabriel suppressed the wicked thought. Perhaps in time Arabella would pose for him in the way he truly wanted. But not today.

"Any way you like," he replied, rising from his seat and removing his jacket. He tossed it over the back of his chair, then untied his cravat and loosened the neck of his cambric shirt. He smiled inwardly when he caught Arabella staring at his exposed throat and collarbones. "As long as you are comfortable. Just let me get my things. I'll be back in a minute."

When Gabriel returned, it was to discover that Arabella was still sitting at the table; she toyed with her glasses.

"I'm not sure if you'd like me to wear these," she said as he reclaimed his seat.

"It's up to you." Gabriel flipped open his sketchbook to a fresh page. "You are gorgeous with or without them."

As he expected, Arabella's cheeks pinkened again. She really wasn't used to receiving compliments of any kind. "Perhaps I'll hold them," she said. "Then you can see my eyes. Would that be all right?"

"Of course." Gabriel loosened his cuffs and rolled up his sleeves. He was quietly amused to see Arabella sneaking another peek at him as he exposed his forearms. When he caught her gaze, she quickly looked away.

"And would it help if I sat closer to the arbor?" she asked in a voice that sounded more than a little breathless. "It might look nice if there were flowers behind me."

He picked up his charcoal pencil. "Another wonderful idea."

Arabella moved her chair so that she was framed by the arched trellis of roses. At her back was a heavenly view of deep blue water and towering mountainside. She sat perfectly straight and perfectly still, her serious gaze trained on the lake.

Gabriel bent to his task, chatting to her about inconsequential things as he drew her slender, elegant form, and by degrees, she began to relax and smile again. When he asked her to turn her head a certain way so he could accurately render the line of her small, straight nose and petite yet determined chin, she complied without hesitation. He was most careful not to draw attention to the fact that he was studying the swell of her pert breasts as they rose above the cream and gold bodice of her gown.

He'd love to paint her—to capture the precise golden hue of her hair, the soft rose pink of her delicate mouth. The creamy smoothness of her satiny skin. The clear hazel of her eyes and the rich golden brown of her lashes and finely arched eyebrows.

Try as he might, he couldn't stop himself from imagining the delightful body hidden beneath her beautiful wedding gown. If Arabella weren't an innocent, he'd be tempted to strip her bare on this very balcony and take her on the table among the plates of delicacies and glasses of champagne. He was certain she would taste far sweeter . . .

He put down his charcoal pencil and took a rather large swig of champagne, hoping it would quell the rampant fire running through his veins. He'd best focus on the job at hand. There was plenty of time for bed sport.

All the time in the world in fact.

Within the space of a quarter hour, Gabriel had completed the sketch to his satisfaction. "I will add more detail later," he said as he handed the book to Arabella. He very much hoped she would like it. He also hoped she hadn't noticed the telling swell at the front of his snug pantaloons. Well, not yet anyway.

She slipped her glasses on, and as she studied the drawing, he was pleased to see her eyes light up. "That's . . . I look quite pretty for once," she said with a genuine smile. "How very clever of you. Thank you, Gabriel."

"It was my pleasure. And you look pretty all the time, Arabella. At least to me."

A small crease appeared between her brows and he added, "You doubt my sincerity again."

She looked up and met his gaze directly. A small, sad smile tugged at her mouth. "I don't want to. But yes, I do." She shrugged a slender shoulder. "I can't help it."

Before Gabriel could think of another way to convince her that he spoke the truth, Arabella sighed and added, "I can see what you're doing here. Employing all these grand, romantic gestures. Even though we're not a love match—indeed, we barely know each other—you're trying to reassure me that I'm wanted, at least in a physical sense. And I do appreciate the effort. Truly. No one has ever done anything like this for me before. Or paid me such lovely compliments. But no matter how much effort you expend on wooing me this afternoon"—she made an expansive gesture encompassing the balcony and the wedding breakfast—"or plying me with champagne to reduce how anxious I feel, I'm still going to fret about what's going to happen later tonight in the marriage bed. Even though I possess medical knowledge of . . . of copulation, I'm a complete novice in all other respects. Whereas I've heard you're quite the expert. And despite my bout of nerves"—she gave him a shy smile and Gabriel's heart was touched in the oddest way—"it seems I'm tipsy enough to concede that I might be more than a little curious about it all. In fact . . ." A bright red blush bloomed across her cheeks. "I can't stop thinking about it."

His mouth kicked into a grin at her admission. "You're not alone there."

"So . . ." She rose from the table, drew a deep breath, and extended her hand. "Rather than delaying the inevitable, let's get the deed done, Gabriel. Make me your wife in truth. I can't bear the suspense a moment longer."

To say Gabriel was surprised by his wife's directness would be an understatement. Desire mingled with another wholly unexpected wave of tenderness as he stood and pressed his lips to her fingers. "I'm more than happy to acquiesce, Arabella," he murmured in a voice that was more than a little husky with want. "Who am I to deny my wife on her wedding day?"

CHAPTER 9

Could I embody and unbosom now
That which is most within me . . .
Lord Byron, "Childe Harold's Pilgrimage"

I'm more than happy to acquiesce, Arabella. Who am I to deny my wife on her wedding day?

At Gabriel's words, Arabella's pulse raced wildly. Even though she was initiating this, her first sexual experience, apprehension still warred with desire. She'd been completely honest when she told Gabriel that she really wanted to get this over and done with. It would be like removing a plaster stuck to a sore spot. It was always best to just rip it off, nice and quick, without thinking about it too much. The anticipation was often worse than the actual business.

But then she recalled Gabriel's kisses, the heat and taste of his mouth, the gentle rasp of his tongue. The feel of his fingers pushing into her hair, and caressing her face as though it were as precious and fragile as the finest porcelain and she might break.

He knows what he's doing. He's an expert, she reminded herself. *He'll make this, my first time, enjoyable, despite my reservations.*

"Come." Gabriel entwined his long fingers with hers and led her toward the doors of her suite. He ran his thumb lightly over the inside of her wrist, and even that small, teasing touch made Arabella's skin tingle. "Truth be told, I can't wait to introduce you to the delights of sexual congress. Or as I like to call it, bed sport."

Bed sport. Arabella hadn't expected Gabriel to describe the act they were about to engage in as making love—neither of them felt such a tender emotion for the other—so it would be a lie to apply it. But the term *bed sport* seemed too trifling, an almost dismissive term that implied their physical union was a mere amusement. An activity of little consequence. Arabella bit back a small sigh. For him it might be, but for her . . . she was about to lose her virginity to a man she desired but barely knew.

At least Gabriel hadn't used a crude term for what they were about to do.

She trusted he would try to make the experience as pleasurable as possible for her. As she'd told him, she knew what was involved from a technical perspective. Hopefully the lust he so easily brought to life inside her would reduce the discomfort she was bound to feel when he took her maidenhead.

They paused by the side of the sumptuous four-poster bed. The counterpane of dusky blue silk figured with embroidered ivory roses, and the fine cotton sheets and pillows, looked too fine and pristine to disturb. Arabella's chest felt tight. She was suddenly so nervous, she could barely breathe or bring herself to look at Gabriel.

Keeping her eyes fixed on the delicate floral carvings in the satinwood headboard, she said, "When penetration commences and you breach my hymen, it will no doubt be uncomfortable, perhaps even painful for me." She was trying to be matter-of-fact, but she was so embarrassed, her words began to tumble out in a great rush. "However, I suspect that if we can manage to achieve a sufficient amount of lubrication to ease your passage and reduce the friction . . ." She started toward the dressing room. "I have a particular ointment in my medical bag that might help. I'll just go and fetch it . . ."

Gabriel followed and caught her hand, staying her. "We won't need that."

"Are you sure?"

He gave her a wicked smile. "I'm positive."

She nodded and her attention flitted back to the bed.

"Arabella. Look at me."

With an effort, she met Gabriel's gaze.

The expression in his eyes had softened, reminding her of moss green velvet. "I promise you that I'll be as gentle as I can be. I like to think my skills as a lover will bring you pleasure. But you're going to have to trust me."

Arabella nodded stiffly. "I don't doubt your expertise will come in handy. I'm just . . ." She worried at her lower lip. How could she say he was the most sexually magnetic man she'd ever met, but she feared she wasn't good enough? That she might fail to meet his expectations? "I know this was my idea, to do this. However, despite my curiosity and . . . and desire for you, now that the moment is upon me, I'm all at sea. I'm worried I won't be any good at this compared to—" She broke off; she didn't really want to talk about all the other women he'd bedded in the past, so she said, "You're so worldly and I am not . . ."

"Arabella." He lifted her chin with gentle fingers, and she couldn't escape his gaze. "There's no one here but you and me, and I've wanted you from the first moment we met. Indeed, part of the reason I kept my distance this past week is that I was worried I wouldn't be able to keep my hands off you." He tilted his hips forward, and she realized he spoke the truth when the evidence of his arousal brushed against her belly. His thumb caressed her bottom lip as he murmured, "If your kisses are anything to go by, I have no doubt at all you will be *very* good at this. We'll take things slowly, all right?"

She exhaled shakily. "All right."

"Excellent." Gabriel brushed a finger down her nose. "May I take your glasses off and then let your hair down?"

"Yes . . ."

After he'd carefully removed her spectacles and placed them on the bedside table, he patted the gilt back of an elegant shepherdess chair. "Sit here and I will play lady's maid."

Arabella subsided into the seat and closed her eyes as

her husband slowly but surely removed the hairpins taming her curls. Gabriel's touch was light and deft, and within a few minutes, her hair cascaded about her shoulders and down her back.

"Beautiful." Gabriel ran his fingers through the thick, riotous mass, and as he bent his head to her ear, she caught his rich masculine scent—musk and spice and citrus. "I can't wait to see this and nothing else draped about you."

Oh, my goodness.

Sweeping her hair to one side, he grazed a kiss along her jaw. "It's time to get undressed, Bella."

Bella? No one had ever called her Bella. Before she could think further on it, Gabriel was kneeling at her feet, sliding off her slippers. Lifting her skirts, he then proceeded to tug her ribbon garters loose before slowly rolling down each stocking. Delicious tremors of anticipation shimmered over her skin wherever his fingers brushed.

Once her legs were bare, he stood and encouraged her to rise with him. Catching her against his body, her back to his front, he pressed kisses to her temple and the curve of her ear. Then her neck. The slide of his hot mouth made her shiver, and liquid heat bloomed low in her belly. She could feel the jut of his engorged penis against her bottom.

Then his clever fingers were everywhere, tugging at the fastenings of her gown, stays, and petticoat until everything was loose and sagging open and sliding to the carpeted floor.

With nothing on but her new necklace and flimsy shift, Arabella felt vulnerable indeed.

Gabriel's large hands skimmed over her rib cage to cup her breasts. "They're just as I imagined," he whispered against her fevered cheek. "Firm, and round, and they fill my palms perfectly." Through the fine lawn of her shift, he caught her nipples between his fingers, pinching them before tugging gently. Arabella gasped as desire sparked, hot and bright. She squirmed against Gabriel's hard, lean body and he groaned. The deep, throaty rumble seemed to reverberate through her.

"Sweet Jesus, Bella. If you keep that up, I'll be coming in my breeches like a green boy."

She smiled and turned her head to the side. "You say just the right things to make me feel better."

"Remember, I'll only ever tell you the truth. And I'm sure you can feel how much I want you." He spun her around and caught her mouth in a brief, but searing kiss. "I'm desperate for you."

Gabriel pulled at the tie securing the neckline of her shift, and within moments, the gossamer garment had puddled on the floor with her other clothes.

The slow, deliberate sweep of Gabriel's gaze over her naked body made her nipples tighten into hard, aching points, and her belly did an odd little flip. Even though his green eyes were shielded by his long dark lashes, Arabella gained the distinct impression he liked what he saw . . . especially when his wide mouth curved into the most sinful smile she'd ever seen.

"Bella . . . I'm in awe." Gabriel's deep voice was hoarse yet soft, his expression reverent. He reached up and brushed a finger over one of her taut nipples. "You'll be lucky if I ever let you put clothes on again."

Arabella was sure she blushed from the top of her head to the tips of her toes. Surely he couldn't mean that. She lifted her hair and touched the diamond and emerald necklace. "Will you help me take this off?"

Gabriel shook his head. "No. I don't think so." He traced along her collarbone with the tip of one finger, raising gooseflesh. "I like seeing it around your pretty neck. I find it quite arousing to see you thus."

Oh. Arabella swallowed. Her throat was tight with a strange combination of nerves and longing. "I think it's a trifle unfair that I am wearing nothing at all, but you are almost fully dressed." She reached out to undo the buttons of his brocade silk waistcoat and he stayed her hand.

"Not so fast, sweetheart," he purred. "There are other things I want to do with you first." And then he was kissing her, his mouth hot and hungry; his hands slid around her back and cupped her buttocks, urging her hips forward so that her sex was pressed up against his steel-hard erection.

Gripping Gabriel's wide shoulders, Arabella moaned as

she submitted to his ravaging kisses. The yearning ache inside her was growing, and she knew her body craved more.

As though in tune with her rising need, Gabriel walked her back toward the bed and then pushed her down onto the soft mattress. Taking his weight on one forearm, he stared down at her, his eyes hooded, his gaze smoldering with dark green fire.

"You have no idea what you do to me," he grated out. "I've never been so consumed with desire." He buried his face in her neck, dragging his teeth along the tendon below her ear. "I need to slow down, but God help me, I don't know if I can."

Arabella touched shaking fingers to his sharply cut jaw. "Take your waistcoat and shirt off, Gabriel. I want to touch you."

"In a minute." Gabriel bent his head and licked one of her nipples, and Arabella's whole body jolted as though she'd been struck by a sizzling bolt of electricity.

*Oh, my God. That felt so—*All thought disintegrated as Gabriel covered her other nipple with his mouth and suckled delicately. Then he transferred his attention to the other breast again, tormenting her with rapid flicks of his wicked tongue before drawing on her with a long slow suck.

Spearing her fingers into his hair, Arabella arched her back, flagrantly pushing herself into the hot cavern of his mouth. She never imagined torture could be so exquisite. So all-consuming. Her body was aflame, her sex pulsing in time with the desperate throb of her heart.

When Gabriel dragged his mouth away, an involuntary mewl of protest escaped her. "Climb up to the head of the bed." His voice was little more than a rough, low growl as he ripped at the buttons of his waistcoat with jerky movements.

Arabella complied with his request, settling onto the plump pillows. She was about to pull the counterpane over her body when Gabriel moved closer and caught her wrist. "Don't hide from me, Bella. I want to see you. All of you."

She nodded, unable to resist the raw tone of his command or the blatant lust in his gaze. Seeing him in such a state of acute need sent a dark thrill coursing through her body. And then a frisson of fear as she realized his power over her was so great, she'd be hard-pressed to deny him anything.

He straightened, and heedless of the injury to his shoulder, he tugged his shirt over his head and tossed it away in one fluid movement.

Even though Arabella had already seen his naked torso, she found herself riveted to the sight of him. The swell of hard, lean muscles. The rigid lines of bone and sinew beneath sleek flesh. The smattering of dark hairs across his chest and the intriguing hawk's head tattoo on his right bicep. Her fingers twitched at the memory of touching him. It was hard to believe she had tended to his injury without melting into a puddle at his feet.

Within a flash, he'd also made short work of his black Hessian boots and hose. And then he began to release the button fastenings of his pantaloons . . . The form-fitting ivory fabric left little to the imagination, but even so, as the fall front came undone, Arabella couldn't help but gasp at the sight of his erect manhood as it sprang forth from its nest of tight black curls.

She swallowed and clutched the silk counterpane. Gabriel was going to put *that* enormous organ inside her?

"I can see you're shocked by the sight of me," he said after he'd removed every last stitch.

"I . . . you're quite a fine male specimen," she whispered. His thighs were heavily muscled, dusted in fine black hair. His hips were lean, and the plane of his belly as taut as a drum. "I must say, I'm quite impressed by the size of your . . ." She gestured helplessly toward his groin.

His eyes glinted wickedly. "My cock?" Climbing onto the bed, he began to crawl toward her like a beast about to devour her.

She blushed hotly. Though part of her couldn't deny that the crude term aptly described that part of his anatomy. "Yes."

"I promise I'll be as gentle as I can when I enter you." He settled alongside her, propping himself on one elbow. His beautiful, hard body felt as hot as a furnace as it pressed against her naked skin. His leg hairs tickled her inner thighs as he used his knee to nudge her legs apart.

Cushioned by a soft bank of pillows, Arabella stared up into Gabriel's handsome face, framed by its cloud of black curls. Up this close, she wished she could see him better. The expression in his eyes. She lifted a hand and placed it against his lean cheek. "I believe you."

Gabriel groaned, pressing himself into her palm. "Your touch excites me, Bella."

"It does?" She slid her hand lower and ran her fingers through his chest hair.

When she grazed one of his nipples, the little bronze nub furled tight, and he groaned again. "Yes . . . Hell, yes . . . touch me wherever and however you want."

Her husband's invitation was impossible to resist. Curiosity at last overcoming her timidity, Arabella skimmed her fingertips down Gabriel's rib cage and over one lean hip bone to cup his buttock. Then she gasped.

Her fingertips had encountered scar tissue. A raised, jagged line puckering the skin on Gabriel's firm rump.

"What happened to you?" she breathed.

"It's only an old war wound. I was shot at Waterloo. I'll admit it was difficult to sit for a while but it doesn't bother me anymore."

Arabella frowned. "How awful. And yes, painful." Judging by the size of the scar, the bullet must have done more than a wee bit of damage. "I'm glad nothing vital was injured."

Gabriel's mouth twisted in a wry smile. "Well, my pride was, but I eventually got over that too."

Arabella slid her hand back to his hip. She was beginning to notice her husband sometimes used humor to hide how he really felt. She wanted to delve deeper, learn more about his past, but now didn't really seem like quite the right time. Not when she and Gabriel were both naked in bed and his rampant arousal kept nudging her.

She decided to resume her exploration of her husband's beautiful body. Holding her breath, she dared to wrap her fist around his manhood. As hard as iron yet encased in hot velvet, it seemed to pulse between her fingers. With her other hand, she gently rolled the tightly bunched testicles beneath, and he swore beneath his breath.

"That's it, sweetheart," Gabriel gritted out from between clenched teeth. "Don't be afraid to explore. I won't break."

Emboldened by his words, Arabella gave his shaft an experimental squeeze and he groaned, low and deep. "Oh, God, Bella. I want you so much." In the next instant, Gabriel was kissing her again, his tongue pushing into her mouth, stroking and tasting. His fingers plucked at one of her nipples before tracing a teasing path across her hips and then down her belly until they feathered through the blond curls covering her sex.

Arabella's breath quickened as the tip of one wicked finger slipped into the hidden furrow between her thighs. He'd been right. They wouldn't need to apply any sort of ointment.

"Yes, Bella, yes," crooned Gabriel against her mouth. "You're so slick. Wet with desire. Open your legs. Let me tease you. Just there. Yes?"

Oh, yes. How did he know that little hooded nub at the apex of her sex—her clitoris—was so excruciatingly sensitive and exactly the place she wanted him to touch? Arabella moaned as he tormented the spot with the pad of his finger, circling and flicking and delicately rubbing it until she was writhing, parting her legs wider, not caring how wanton she'd suddenly become. She sought Gabriel's mouth and clung to his wide shoulders as though they were her only anchor in the wild storm of unfamiliar sensation that seemed to be rapidly engulfing her.

And then Gabriel slid another agile finger between her feminine folds. It gently probed her virginal entrance before abruptly pushing inside. Arabella immediately stiffened and her eyes flew open. The slight burn of his incursion felt odd but also so very right.

Gabriel stilled too. "Did I hurt you?" he murmured, catching her gaze. "I can stop."

She shook her head. "No. I . . . wasn't expecting you to . . . to do that just yet." She swallowed and firmed her voice. "I want this."

He brushed a kiss across her lips. "It will help ease my way later if I touch you like this first."

"I understand." She closed her eyes and tilted her hips so

Gabriel's wicked finger slid deeper. The friction was not unpleasant. In fact, Arabella thought she might like it. "Do what you will. I trust you."

Gabriel answered her with a tender, lingering kiss before he slid another finger inside her, gently stretching her untried tissue. And then he began to rhythmically stroke her inner softness, curling his fingers as he thrust. All the while his wicked thumb toyed with her clitoris, circling languidly yet steadily.

As Gabriel played, Arabella soon found she couldn't resist the overwhelming urge to move her hips. Tiny, uncontrolled gasps and mewls she had no hope of containing kept tumbling from her throat as she rocked mindlessly against Gabriel's hand. His intimate caresses were driving her mad. Her heart pounded. Her sex pulsed, clenching tighter. She was racing toward something just out of reach. Something wonderful. She moaned as desire flared hotter and brighter, a beckoning, irresistible flame.

"That's it, Bella." Gabriel's wicked words were a dark whisper in her ear. "Ride my hand. Use me. Let pleasure take you."

And then it did. All at once Arabella was soaring. Flying heavenward into blissful abandon. She cried out, and her whole body shuddered and jerked as waves of euphoria washed through her.

When she'd subsided into a quivering, exhausted mass, Gabriel gathered her against him and nuzzled her neck. Nibbled her earlobe and stroked his hands up and down her back.

"It's time to truly make you mine," he whispered against her temple. "I won't use a sheath but I'll pull out of you before I come."

Still breathless and too overwhelmed to speak, Arabella simply nodded and let him turn her onto her back. Gabriel rose over her, graceful yet fearsome. She might not be wearing her glasses, but she could feel the searing intensity of his gaze. The purpose in each and every one of his movements.

He fondled her, spreading the moisture that had welled between her folds up and over the swollen bud of her clitoris, mercilessly arousing her all over again. If she wasn't so spent, she might have been embarrassed by how wet she was. Or how much she already craved Gabriel's wicked touch. She couldn't help but press herself into his hand.

"I'm going to put myself inside you now," he whispered huskily, settling over her. "Good Lord, you are so sweet. So lovely. I can't get enough of your kisses." He raked his mouth across her cheek before tasting her lips. Taking his weight on one arm, he grasped his shaft, then pressed his hips forward, the hot, smooth head of his penis seeking her drenched entrance.

Arabella sucked in a startled breath as he pushed again and the burning sting of his invasion intensified. Clutching at his biceps, she stiffened and tried not to cry out as he thrust even deeper. Surely she would split in two. Filled to bursting point, pinned to the bed beneath Gabriel's substantial weight, there was nothing she could do but try to breathe through the pain.

Gabriel thrust one last time and then he held very still. Her heart thudding in her ears, Arabella blinked away tears. It didn't seem at all fair that their joining should be so painful. Especially when he'd taken so much care with her beforehand.

"I'm sorry for hurting you, my brave darling. And I hope the worst is over for you." He feathered kisses over her forehead and down her nose. "I'll be ever so gentle as I take my pleasure. I'll try very hard to help you find yours again too."

Arabella gripped the back of his strong neck, steeling herself for what would happen next. "Don't mind me. Do what you must."

Gabriel dipped his head and kissed her with such tenderness, Arabella's throat tightened. In that moment, she almost believed that he cared for her.

Leaning on one arm, he caressed her breast with his free hand as he began to carefully work himself in and out of her body. His sliding thrusts were long and slow, deliberate yet gentle, and it wasn't long before sweat sheened his back. He bent his head to kiss her and Arabella welcomed him, opening her mouth and tangling her tongue with his. The pain of his incursion was receding, and desire flickered to life deep in her womb.

If Gabriel could increase his pace just a little . . . Arabella lifted her hips to meet his and then Gabriel's whole body spasmed. "Christ." His chest heaved as he dragged in a ragged breath. "You feel so damned good. Too good. I can't . . . Fuck." All of a sudden, he wrenched his body away. Gripping his manhood, he shuddered and groaned as he spent his hot seed all over her belly and the inside of her thighs.

Oh. Arabella blinked at the curious sight, then frowned in dismay when she realized what a mess they'd both made on the blue silk counterpane.

Gabriel collapsed onto the bed beside her. Lying on his back with his eyes closed, one arm was flung over his forehead while the other hand reached for her. His fingers threaded through hers, and then he brought her hand to his lips. "Good Lord, Arabella. That was a narrow escape we just had," he rasped. "I almost didn't pull out in time."

Arabella didn't know what to say. If he *had* spent inside her, surely that wouldn't be so bad. Despite the threat to his title, they were married after all. Aloud she said, "I'm glad you achieved satisfaction. And that the deed is done, so to speak." She felt strange and unsettled—oddly hollow and yearning.

"Yes. On both counts." Gabriel rolled over and propped himself on one elbow. He crooked a finger beneath her chin, forcing her to look at him. "But what about you? I'm quite certain you didn't come a second time. I'm sorry I lost control and ended things too quickly."

"No, I didn't. But that's all right. Once was enough." She fell silent, suddenly overwhelmed by the enormity of what they'd just done. She was Gabriel's wife in truth and no longer a virgin. And surely she should be pleased her husband was a considerate lover. No, he was more than that: he was an accomplished lover.

An amazing lover.

Gabriel kissed her gently on the forehead. "I swear I'll make it up to you a little later on when we are both rested. But for now . . ." He slid from the bed and, apparently comfortable in his own skin, padded stark-naked toward her dressing room. "Let me clean you up, my sweet."

Arabella pushed herself up higher on the pillows, wincing as her body protested at the change in position—as was to be expected, her nether region was quite sensitive and sore.

A minute later, Gabriel returned with a towel, a basin of water, and a soft washcloth. Another towel was slung low around his lean hips. "I'm sorry this isn't warm," he said as he squeezed the excess water from the cloth. He began to ever so carefully wash away the stickiness from between her thighs.

"That's all right." Arabella blushed hotly as she noticed pinkish streaks of blood on the cloth. Even though Gabriel had already seen and touched her most intimate places, she still felt terribly self-conscious and had to resist the urge to cover herself with the counterpane yet again.

Perhaps sensing her discomfort, Gabriel said softly, "I'll order a hip bath for you if you'd like."

Arabella offered him a grateful smile. "Yes, please. That would be lovely." Part of her really wished he wasn't being so sweet. He confused her. How could he be so kind and thoughtful on the one hand, yet claim he was a heartless rake on the other?

A little while later, as Arabella lay soaking in a large tub of lavender-scented water in her dressing room, she realized that the feeling of discontent that sat heavily inside her breast was disappointment. And apprehension.

Her husband didn't love her, and he never would. Nor would he ever be faithful. He'd told her that at the outset. But after experiencing Gabriel's lovemaking—although Arabella knew love had naught to do with it—she was forever changed.

Even though she'd told herself over and over again that she was not made to be loved—that she was practical and sensible and unromantic—it seemed her foolish heart had other ideas. Why else would it beat double time when Gabriel smiled at her? Why else did she wish he meant it whenever he told her she was beautiful?

Why else did she despair that their physical union had

been little more than "sport" to him and that's all it would ever be? Yet what they'd done had meant so much more to her. Although her body thrummed with excitement when she thought of having sexual congress with Gabriel again, her head told her it would be most unwise for her to do so—well, at least until it was absolutely necessary.

She would keep to her end of the bargain and share his bed when the time came to beget his heir. But until then, it would all be for the best if she kept her distance from him. It would hurt too much to pine for something she could never have.

Charlie had once said that in order to catch a rakehell, you needed to make him fall in love with you. However, Arabella realized she'd done things all back to front—she'd snared herself an earl, albeit accidentally, but she now feared the second thing was an impossible feat. She had no clue how to begin or if it were even possible for Gabriel to fall in love with her.

One thing was certain: *she* certainly couldn't afford to fall in love with her wickedly handsome but fickle-hearted husband, because doing so would surely destroy her.

When Gabriel emerged from his dressing room after luxuriating in his own bath, it was to discover his lovely young wife was sitting on the balcony, brushing her glorious blond locks. The curls shone like liquid gold in the afternoon sunshine, and Gabriel itched to run his fingers through them. Per his instructions, the servants had cleared away the remains of their wedding breakfast, leaving nothing but a fine lace tablecloth, a decanter of claret, and two crystal glasses.

Throwing on an emerald green silk banyan over a pair of loose linen trousers, he scrubbed at his dripping hair with a fresh towel as he wandered out to join Arabella.

Then something blue caught his eye. Something that didn't belong on the balcony.

What the hell?

Arabella's counterpane was draped over the railing, one ruffled edge flapping lightly in the gentle breeze. It looked as though a section of it was damp.

"You don't have to do your own laundry, you know," Gabriel said as he approached his wife. He tossed his towel over the back of a chair. "I have . . . I mean *we* have more than enough staff here."

"I know . . ." Arabella put down her silver-backed brush. Her cheeks were bright red as she met his gaze. "It's just there was such a mess after we . . ." She lifted her chin. "I was embarrassed about it. Aside from that, I'm used to being self-sufficient."

"Oh, Arabella." Gabriel raked a hand through his hair. "You don't need to worry so much about what everyone thinks. Not anymore. The maids won't care what state we leave the bed linen in. To begin with, it's none of their business and we *are* married."

"Yes . . ." Arabella began to brush her hair again. Her expression had turned serious. No, it was more than that; she was withdrawn. Her gaze was now trained on the flagstones at his feet, and a slight frown creased her brow.

Gabriel frowned, too, unsure of what was wrong. He didn't think he'd used a stern tone when he'd gently rebuked her. Wanting to dispel the awkwardness between them, he took the brush from Arabella's hand. "Here, let me do that, sweetheart."

To his surprise, she stiffened a little as their fingers touched, but she didn't naysay him.

"I hope you are feeling refreshed," he said as he began to gently tug the brush through her still-damp hair. He rested his hand on her slender shoulder and skimmed his thumb across the satiny skin at her nape, just above the white muslin neckline of her gown. "Although it's a pity Villa Belle Rive hasn't anything larger than a hip bath. I rather think I'd enjoy sharing a tub with you."

Arabella made a soft sound at the back of her throat, which he took to mean she agreed. With her eyes closed and her head tilted back, she reminded him of a contented cat, sunning itself. At least her frown had gone.

As he only just resisted the urge to kiss her, his gaze fell to the table where her glasses lay on a slim, leather-bound volume.

"What are you reading?" he asked as he encountered a particularly stubborn snarl.

"It's a travel diary by Mary Shelley," she replied. "She documents her tour of the Continent, including her stay here in Switzerland. Aside from Lord Byron's "Prisoner of Chillon," I've also been reading "Childe Harold's Pilgrimage." I picked it up at Hatchards before I left."

"I must borrow it from you sometime." The brush snagged on another knot. "I didn't pack many books before I left London. Have you read Rousseau's *Julie, or the New Heloise*? I believe he penned it while he was residing at Vevey."

Arabella replied she had and that she had a copy in her trunk if he cared to borrow that too.

They lapsed into uncomfortable silence again, and Gabriel wondered what she would like to talk about. He wanted to get to know his wife better. After bedding her, he'd learned small, intimate details no one else knew. That her nipples were a dusky rose pink. The little sounds she made in the throes of passion. His cock stirred and he steered his thoughts in another direction. It probably didn't help that he'd been living the life of a monk since he left London.

As much as he desired Arabella, he shouldn't be thinking about rushing her off to bed again straightaway given that he'd just taken her maidenhead. Although intercourse was out of the question right now, there were plenty of other things they could do that he was certain she would find pleasurable. Perhaps later this evening . . .

He cast his mind back to what they'd chatted about when he'd drawn her earlier: their mutual friends, Nate, Charlie, and Sophie. Her travels so far. As much as he wanted to learn more about her past—what it had been like in the orphanage—and her passion for medicine and philanthropy courtesy of her grandfather, those topics seemed too serious to explore today. He certainly didn't want to dredge up any painful memories for Arabella.

Lord knew there were episodes in his past that he avoided revisiting like the plague.

Arabella shifted in her seat, and because he was standing so close, he caught a tantalizing glimpse of her cleavage. He still had no idea why she was so insecure about her appearance. Perhaps someone close to her had undermined her self-confidence—her shrew of an aunt for instance. He could well imagine the woman would harp on about her niece's "flaws" just to keep her under her thumb. The thought that someone would do such a thing made him unaccountably angry.

Arabella jumped. "Ow."

"Sorry," he said. He'd been gripping the brush too tightly and not paying enough attention to what he was doing. "I think that's the last of the tangles gone." He handed the brush back and reached for the claret.

"Can I get you anything?" he asked as he took a seat and poured himself a sizable glass. "If red wine isn't to your taste, there's still a crateful of champagne left."

Arabella slipped her glasses onto her nose and picked up her book. "A cup of tea would be lovely," she said in such a subdued tone that the alarm bells that had been quietly ringing in his head began to clang louder. "If it's not too much trouble."

Gabriel's brows plunged into a deep frown. *What?* They were sitting in the summer sun on a balcony overlooking heaven, yet his new wife wanted to read her book and drink tea like an elderly maiden aunt? Of course this wasn't a love match—they both knew that—but this was their wedding day for God's sake. The beginning of their honeymoon.

A time for both of them to get to know each other in every conceivable way. To have fun.

He wanted her and she'd admitted she desired him, too, but something was definitely wrong. Gabriel's visions of getting pleasantly soused with Arabella and then discovering all the ways he could bring her pleasure with his hands and mouth alone were dissolving faster than a sugar lump in a blasted cup of tea.

He put down his claret. "What's the matter?" he asked,

his tone light and teasing. "Are you having misgivings about our marriage already?"

Arabella removed a pretty scrap of embroidered linen that marked the place in her book. "No." She looked up and gave him a small smile that didn't reach her eyes. "I'm just a wee bit tired, that's all."

Little liar. Gabriel's uneasiness intensified. He knew he'd caused her great pain when he first entered her, but she seemed to enjoy everything they'd done before that. But what if he was wrong? "Bella, be honest with me. Are you upset about what happened in the marriage bed? Was I too rough or did I frighten you?"

She shook her head. "No. Nothing like that. You were wonderful and as gentle and considerate as could be."

"Did you . . ." Gabriel swallowed and forced himself to untether his tongue and ask her a difficult question—for him at least. "Did you achieve an orgasm at all? I thought you did, but perhaps I was mistaken. I've always striven to be a generous lover, so I don't want you to lie to me about something so fundamentally important."

Arabella blushed. "You know that I did. It was . . . it was marvelous. Quite a revelation. I had no idea that such a pleasurable rush could be had by a woman too. And I thank you for it."

Thank God. His male pride appeased a little, Gabriel lowered his voice to a seductive purr. "You know you can have as many orgasms as you like. Whenever you like."

But Arabella pressed her lips together and shook her head. "I . . . I don't want any more."

Confused, Gabriel frowned. "But you just said you enjoyed the first one. I know you must be quite tender at the moment, but that will pass. And there are other things we can do . . ."

"No." She shook her head again. "We've consummated our union. When we became engaged, that's all we agreed to do. Until you are ready to begin a family of course. Then I will come to your bed so that you might get me with child."

Gabriel raked a hand down his face. *No, no, no.* This was *not* what he had in mind. At all. "But why shouldn't we enjoy ourselves?" he demanded, his tone gruffer than he intended. "We are wed. It is allowed. And as your husband, it is my right . . ." He took a deep breath and attempted to temper his tone. He didn't want to sound like a bombastic oaf. "And I want you so very much, Bella. You *know* this to be true."

Arabella's expression hardened. "Don't. Please stop calling me that. It doesn't suit me. And you don't need to keep pretending I'm attractive when I'm clearly not. You've had me, so your pretty words are just a waste of breath from now on."

"I'm not pretending," Gabriel snapped. "You are beautiful, god damn it. Why won't you believe me? You're my wife and I want you. It couldn't be simpler."

Arabella's lower lip quivered and she looked away from him. "I wish I could make you understand. And it's far from simple."

Damn, his flash of temper had made her cry. Gabriel's heart twisted in the most peculiar way—a strange occurrence to be sure because the sight of a woman weeping usually made him want to run a mile. Pushing aside his own pique, he gentled his voice. "Then tell me." He leaned forward and grasped her hands, but to his great dismay, she tugged them away.

"What we just did"—she gestured toward her bedroom—"was more than 'sport' to me. But it will only ever be sport to you. I know this isn't a love match, but I've realized I can't share a bed with you unless it *does* mean more. I want my husband to make love to me, and not just in a figurative sense. I fear . . ." She swallowed. "You're difficult to resist, Gabriel. You have a way of effortlessly weaving a spell over a woman, and I fear that despite my best efforts, I *will* fall in love with you. And I don't want to because in the end, you'll only break my heart. As I'm sure you've broken other women's hearts. I won't . . ." She lifted her chin. Behind her glasses, her eyes glimmered with tears. "My mother was destroyed by a man who didn't love her, and I won't suffer the same fate."

Gabriel grasped his chin and stared hard at Arabella.

What could he say to that? It was true he'd broken many a heart over the years. Grimacing inwardly, he tried to push away the thought of Lady Astley and how he'd burned her last letter to cinders—she was a married woman and should have known their illicit affair would go nowhere.

He sighed heavily. Why was it that females always had to attach so much emotion to sexual congress? He'd foolishly assumed that Arabella—rational and practical yet undeniably passionate—would be different. That they'd have their fun, she'd bear him a child or two, and then they'd both seek sexual satisfaction elsewhere. Wasn't that the way of most ton marriages? And hadn't she agreed to that when he'd offered for her hand?

"Any number of women would want me in their beds, Arabella." As soon as the words were out of his mouth, Gabriel regretted them. The stricken expression on his wife's face made him feel like the lowest heel ever to walk the earth. "I'm sorry, I shouldn't have said that. It was cruel. I'm just so very confused and disappointed."

"I accept your apology, but it would be foolish of me not to heed your warning, Gabriel. Women *do* want you. And you probably aren't used to being denied."

"No. I'm not." It was true he usually got what he wanted, at least where women were concerned. "I would never take you against your will," he added gravely. "But do you really expect me to take a vow of priestly celibacy? I have needs, Arabella, and you are my wife. I will ask you to reconsider before you banish me from your bed."

She shook her head sadly. "I'm sorry, Gabriel, but I won't." And then she closed her book and quit the terrace, leaving him all alone with his claret, his bruised male pride, and more than a little bit of sexual frustration.

CHAPTER 10

The morn is up again, the dewy morn,
  With breath all incense, and with cheek all bloom,
  Laughing the clouds away with playful scorn . . .
  Lord Byron, "Childe Harold's Pilgrimage"

Villa Belle Rive, Villeneuve, Switzerland

July 10, 1818

When Arabella woke the next morning, it was to discover someone had left a fragrant white rosebud on the pillow beside her head.

Of course, that someone must have been Gabriel. She frowned at the bloom, confused. Did this mean he was still trying to court her in the hope of inveigling his way into her bed? Or was it his way of apologizing for brooding and ignoring her for the rest of the afternoon and last night? Indeed, after she'd quit the balcony and retired to her room, she barely saw him.

Well, that wasn't quite true. She *had* seen quite a lot of his strong back. After she left the balcony, he stayed seated at the wrought iron table, drinking his claret and rendering sketch after sketch until the sun had completely set. At one point, he even smoked a cheroot cigar; the tip glowed in the twilight, and the rich, smoky smell drifted through her open door, reminding her of her husband's potent masculinity.

When he eventually knocked on her door, her stomach flipped; his appearance had been truly forbidding—still attired in only a banyan and trousers, his black hair was wildly ruffled, and his jaw shadowed with black stubble. His gaze, when it dragged over her as she sat propped up in bed with a book, had a dark, smoldering edge. But to her relief, he simply bid her a brief and perfunctory good night before disappearing into his own rooms next door.

She pushed herself up on the pillows and picked up the barely open bud. She only had herself to blame for her husband's bad mood. She'd rejected him on their wedding day. He wasn't vainglorious, but he was a much-vaunted rakehell, and as he'd already told her, he possessed a great carnal appetite. No doubt, she'd frustrated him and dented his pride by barring him from her bed. While she was relieved he hadn't tried to persuade her to change her mind last night—as her husband, he certainly did have conjugal rights—she also felt terrible that they were already estranged.

Arabella rang for her maid, Colette, and after she'd washed and dressed in a simple gown of pale green muslin and a white silk shawl, she emerged to find Gabriel taking breakfast on the balcony.

What would his mood be like this morning? Would he welcome her company? The rose was clearly a peace offering. Nevertheless, Arabella felt her stomach tumble with apprehension as she pushed open the French doors.

Gabriel stood and bowed as soon as he heard her. He was dressed in a burgundy banyan and loose linen trousers, and to Arabella's relief, a fresh cambric shirt; she'd blush like a ninny if his bare chest and muscular torso were still on display. "My lady wife, I trust you slept well," he said with a perfectly polite smile. A liveried footman, who'd been waiting by a potted fir at the edge of the balcony, stepped forward and pulled out a chair for her.

"Aye, I did." It wasn't a lie. After her emotionally tumultuous wedding day, she'd slept soundly. She smoothed her skirts as she sat, and the footman draped a linen napkin over her lap. "And you?"

"Dreadfully." As Gabriel folded his tall frame into his

seat, Arabella noted he did indeed have the look of some-one who hadn't slept well; there were smudges of fatigue beneath his eyes, which were ever so slightly bloodshot.

"Would you like tea or coffee, or even hot chocolate, my lady? The coffee has just arrived, but Soames here"—he nodded at the footman—"can fetch whatever you like."

My lady, is it? Well, she *had* asked him not to call her Bella. She supposed he wouldn't call her *sweetheart*, or any other term of endearment now either. Which was for the best really. Summoning a scrupulously polite tone to match his, she responded, "Tea would be wonderful. Thank you."

Soames quit the terrace, and as Gabriel sipped his coffee, his gaze fell on the rosebud she'd pinned to her bodice. But he didn't remark upon it. Instead he removed the silver lids on all the serving dishes set out on the table and invited her to help herself to whatever she wished.

Arabella selected a slice of ham, a coddled egg, and a fresh roll. She hadn't sent for a supper tray last night and was quite hungry.

Gabriel piled a few more rashers of bacon and another egg onto his already quite full plate. "What are your plans for the day?" he asked before he took a sizable bite of egg-smeared toast.

Arabella concentrated on buttering her roll as she considered his question. "You know, I'm really not sure, to be perfectly honest. For such a long time, I've been at the beck and call of Aunt Flora and Lilias, so it's quite a novel experience to be at a loose end for once. But I suppose I could explore the villa and the garden. And talk to your house-keeper and cook about the menus . . . If that aligns with your plans, of course."

Gabriel attacked a kidney before responding. "My in-quiry agent is visiting at eleven o'clock to provide an update on his progress in locating my mother. I'll be sending off some correspondence to London via a courier around noon, so you might like to dash off some quick letters to your friends—Lady Charlotte, Lady Malverne, and Miss de Vere. I'd be happy to include them in the packet."

"Oh . . ." Arabella's spirits lifted immediately. "I would like that indeed. Thank you so much, my lord."

His lips twitched with a fleeting smile. "Think nothing of it, Arabella." He studied her over the rim of his coffee cup for a long moment before adding, "I had also originally planned on sailing us about the lake and then stopping somewhere for a picnic this afternoon . . . but given our current situation"—he shrugged—"I would understand if you didn't feel comfortable accompanying me on such an excursion. It does seem a tad too romantic, and I don't want you to feel uncomfortable or awkward. I will also admit that my shoulder is a bit sore today, so perhaps it's for the best that we don't go for that reason too."

Ouch. Arabella dropped her gaze to her plate. Guilt flooded her heart. There was now no doubt in her mind she'd hurt Gabriel's feelings. Sailing and a picnic sounded wonderful, but he was right, it smacked of romance. It would be far safer and easier—for her at least—to avoid such an activity.

"You should rest your shoulder then. I can fetch you some more liniment for it after breakfast if you'd like . . ."

"Thank you. I'll have Ryecroft apply it later when I get dressed."

What, he wasn't going to make a quip about her rubbing it in? Soames returned with a tea tray, and Arabella focused on dispensing a cup for herself. Why was she being so annoyingly contrary? Yesterday she'd been quite decided that she didn't want Gabriel to woo her or take her to bed so she could protect her heart. But now, when he was behaving like a perfect gentleman, she missed seeing his rakish side.

She sighed, and after she'd finished picking at her breakfast—her appetite seemed to have fled—she excused herself and went to her dressing room to retrieve the liniment. Opening up the bag, she rummaged about, then frowned when she picked up the bottle of laudanum.

It was empty. Bone dry.

Annoyance bristled. Had Aunt Flora helped herself when she wasn't looking? How abominably rude of her. Aside from that, she was concerned her aunt would take too much. It was a stronger concoction than she was probably used to and had to be dispensed carefully.

When she returned to the balcony, Gabriel immediately noticed her disgruntled expression. "Is everything all right?" he asked as he put down his coffee.

Arabella handed him the small pot of liniment. "No. I've just discovered my bottle of laudanum has been drained dry. I'm worried my aunt has taken it."

Gabriel's mouth twisted. "It wasn't your aunt. It was me. When your bag arrived along with your trunk, I tipped it out."

Arabella gaped at him as anger warred with confusion. "Why would you do such a thing?" she demanded when she could manage to draw breath. "Not only did you have no right to go through my belongings, you shouldn't have disposed of it. It's a special blend made by an apothecary in Edinburgh whom I trust implicitly. What if I need laudanum to treat someone who is ill or in pain?"

Gabriel gave her a long look, his expression inscrutable, but Arabella refused to break eye contact. She lifted her chin. "Well, I'm waiting for an explanation, my lord."

To her surprise, Gabriel sighed heavily, then shook his head as though a great weight had just settled upon him. "I can't bear the stuff for several reasons," he said quietly, his eyes glimmering with an emotion she couldn't quite identify. "But the most pertinent one is, two years ago, my father took too much and died. The coroner ruled his death was accidental, but I'm not convinced he didn't take his own life. You see, at the risk of being indelicate, his physician also informed me that he had syphilis."

Oh, dear Lord above. "Oh, Gabriel, I'm so, so sorry. I had no idea." The sense of guilt assailing Arabella was so strong, she felt as if she'd just been punched in the midriff and winded. "How shocking and tragic."

Gabriel shrugged. "My father and I had a complicated relationship. It may sound terrible, but I did not mourn his passing overly much. He wasn't a good man."

Arabella wanted to take Gabriel's hand in hers, to offer some sort of comfort, but she wasn't sure if her display of sympathy would be welcome.

Perhaps sensing her distress on his behalf, Gabriel cast her a small, crooked smile. "I apologize for invading your privacy, but when I saw your bag, just knowing there was a bottle of laudanum in there was too—" He broke off and a sigh shuddered through him. "I do hope you can see your way to forgive me."

Arabella did reach out and touch his forearm briefly. "I do. Unreservedly." Laudanum was easy enough to come by, so she could replace it. The problem was, if she did, she would have to do so surreptitiously. She didn't want to keep secrets from her husband, but it seemed that she must.

An hour later, Arabella sat at a small satinwood table by one of the wide windows in her room, sharpening her quill so she could pen a letter to Sophie. She still couldn't quite believe her dear friend was a viscountess. According to Charlie's letter, Sophie was blissfully happy, and Nate, her husband, was thoroughly smitten.

While Arabella was thrilled for Sophie, she couldn't help but compare their situations. Would that Gabriel was smitten with his own wife. Arabella sighed as she dug out her inkpot. There was no point in pining for the moon—she'd learned that lesson long ago when she'd lived in the orphanage in Glasgow. When they returned to London, she would try to focus on her charity work just as she'd always planned. At least that was something she could look forward to.

As she pondered how to begin her letter, her gaze wandered inexorably outside. With the curtains pulled back, she had a marvelous view of the balcony, and although she told herself she was simply drawn to the vista of lake and mountains and cloudless sky, that's not what really snared her attention; Gabriel's valet, Ryecroft, was currently shaving his shirtless master.

Gabriel was sprawled negligently in a chair, his dark head tilted back at a slight angle as Ryecroft slid the razor along his master's well-defined jaw. His wild black locks shone like a raven's wing in the morning sunshine. If he liked to laze about in nothing but buckskin breeches, no wonder his sleek skin was such a glorious bronze. Arabella swallowed as an unexpected wave of longing washed through her. She fervently wished she weren't so physically attracted to her husband. It would be easier to rid herself of this useless yearning if she wasn't.

And it would certainly be easier to focus on her letter writing. Forcing herself to drag her admiring gaze away, she dipped the nib of her quill into the ink and began to write, *My dearest Sophie . . .*

She'd written only a few lines, when she was distracted by a movement in the corner of her vision. Looking up, she discovered the young maid Colette was in the room. She stood by the French doors, apparently wiping a smudge off the glass pane with her white cotton apron, but her gaze was steadfastly trained on Gabriel.

The little minx.

Arabella supposed she couldn't blame the girl for gawking. She wanted to gawk too. Ryecroft had finished shaving Gabriel and was now rubbing liniment into his master's heavily muscled shoulder and back. Indeed, the sight was enough to make one's mouth water.

Colette had given up pretending to wipe the spot from the window, and Arabella frowned. The prickle of annoyance inside her intensified. She really *should* shoo the girl away. All things considered, it was most unseemly as well as disrespectful for her to be so blatantly ogling her master in front of his wife.

She called Colette's name and the maid jumped before blushing bright red. Arabella coolly requested a pot of tea, and the girl scurried from the room, as well she might.

Arabella picked up her goose feather quill again, but she couldn't concentrate. She removed her glasses and massaged the bridge of her nose as a sense of despondency settled over her; it felt like a cloud had suddenly covered the sun.

It would always be this way. Women were bound to stare at—and no doubt actively pursue—her breathtakingly handsome husband. And it wouldn't be long before Gabriel, who was ostensibly as libidinous as an alley cat, decided to stray. Especially in light of the fact that she'd just informed him she didn't wish to have marital relations for the foreseeable future.

Imagining him with another lover, whether a noblewoman or a prostitute—kissing her, undressing her, *pleasuring* her—hurt as much as a physical blow to Arabella's chest. A stab to her heart.

Tears stung the back of her eyelids. She'd been worried she might fall in love with Gabriel, but the way she felt right at this very moment, she rather suspected she'd already started to.

The idea of Gabriel being unfaithful wasn't the only thing that troubled her deeply. He was promiscuous, and with that came the risk of infection. He'd already mentioned he used condoms regularly, but they weren't a perfect method of protection by any means. She'd heard her grandfather inform his patients often enough. Abstinence was the only sure way to avoid contracting terrible diseases such as syphilis and gonorrhea.

Putting down her quill, Arabella realized she was going to have to instigate another difficult conversation with her husband.

W hen the inquiry agent, Monsieur Rochat, took his leave, Gabriel's gaze landed on the crystal decanter on the other side of Villa Belle Rive's study. Was half past eleven in the morning too early to start drinking brandy?

Rochat had just delivered news he hadn't wanted to hear: his mother was nowhere to be found in and around Vevey, Clarens, Montreux, or indeed any of the other Swiss lakeside towns between here and Geneva. Gabriel had left word in each and every place he'd visited—in Switzerland and Italy—that he was searching for his mother, hoping beyond hope she, or someone of her acquaintance, might come across one of his messages and reach out to him. But so far, his search had been in vain. The château she'd stayed at in Cologny a year ago was vacant except for a skeleton staff, and no one seemed to remember her. The house's owner was "abroad."

Such had been the case here at Villa Belle Rive—his mother had apparently stayed at this château for a whole month last summer, but the property agent in Villeneuve had no record of a Caroline Holmes-Fitzgerald, or Lady Langdale, renting this house, and the owner, a wealthy merchant, was presently touring Greece and Turkey. The villa's staff couldn't readily recall the names, or indeed anything much at all about past guests.

There was one tiny glimmer of hope. Rochat mentioned he'd heard a rumor that an English baroness—a certain Lady Wilfred who was supposedly an old friend of his mother's—was currently renting a villa not far from the small town of Nyon, just outside of Geneva. When Rochat sought an appointment with her, the woman had refused to meet with him.

Other than trying to secure an audience with the uncooperative Lady Wilfred himself, Gabriel really had no idea what to do next.

His mother could be *anywhere*, and it wouldn't be long before Timothy made moves to challenge for the title. And to have *any* hope at all of refuting his claim, Gabriel needed to be in London.

He really couldn't afford to stay away any longer. Tomorrow, he'd begin the long journey home, stopping at Nyon along the way. If he set out early, he'd be at the lakeside town by early afternoon.

Gabriel abandoned his seat behind the oak desk, threw off his superfine coat, and loosened his damnably tight collar and cravat.

He needed to do something to relieve the tension vibrating through him, and—as swiving his wife was definitely out of the question—imbibing brandy seemed like the next best option.

Taking up a position by the French doors, he sipped his drink and studied the lake. The sailing boat he'd hired floated at the end of a small wooden pier; yesterday, he'd harbored visions of ferrying Arabella about, sharing a bottle of wine, and then making slow, sweet love to her on a secluded, shady bank.

But it wouldn't be making love, would it? Gabriel sighed. Arabella had a point. He was loath to call what he wanted to do with her *fucking. Swiving* seemed too crude a term as well. He wanted her with a passion that defied explanation, a passion that only seemed to have intensified since he'd bedded her. Last night he'd tossed and turned into the wee hours, torn between the urge to slide into bed with Arabella and kiss her into submission, or to just admit defeat and scratch his own itch. Which would hardly be satisfying compared to the former option. In the end, he'd done neither, and as a result he was exhausted and out of sorts with a bad case of aching cods.

He briefly contemplated the idea of securing a mistress when they returned to London, but he knew deep down that such an arrangement wouldn't satisfy him. Not only that, he suspected he'd be plagued by a most inconvenient sense of guilt if he did stray. He seemed to be feeling that particular emotion a lot where Arabella was concerned.

He really didn't want to think why that should be so.

When Arabella admitted that she feared she might fall in love with him, Gabriel was certain she only felt that way because he'd been the one to take her maidenhead and show her physical pleasure for the very first time. She was simply casting him in a romantic light because, in her mind, it would be unseemly to enjoy sexual congress unless she and her bedmate shared an emotional attachment.

His mouth curved into a cynical smile. In time, she'd come to realize that he really wasn't worth falling in love with. Smart, compassionate, strong—and yes, beautiful—Arabella was far too good for a debauched libertine like him. Yet here they were, stuck with each other . . .

Gabriel tossed back his brandy, then sighed. A single nip wasn't enough to soften the edges of his discontent. He'd just replenished his glass when the door clicked open.

Arabella. How was it possible that such a range of conflicting emotions—hope, longing, and much to his shame, a modicum of childish petulance that she'd rejected him—could swirl about inside him all at once?

"My lord," she began as she advanced into the room before stopping in the middle of the rug. "I hope I haven't missed the courier. I've several letters—four actually—for my friends."

Gabriel smiled. "You're not late at all."

She gave him a hesitant smile in return. "I'm much relieved." In one hand, she held a small bundle of parchment while with the other, she clutched her silk shawl about her shoulders. "However, I'm afraid I've run out of sealing wax. Each letter is clearly addressed. If it's not too much trouble, would you be able to seal them for me?"

In light of the laudanum incident, Gabriel was unexpectedly touched that she still trusted him with something as personal as her private correspondence. "Of course," he said and, glass in hand, gestured toward the desk. "Although, I don't think we will be here much longer. I need to return . . . Sorry, I mean *we* need to return to London sooner rather than later."

"Oh . . ." She frowned. "How soon?"

"I'd like to leave early tomorrow morning if possible. The courier will make faster time than us, and I imagine your letters will arrive home at least a few days before we do. Unless you want to deliver your news in person . . ."

She shrugged. "They're written now, so I may as well send them on ahead." Crossing to the desk, she placed her letters on the leather blotter. "I don't wish to pry, but judging by your mood"—her gaze flitted to his glass of brandy before returning to his face—"I suspect the inquiry agent didn't impart anything useful about your mother's whereabouts then?"

His mouth twisted with a cynical smile. "I had hoped for better news," he admitted, then gave a brief recount of Monsieur Rochat's report. "If there's even a slim chance of meeting with a friend of my mother's, I must take it. However, if I don't ferret out any useful intelligence in Nyon, I'll have effectively exhausted every possible avenue of inquiry.

I'm beginning to think my mother decided to move to the North Pole or the antipodes."

Arabella's frown deepened. "I . . . I hope she is all right."

Gabriel sighed heavily. "So do I." It wasn't a lie.

Arabella nodded and worried at her lower lip for a moment before adding quietly, "I know this might not be an opportune time, but I need to talk to you about something of a rather delicate nature."

Gabriel's interest sharpened. Had his wife had a change of heart about allowing him into her bed? "Of course." He approached the desk. "Would you care to take a seat?"

"Thank you." Arabella sat carefully in a leather upholstered bergère and then spent an inordinate amount of time smoothing the light green muslin fabric of her skirts.

Gabriel took the seat on the other side of his desk and sipped his brandy while he waited for Arabella to collect her thoughts. Whatever she wanted to talk about must be serious indeed. Foreboding prickled at his nape.

"What, you're not thinking of asking for an annulment, are you, Arabella?" he quipped. "Because that won't work. No one will believe I'm impotent and that our marriage wasn't consummated. According to the London newspapers, I'm the 'Errant Earl,' the randiest rakehell in Christendom. A filthy libertine."

Arabella lifted her gaze and met his directly. Her cheeks were bright with color. "Unfortunately, even though it is an awkward topic, your libidinous nature is exactly what I need to discuss with you, my lord. Despite the fact that we are married, you've told me time and again that you are not willing to give up your licentious ways."

Exasperation flared. "At the moment, you are giving me little choice."

"I know . . ." She lifted her chin. "At the risk of deepening our estrangement, I'm going to say something you won't like. But I must because it impinges upon my well-being . . . and if we should be so lucky, the well-being of any child we might have in the future."

Gabriel put down his glass. Apprehension slithered along his spine. "Go on."

Arabella swallowed. Her entire face turned scarlet. "I know this will be difficult for you to accept, but . . . I'm going to ask you to abstain from sexual congress altogether until it's time for us to beget a child. I worry . . . I worry if you take up with a cyprian, or indeed any other woman, you might contract a venereal infection. I know you've been careful up until now, but there's always a risk the measures you take won't be sufficient. Sheaths can develop holes, or split, or . . . or fall off during the act. When I worked alongside my grandfather, I saw what syphilis could do too."

"But it could be months and months until we try for a child, Arabella," Gabriel snapped, his tone harsh. "You're asking too much. I'm not a goddamned saint."

Arabella flinched at his display of temper, and remorse immediately washed over him. He gentled his voice. "I apologize for my fit of pique. I assure you, I'm not usually so inclined. I'm just . . . I'm frustrated, and I can see it in your eyes that you won't be swayed."

"No," she said flatly. "I won't."

Gabriel raked a hand through his hair. "You know I only want *you* right now, don't you, Arabella? This will not be easy. Especially on our journey home. To be so close to you for days on end, but not to have you . . ." He shook his head. "It's going to be torture."

"I know. If it's any consolation, it will be difficult for me too. You're not the only one who is struggling to suppress a most inconvenient desire." Even though Arabella's countenance was still bright red, her gaze remained steady. "As I've said before, I won't risk giving my heart away to a man who doesn't want it, so it's the way it must be. I know I've hurt you by rejecting you, and I'm sorry for that. But if you have any regard for me whatsoever, you will accede to my wishes."

"And if I don't agree to your terms?" he demanded. He loathed sounding like a mulish prick, but right at this moment, he couldn't seem to help himself.

"While I recognize you do indeed have conjugal rights, you promised me you would never take me against my will. And as to whether you seek satisfaction elsewhere . . ." She shrugged. "I suppose you could hide an affair easily enough if you were so inclined . . . even though you also assured me you'd never lie to me. But if I *did* find out you'd been with another woman, I'd have no other choice than to live apart from you. And because you'd broken faith with me, I would not be inclined to come to your bed willingly for the purposes of begetting a child. No doubt that would lead to all sorts of inconvenient questions. I'm certain Lord and Lady Malverne and Lady Charlotte would be most curious about the true state of our marriage. Of course, I'm happy to pretend we are content if you can keep yourself in check. At least until you have your heir. After that, you can bed whomever you please."

Damn it all. Arabella was right on every score. She was far too clever, this wife of his. Resentment warred with grudging admiration as Gabriel studied her, sitting on the other side of the desk, her back ramrod straight with a determined glint in her hazel eyes. She might only be one-and-twenty, but she had a will of iron and a mind sharper than a bayonet.

Gathering her shawl about her shoulders, Arabella stood. "I realize I'm asking a lot of you, Gabriel. But surely you cannot blame me for wanting to protect my heart as well as my physical health. And the health of any babe we might have."

Gabriel rose to his feet as well. He suddenly felt exhausted. Defeated. "Of course, I'll respect your wishes, Arabella," he said gruffly. "Though God knows, it won't be easy."

"Thank you." Arabella inclined her head. "It means a lot to me that you would make such a sacrifice. I'll . . . I'll begin packing."

As she crossed the room, some devil inside Gabriel made him say, "If you ever change your mind, my dear, my bedroom door is always open . . ."

"Well, mine will be firmly closed, my lord," she replied in a clipped tone. "And as I've said before, I *won't* change my mind."

As the door clicked shut, Gabriel dropped into his seat. He really hoped Arabella had something in her medical bag that was an effective treatment for soothing calloused palms and blisters. Because in the coming months, his hand was going to get very sore indeed.

As Gabriel picked up his brandy again, his gaze strayed to the small pile of letters, and the name printed neatly on the uppermost one leapt out at him.

Dr. Graham Radcliff.

Gabriel's brows snapped together. What the hell was his wife doing sending mail to another man?

Of course, he shouldn't jump to conclusions; it was likely this Dr. Radcliff was simply a former acquaintance of her grandfather. Yes, he was probably some gray-haired gentleman with a stoop and a walking stick and Arabella had written to him about something completely innocuous related to some obscure medical topic or a particular philanthropic endeavor they were both interested in.

But then, why write to the man at all if the matter was of little consequence? She would be in London soon anyway.

Gabriel drummed his fingers on the blotter for a moment before sifting through the other letters. There was one for Lady Charlotte Hastings, another for Lady Malverne, and the last one was for Miss Olivia de Vere. All of her friends from the young ladies' academy.

Gabriel picked up the letter to the doctor and tapped it on the edge of the desk. A better man wouldn't be so suspicious. A better man would resist the temptation to look inside, thus betraying his wife's trust. A better man would simply seal it shut . . .

Fuck it. He wasn't a saint. He was going to look inside to discover exactly why Arabella had written to this Dr. Graham Radcliff fellow, whoever he was.

Gabriel swiftly unfolded the letter before his conscience got the better of him.

To his relief, the contents were generally unremarkable. The tone was light and friendly. Arabella mentioned that she wasn't sure if the doctor had received the missive she'd sent from Paris in April, but she was returning to London soon. She also expressed interest in visiting a dispensary he was opening in Seven Dials.

Gabriel arched an eyebrow. *Not bloody likely.* The area was a cesspit and too dangerous a place for Arabella to set foot in.

Arabella also talked about the Foundling Hospital, hinting that because he, Dr. Radcliff, was on the board, perhaps he could discuss budgetary considerations with her at a mutually convenient time. Gabriel's interest was piqued by that particular tidbit; he knew Arabella was interested in improving the conditions in orphanages, so perhaps she simply wished to cultivate a working relationship with the man. She'd ended the letter by informing the doctor she'd recently wed the Earl of Langdale.

And that was all.

Gabriel blew out a sigh. Yes, he was a heel, but at least his concern—that his wife harbored a tendre for a man of medicine—had been laid to rest. He folded the letter and then sealed it, using his signet ring emblazoned with the Langdale family crest—a hawk's head—to mark the red wax.

He smirked. He wondered what the good doctor would make of that.

And then he frowned as an altogether unsettling thought slid into his mind. Good God, could it be that he'd actually felt a pang of jealousy for the first time in his life? It was not like him to be so possessive . . .

Gabriel tossed back the rest of his brandy in one gulp. Steadfastly pushing away the notion that he might actually be starting to feel anything beyond desire for Arabella, he sealed the rest of the letters, then gathered together the correspondence he wanted to send off with the courier.

He made a mental note of what he would need to get done today. It wouldn't take long for Ryecroft to pack his things. He'd send word to the estate agent that he was vacating Villa Belle Rive. He'd paid in advance for the month's rental so the account was already settled. He supposed Arabella might like to farewell her family, so perhaps a quick stop at Clarens on their way to Nyon might be in order. He'd ask her this evening if that would suit.

Which meant the rest of the day could be spent at leisure.

Gabriel helped himself to another brandy, then picked

up his sketchbook, which he'd left on the desk. Damn, what he really wanted to do was draw Arabella naked, in his bed, or on the balcony, or even on a picnic blanket with her hair tumbling about her like sunlit honey.

Yesterday, on their wedding day, he confirmed what he'd suspected from the first moment he'd met her—that Arabella was a passionate creature beneath her demure, bespectacled facade. Indeed, her sexual responsiveness in bed had thrilled him.

And now he knew for a fact that the wanting in this relationship was far from one-sided. Arabella's choice of words might not have been flattering when she'd stated she was "struggling to suppress a most inconvenient desire," but it *was* an admission that she wanted him nonetheless.

To him at least, that was a relief. It was a start. If nothing else, Arabella was proving to be a most intriguing puzzle, and he was always up for a challenge. How ironic that the first woman to ever kick him out of her bed with a flea in his ear was his wife. As he'd suspected from the very start, a different tack was required to win her over.

But what?

Gabriel sighed and replenished his drink yet again. He had no bloody idea. For once in his life, he was dumbfounded. He suddenly wished his friends—Nate Hastings, Hamish MacQueen, and Max, the Duke of Exmoor—were here. Nate, a newly wedded groom himself, would certainly be able to give him some advice. But by all accounts, Nate had fallen in love before he proposed to his Sophie.

Showering Arabella with romantic gifts and compliments and introducing her to pleasure clearly hadn't been enough. But Gabriel was afraid that what she truly wanted, his undying love and fidelity, he really *was* incapable of giving.

The time had come for him to find the middle ground.

Of course, he would try to make their relationship amicable. And he'd do his very best to suppress his carnal urges during this enforced period of abstinence. While a not-so-charitable part of him was inclined to make Arabella ache with longing, too, he would be a right royal bastard to do so.

Gabriel pushed through the French doors and wandered out to the terrace with his brandy before settling himself on a stone bench beneath the shade of a willow tree. Lake Geneva sparkled in the sunshine, beckoning him to go sailing. But it wouldn't be the same without Arabella beside him.

He took a large sip of his drink; the alcohol was at last having a mellowing effect, melting away the sharp edges of his discontent. It was not within him to play the part of a perfect gentleman. Yet, clearly patience and a delicate, teasing approach were required to win Arabella over, just as he'd originally intended. While he wouldn't set out to deliberately seduce her, surely a little harmless flirting was permitted to remind her of what she was missing out on.

Praise be to God, his vexing-but-oh-so-tempting wife hadn't forbidden him to do that.

CHAPTER 11

Childe Harold had a mother—not forgot,
    Though parting from that mother he did
shun . . .

Lord Byron, "Childe Harold's Pilgrimage"

Nyon, Canton of Vaud, Switzerland

July 11, 1818

By the time they reached the small lakeside town of Nyon, it was almost three o'clock in the afternoon.

Arabella put aside "Childe Harold's Pilgrimage" and regarded Château de Nyon, a whitewashed, medieval castle perched on a rise above Lake Geneva, with interest as Gabriel's carriage drove by.

"I imagine we'll arrive at Lady Wilfred's villa in about a quarter of an hour," remarked Gabriel in a scrupulously polite tone. "I'm sure you'll be glad for the opportunity to stretch your legs. I know I will."

"Aye," replied Arabella in an equally civil manner. They'd set out just after breakfast, and aside from a perfunctory visit to Maison du Lac to bid her family farewell, and several brief stops at coaching inns to change the horses, they'd been traveling steadily for hours and hours. "But more than that," she continued, "I hope Lady Wilfred will grant you an interview."

Gabriel cast her a tight smile. "Thank you. I hope so too."

Sitting on the opposite bench seat, Gabriel canted his long, muscular legs away from Arabella, so there was no chance of his booted feet accidentally bumping against hers. His attention returned to the passing scenery of the deep blue lake and the cloudless sky above. No doubt he was preoccupied with thoughts of how fruitful the coming interview with the baroness would be. Arabella couldn't blame him given what was at stake.

Indeed, Gabriel's demeanor had been cordial but distant since they'd left Villeneuve early that morning. Arabella told herself she preferred it this way. That it augured well for the days to come that Gabriel was respecting her wishes. It proved they *could* have a courteous, perhaps even congenial relationship based on friendship and mutual respect. Even so, there was a perverse part of her heart that longed for one of his lopsided smiles. The flash of mischief in his green eyes when he said something calculated to make her blush.

If she were truly honest with herself, she'd admit she already missed his flirting—how it caused her pulse to race and made her think she might be special to him in some way, even when she wasn't.

She was such a contrary fool.

Directing her gaze to the verdant vineyards flashing by her carriage window, Arabella sent up a silent prayer to heaven that Gabriel would find his mother. She'd give anything to learn more about her own mother, Mary—she didn't even know where her final resting place was. Her grandfather had presumed it was in Glasgow.

She reached for Byron's volume of poetry and wrapped the ribbon-like scrap of fabric marking her place around her fingers. A rectangular strip of pale green linen embroidered with tiny lilies of the valley, it was a much-treasured keepsake. She'd tatted a delicate border of white lace around the edges to keep it from fraying; one of the threads was loose, so she'd have to repair it. There was a needle and thread in her medical bag, stowed away with her traveling trunk on the roof . . .

She felt the weight of Gabriel's stare and lifted her gaze.

"I've noticed you're quite fond of that ribbon." He gestured toward her hand. "Was it a gift from someone special?"

"Oh . . . it's more of a sentimental token than a gift." Arabella's mouth lifted into a faint smile. "I believe it's the remnants of an old handkerchief that once belonged to my mother. It's all that I have left of her . . ."

Compassion filled Gabriel's eyes. "I'm sorry."

Touched by her husband's expression of sympathy, Arabella had to swallow past the lump of emotion jamming her throat before she could speak again. "Thank you. My grandfather once told me that my mother posted this piece of the kerchief to the family home in Edinburgh just before she died. Apparently when Mary left me at the Great Clyde Hospital in Glasgow, she'd attached the other half of the kerchief to my admission papers, the idea being that if anyone from my family *did* come for me, the staff would know that person's claim was genuine because he or she possessed the matching piece."

"That was very clever of her."

"I believe it's a fairly common practice in foundling hospitals. Sadly, not many of the babes who are given up are ever reunited with their families."

"I'm glad your grandfather found you. And that you were loved," murmured Gabriel.

Oh, why did her husband have to look at her with such softness in his gaze and in his smile? He was supposed to be agreeable and polite, not kindhearted and considerate. In a way, such displays of tenderness were even more dangerous than any overt attempts at physical seduction. Crushing down an unwanted surge of hopeless yearning for a man she'd be unwise to want, Arabella made herself smile back at him. "So am I. God willing, you will be reunited with your mother."

Gabriel inclined his head. "Thank you. I do hope Lady Wilfred will be able to offer some assistance. And if she doesn't . . ." He shrugged. "I suppose I'll have to do battle with my cousin Timothy on my own."

* * *

"I am sorry, Lord Langdale. But I'm afraid my mistress is not in the habit of receiving *gentlemen* callers," declared Lady Wilfred's decidedly poker-faced English butler as he regarded Gabriel's card with undisguised distaste. "Especially those who are complete strangers and have not arranged an appointment with her ladyship via her personal secretary."

Standing on the wide, front steps of the elegant Château de Céligny with Arabella at his side, Gabriel prayed for patience. Good God. He'd never encountered such a puffed-up, irritating servant in all his life. No wonder Monsieur Rochat did not get very far.

Unclenching his back teeth, Gabriel drawled in the most disdainful, aristocratic manner he could muster, "Well, I'm not just *any* gentleman caller, and I'm hardly by myself. I'm the Earl of Langdale, and this lovely woman beside me is my wife, Lady Langdale. Aside from that, I'm by no means a complete stranger. My mother, the Dowager Countess of Langdale, is a good friend of your mistress's. I would strongly suggest you present her with my card." Gabriel couldn't be sure that the rumor Rochat had heard was true, but he sure as hell wasn't going to leave here without at least talking to Lady Wilfred.

The butler sniffed. "So you claim. In any case, I doubt Lady Wilfred will agree—"

"I really don't give a fig about your opinion. It hardly signifies." Gabriel waved a dismissive hand. "Now go and present my card to your mistress and be quick about it. I haven't got all day."

The man's eyebrows shot up, and a dark red flush stained his neck then flooded his cheeks. He clearly hadn't been challenged quite like this before.

However, Gabriel's strategy worked. The butler made a quick bow, then opened the front door of the château to admit them. "This way if you please, Lord Langdale." He bowed a little more deeply as Arabella approached. "Lady Langdale." After a liveried footman stepped forward to take their hats and gloves, he gestured toward a pair of gilt-legged chairs by a large arrangement of summer flowers in the entry hall. "You may wait here. I shan't be long."

"What a horrid man," Arabella murmured as she selected a seat. "I'm glad you were able to convince him to speak with Lady Wilfred."

Gabriel couldn't resist casting her a rakish grin. It seemed he could only behave himself for so long. "What can I say?" he replied, and flipped out his coattails as he claimed the opposite chair. "I've mastered the art of persuasion."

Even though Arabella pressed her lips together, he detected a twinkle of amusement in her hazel eyes. "Hmm. Let's hope you're able to persuade Lady Wilfred to reveal your mother's whereabouts just as easily."

He inclined his head. "Agreed."

Within a few minutes, the butler returned and escorted them to the back of the château. "Lady Wilfred will receive you on the terrace, where she is taking tea with her grandson and daughter, Lady Brinsley," he said stiffly. "She trusts you won't stay long."

So, Gabriel was to be treated like an inconsequential distraction in the baroness's day. That wasn't an encouraging sign. Nevertheless, having the opportunity to speak with her was better than nothing.

Lady Wilfred, a birdlike, stylishly attired woman of middling age, seemed in no hurry to put aside her teapot as Gabriel and Arabella were announced. She dispensed sugar lumps and milk into her own cup and her daughter's before shifting her attention to her visitors. When her bright brown eyes flickered over Gabriel and her mouth twitched with a moue of distaste, he wondered if she knew he was London's notorious Errant Earl.

Also quite telling was the fact that she didn't invite him or Arabella to take tea with her and her daughter. Lady Brinsley, an attractive young brunette, sat quietly beside her mother at a wrought iron table set with a ridiculous amount of fine bone china and silver platters overflowing with a variety of delicate cakes and sandwiches. It was enough to feed a battalion of starving soldiers.

"Lady Wilfred," Gabriel began without preamble when it was clear the baroness wasn't going to address him unless he spoke first, "I sincerely appreciate that you have agreed to meet with me and my wife at such short notice."

Beneath the fine lace brim of her cap, the baroness arched a brow. Her tone was cool as she said, "Lord Langdale, you claim that I am a good friend of your mother's."

"Yes. I was hoping that was indeed the case," he replied smoothly.

"Oh, you don't know?" she rejoined.

"One hears things," he said. "I am trying to locate her as I need her assistance with a private matter of some importance. In fact, one might even say it's most urgent."

Again she arched her brow. "Might one?"

"Yes."

At that moment, an almighty, wince-inducing wail splintered the silence. Gabriel sensed Arabella stiffening beside him. "Oh, dear," she murmured. "That doesn't sound good."

Lady Brinsley, who'd been silent throughout Gabriel's exchange with her mother, visibly paled. Rising to her feet, she cast aside her white linen napkin. "If you'll excuse me, Mama. I think Christopher has taken another tumble."

The baroness let out an impatient sigh. "Louisa, I'm sure your nurse is perfectly capable of dealing with the problem."

But it seemed Lady Brinsley would not be dissuaded. "You know he always settles better when I attend to him," she said. Picking up her pale lavender skirts, she rushed onto the lawn, heading for a nearby shrubbery from whence the crying seemed to be emanating.

Lady Wilfred rolled her eyes. "Sir Giles, my son-in-law, recently bought my grandson a spaniel puppy for his fifth birthday," she said by way of explanation. "Heaven knows how we are going to get the dog home to England when it's time to return at the end of summer." Her slight frame trembled with a delicate shudder. "There's bound to be a great hullabaloo."

Gabriel inclined his head. "No doubt. Does Sir Giles happen to be in?" He was certain he'd seen Sir Giles Brinsley's name on the membership list at White's. If Lady Wilfred wasn't forthcoming, perhaps he could have a word with the man. Not that the baronet would necessarily know all of his mother-in-law's friends—

"No, he's not," said Lady Wilfred decisively. She pushed back her chair and stood. "He's attending to business in Geneva today. So, if that's all, Lord Langdale—"

"My apologies for interrupting, my lady, but you still haven't confirmed or denied that you're a friend of my mother's."

At that moment, Lady Brinsley returned with her sobbing child on her hip and a tan and white King Charles spaniel nipping at her heels. A visibly distressed nursemaid followed close behind.

"Oh, Mama," cried Lady Brinsley. "My poor Christopher. Just look at what he's done to himself on the gravel path. I'm worried he's broken something." Heedless of the chinaware and the array of food, she deposited her son on the table and proceeded to ineffectually dab at his palms with a napkin.

Gabriel grimaced. The child had indeed scraped his hands and one of his knees quite badly.

Lady Wilfred's face took on a decidedly green cast and she promptly sat back down. "Oh, heavens," she said fanning herself with her own napkin. She clearly couldn't abide the sight of blood. "We must send for the doctor in Nyon."

"I might be able to lend some assistance, Lady Wilfred. Lady Brinsley," said Arabella, stepping forward. Her clear hazel gaze was direct and her manner unruffled as she added, "I have medical training courtesy of my grandfather, Dr. Iain Burnett. He was a well-regarded doctor in Edinburgh and a member of the Royal College of Physicians."

The baroness waved at her. "Well, do get on with it then."

Ignoring the arrogant woman's blatant rudeness, Arabella simply inclined her head. "Of course, Lady Wilfred." She turned back to Gabriel and touched his arm. "Would you mind fetching my medical bag from the carriage?"

"You don't have to do this, you know," murmured Gabriel. He'd had enough of the baroness, and he couldn't imagine why his mother would be friends with such a self-involved creature.

"I know. But I want to," she whispered back. "It's not wee Christopher's fault that his grandmother is being difficult."

Gabriel nodded. She was right, of course. "I'll be back in a moment."

By the time he returned, the little boy's sobs had subsided to watery sniffs. Arabella had drawn up a chair and was carefully checking his small fingers and thin wrists. "Everything is in perfect working order," she informed Lady Brinsley with a reassuring smile.

"Are you sure there's nothing broken?" asked Lady Wilfred.

Arabella turned to regard the woman. "I'm absolutely certain. I see no signs of swelling, bruising, or stiffness. Each joint moves freely through its full range of motion without pain." Her tone was so cool, confident, and professional, the baroness simply nodded in return.

Gabriel's chest swelled with pride. "Here's your bag, my lady wife," he said, placing it on a chair beside her.

She cast him a grateful smile. "Thank you. Would you mind opening it for me?" Her attention returned to the child. "Now, Christopher, I'm going to clean your scrapes and then apply some soothing ointment and a few plasters," she explained gently. "The cleaning part will sting a little, but it's for the best. Would that be all right with you?"

The child's lip wobbled, but he nodded and replied yes in a voice that wavered only a little.

Lady Brinsley ruffled his hair. "My brave strong boy. When Lady Langdale has fixed you up, then you can have as much cake as you like."

After the cleansing and bandaging were complete, and young Christopher was ensconced on his mother's lap with a plate of petit fours, Gabriel thought it might be safe to at last finish questioning Lady Wilfred.

As he accepted a cup of tea from the baroness—it seemed her attitude had softened a little since Arabella had stepped in to help her grandson—he ventured to ask yet again if she was a friend of his mother's and if so, could she share her current location.

"Yes, I did know her," Lady Wilfred replied carefully as she replenished her own tea. "However, I haven't had any contact with her for some years, Lord Langdale. I'm afraid I have no idea where she might be residing at present."

Gabriel regarded her over the rim of his cup. The woman was lying, he was sure of it. But accusing her of such a thing would not further his cause. Instead he said, "That's such a shame. Even though my parents were estranged for some time, it seems my mother wished to remain in contact with me at least. Indeed, she wrote to me every year without fail. However, my father kept her letters from me, and it wasn't until he'd passed away that I discovered them. Ever since, I've harbored hopes that we might reconcile. Her last letter mentioned she'd spent time here in Nyon. Last summer in fact . . ." He shrugged. "So here I am."

Lady Wilfred's eyes narrowed. "Yet earlier on you claimed you needed to see your mother about an 'urgent matter.'"

Gabriel put down his cup. He didn't want to air all of his family's dirty laundry, not if this woman didn't know his mother all that well. "It's a business matter related to the estate," he said. "I hoped she might be able to shed light on some of the details."

"Hmm." The baroness added a lump of sugar to her second cup of tea and stirred. "I'm sorry, but I really can't help you at all. As I said before, I haven't seen her for some time, and I don't have her direction."

"Well, if you do remember anything at all," said Gabriel, "you have my card. I'm actually on my way back to London, so you'll be able to reach me at Langdale House in St. James's in a fortnight if you recall anything, or better yet, have any news."

"Quite," replied Lady Wilfred with a tight-lipped smile. "I wish you and Lady Langdale"—she directed a warmer look at Arabella—"a safe and pleasant journey."

A short time later, Gabriel escorted his clever wife back to the carriage. "You were simply marvelous," he said as he handed her in along with her medical bag. "I don't think that woman would have admitted she knew my mother at all if you hadn't come to her grandson's rescue."

Arabella blushed as he dared to join her on the bench seat, her bag between them. "'Twas nothing really. I was happy to help the boy." She shrugged a slender shoulder. "It's what I do."

"A most admirable quality." Gabriel settled himself into the corner and removed his beaver hat. "The desire to help others."

A shy smile tugged at the corners of her pretty mouth as she removed her own bonnet. "Thank you."

The carriage moved off, and Arabella undid the buckles on her medical bag. "I do hope Lady Wilfred has a change of heart and decides to help you."

"Ah, so you also got the feeling she knew something about my mother but wouldn't share it?"

"Aye." Arabella reached into the bag and fished around for a brief moment before withdrawing a thin needle and a reel of fine white cotton. "I did."

"Alas, it seems my persuasive skills weren't quite per-suasive enough this time," Gabriel said with a sigh. He watched with interest as Arabella cut a piece of thread with her silver scissors and then proceeded to thread the needle with a deftness that was impressive. "Is there anything you *don't* have in that physician's bag of yours?" he said, peer-ing inside.

When he reached in and pulled out a wicked-looking scalpel, Arabella aimed a severe look his way. "You might want to put that down, my lord," she said in such a quelling tone that even a battle-hardened soldier would've been re-duced to quivering jelly. "It can slice through flesh like a scorching-hot knife through butter. I wouldn't like to think what damage it could do if we went over an unexpected bump."

"Neither would I, Doctor." Gabriel replaced the scalpel in its leather pocket, then returned his attention to his wife. She was carefully repairing a section of the lace on her kerchief. "My question beforehand was a serious one. *Is* there anything you're missing? Anything you'd like?" He inwardly grimaced. *Aside from the laudanum I cavalierly disposed of.*

Arabella's brow wrinkled in thought for a moment. "Well," she began, "when I was last in Paris, I visited L'Hôpital Necker and met a young physician—Laennec was his name—who'd invented the most remarkable but simple implement. He called it a *stéthoscope.*"

"A *stéthoscope*?" Gabriel had never heard of such a device. "And what does a *stéthoscope* do?"

"It's simply a slender wooden tube that allows one to auscultate vital sounds within the chest: the beating of the heart and the movement of air within the lungs. It amplifies these sounds, making it much easier for one to detect if anything is amiss."

"And you'd like one of these *stéthoscopes*?"

She smiled at him. "Aye. When we return to London, I was hoping to have one made based on Laennec's design. It looks a little like a spyglass, but it's completely hollow."

"Hmm. Who would've thought something so simple could be so useful?"

"Yes indeed. Docteur Laennec is very clever."

Gabriel studied his wife as she continued to sew tiny stitches. It was such a shame that society prevented someone as gifted as Arabella from practicing medicine, just because she was a woman.

Although, now that she was the Countess of Langdale, at least she could perhaps fulfill some of her other dreams; Gabriel was sincere when he'd promised to support her philanthropic endeavors. She might even be the mother of his children one day if he could successfully fend off Timothy's challenge and retain the earldom.

As far as Gabriel was concerned, the day when he defeated his cousin couldn't come soon enough.

CHAPTER 12

The evening was most beautiful . . . the moon rose,
and night came on, and with the night a slow, heavy
swell, and a fresh breeze.
    Mary Shelley, *History of a Six Weeks' Tour*

Hôtel Dessins, Rue de la Mer, Calais, France

July 25, 1818

Gabriel had been right. The journey home was absolute
torture.

How else could Arabella describe the experience of being sequestered in the close confines of a carriage for hours
on end, day after day with a man she wanted but, for very
sound reasons, shouldn't have? And when that man in question happened to be her husband, it only made matters
worse because by rights, she *should* be able to snuggle into
his wide chest and fall asleep in his arms, even seek his
breath-stealing kisses whenever she wanted. She should be
able to share his bed each and every night without shame,
instead of insisting on her own room at whichever inn they
stayed at. This self-imposed denial was wreaking havoc on
her equilibrium. And she hadn't expected that.

By the time they reached Calais, Arabella was more
than a little bit beside herself with longing. Throughout the
long journey through Switzerland and France, Gabriel—for
the most part—had been nothing but the perfect gentleman.

When she'd accidentally fallen asleep on his shoulder on more than one occasion, he hadn't taken any liberties with her person.

Although, there had been one time when, on the edge of wakefulness, she wondered if he might have pressed his lips against her temple as though he cared about her. But then again, perhaps she'd only dreamed about such a lovely moment.

It was strange and most vexing that even the smallest, ordinary things that Gabriel did began to have a peculiar effect on her. The gentlemanly touch of his hand at her elbow or on her back, or the brush of his muscular thigh against hers in the carriage seemed to penetrate her clothes, branding the flesh beneath. Sometimes when she looked away from the passing scenery or glanced up from the book she was reading, she caught him studying her. He never looked embarrassed when their eyes met; indeed, she was the one who blushed like a silly chit, especially when he smiled at her.

And then there were numerous occasions when she had unseemly thoughts and behaved in a most unladylike way. Just like the smitten maid Colette and so many of the other chambermaids they encountered at inns along the way, she couldn't stop stealing lascivious glances at her husband. At the end of each day, the black stubble shadowing Gabriel's lean jaw made her fingertips twitch with the need to explore the rough texture. When he slept, she was transfixed by the sweep of his black eyelashes on his high cheekbones and how his features softened, making him seem angelic rather than devilish. Because of the hot weather, he developed a habit of removing his jacket and loosening his collar and cravat so that the strong column of his throat and a tantalizing tanned patch of his chest were on display. And then all she could think about was inhaling his potent scent and pressing her lips to his neck where his pulse beat beneath his smooth skin.

At other times Gabriel read, or—if the road wasn't too bumpy—he sketched the scenery. On these occasions, Arabella found she became quite captivated by his hands: the way his long, elegant fingers splayed along the spine of the book, the deftness of his movements when drawing, or how a knuckle or the heel of his hand became charcoal smudged. She dared not think about what her husband could do with those clever, beautiful hands in the intimate moments they'd shared on their wedding day. But sometimes, despite her best efforts, she did.

Of course, throughout the journey there were endless opportunities for discussion, and they talked about anything and everything; although Arabella observed they both steered clear of anything too personal or painful. When Gabriel showed genuine interest in conversing about topics of a medical nature, she was quietly touched. She learned Gabriel had attended Eton and Oxford and had served in the infantry in Wellington's army for two years. She gathered his relationship with his father had been far from amicable—in fact Gabriel did not like to talk about him at all. She also suspected that after his mother left his father—when Gabriel was thirteen—that he'd felt quite abandoned. He admitted he didn't quite recall *why* he decided to get a tattoo, but it had been during a drunken spree after he'd returned to England after Waterloo.

Gabriel made a concerted effort to secure separate bedrooms at all of the inns and hotels where they spent the night. Although, there was one occasion when they were obliged to share. In the small French town of Provins, the inn had only one room of inferior quality to spare. Even though Gabriel offered to sleep on the dusty floorboards, Arabella insisted he share the tester bed; she built a wall of pillows and blankets down the center of the lumpy mattress, and Gabriel—much to his credit—had stayed on his side. However, in the morning, Arabella was both shocked and mortifyingly aroused when she woke and noticed that her husband, who was bare-chested and lying flat on his back fast asleep, sported an enormous erection, which tented the bedclothes in a most curious manner. For a moment, Arabella pretended Gabriel was dreaming about her, and indeed, it had taken a considerable amount of effort on her part not to kiss him awake to see what would happen next.

Telling herself it would be foolish of her to succumb to

temptation, she forced herself to rise and dress, and then went in search of breakfast in the public room downstairs. By the time she returned to their room, Gabriel had awoken also and thankfully, his erection had subsided. He was miffed with her for visiting the public room without an escort—she didn't have a maid, and he was concerned she might have been accosted by some of the disreputable characters about. However, Arabella had been reluctant to defend her decision to scout for breakfast on her own because she didn't want to mention the real reason she'd left—her husband's rampant arousal seemed like a veritable hornet's nest of a subject, given the circumstances. In the end, she took the path of least resistance and simply apologized, assuring Gabriel she wouldn't go off on her own again. She really couldn't blame him for being concerned about her safety.

And now, on their last night in France, they were staying at the Hôtel Dessins in Calais. It was a well-appointed hotel in quite a grand house, and their ground-floor suite looked out onto a courtyard garden that contained well-tended parterres of flowers.

The sun was setting as the concierge of the hotel showed them to their elegant apartment, informing them quite proudly that Napoleon Bonaparte had stayed within this very suite as he threw open a set of French doors to let in the sea breeze.

Gabriel simply arched an eyebrow, then nodded at Ryecroft to give the man a tip to shoo him away; the vanquished French emperor might have stayed here once, but that knowledge clearly wasn't enough to put her husband off occupying the same rooms. Judging by the way he threw himself onto a settee upholstered with red silk damask and propped his dusty Hessians up on a low mahogany table, Arabella thought he might even be taking perverse pleasure in the whole experience.

Dinner was taken alone in the main sitting room—plaice with sorrel sauce followed by a platter of cheese and summer peaches, all washed down with a reasonable claret— and when they at last finished, Arabella felt as though she might fall asleep at the dining table. A chambermaid had delivered hot water to each of their respective bedrooms while they were dining, and Arabella couldn't wait to wash off the grime of travel and then slip between the crisp cotton sheets in her enormous tester bed.

When she stood and bid Gabriel a cordial good night, he rose, too, and inclined his head in acknowledgment.

"We shall endeavor to take the packet that sails for Dover at ten o'clock tomorrow morning," he said, loosening his cuffs. Because the night was balmy, he'd discarded his jacket and waistcoat and had eaten dinner in his shirtsleeves. "However, I'd like you to be ready by eight o'clock as there are certain formalities that will need to be completed at the customs house before we embark."

"Of course. I'll be ready," she replied. "Well . . . good night again, my lord."

"Good night, my lady. I hope you sleep well." The heaviness of Gabriel's gaze made Arabella blush, and she made a fuss of fluffing out her crushed, travel-stained skirts as she crossed the sitting room. Indeed, she swore she could feel the seductive weight of his regard until she entered her bedchamber and closed the polished mahogany door.

Curse my too-handsome husband with his fallen-angel looks and smoldering eyes. Arabella pressed her hot forehead to the cool wood panels of the door and waited for her racing pulse to slow. It wasn't as though she could take Gabriel to task for behaving indecorously. It was hardly his fault that his very presence made her tingle with awareness. That he constantly drew her eye.

Why couldn't she be immune to his charms and purge herself of this useless craving? It was like a fever in her blood, and she was certain the only cure was to give in to the overwhelming urge to fall into Gabriel's arms and let him kiss her and strip her bare and take her over and over again.

It would be easier in London. She imagined they would have their own suites so she wouldn't have to come across him in nothing but his banyan and breeches, as she'd accidentally done on several occasions during their journey. They would also lead their own, very separate lives; while

Gabriel was off attending to estate and business matters, she would join various charity boards and, at long last, throw herself into the work that needed to be done to establish her own, well-funded orphanage in Edinburgh. She could even talk to Dr. Radcliff about opening more dispensary clinics for the poor. He'd probably received her letter by now and knew she was married. She wondered what he thought of that. Would he be disappointed she'd wed another, or would he be happy for her?

Sighing wearily, she turned around to face the spacious, well-furnished room. There wasn't much point in speculating about Dr. Radcliff's reaction to her news. She supposed she'd find out soon enough anyway.

Kicking off her slippers, Arabella set about getting ready for bed as well as preparing fresh traveling attire for tomorrow. She didn't have a maid yet—Gabriel had wanted her to hire Colette, but there was no way on earth that Arabella was going to employ a lady's maid who lusted after her husband. So she'd simply informed him that she was used to taking care of herself and would rather secure the services of a maid once they got to London.

After opening her traveling trunk—it had been installed in the adjacent dressing room—Arabella selected a relatively plain gown of striped cotton and a matching spencer, and hung them on a hook so the creases would fall out. Then she washed her face and hands and fished out her night rail and hairbrush from her overnight valise.

Her dusty traveling gown landed in a heap on the floor, along with her petticoats, but as she tried to remove her stays, she ran into trouble. The corset fastened at the back, and evidently, she'd tied the laces far too tightly; she couldn't loosen the knot no matter how hard she tried. After five minutes of twisting and contorting herself into all sorts of positions, she conceded defeat. She needed help.

Cursing under her breath, Arabella slid her gown back on, thrust her feet back into her slippers, and then returned to the sitting room. However, it was deserted. Gabriel had vacated the dining table, and the candles had been extinguished. The French doors were shut, and when she peered out to the enclosed garden, the rising moon cast sufficient light for her to see Gabriel wasn't there either; sometimes he liked to venture outside to smoke a postprandial cigar. He must have retired for the night too.

Following a quick search for a bellpull, Arabella's chagrin increased—there didn't seem to be a way to ring for a chambermaid. Of course, the type of guests who stayed in this suite probably had a surfeit of servants at their beck and call. Arabella supposed she could ask Ryecroft to fetch a maid. But then, he might be helping his master at this very moment.

She was loath to go looking for a hotel servant on her own considering the kerfuffle that had occurred in Provins.

Arabella lifted her glasses and wearily rubbed the bridge of her nose. Unless she wanted to spend an uncomfortable night sleeping in her stays, or take a pair of scissors to them, it looked as though she'd have to call on Ryecroft to assist in her quest for a maid.

Drawing a deep breath, she gently knocked on Gabriel's bedroom door, but there was no answer. Surely he hadn't fallen asleep already. There was only one way to find out . . .

Cracking open the door a fraction, Arabella peered into the room. Candlelight danced over the crimson flocked wallpaper, the mahogany wood paneling, and the tester bed that was very similar to her own—but the bed was empty. The door to the dressing room was ajar, but Arabella couldn't hear any voices or sounds of activity.

She frowned in confusion. Had Gabriel gone out? He hadn't mentioned he had any other plans. Ryecroft was sharing a smaller room with the footman, Soames, but she would have to venture out into the hall and knock on the door to summon him. Though he might know the whereabouts of her husband . . .

Arabella blushed. Lord, how embarrassing that she might have to ask her husband's valet such a thing.

A breeze stirred the white chintz curtains at the open sash window, and the candles guttered. All was silent save for the soft sigh of the sea in the distance and her own nervous breathing.

She was about to shut the door when another sound snagged her attention. A soft, decidedly male groan.

Heavens, was that Gabriel? The low moan had come from the direction of his dressing room. The door stood slightly ajar, and a pool of golden lamplight spilled onto the Turkish rug and the edge of the burgundy-hued counterpane covering the bed.

Arabella hovered on the threshold as uncertainty gripped her. Was Gabriel hurt or unwell?

She inhaled a breath to call out his name, but then he suddenly appeared in the open doorway. And Arabella gasped, her hand flying to her throat.

Oh, Lord above! Gabriel was shirtless and barefoot, his breeches slung low around his narrow hips. But that's not why horrified mortification, perverse fascination, and wicked desire tangled together inside her, rendering her speechless and frozen to the spot.

The fall front of his breeches was open, and in one large hand, he gripped his fully erect penis.

Arabella didn't know where to look—her gaze skittered away into the shadows, but somehow her awareness was still completely focused on Gabriel. Aside from an initial widening of his eyes, perhaps because he was momentarily startled, too, he now appeared completely unperturbed. He leaned nonchalantly against the door, one raised forearm resting on the doorframe. He made no attempt to hide his nudity or aroused state. Indeed, his mouth kicked into a wicked smile as he gave his shaft a long, languid stroke. "Can I help you, my sweet wife?"

Her face aflame, Arabella swallowed to moisten her dry mouth. "I . . . um . . . I came in to . . . But you . . . I mean there was no one . . ." It was no good. She was so breathless and her thoughts so scattered, she doubted she could string a coherent sentence together even if her life depended upon it.

"Have you had a change of heart about inviting me into your bed, Bella?" Gabriel's voice was so deep and husky with lust, it stirred Arabella's blood; it ran hot and fast, straight to her sex. As she blinked at him like a brainless ninnyhammer, he moved his fist with deliberate slowness, caressing himself from root to tip. "Or if you haven't, perhaps you could take pity on me and lend a hand . . ."

Lend a hand? Was he suggesting that *she* stroke him? Without thinking, Arabella began to curl her tongue around the word *yes*, but then sanity prevailed, and she stopped herself. If she gave in to temptation, who knew where things might end. She shook her head. "I . . . no. Gabriel, I'm so sorry for disturbing you. I didn't mean to . . . to interrupt . . ." Somehow, she tore her fascinated gaze from her husband and examined the exotic patterns in the rug at her feet. "I needed . . . I mean I *need* help with loosening my stays. The laces are badly knotted. But there doesn't seem to be a way to ring for a maid, not that I can see, at any rate . . . I was going to ask Ryecroft to fetch someone . . . but he isn't here . . ."

Gabriel sighed and straightened. "What a shame," he murmured. Turning away from her, he began to adjust his breeches. "If you could give me a moment," he called over his shoulder, "I'll help."

"No . . . no it's quite all right. I just need a maid."

"Don't be silly." Gabriel disappeared, and Arabella heard water splashing in the basin. A few moments later when he stepped back into the room, his breeches were buttoned and he was wearing a banyan. "I'm here and happy to do it. I happen to be quite adept at undoing stays."

"I'm not sure if that makes me feel more or less comfortable about this," grumbled Arabella.

Gabriel clucked his tongue like a cross nurse as he padded across the rug in his bare feet. "Here, turn around. The knot will be undone in a jiffy and then you can go to bed. You must be dead on your feet."

Arabella couldn't deny that she was exhausted. And there didn't seem much point in refusing his seemingly sincere offer to help, so she complied.

Once she'd presented her back to Gabriel, she undid the buttons at the front of her gown so it would be loose enough to slide off her shoulders to expose her stays. She was suddenly transported back to their wedding day when Gabriel had undressed her before making her his wife in truth. Stiffening her spine, she made herself resist the urge to sway backward and press herself against his beautiful body.

"I didn't mean to startle you before," Gabriel murmured as he worked at the knot. "I had no idea anyone was in here."

Arabella turned her head to speak over her shoulder. "It's not your fault. I did knock but apparently not quite hard enough."

There was a long pause, then Gabriel cursed beneath his breath as he continued to fumble with the knot. "I shouldn't have acted so crudely either. I hope you'll accept my apology."

"I do." Curiosity tugged at Arabella and before she could stop herself, she added, "Do you . . . do you do that often?"

"I assume you mean come off by my own hand?"

Arabella blushed from the top of her head to the tips of her toes. She'd never dreamed such a thing was even possible, but it seemed it was. "Aye."

"More often than I probably should, but at the moment, it's the only thing I can do to achieve some relief . . . You see, men are base creatures and have strong urges by and large. If we're sexually aroused and don't expend our seed regularly . . ." Arabella sensed that he shrugged. "Our bollocks become quite painful and ache with the need for release."

Oh. "I had no idea," whispered Arabella. It was the truth. She was only beginning to understand how odd the male of the species really was, especially if the man in question was a rakehell. Charlie had been right. There were so many things young women didn't know about men. Or sexual intercourse.

"You could always try it yourself sometime," continued Gabriel in a low voice. "Self-gratification is nowhere near as fulfilling as sexual congress, but it can relieve one's frustration. *If* one is frustrated of course . . ."

Was he fishing to find out if she suffered from a similar affliction? Arabella didn't know what to say. Yes, she was frustrated. Perhaps even more so since she'd come upon Gabriel in flagrante. The image of him stroking himself so casually, so seductively, had burned its way into her brain. But she didn't want to admit her body thrummed with need too. It seemed this man had awoken a hunger in her that couldn't be satisfied.

Well, that wasn't quite true. Gabriel *could* satisfy her, but she wouldn't let him. For very sound, eminently sensible reasons. Though right at this moment, she was very tempted to throw all of them out the window.

She was spared from having to respond as Gabriel at last loosened the knot. "There we go," he said softly.

When Arabella's voice emerged, she was dismayed it contained a telltale husky edge. "Thank you."

Before she could shrug her gown back into place, Gabriel curled his fingers lightly about the tops of her bare arms and she shivered with awareness. He was so close, she could feel his body heat, hear his breathing. She held her own breath, waiting. The air around them trembled with expectation as desire whispered and beckoned. *Lured* . . . She closed her eyes and prayed for strength. The urge to surrender to its pull was almost irresistible.

"These past two weeks, it hasn't been easy, being so very close to you, yet I cannot have you, Arabella." Gabriel leaned close and she felt the brush of his cheek against her hair. "I think you'd best go before I break my word and actually do try to seduce you." He pressed a soft kiss against her temple. "Good night, my lovely lady wife. I wish you sweet dreams."

His hands lightly caressed her arms one last time and then he stepped back, releasing her.

Arabella clutched her loosened gown to her chest with shaking hands and forced herself to walk away, to return to her room before she changed her mind.

CHAPTER 13

❧

England's most Errant Earl has returned to town!

However, many of the ladies of the ton will be disappointed to learn he's married.

Rumors abound about the identity of his new blushing bride and whether or not she'll be able to tame him . . .

The Beau Monde Mirror: The Society Page

Langdale House, St. James's Square, London

July 26, 1818

It was approaching midnight when Gabriel's coach drew to a stop in front of his town house. Despite the fatigue weighing her down, Arabella stared up at the grand facade with its white pillars and shiny black double doors in wide-eyed amazement as her husband helped her to alight.

It would take her some time to become accustomed to residing in houses that were veritable palaces.

"Welcome home, my Lady Langdale," Gabriel said as he took her arm and escorted her up the short flight of stairs to the front door. "I sent word ahead that we would be arriving late tonight, so the staff should have readied our rooms. And knowing my butler, they are probably gathering to greet us as we speak."

Almost too weary to reply, Arabella inclined her head and smiled. "That's very kind."

"Kindness has nothing to do with it, my dear. I pay them well and they ought to show their new mistress due deference."

The butler, a gray-haired slender gentleman of middling age, admitted them. Gabriel introduced him as Jervis; he gave an elegant bow as he greeted Arabella. "My lady, welcome to Langdale House. If there's anything at all that you need, you have only to ask."

Arabella smiled her approval. "Thank you."

"I'm afraid this has been a bachelor's residence for so long, I don't have all that many maids on staff," said Gabriel after he'd introduced her to the middle-aged housekeeper, a short, plump-cheeked woman with kind brown eyes. "But I'm sure you and Mrs. Mayberry here will have that all sorted out soon enough."

"Yes, indeed, my lord," agreed Mrs. Mayberry. She smiled warmly at Arabella. "Ma'am."

The remaining introductions to the assembled footmen and a handful of maids were conducted swiftly, and then Mrs. Mayberry offered to show Arabella to her suite.

Gabriel, still holding Arabella's arm as though he didn't want to release her, accompanied them. "The apartments were once my mother's," he explained as they mounted the left side of a sweeping oak staircase that led up to the next floor. "You might want to redecorate as everything will be outdated and I'm sure you have your own particular tastes in furnishings. So spare no expense. My pockets are deep."

Arabella didn't want to raise a difficult subject, but felt compelled to anyway. "Are you sure? Because if Langdale House is entailed . . ." She didn't need to complete the thought, as Gabriel gathered her meaning straightaway.

To her dismay, he grimaced. "You're right, it's probably best to wait until this title business is sorted out. Curse my cousin."

"It's quite all right," Arabella offered as they climbed another set of stairs to a long, wide gallery. The oak wainscoting and gilt-framed paintings gleamed softly in the muted glow of the wall lamps. "Perhaps I can use a little of the money for other things."

Gabriel patted her hand. "You'll have a separate, generous allowance for a new wardrobe."

"Oh no, I didn't mean for clothes. I'd like to begin donating funds to some of the charitable concerns that are dear to me. If you agree."

"And you shall have a separate budget for that too."

Arabella's gaze whipped to his. "Are you sure?" How much money did this man have?

"Of course. I wouldn't offer if I didn't mean it," he said. "Besides, we had an agreement, remember?"

"Yes . . ." She would provide him with an heir and he would support her charities.

She wasn't able to add anything further, as Mrs. Mayberry was opening a set of double doors. "Your rooms, Lady Langdale," she said as she stepped back to let her and Gabriel pass through into the suite beyond. "I trust they meet with your satisfaction. But if anything is amiss, or you require anything else, just let me know. There's hot water already waiting in the dressing room."

Arabella inclined her head. "Thank you." And then she gave a soft gasp.

The sitting room was beautiful. The plush Aubusson rug, the curtains, armchairs, and sofas were all decked out in soft shades of gold, cream, and dusky rose. A Boulle clock and a large bunch of deep pink roses and lilies graced the white marble mantelpiece, and silk wallpaper featuring a delicate pattern of pink peonies, butterflies, and dragonflies lined the walls above the honey-hued satinwood paneling. After Mrs. Mayberry showed her the bedroom with its elegant four-poster bed, Arabella turned back to Gabriel, who was waiting by the fireplace, watching her. "I'm telling you now, I won't need to redecorate," said Arabella. "I've never seen such lovely rooms."

"I'm pleased to hear they meet with your approval, my lady." Gabriel's mouth tipped into a rakish half smile, and Arabella's heart skipped a beat. "I'm not far away"—he nodded toward a door on the other side of the sitting room—"if you ever want me."

Oh, my. Of course she wanted her husband. Too much.

Despite her fatigue, desire began to hum inside Arabella and she barely heard the knock on the door heralding the arrival of several footmen bearing her traveling trunk, medical bag, and valise. Mrs. Mayberry directed them to the dressing room, and then all the servants quit the room, leaving her and Gabriel quite alone.

Gabriel rested one arm along the mantel. He picked up a stray pink rose petal and rubbed it between his fingertips. "In the morning, I'd suggest you talk to Mrs. Mayberry about securing a lady's maid. She'll be most helpful in that regard."

"I'm sure she will." Arabella was relieved Gabriel seemed to be focusing on mundane, practical matters again.

"And tomorrow, I will seek an audience with the Archbishop of Canterbury to obtain a special license. I'd like us to wed the day after, here at Langdale House as I'd rather not cause a fuss. I'll see if the minister at St. George's is available for an afternoon service. As you know, I don't want anyone to be able to challenge the validity of our marriage."

Arabella nodded. "I understand. And I agree."

"Good." Gabriel dropped the crushed rose petal and regarded her for a moment before he added, "I'd like to hold a gathering here afterward. With all of our friends."

"Oh, that would be wonderful," declared Arabella. Happiness flooded her heart. She couldn't wait to see Charlie, Sophie, and Olivia. Perhaps she could even arrange to meet with them tomorrow. A reunion at Gunter's perhaps?

Gabriel was speaking again. "Do order whatever flowers you'd like to decorate the house. I'm sure Mrs. Mayberry will be able to handle the catering for the wedding breakfast, but you may wish to consult with her to ensure the arrangements meet with your satisfaction. And if you wish, feel free to take my town coach and visit whichever modiste you would like in order to obtain a new gown for the occasion. Just set up an account in my name."

"Thank you," Arabella replied. "But I'm more than happy with the one I wore on our wedding day in Clarens. It's exquisite. It would be a shame not to wear it again."

"You are very easy to please, Arabella, and I am most grateful. I will see you on the morrow then . . ." His mouth kicked into a wicked grin. "Unless, of course, you have trouble with your stays again . . . As you know, my door is always open."

Arabella made herself frown. "Have I ever told you that you're incorrigible?"

Gabriel gave a deep, throaty chuckle. "Sweetheart," he said as he headed for his room, "I think I have a new aim in life. My day will not be complete unless I've heard you call me incorrigible at least once."

Arabella couldn't help but smile. At least her incorrigible husband was good-natured about his shortcomings. Left alone, she retired to her own bedchamber and began to get ready for bed. The next two days would be busy indeed, but she didn't mind. She'd be surrounded by the people she loved most in this world, her friends.

But then a wave of sadness welled. She'd have to pretend that her marriage to Gabriel was a blissful love match, just like Sophie's. Because how could she admit to Charlie, Sophie, and Olivia that her bridegroom had merely offered for her out of a sense of obligation and that the nature of their union was purely transactional?

She didn't want to lie, but sharing the unadulterated, perhaps even ugly truth would be difficult indeed.

28 Russell Square, London

July 27, 1818

"I'm sorry, Lord Langdale, but my master has given orders that you are not to be admitted under any circumstances."

Gabriel ground his teeth as he leveled a hard stare at the weak-chinned butler attempting to guard the front door of his uncle's town house. He almost felt sorry for the chap because he was about to discover *no one* stood in the Earl of Langdale's way. His uncle was still alive and he *would* see him.

"Whose orders exactly?" he demanded in a low, gravel-laced voice and braced a forearm against the door to stop the man from closing it in his face. "My cousin's or my uncle Stephen's?"

The butler swallowed and his jowls quivered. "Captain Holmes-Fitzgerald's of course. He's not home at present and his father is indisp—" He broke off as Gabriel gave the door a quick, forceful shove, unbalancing the servant. "Now, see here! You can't just barge in—"

But it was too late, Gabriel had already pushed past the stumbling butler and was striding toward the stairs that led to the bedrooms on the next floor. "Yes I can. I'll see my uncle whenever I like."

None of the other servants challenged him as he mounted the stairs, two at a time, and marched down the corridor. Considering that Timothy was probably using Gabriel's coin to pay their wages, they bloody well should mind their own damned business.

Stopping before his uncle's door, Gabriel drew a steadying breath to collect himself. The report he'd received from Nate a month ago indicated his uncle was in a very frail state. Indeed, it seemed like a miracle that Uncle Stephen had managed to hang on to life for this long.

Gabriel didn't want to disturb him when he was so unwell, but he feared that he must. This might be his last chance to glean any additional information about his parents' marriage before Timothy acted. Perhaps Uncle Stephen knew something about the two witnesses who'd been present at his parents' anvil wedding. Their names appeared on the certificate, but he feared that wasn't enough. He'd always assumed they were local villagers from Springfield, but then again, they might very well have been acquaintances of his mother or father. Or even servants in his father's employ. Surely it would help if at least *someone* was able to attest before the Committee for Privileges that a lawful Scottish marriage ceremony had indeed taken place.

Although that might mean little under the terms of the Hardwicke Marriage Act if Timothy pressed his claim.

Christ. Gabriel removed his beaver hat and ran a hand

down his face. He was suddenly gripped by a smothering sense of desperation unlike anything he'd ever felt before. Because it wasn't just his own future he needed to consider. So much more was at stake now that he had Arabella in his life. It was vital that he secured his right to the earldom for the sake of their future children.

And at the moment, he didn't have a hope in Hades of Arabella sharing his bed again unless and until he succeeded.

But standing about in a hallway quietly panicking about the situation wasn't going to help matters. And Timothy might turn up at any moment and attempt to have him ousted. He drew another bracing breath and opened the door.

Even though the bedroom was dimly lit—the heavy velvet curtains were still drawn, blocking out the morning sun—Gabriel could see the bed was occupied. However, the slight figure huddled beneath the covers barely resembled the man he remembered. His uncle had always been a tall, vigorous man with an athletic physique, and to see that he had withered away to almost nothing was shocking indeed.

Also shocking was the realization that no one else was in the room—not a nurse, not a valet, not even a housemaid. The room was stuffy and smelled of unwashed male and unemptied chamber pots.

Gabriel swore beneath his breath, and his gloved hands curled into fists. How dare Timothy leave his father alone when he was in such a state. If his cousin were here right now, Gabriel would be hard-pressed not to beat the sniveling, drug-addled swine to a pulp.

He twitched the curtains open to let in a little more light, then cracked the window to let in some fresh air. "Uncle Stephen?" he said softly as he approached the bed. "It's me, Gabriel. Your nephew."

His uncle didn't stir, and for one blood-freezing moment, Gabriel feared the worst. But then the covers moved and his uncle inhaled a rattling breath.

Moving to the side of the bed nearest to the window, Gabriel took a seat in the bedside armchair. He tugged off his gloves and placed them, along with his hat, on the bedside table. Now that he was closer, he could see how rail-thin his uncle was; his cheeks were hollow and his eyes had all but sunken into their sockets. Except for the dark bruise-like shadows beneath his eyes, his skin had a waxy pallor. If Gabriel hadn't heard his uncle draw breath, he might have believed he'd already passed from this world.

"Uncle Stephen?" Gabriel reached out a hand and gently squeezed his uncle's shoulder; he was nothing but skin and bone. The belly canker seemed to be devouring him alive. He suddenly wished Arabella were here with him, to offer advice. To hold his hand.

He brushed a tear from his cheek and tried again. "Uncle, can you hear me? I'm so sorry I haven't come to see you sooner . . . I've been away. On the Continent. I pray you can forgive me."

His uncle inhaled another shaky breath and coughed a little. His eyes flickered beneath blue-tinged eyelids, but then he grew still again. Gabriel knew his uncle hadn't much time left, yet here he lay, all alone. Forgotten and unloved.

Stephen's wife, Susanna, had passed away a decade ago. Gabriel hadn't been particularly close to her—she'd always been a quiet, prim woman who kept to herself. Although his uncle Stephen was also a man of subdued character, he possessed a strong will and a deep sense of moral decency. He seemed to understand Gabriel . . . unlike Michael, his own father, who'd resented the fact that his adolescent son would rather read, draw, and paint than drink and fuck morning, noon, and night. During Gabriel's adolescence, his uncle had been his champion on more than one occasion, removing him from his father's immediate sphere when he was in the throes of his worst drunken excesses.

Gabriel thrust away the dark memories crouching at the back of his mind, waiting to spring forth if he let them. He'd always be grateful for his uncle's intervention; it had given him a much-needed respite from the riotous storm his life had become after his mother left. Indeed, for many years, Eton and his uncle's home were the only safe havens he'd had.

He suddenly realized that he craved his own safe
haven—a true home—and that a better man could create
that with Arabella. But his soul had been corrupted long
ago. Arabella was too good for him, and he would surely
destroy her if he pretended to be something he could never
be—a faithful, loving husband.

Perhaps it was best that she kept her distance.

His uncle coughed again, the sound weak and wet. Gabriel rose and adjusted the pillows so he was propped up a
little more. Horror lanced through his gut when he lifted
his uncle's shoulders and discovered he weighed little more
than a child.

"Thank you." The thread of sound escaping Uncle Stephen's lips was so soft, Gabriel almost missed it.

"That's quite all right, Uncle." Gabriel sat carefully on
the side of the bed. His uncle studied him from beneath
veined, paper-thin lids. His eyes were pain-glazed but he
seemed lucid enough. Gabriel fought to keep his voice
steady as he added, "Is there anything else I can do? Would
you like a sip of water?" There was a china jug and a tumbler on the bedside table.

Uncle Stephen moved his head a little—the shake was
almost imperceptible. His Adam's apple rose and fell in an
ineffectual swallow before he coughed again. "No . . .
it's . . . it's good to see you, Gabriel."

"It's good to see you too, Uncle . . . I have some news."
He forced himself to smile, to keep the tone of the conversation light. "I'm married."

Uncle Stephen's lips twitched. Was that an attempt to
return his smile? "Wonders . . . wonders will never cease,"
he whispered, his voice little more than a harsh rasp.
"Who's the unlucky woman?"

"Her name is Arabella."

"Pretty name. Knowing you, I'm sure she's pretty as well."

"Very. I cannot keep my eyes off her. Clever too."

"I wish you well."

"Thank you."

All of a sudden, his uncle's expression changed—his
thin chapped lips turned down at the corners. "I've recently

heard . . . I know what Timothy is trying to do . . . to you.
How he's planning to steal your title . . . He thinks I don't
listen . . . but I do. . . . You need to know . . ." He clutched
at Gabriel's arm, his bony fingers hooking into the sleeve
of his superfine coat like a bird of prey's talons. "You need
to know he hasn't a leg to stand on . . ."

Uncle Stephen's eyelids fluttered closed. His chest rose
and fell weakly as he sucked in air, his gasps rapid and
shallow, and his lips were tinged with an alarming shade of
blue. Speaking this much was clearly sapping what little
strength he had left.

Gabriel patted his shoulder. "It's all right, Uncle. You
don't need to talk any—"

"I was there . . ."

What? Gabriel stared at his uncle, not daring to believe
what he'd just heard. "Uncle Stephen, are you saying
you were present at my parents' wedding? In Springfield,
Scotland?"

"No . . ." His uncle gave a great shuddering sigh and
sank into the pillows. His mouth grew slack, and his breath
began to rattle in and out of his chest again.

*God damn it. What did he mean? He was either in
Springfield or he wasn't.* Gabriel squeezed his uncle's hand
and shoulder and called his name but it was to no avail. His
uncle had slipped back into unconsciousness again and
couldn't be roused. He recalled Timothy's visit to Langdale
House in April and how he'd laughed about the fact that his
father was addicted to laudanum. Gabriel couldn't blame
his uncle for wanting to relieve his pain, but the drug could
knock one out if a large enough dose was taken.

Gabriel scrubbed a hand through his hair as acute frustration and disintegrating hope ripped through him like
shards of glass. If his uncle was under the influence of laudanum, anything he said couldn't be relied upon anyway.
Stephen Holmes-Fitzgerald was *not* one of the names on
the marriage certificate. He clearly hadn't been a witness at
the wedding ceremony.

Gabriel's gaze shifted to the bedside table and he swore.
Fuck. He hadn't noticed it before because it was in deep

shadow, but there, behind the porcelain water jug, sat a dark bottle of Kendal's Black Drop. Gabriel's hands curled into fists so tight his knuckles cracked and his breath came in short, sharp spurts. Acute need clawed its way up his throat and he grappled with the overwhelming urge to snatch up the bottle and down its potent contents when he really should hurl it against the wall.

He couldn't stay. He was standing so close to the edge of the precipice of no return, he couldn't even afford to farewell his uncle. His hands shaking, Gabriel grabbed his hat and gloves and quit the room as if the hounds of hell were nipping at his heels.

Time was fast running out for both him and his uncle, and in both cases, it seemed there was nothing he could do to prevent the worst from happening.

CHAPTER 14

❧

The new Countess of L. was once a Disreputable Debutante!

Loyal readers of our most esteemed publication may recall a certain scandal at a young ladies' academy three years ago . . .

The question on the tips of everyone's tongues is: Will Lady L. turn out to be as errant as her husband?

Time will surely tell . . .

The Beau Monde Mirror: The Society Page

Berkeley Square, London

July 27, 1818

Arabella sighed with contentment as she finished the last spoonful of her elderflower-and-lemon-flavored ice. Settling back against the red leather seat of the barouche, she addressed her magnanimous hostess, Charlie's aunt Tabitha, a dowager marchioness, no less. "Lady Chelmsford, I cannot begin to thank you and Charlie enough for this excursion. It's just what I needed."

"Yes, thank you so much," agreed Sophie, Lady Malverne. Her eyes were as blue as the summer sky that could be glimpsed through the branches of the plane trees above their heads. "It's such a warm day and Gunter's ices are just the thing."

Lady Chelmsford's mouth curved into a smile beneath her plump cheeks. The jaunty peacock feathers in her silk capote bonnet nodded in the gentle breeze crossing the square. "It is my absolute pleasure, my dear gels. When Charlotte mentioned this morning that you were both in town, I thought a trip to Gunter's was definitely in order. There is much to celebrate."

"Yes indeed," said Charlie with a bright smile. "Two of my dearest friends have found the men of their dreams and are happily wed." The sparkle in her topaz brown eyes dimmed a little. "It's a shame Olivia can't be here with us though. But I'm sure she's having a delightful time in Brighton. The sea air is sure to do her a world of good."

Sophie nodded. "Yes. Being cooped up in a London town house, no matter how grand, cannot be good for one's constitution. I was more than a little surprised her pernickety aunt and uncle let her attend my wedding at Nate's country estate. I do believe I have you to thank for making that happen, Lady Chelmsford."

The marchioness waved a dismissive hand. "It was nothing in the end. The promise of a few Almack's vouchers for her daughters and Olivia next Season was all it took. When I met with her, I got the distinct impression that she hopes her own daughters will climb the rungs of society's ladder all the way to the very top." Her expression grew grim. "Although I gather she wants Olivia to remain firmly under her thumb."

"Aye," agreed Arabella. "I suspect she sees Olivia as a threat to her own daughters' success in the marriage market so she keeps her hidden away."

Charlie's eyes sparked with indignation. "I firmly believe the only thing Olivia's family cares about is her money. I cannot wait for the day she's free of them. At least she'll be turning twenty-one soon so she won't need her uncle's permission to wed. If she finds herself a suitable husband, that is. It won't be easy, but I think it is incumbent upon us, as the Society for Enlightened Young Women, to continue to help her gain her independence and find fulfillment, in whatever way we can."

Arabella, Sophie, and Lady Chelmsford—Charlie had made her an honorary member—agreed wholeheartedly. A waiter from Gunter's appeared at the side of the barouche, and as he removed all their empty dessert dishes, the conversation turned to Arabella's upcoming nuptials at Langdale House.

"I still cannot believe that you are already married, Arabella. And to Gabriel, Lord Langdale, no less," said Charlie. "I'm so thrilled for you. And the way you met is beyond romantic. Indeed, your match was clearly fated."

Arabella forced herself to smile. "I'm not sure if a dungeon is actually all that romantic a setting, and I think it was happenstance rather than fate that caused our paths to cross."

"Oh pooh, Arabella," said Charlie with a mock frown, "you can be far too practical sometimes. But whether it was your destiny to meet or pure chance, it's wonderful you are now wed. I'm sure Gabriel is as head over heels in love with you as my brother is with Sophie."

Keeping her smile in place was one of the hardest things Arabella had ever done. Heat stung her cheeks and her mouth suddenly felt as if it were full of sand. She had no idea what to say. Should she tell her friends the truth—that Gabriel didn't love her and never would? That she was no better than a mercenary because she wanted to use her husband's wealth to advance her own charitable causes? That she didn't love him either?

But that wasn't entirely true . . . Deep down, Arabella knew she was falling in love with her husband, despite her best efforts not to.

Thankfully, Lady Chelmsford spoke. "I do think it's very sensible of your Lord Langdale to arrange a second ceremony here in London. Heavens, I remember the enormous to-do over the Earl of Westmorland's marriage to the banking heiress Sarah Anne Child. The pair eloped to Gretna Green, but then Sarah's father demanded they also be wed in an Anglican ceremony when they returned to England. And quite rightly so."

"Yes," agreed Sophie. "Even though a Presbyterian minister married you and Gabriel, Arabella, Nate says it's best to repeat the ceremony to avoid any difficulty in the future."

Arabella suddenly wondered if Sophie knew about Gabriel's looming troubles. Gabriel had shared his situation with Nate some time ago, so Sophie *might* be aware of what was going on. However, if she did, she gave no indication of it now. Sophie's smile was guileless as she added, "You must be excited about tomorrow. I can't wait to see your wedding gown."

"Which reminds me," said Lady Chelmsford, "we really should be on our way to Madame Boucher's. She's one of the best modistes in London, Arabella. As the Countess of Langdale, you are going to need a whole new wardrobe. And there's no time like the present to begin filling it."

Charlie grinned. "Yes, you will indeed need a suitable wardrobe, Arabella. I remember when Aunt Tabitha and I took Sophie to Madame Boucher's at the beginning of the Season. I made Nate come too. It was such torture for him, poor boy, to see Sophie all dressed up to the nines. He couldn't stop staring at her, yet he was determined to pretend he *wasn't* smitten. He was such a stubborn clodpoll for weeks—it was probably his rakish pride that blinkered his vision—but he saw the light in the end."

"Yes, my nephew is definitely besotted with Sophie," agreed Lady Chelmsford. "As I've always said to Charlie, reformed rakehells often make the best husbands."

Oh. Arabella blinked. She had no idea Lord Malverne had taken so long to realize he was in love with Sophie. But it would be foolish of her to think all rakehells were cast in the same mold. Gabriel had warned her what he was truly like, and she would be a fool not to believe him.

Lady Chelmsford had just begun to instruct her driver to take them all to the modiste's boutique on Conduit Street, when Sophie gave a little gasp.

"Is anything wrong?" asked Arabella. She followed the direction of Sophie's gaze but saw nothing out of the ordinary. Just the usual traffic—hackney coaches, other barouches, town coaches, the occasional phaeton or curricle—as well as pedestrians making their way around the square. Although, there was a very beautiful, stylishly attired woman with pale blond hair standing in the doorway of Gunter's as she wrestled with her pastel blue parasol.

When Arabella returned her attention to Sophie, she caught her trading a glance with Charlie. She narrowed her eyes. "What is it, you two?" she asked as the barouche moved off. "What are you both so worried about? And don't tell me it's nothing. I can see by your expressions it's not."

Sophie sighed and looked contrite. "I'm sorry, Arabella. It *is* nothing really. I simply caught a glimpse of the Countess of Astley across the street. She was leaving Gunter's."

Arabella's brow knit with confusion. "The blond woman in the doorway? I don't understand. Aside from the fact that she's very attractive, Lady Astley seemed perfectly ordinary to me."

The look of sincere sympathy in Lady Chelmsford's eyes made Arabella's nape prickle. "I suppose we should tell Arabella about Lady Astley, my gels," she said to Charlie and Sophie. "Because she's bound to find out."

"Find out what?" The prickle turned into a frisson of panic that tripped its way down the entire length of Arabella's spine. "I wish someone would speak plainly."

Charlie met her gaze directly. "At the beginning of the Season, Gabriel began an affair with Lady Astley."

Oh. Arabella pressed her lips together. She tried to maintain a calm expression even though the knowledge stung her like she'd just been cut.

"But that's not all." Sophie reached out and touched her arm, alarming Arabella even further. "You see . . . Lady Astley is married."

Arabella curled her fingers into her muslin skirts. How shocking. And mortifying. Her husband had engaged in an adulterous affair. But really, she shouldn't be that surprised. After all, Gabriel was a rakehell. A libertine. Of course he would have dallied with all kinds of women—debutantes, widows, cyprians, chambermaids, and yes, other men's wives. Arabella's vision misted and she inwardly chided herself for being so sensitive.

But then, she supposed the difference was she'd never

encountered any of the women he'd actually bedded before. They were just shadowy figures in her mind. But she'd just seen Lady Astley in the flesh and she was beautiful.

And she was in London.

Arabella forced herself to take a calming breath. "You said Gabriel *began* an affair."

Charlie was quick to reassure her. "Oh, it's definitely over," she said. "In fact it ended in April, right before Gabriel left for the Continent. My aunt, Sophie, and I were all at Astley House the night Lord Astley confronted Gabriel about it . . . right in the middle of his ballroom."

Arabella's hand flew to her lips. *Oh, good heavens.*

"They came to blows," Sophie continued, "but Nate stepped in and managed to stop Lord Astley from calling Gabriel out." She grimaced. "I'm afraid there was a story in the *Beau Monde Mirror* about it. And a few of the other newspapers as well."

So the entire ton knew her husband had cuckolded the Earl of Astley. Arabella closed her eyes and willed herself not to cry. How humiliating.

"Oh, Arabella. I didn't mean to upset you so," murmured Sophie. She placed a slender arm about Arabella's shoulders and gave her a little hug. "Nate told me Gabriel never cared at all for Lady Astley, so there's no need to worry. You're his wife and he loves you and you alone."

But he doesn't . . . and he never will.

She wanted to tell Charlie and Sophie, but the words seemed to stick in her throat. Somehow, she managed to plaster a bright smile on her face as she hugged Sophie back. "You know, you are the best friends in the world," she said. "And I'm so lucky to have you."

At least that wasn't a lie.

White's, St. James's, London

"Good God, I can't believe you two are both bloody married," declared Hamish MacQueen, the Marquess of Sleat, as he settled back into the leather wing chair in their favorite corner of White's club for gentlemen. The fronds of a nearby potted palm brushed his bulky shoulder as he adjusted his eye patch. "It looks as though Max and I are the only sane ones left in this group."

Max Devereux, the Duke of Exmoor, chuckled over his glass of claret. "I think you're right, MacQueen. It seems love can make a man do the maddest things. Who, in their right mind, would want to be leg-shackled when he's in his prime?"

Gabriel snorted. "I'd say you and MacQueen are both well past your prime already. By my calculations, you should have been married at least five years ago."

Nate laughed, his brown eyes alight with good humor. "I don't give a farthing about any of your opinions. I couldn't be happier, so I'm impervious to any of the barbs you fire at me."

"Quick, somebody get me a bucket because I think I'm going to be ill," said MacQueen with a smirk.

Max stretched out a long leg and nudged Gabriel's chair with the toe of his boot. "It's you who's shocked us the most, Langdale. It was clear Nate was besotted with his Sophie from the very beginning of the Season. But you, old chap? What the deuce happened to you in Switzerland? Did you simply get swept up in the romance of the place, or did someone from the poor girl's family threaten you with bodily harm after you seduced her? Because all jokes aside, I'm sure you're not *really* in love."

Gabriel gave a wry smile. "As you well know, I never do anything I don't want to."

"Now that's an evasive answer if ever I heard one," replied Max drily.

"Next he'll be telling us a gentleman doesn't kiss and tell," said MacQueen. His one good eye glimmered with mirth. "Which is quite ironic when you think about it, because—and I'm sure you'd agree, Langdale—you are the least gentlemanly out of all of us."

Gabriel leaned forward and poured himself another glass of claret from the decanter on the low table in front of him. For Arabella's sake, he didn't want to let on that he wasn't in love. He certainly didn't want to admit his wife had also banned him from her bed. He already felt emasculated enough. So he said, "Perhaps I've met the perfect woman and have decided to settle down."

At that remark, his three friends all burst into laughter.

"I'm sure Arabella *is* perfect," said Nate. "I mean she must be if she's a friend of Sophie and my sister. But I can't see you ever settling down, my friend. You've too much fire in your soul."

Gabriel was about to respond, when Max let out a low whistle. "Don't look now but Lord Astley has just walked in."

Damn. The last thing Gabriel needed was an irate spouse breathing down his neck. Sitting in a shadowy corner on the other side of the potted palm, he prayed the middle-aged earl wouldn't notice him. "I didn't know he was in London," he murmured.

"The election has kept many in town this month," remarked Max. "But perhaps he'll see you as less of a threat to his marriage now that you're also wed."

"I'm no threat. You all know I never cared for Camilla and besides, she and I were finished months ago."

For several moments they all watched Astley make his way across the club floor before he disappeared into the dining room, then Nate leaned forward. "I believe Camilla is still in town too. But as far as I know, she hasn't taken up with anyone else. So perhaps they've sorted things out."

Gabriel took a large sip of his own claret. "I damn well hope so. I've got enough to contend with at the moment."

MacQueen cocked a dark brow. "I gather you're referring to this business involving your cousin and his ridiculous claim to the title?"

As Gabriel nodded, Nate met his gaze. "I hope you don't mind that I told Max and MacQueen after you wrote to me from Italy," he said quietly. "I thought they might be able to offer some advice if need be. In a case like this, four heads must be better than one."

Max's brow plunged into a scowl. "Speak of the devil . . ."

Bloody hell. Timothy had appeared in the doorway to the card room. "When did *he* join?" growled Gabriel. After visiting his uncle this morning and witnessing the lack of care he'd been receiving, Gabriel felt his whole body tense. If they weren't in White's, he'd hurl his cousin against the nearest wall and go to work on him with his fists.

"I'm not sure," murmured Max. They watched Timothy have a word with one of the club's attendants before he disappeared back into the card room. "I'm sure I can get his membership canceled."

MacQueen cracked his knuckles. "And if you'd like, I could drag him out to the back alley and see if I could change his mind about challenging you for the earldom. I haven't been to Gentleman Jackson's this week so I wouldn't mind a bit of bare-knuckle boxing."

Gabriel knocked back his claret. He was suddenly in a foul, reckless mood, and he needed to leave before he did something that might get him arrested and banned from White's for life. "I have a better idea. Let's all go to the Pandora Club and raise hell. For old time's sake."

Max and MacQueen readily agreed but Nate arched a brow. "You know I'll only take part in gaming now. And if any of you tell Sophie where I've been, I'll have to kill you."

Gabriel gripped his shoulder. "Do whatever makes you happy, old chap. I certainly won't judge you. But I'm getting married for the second time tomorrow, and this might very well be the last time I ever set foot in Pandora's."

As they all trooped out onto St. James's Street—the Pandora Club was but a short walk away—Gabriel prayed to God no one told Arabella he'd been to the gaming-hell-cum-brothel either. He shivered and his bollocks contracted. There was no doubt in his mind that his wife knew how to wield a scalpel and could probably castrate him if she chose to.

Langdale House, St. James's Square, London

July 28, 1818

Arabella couldn't sleep.

The uncertain light of a single, low-burning candle on a

nearby table illuminated the face of the Boulle clock just enough for her to make out the time; it was almost half past two in the morning.

And Gabriel wasn't home . . . Perhaps his absence wouldn't have bothered her so much if today wasn't actually their second wedding day.

Arabella sighed heavily and slipped from her bed. Her eyes were gritty with exhaustion as she slid on her glasses and began to aimlessly explore her bedroom and then the sitting room.

She picked up a discarded medical text on smallpox vaccination from one of the damask-covered settees gracing the rug before the empty fireplace, but then cast it aside once more—before she'd retired, she tried to read it, but nothing could hold her attention. She didn't want to describe the restlessness knotting up her belly as fretting . . . but that's exactly what she was doing.

If she were truly honest with herself, she would also acknowledge that she was irritated beyond measure. Indeed, her emotions fluctuated wildly between anxiousness and exasperation, perhaps even anger. She had no idea where her husband was or if he was safe. He wasn't being fair.

After Charlie, Sophie, and Lady Chelmsford dropped her back at Langdale House in the late afternoon, Jervis, the butler, handed her a message from Gabriel. The note was brief—apparently, he'd secured the special license from the Archbishop of Canterbury, and the Anglican minister from St. George's would be conducting their wedding ceremony at three o'clock tomorrow afternoon at Langdale House, just as they'd planned. He hadn't mentioned his plans for the rest of the day and evening, but Arabella assumed he would return home for dinner.

With that in mind, she met with Mrs. Mayberry to discuss the dinner menu and to check that everything was ready for the morrow. The flowers that would decorate Langdale House's ballroom, drawing room, and dining room—great bunches of roses, lilies, and peonies—would be delivered in the morning. And Mrs. Mayberry assured her the catering was well in hand . . . with a little help from

Gunter's and Fortnum and Mason; Gabriel apparently had accounts at both stores and would often avail himself of their services when holding any type of soiree at Langdale House.

As the soft, warm summer twilight melted into night, Arabella realized Gabriel wasn't coming home. She abandoned her post at the enormous mahogany table set with fine bone china and gleaming silver cutlery in the dining room downstairs and instead ate alone in her sitting room. Well, she attempted to eat, but her appetite had all but fled. The perfectly cooked fillet of beef in pastry with tiny, buttered potatoes and asparagus spears on her plate had hardly been touched when the footman took her tray away. She'd have to apologize to the cook, Mrs. Simpkins, in the morning. She didn't want her to be offended.

As Arabella prepared for bed much later, she prayed this wasn't how their married life would always be—her rattling about an enormous house with no one to talk to but the servants.

The idea was enough to make tears well in her eyes.

What had she got herself into? The idea of being in a loveless, lonely marriage was depressing indeed.

The clock struck the half hour and Arabella wandered into Gabriel's sitting room, heading for his bedchamber. The moonlight filtered through the diaphanous white curtains at the windows so everything within the room was painted in soft shades of gray, silver, and velveteen black. She'd opened the communicating doors between her suite and Gabriel's before she went to bed, so she already knew her husband hadn't arrived home—she hadn't slept at all, so she was certain she would've heard him come in. Ryecroft wasn't to be seen either; Arabella suspected he retired to his own room farther along the gallery while she'd waited in vain in the dining room.

A lamp burned softly on a polished oak table near Gabriel's bed, a grand four-poster just like her own. Arabella trailed her fingertips along the emerald green counterpane and wondered what would happen if she crawled between the crisp white sheets to wait for Gabriel.

Would he be pleased with her? Did he still want her? She'd constantly rebuffed him since their wedding day in Clarens, so she only had herself to blame if his ardor had faded and he rejected her instead.

While part of Arabella yearned to climb into Gabriel's bed, her pride along with a healthy dose of chagrin stopped her from giving in to temptation. What if Gabriel had already broken his word and, at this very moment, was lying in another woman's arms? Someone beautiful and accommodating like Lady Astley . . .

Stop torturing yourself, Arabella. You're jumping to conclusions. Gabriel might just be out carousing with Lord Malverne and his other friends. Remember Charlie told you they were all in town and it's been months since he's seen them.

Her gaze slid to the bedside armchair where Gabriel's sketchbook and a discarded shirt lay. Even though she knew that what she was about to do was tantamount to spying, Arabella couldn't resist the urge to look through his sketches—her husband was quite a talented artist, and his work deserved to be admired.

Flipping through the book, her eyes widened with astonishment; page after page was filled with drawings of her. There was the lovely portrait Gabriel had rendered on the balcony of Villa Belle Rive on their wedding day as well as a series of sketches of her face, some with and some without her glasses. One sketch even depicted her sleeping in his carriage; another showed her gazing dreamily out the window.

Arabella frowned; she didn't know how she felt about being Gabriel's muse. A little confused perhaps but also disconcertingly touched. His depictions of her countenance were flattering indeed and she wondered if he really did see her as pretty. Only the Lord above knew why though.

She sighed and after returning the book to its place on the chair, she picked up Gabriel's discarded shirt; Ryecroft had obviously forgotten to put it away. Rubbing the fine fabric against her cheek, Gabriel's scent—his spicy cologne and the trace of something that was entirely masculine—

filled her senses, and tears pricked at her eyes. Despite her annoyance, she missed him. After spending day after day with Gabriel in close quarters, she felt his absence keenly.

She wasn't sure why, but she was suddenly possessed by the mad impulse to wear his shirt as a nightgown. Throwing off her own cotton night rail, she slipped the cool cambric shirt over her head. It was voluminous and she'd have to roll up the sleeves, but it wasn't too long; the hem sat at midthigh. For the first time that night, Arabella smiled. Yes, her husband's shirt would do nicely.

Gathering up her night rail, Arabella returned to her own room, extinguished the candle, and, after removing her glasses, slid back into bed.

Steadfastly pushing away the thought of her husband making love to someone else right at this very moment, she hugged a pillow to her chest and pretended Gabriel was with her instead.

S omething woke her. A low grumbling sound that called to mind the roll of distant thunder.

No, not thunder . . . Was that a snore?

Is that Gabriel?

Arabella prized her heavy eyelids open and blinked blearily into the darkness. The gentle rumbling came again from the direction of her sitting room and she frowned. Yes, it was definitely a snore. But as far as she knew, Gabriel was a quiet sleeper. She'd never heard him snore in the carriage on their journey home.

Although, she recalled Lilias had often complained that Bertie snored when he'd had too much claret with dinner. If Gabriel had been out with his rakish friends, it was highly likely he'd imbibed too much alcohol. It *had* to be her errant husband.

There was only one way to find out.

Her hectic heartbeat thudding in her ears, Arabella rose from the bed and padded quietly to the sitting room doorway. Relief tangled with resentment and confusion when she saw it was indeed Gabriel.

A wash of pale moonlight revealed that he was sprawled on the damask settee, fast asleep with his booted feet propped on the table and his arms spread wide along the headrest. His head was thrown back at an awkward angle, his mouth slack and slightly open as another snore tumbled forth.

Arabella gripped the doorjamb as all her anger rose in a hot wave; she was glad he was safe and sound, but how dare he arrive home so late! How dare he go out without telling her first! It was more than inconsiderate. It was appallingly rude.

Then another thought came to the fore: Why on earth was he in her sitting room?

He couldn't be comfortable and she wouldn't be able to sleep unless he stopped snoring—she was certain she'd still be able to hear him even if she closed her bedroom door— so she had to wake him.

Tamping down her irritation, Arabella crept toward her drunk, unconscious husband in the manner of someone approaching a sleeping lion. How best to wake him without startling him? While she was tempted to throw the pitcher of water in her dressing room over him, she'd also likely ruin the silk damask upholstery on the sofa and she didn't want to do that.

Holding her breath, she reached out and touched his pantaloon-clad lower thigh, just above his knee. Her fingers encountered warm, solid muscle beneath the snug fabric. "Gabriel. You need to wake up," she murmured hesitantly.

He didn't stir.

"Gabriel . . ." She gave his leg a slight shake and raised her voice to make herself heard over a louder snore. "Gabriel, wake up."

He snuffled and closed his mouth, then wiped a hand down his face.

Good, he was coming to. "Gabriel . . ." Arabella placed a hand on his shoulder. "You need to go to bed."

He mumbled something but Arabella couldn't make out the words. "What was that?" she asked.

Gabriel's words were slurred but this time she understood him. "What's the time?" he repeated.

"I have no idea but—" Just at that moment, the clock helpfully chimed the hour. "Four o'clock."

"Christ . . ." Gabriel opened his eyes and straightened in his seat. His groggy gaze lifted to Arabella's face. And then he smiled. "Bella . . ." Before she could blink, he reached out and wrapped his fingers around her wrist. "I was dreaming of you."

Arabella fought to keep her ire aflame. Even in an inebriated state, her husband was charm personified. "Where have you been all night?" she demanded. "I've been worried sick about you." *Worried sick you might be making love to someone else . . .*

He frowned. "No need to worry, pet." He scrubbed at his face again. "I was just at the Pandora Club."

"The Pandora Club?"

Gabriel yawned. "Yes. It's a gaming hell and a brothel."

"You went to a brothel?" Arabella gasped. She couldn't hide her shock.

Gabriel waved a dismissive hand in the air as though he were clumsily swatting away a fly. "S'nothing. No need to get out your scalpel."

What on earth was he talking about? "It's not nothing, Gabriel." Arabella shook his other hand off her wrist. "You promised me—"

"I didn't break my promise," he said, his tone indignant. "I didn't do anything at all. Just gambled. I didn't even look, let alone tumble anyone . . ." His eyes were heavy-lidded, his smile lazy and almost boyish as he looked up at her again. "I didn't want to because I have you."

Arabella's horror quickly dissipated at that last pronouncement. She didn't know why, but she believed he hadn't been unfaithful.

"Was Lord Malverne there too?"

Gabriel removed his feet from the table and leaned forward, his elbows resting on his thighs, his head bowed. "Yes, but he didn't do anything either. We played faro most

of the night. Bloody boring game, if you ask me." He
scratched the back of his head and yawned again. "But
don't tell Sophie. Nate didn't want to upset her. He's absolutely besotted with her, poor bastard."

Arabella pressed her lips together. She wasn't sure what
she'd do. But she'd worry about that tomorrow. "You need
to get to bed," she repeated.

"Yes." Gabriel suddenly lurched to his feet and for one
heart-stopping moment, he teetered to one side. Arabella
caught him about the waist.

Gabriel squinted down at her as though he was trying to
focus his gaze. "I can see two of you . . . I might need some
help."

"Aye, I won't disagree."

By the time Arabella had safely steered Gabriel into the
armchair beside his bed, she was out of breath and had a
bruised shin; at one point, Gabriel had stumbled and she'd
collided with a gilt-edged occasional table in his sitting
room.

She supposed she could ring for Ryecroft to help him get
undressed—especially when she almost lost her balance
tugging off his boots—but it seemed like too much effort.
Aside from that, she was secretly enjoying the fact that she
was doing something wifely. And for once, her inebriated
husband was as docile as a lamb . . . until he noticed what
she was wearing.

She'd just helped him shrug off his waistcoat when he
caught her hand, drawing her close. "What the hell are you
wearing, Bella?" His brows crashed into a confused frown
as he looked her up and down. "Is that one of my shirts?"

Arabella blushed, suddenly overcome with shyness. In
all the fuss of finding Gabriel asleep in her sitting room,
she'd completely forgotten she wasn't wearing her sedate
cotton night rail. She also suspected the bedside lamp was
shining through the thin cambric and revealing a good deal
more of her person than she'd like. "It's um . . . I went shopping with Sophie, Lady Charlotte, and her aunt and purchased a few things for my wardrobe. This is a new style of
nightgown. They're all the rage." Telling a white lie seemed

easier than admitting the truth . . . that she'd missed him so much she'd wanted his scent to surround her.

Gabriel's mouth curved into a slow, sinful smile as he made another leisurely perusal of her attire. He seemed to spend an inordinate amount of time inspecting her bare legs. "I like it," he murmured huskily. "Very much."

"I, ah . . . thank you." Arabella's breathing quickened and desire gathered low in her belly as Gabriel lifted his gaze to her face. The lamb had gone and the lion was back. And there was a smoldering hunger in his eyes.

Arabella's heart began to crash against her ribs. What if she threw caution to the wind and just gave in to temptation? Leaned down and touched her lips to her husband's?

To her surprise, Gabriel sighed and released her hand. "I must apologize, Bella," he said as he pulled his shirt from his pantaloons. "Even though I'm foxed to the eyeballs, I'm afraid I'm beginning to develop a fearsome cockstand. It's just been so long since I've had sexual intercourse . . . and the way you look in that shirt . . ." He shook his head. "I hope you understand my arousal isn't intentional."

"It's all right," she whispered. Disappointment settled over her. Which was ridiculous because Gabriel was clearly respecting her wishes . . . Only, it seemed her wishes might be changing. "If you don't need me—"

Gabriel stood. His balance was steady now. His fingers came up to gently capture her chin. Tilting her head up, he trapped her gaze. "There's no question in my mind that I need you, but now's not the right time to act upon my desire. And you know . . ." His green eyes searched hers for one long moment, "I think that if I *could* fall in love with anyone, it would be you, Bella."

Arabella's heart twisted with pain and longing. Why did he have to make her feel this way? Or feel anything at all? Could there be anything worse than desperately wanting the love of a man who couldn't love you in return? She didn't want to love him, but she couldn't hide from the truth anymore. She drew a shivering breath. "You're incorrigible," she whispered.

"Yes I am," he said softly. He dropped a gentle kiss on

her forehead. "Now go to bed, sweetheart. We're getting married later today and you need your rest."

As Arabella crossed to the door, Gabriel extinguished the bedside lamp.

If only her own love for this complicated, impossible devil of a man could be snuffed out so easily.

CHAPTER 15

A "special" occasion in St. James's?

Hampers of gastronomic delights, crates of champagne, and a cartload of summer blooms were recently delivered to the home of a certain Errant Earl . . .

It appears as though the earl and his new lady wife held quite an exclusive gathering at their St. James's residence. But the curious thing is, one of the guests was a man of the cloth, the Rev. R. G. from a cathedral in H. Square . . .

If the earl wasn't already leg-shackled, one might have good reason to suspect another wedding had taken place.

But whose?

The Beau Monde Mirror: The Society Page

Langdale House, St. James's Square, London

July 28, 1818

Arabella, you look beautiful," declared Charlie. "Doesn't she, Sophie?"

"Yes indeed," agreed Sophie with a warm smile. "Arabella, you are the prettiest bride in the whole of London."

"Oh, stop it, you two. You are making me blush," said Arabella. She studied her reflection in the full-length oval looking glass in her bedroom. Charlie's lady's maid, Molly, had styled her hair into an elaborate arrangement of cascading curls threaded with seed pearls, and the cream and gold couture wedding gown suited her slight figure well. And of course, the diamond and emerald necklace— Gabriel's gift to her on their first wedding day—matched beautifully too. Arabella's blush deepened as she recalled the last time she'd worn it . . . along with nothing else.

Gabriel had also surprised her this morning with an additional wedding present. Two presents in fact. Gifts so thoughtful, Arabella had been alternately stunned and thrilled and then moved to tears. When she woke, it was to discover a satin-lined wooden box on her bedside table containing a banknote made out to Arabella Holmes-Fitzgerald, the Countess of Langdale, in the amount of one thousand pounds for her charity work, along with another item of immeasurable value, at least to her. It was a *stéthoscope*, exactly like the one René Laennec had shown her in Paris. In fact, Arabella was certain that it might actually be one of the good doctor's *stéthoscopes* as she examined it with trembling fingers. The initials *R. L.* were carved into the wood at one end.

So that's why Gabriel insisted we stop for a whole day in Paris, Arabella had thought as she placed the *stéthoscope* carefully back in its case. When he'd been "attending to business," he must have gone to see Dr. Laennec at L'Hôpital Necker. The whole notion made her head spin.

The *stéthoscope* and bank check seemed to serve as a wedding gift, apology, and a peace offering because the note Gabriel left with it read: *To my clever, beautiful Bella. I hope you can forgive me for being such an inconsiderate, drunken dunderhead last night. I can't wait to marry you all over again. G*

Just recalling Gabriel's words and his gifts filled Arabella with bittersweet longing, and she had to dash away a surreptitious tear lest her friends see. Of course, she would forgive Gabriel—how could she not after he'd presented her with such treasures? However, she also wanted to talk to him about last night's incident and how sick with worry she'd been . . . But then she'd be in danger of betraying how she really felt. She didn't want him to know she'd fallen in love, not when he didn't love her back. Her mind tumbled with frustration and confusion. Gabriel seemed to want her, at times it felt as though he even cared for her, yet lately, he kept pushing her away . . .

But wasn't that exactly what she was doing to him? And she was the one who'd started it all. Everything was such a mess.

"Do you need your glasses?" asked Sophie, drawing her out of her tangled thoughts; she held out her usual pair but Arabella shook her head.

"No, call it vanity, but I'm going to try using a quizzing glass today," she said. "Courtesy of Lady Chelmsford."

"Yes, I swear my aunt has a hundred of the things," said Charlie as she stepped forward and fastened the chain of the small, gilt-framed eyeglass to Arabella's cream silk bodice with a pearl brooch. "There. Now you can peer at us all imperiously, Lady Langdale."

Arabella laughed. "I don't think I have an imperious bone in my body."

"Nor I," replied Sophie. Radiant in a well-cut gown of azure blue silk that matched her eyes perfectly, and with sapphires and diamonds at her throat, she was the epitome of a refined ton beauty. "I confess that half the time some-one addresses me as Lady Malverne, I haven't realized I'm the one being spoken to."

Charlie waved a hand. "You will both get used to it. Now, are you ready to wed again, my dear Arabella? I do believe the clock just struck three and your eager bridegroom—or should I say husband?—awaits."

Arabella nodded and smiled, hoping her friends wouldn't see the merriment in her eyes had dimmed. Since last night, she'd hardly seen Gabriel at all.

When she'd knocked on his closed sitting room door to thank him for her wonderful gifts and tell him she had in-deed forgiven him, it was Ryecroft who answered and in-formed her Gabriel had gone riding in Hyde Park. They'd eventually crossed paths in the drawing room just before noon when Arabella was supervising the placement of the floral arrangements with Mrs. Mayberry. Gabriel stuck his head around the door—Arabella marveled at the fact that he was so bright-eyed given how drunk he'd been last night—and stated he couldn't wait for three o'clock. And then he disappeared.

Arabella had wanted to go after him, but by the time she'd finished checking all the last-minute details of the wedding breakfast with the housekeeper, Sophie, Charlie, and her maid arrived, and then she'd been caught up in her own preparations for the wedding.

Despite the fact that Gabriel had written her a note stating he couldn't wait for their nuptials, it worried her deeply that he seemed to be actively avoiding her. She didn't want to believe his so-called eagerness was nothing but pretense. That his thoughtful gifts were nothing but hollow gestures—a "means to an end"—so she'd forgive him the worst of his excesses, last night being a case in point.

Well, she was about to pretend, too, for the whole afternoon in fact, so everyone believed she and Gabriel were blissfully happy. Fixing a bright smile in place, she picked up a nosegay of ivory rosebuds from a nearby satinwood table and turned to face her friends, hoping they wouldn't notice she was lying. "Aye, I'm ready."

Forasmuch as Gabriel and Arabella have consented together in holy wedlock, and have witnessed the same before God and this company, and thereto have given and pledged their troth either to other, and have declared the same by giving and receiving of a ring, and by joining of hands," declared the gray-haired Reverend Robert Hodgson with a benign smile, "I pronounce that they be man and wife together, in the name of the Father, and of the Son, and of the Holy Ghost. Amen."

Over the claps and cheers of their friends, Gabriel murmured, "It's done, Bella." He lifted her hand and feathered a kiss across her knuckles. "It's done."

The rapt look in her husband's brilliant green eyes made Arabella's heart race and with so many others watching them, a fiery blush scalded her cheeks. She could almost convince herself that Gabriel cared for her, that the intensity in his gaze wasn't all just for show. "Yes," she whispered, even as relief and despair flooded her.

There was no turning back now. They were legally, irrevocably wed.

After Lady Chelmsford and Maximilian Devereux, the charming Duke of Exmoor, witnessed the marriage lines, Reverend Hodgson presented them to Arabella for safe-keeping. For better or worse, no one would ever be able to question the validity of their marriage now.

Except, it wasn't the marriage Arabella wanted.

Throughout the opulent wedding breakfast—a cold buffet served with chilled champagne—Gabriel played the attentive husband and host, regaling everyone with the story of how they'd first met at Chillon Castle, and how Arabella had come to his rescue during the storm after he'd attempted to deliver Charlie's letter. Arabella was grateful he glossed over some of the more salacious details of that particular incident, namely how he'd been sans shirt when she'd fixed his shoulder, and how he'd kissed her. He'd explained away their sudden engagement by stating, "The first time I saw Arabella in that dark, chill dungeon, I knew I had to have her," and everyone seemed to believe that meant he'd fallen head over heels in love. His glib delivery and play on words was clever, but in a way, deceitful.

Her husband certainly had a silver tongue.

A horrible thought suddenly pricked at Arabella like a burr in her shoe: Gabriel had sworn he would always be honest with her, but was that really the case? Perhaps he was just adept at telling others what they wanted to hear.

What if he had taken up with Lady Astley again? What if he had dallied with a demirep at the Pandora Club?

Last night, he'd said that if he *could* fall in love, it would be with her, but what if his pronouncement was a lie?

Within the space of two hours, Arabella's mouth ached with the effort of constantly maintaining a false smile. Feigning happiness was exhausting. She loved Charlie and Sophie with all her heart, but right now she wished she could be alone. Though feigning happiness was far easier when one was a little tipsy, she decided after she'd helped herself to her fourth glass of champagne.

Taking up a position by an open set of French doors that looked out upon Langdale House's courtyard garden, Arabella sipped her wine. Her gaze skipped between the flagged terrace, just beyond the doors, and the elegantly furnished drawing room. Inside, Charlie and Nate's father, the Earl of Westhampton, conversed with the very roguish Scottish Marquess of Sleat and Lady Chelmsford. Max, the Duke of Exmoor, chatted with Gabriel, Nate, and Sophie on the terrace. A short time ago, Arabella had seen Charlie talking and laughing with the exceedingly handsome, blond-haired duke by an espaliered orange tree. She wondered about the nature of their relationship. Charlie had put his name at the top of the list of most eligible bachelors they should target in their quest to find perfect matches.

Nate leaned down and whispered something in Sophie's ear that made her blush and bite her lip as if she were trying to suppress a giggle. Seeing how blissfully happy they were together was difficult, to say the least. The way they looked at each other, with adoration in their eyes, made Arabella's heart clench. She was thrilled for Sophie, of course, but it highlighted what was missing in her own relationship with Gabriel—love.

Charlie appeared beside her. "Why are you over here on your own?" she asked quietly.

Arabella donned her fake smile. "I'm just enjoying the scenery while I drink my champagne."

"Hmm." Charlie laid a hand on her arm. Her brow creased with a concerned frown. "What's wrong, Arabella? You don't seem yourself."

Arabella fiddled with the stem of her glass. "Whatever do you mean?"

"You and Gabriel . . . Something's not right, I know it. Your smile is as brittle as that champagne glass you're holding."

"Everything's fine."

Charlie snorted in disbelief. "Now I know something is definitely amiss."

"Oh, Charlie . . ." Arabella sighed and shook her head. "You see right through me."

"We did share a room together at Mrs. Rathbone's Academy. Come . . ." She linked her arm through Arabella's. "Let's take a turn about the garden and you can confess everything to me. You know I'll be the soul of discretion."

Arabella was aware Gabriel tracked her progress as she and Charlie crossed the terrace and descended the steps to the gravel path that meandered through the walled garden. His expression was mildly curious and pensive at the same time. Arabella was grateful that he didn't follow.

When they were well out of earshot of everyone, Charlie paused beneath the boughs of an enormous horse chestnut tree. "Now out with it, Arabella," she said as she took a seat on a stone bench and Arabella did the same. "Has Gabriel done something to hurt you? Because if he has—"

Arabella shook her head. "Not really. I'm afraid it's rather more complicated than that. Although we've been pretending otherwise, Gabriel and I, we are not a love match." Her chest rose and fell with a despondent sigh. "Perhaps I should start from the beginning." And then she told Charlie everything. She described exactly how she and Gabriel met and how he compromised her, although she'd been a very willing participant. How Gabriel had done the honorable thing and proposed to her to avoid a scandal. And the terms they'd both agreed to once they'd wed—that they'd only try for a child when Gabriel's title was secure— Charlie had clearly been shocked to hear Gabriel's cousin would try to claim the earldom for himself. And then Arabella confessed that because Gabriel couldn't promise fidelity, she'd added further caveats that curtailed him from having a physical relationship with not only her, but anyone at all.

"Hmmm." Charlie gave Arabella a considering look once she'd finished her story. "So just to be clear, you're telling me that since you consummated your marriage, nearly three weeks ago, you and Gabriel haven't been intimate? At all?"

Arabella shook her head. "No. We haven't even kissed."

"My goodness." Charlie glanced toward the terrace where Gabriel was talking to her brother, then met Arabella's gaze again. "I understand you're risking your heart by inviting Gabriel into your bed, but . . . but aren't you at all tempted to . . . I mean, Gabriel is . . ." Charlie blushed then, and she was not one to blush easily. "By all accounts, Gabriel is a wonderful lover. Indeed, the whole of London knows it. I imagine it's been very difficult for both of you, not to give into desire. I honestly don't know how you have the strength to deny him."

It was Arabella's turn to blush. "He is . . . wonderful." She bit her lip as tears brimmed. "Oh, Charlie, I feel like I'm going about this the wrong way. And the worst part is, it seems I've fallen in love with him anyway, despite my best efforts not to. But he doesn't love me. At least he doesn't think he ever will. And he's also told me countless times he doesn't believe he can be faithful. And I don't think I can bear it." She bit her lip and shook her head. "I wish I knew how to make my husband fall in love with me."

Charlie squeezed her hand. "Oh, Arabella, are you sure he doesn't care for you? I've seen the way he looks at you."

"What do you mean?"

"He can't take his eyes off you. While we've been sitting here, he keeps glancing over to you. When you speak, he hangs on your every word. I don't know Gabriel that well, but I've never seen him behave that way around other women before."

Arabella shook her head, unconvinced. "It sounds like you are talking about Sophie and Nate, not Gabriel and me." And then she recalled Gabriel's sketchbook. He did seem to like looking at her . . .

Charlie smoothed a curl away from Arabella's cheek. "Having a brother like Nate, I do believe I have a little insight into the male mind. One thing I've learned is that men are physical creatures, driven by strong primal urges, and *I* think pushing Gabriel away is the worst thing you can do.

Give a little, it might give Gabriel the nudge he needs to realize that what he shares with you is more than just base lust. I watched Nate falling in love with Sophie, even though he'd convinced himself he never could do such a thing, and that was partly due to the fact she took the initiative. *She* wooed him. She told me that as they became more physically intimate, she sensed Nate was opening his heart. It will take time, but keeping your husband at arm's length, I don't think that will help."

Arabella's gaze wandered to Gabriel. "I'm afraid," she whispered.

Charlie's smile was gentle. "He probably is too. But I think it would be foolish of you to let fear stop you from going after what you really want. You already love him, so what have you got to lose?"

G abriel watched Charlie conversing with Arabella. Even though they were some distance away and in dappled shadow from the horse chestnut canopy, he got the distinct impression that whatever they spoke about was serious; Arabella's expression was grave, perhaps even desolate, and her slim figure radiated tension, even when Charlie slipped her arm around Arabella's shoulders and gave her a hug.

Uneasiness stirred and he frowned. His wife was unhappy on their wedding day, and he suspected—no, he *knew* that he was to blame.

As soon as Charlie left Arabella's side and returned to the terrace, Gabriel excused himself from his conversation with Max, Nate, and Sophie and sought out his wife. He needed to make amends.

"Why are you over here on your own, Bella?" he asked gently as he approached.

She gave him a small smile that didn't quite reach her eyes. "I'm a wee bit tired. That's all."

"I'm afraid that's my fault," he said as he flipped out his coattails and took a seat on the bench beside her. He studied her lovely hazel eyes. The breeze stirred the leaves of the horse chestnut, highlighting the flecks of green and gold in her irises. "Is something else the matter though? You don't seem yourself."

A short laugh that contained no mirth at all escaped her. "That's exactly what Charlie said." Her gaze fell to the gravel at their feet and Gabriel frowned. Was that the glimmer of tears he saw on the tips of her golden brown lashes? Or was it a trick of the light?

He imbued his voice with every ounce of sincerity that he could. "The fact that I visited the Pandora Club and got horribly drunk last night has upset you, hasn't it? You can be honest with me, Bella."

Her gaze whipped up to his again. Her expression had turned indignant. "It's not just that. I'm upset that you've been avoiding me. I don't want to sound needy or come across as a managing female, but last night, I was worried sick about you. I had no idea where you were. Or who you were with. You told me you didn't bed a prostitute at that club, and for reasons I can't quite explain, I do believe you on that score. All the same, I waited alone in the dining room for you . . . for hours . . . and then I couldn't sleep." She shook her head and looked away. "It was humiliating. And distressing."

Guilt plunged through Gabriel's gut like a knife. "Oh, God. I'm sorry. I didn't think. I've been utterly thoughtless and selfish."

Arabella didn't disagree with him. "And this morning, I wanted to thank you for the *stéthoscope* and the money for my charities. I've never received gifts quite so wonderful or thoughtful in my entire life. But when I did see you, we barely exchanged two words. You seemed far too busy. I don't expect us to live in each other's pockets, but last night and this morning, I felt like an afterthought."

Another stab of guilt sliced through Gabriel. "Again my fault," he said softly. "I went for a ride to clear my head, and then I had to see my man of affairs and my solicitor about some pressing business matters." Threading his fingers through Arabella's, he raised her hand to his lips. "I sincerely apologize for upsetting you so much, and I'll endeavor to keep you abreast of my movements in the future."

"Thank you." Arabella squeezed his hand. This time when she smiled, it reached her eyes. "Your apology is accepted and all is forgiven."

Gabriel breathed an inward sigh of relief and smiled back. He was suddenly struck by something significant Arabella had revealed. "So you were worried about me?" he asked in a low voice meant to stir her.

Arabella's gaze dipped to their hands; their fingers were still entwined. "Yes . . ."

A strange warmth suffused Gabriel's chest. "I suppose this is the first time that I've had to account for my whereabouts. It's never really mattered to anyone until now. I must confess, it is a novel concept, Bella."

"Oh . . . how dreadful," she said softly. "That no one would care." Her eyes were filled with compassion. "I've been thinking . . . about tonight. It is technically our wedding night and—"

Gabriel frowned. "You don't need to worry. I'll respect your wishes."

"Thank you, but I . . ." Bright color flooded Arabella's cheeks. "How shall I put this . . . ? The distance between us, I don't like it, Gabriel. And on today of all days. I was wondering . . . I mean . . . I don't know how to say it." Her blush deepened as her eyes locked with his. "I'll permit kisses."

Gabriel's blood surged. "Kisses. I like the sound of that. Very much, Bella. May I have one now?"

She swallowed nervously. "You want to kiss me . . . in front of everyone?" Her gaze darted to the terrace before returning to his face.

"Why not?" He shrugged a shoulder and offered her a crooked, thoroughly wicked smile. "We are married. Twice over in fact. I think it's allowed. And no one will mind." He trained all his attention on her pretty, entirely delectable mouth. "It will keep me sustained until later when our guests are all gone."

"Very well," she whispered.

Gabriel lifted a hand and cradled Arabella's face as though it were a precious, delicate bloom. This was the first time in weeks that she'd invited him to taste her sweeter-than-honey mouth, and he didn't want to frighten her with the strength of his ardor. Or waste the opportunity to fan the flames of her own desire. Anticipation spiraling through him, Gabriel's heart galloped crazily as he ever so slowly leaned in for the kiss. His strategy of teasing her with heavy looks, fleeting touches, and glimpses of his physique had definitely wreaked havoc on his own equilibrium, if not hers.

As his mouth roved over Arabella's, he endeavored to rein in his passion and keep the kiss gentle and light. But it seemed he fought a losing battle. Her scent—roses and something deliciously feminine—teased his senses, sharpening his lust, and despite his best efforts to remain in control, the kiss deepened. When Arabella's lips parted so he could delve inside and taste her thoroughly, he couldn't stifle a groan. His cock twitched, his body burned, and an unfamiliar ache akin to yearning took up residence in his chest.

Arabella's warmth, her sweetness, her enthusiastic surrender were headier than the champagne he'd been quaffing all afternoon.

Christ, he needed this woman with an intensity that shook him to his very core. How he'd gone this long without having her in every conceivable way, he couldn't fathom at all. He hoped this was but the first step in enticing Arabella back to his bed. Because he wouldn't truly be satisfied until he was buried deep inside her and she was crying his name to the heavens.

Thank goodness it was all over.

Alone in her bedroom at long last, Arabella kicked off her gold slippers and took a seat at her satinwood dressing table. She began to remove the strands of seed pearls from her hair. Talking to Charlie about her troubles had certainly helped to ease her mind. Hearing Nate had taken a little while to realize he'd fallen in love with Sophie gave Arabella a small glimmer of hope that perhaps, in time,

Gabriel might come to care for her. And then maybe he wouldn't stray and break her heart.

Touching her fingers to her lips, Arabella revisited their kiss in the garden. Her mouth curved in a smile. It had been lovely. Wonderful in fact. And heaven help her, she wanted more. She wanted her husband's lips on hers and his tongue in her mouth. His fingers to caress her skin . . .

She was so confused. Should she reveal how she felt? That she had fallen in love? She didn't want to come across as needy and desperate, because that might drive Gabriel away too. No, she couldn't afford to let him see how she really felt, not until she was sure he was beginning to care for her. He *had* seemed genuinely touched when she let slip that she'd been worried about him . . .

With a heavy sigh, she raised her hands to her neck to unclasp the necklace. Charlie was right. One thing was certain, she couldn't keep pushing Gabriel away. Because then he *would* look elsewhere.

"Can I help you with that, sweetheart?"

Arabella looked up. In the reflection of the dressing table mirror, she could see Gabriel lounging against the doorframe, a seductive smile on his lips. He'd discarded his coat and waistcoat and was in the process of rolling up his sleeves to reveal his well-muscled forearms with their dusting of fine black hairs; he had such beautiful, masculine hands. "Yes. You may."

"No lady's maid yet?" he asked, pushing away from the doorjamb.

"No, unfortunately. Mrs. Mayberry said she would begin interviews tomorrow."

"Very good." His long fingers caressed her nape as he reached for the clasp of the necklace. "It pleases me greatly to see you wearing my wedding gift."

Could he see the gooseflesh pebbling her skin and the wild flutter of her pulse in her neck? "I enjoy wearing it," she murmured, aiming for an unaffected tone but failing dismally. Her voice was noticeably husky. "I feel very spoiled."

"And so you should be. You deserve nothing but the best, Bella."

Arabella focused her attention on removing Lady Chelmsford's pearl brooch and quizzing glass from her bodice. She was suddenly so self-conscious, and so acutely aware of Gabriel—the heat of his fingers, the sound of his breathing, the scent of his sandalwood-laced cologne—she didn't know where to look, or how to act. No doubt he'd come to collect more kisses. The thought made her dizzy with desire. She was a hopeless case indeed.

Gabriel began to remove the pins from her elaborate coiffure. "What are your plans for tomorrow, sweetheart?" he asked as her curls started to fall about her shoulders. "Aside from finding a lady's maid."

"I . . . ah . . . Lady Chelmsford would like to talk more to me about my interest in philanthropy. About my plans to establish an orphanage one day. She's a member of the Mayfair Bluestocking Society and they . . ." She lost her train of thought and closed her eyes as Gabriel's fingers threaded through the tumbling tresses at the back of her head and he began to massage her scalp. If she were a cat, she would have purred. "Heavens, that feels good . . ."

She felt rather than heard Gabriel chuckle. Her hair was pushed to the side and he rained a trail of hot kisses across her shoulder. Arabella's toes curled in her silk stockings, and she clutched the polished wood tabletop before her.

"And how does that feel, pet?" he purred. As he spoke, his lips caressed her skin, making her shiver with anticipation all the more.

"I think you know." Looking up, her gaze locked with his in the mirror.

His smile was pure sin right before he gently tugged on her earlobe with his teeth.

"I said kisses not bites were permitted," she whispered.

"Well then . . ." Gabriel feathered a kiss across the top of her ear, then her temple. "Kisses alone it will be."

Before she knew what he was about, Gabriel swooped down and swept her up into his arms.

"What are you doing?" she gasped. He carried her

through to her sitting room with floor-eating strides as though she weighed nothing at all.

"Carrying you to the sofa, sweetheart, where we'll both be a lot more comfortable."

Arabella wasn't going to argue with his reasoning.

As Gabriel gently laid her on the red damask sofa, he followed her down, his mouth on hers, claiming her in a hungry, ravaging kiss. One hand came up to cup her jaw, and his tongue caressed hers with long, slow, languorous strokes.

Arabella moaned, and her arms twined about him, her fingers curling into his hair. With one foot on the floor, Gabriel pushed his other knee between her thighs. His hand covered her breast, squeezing gently.

Why, oh why had she foolishly denied Gabriel and herself this exquisite pleasure for so long? But then a little voice whispered: *Because one day, he will also make someone else feel this way, Arabella. He's your husband but he hasn't promised to stay true to you.*

She stiffened in his arms and Gabriel broke the kiss.

"What is it, Bella?" he murmured. The hand cradling her face slid to her neck. His thumb caressed the spot just above her collarbone where her pulse beat hard and fast. "Am I being too rough?" He grazed a burning kiss along her jaw. "It's just been so long and you taste so damned good."

She swallowed and shook her head. "No . . . you're not being too rough. It's just . . . I find it difficult to be like this with you, when I know that you don't love me and that one day you will bed another."

He placed his forehead against hers, and when he spoke, his warm breath fanned across her lips. "You think too much, Bella. There are so many things we could do to relieve our frustration, to give each other pleasure, if only you'd live in the moment and let go. There's nothing wrong with giving in to passion." He nuzzled her ear. "We're married, remember? We can do whatever we like."

She shook her head. "I want to relent, but I can't. I'm not like you. I've said it before. I want to be more than just a

quick tumble. A bit of sport. I'll not go back on my word
about giving you a child when the time is right. But until
then, the only way I'll welcome you back into my bed is if
you can promise me you'll be faithful. Or better yet, if you
can profess your love for me. In any case, we both know
you won't do either of those things."

"What if . . ." Gabriel drew back a little. His green eyes
were so dark, they were almost black. "What if I said you
make me want to do those things . . . Would that be enough
for you?"

What? Arabella's breath caught and she pushed herself
up on the silk cushions. *Is he sincere or telling me what I
want to hear?* She stared into his eyes, trying to read his
expression. She suddenly wished she had her glasses on.

Gathering her thoughts, she said quietly but firmly,
"Good intentions are not enough. Your promises and any
declarations of love have to be real and heartfelt, Gabriel.
To offer me the moon and the stars and then snatch them
away, that would be cruel indeed."

Gabriel gave her a maddening, devilish smile. "Are *you*
falling for me, Bella?" His voice was a velvet caress, and
his thumb stroked over her cheekbone. "Is that why you're
asking me if I feel the same way?"

Arabella sighed and brushed the raven curls back from
his forehead. He was trying to avoid the issue by turning
the focus back onto her. But she wouldn't confess her love
for him, not yet. He wasn't ready to hear it and she wasn't
ready to tell. "You're a conceited peacock, did you know
that?"

"I know." His smile widened to a grin. "But you're
avoiding my question."

"I could say the same about you," she countered.

He sighed and adjusted his position so he was sitting
beside her. "I'm afraid I don't believe in love at first sight. I
do believe one can feel lust at first sight though. The rush I
got when I first saw you was incredible. Indescribable. I've
never felt anything like it."

Sadness filled Arabella's heart. It seemed they were at

an impasse. "But I want more than lust from you. Lust isn't enough."

"It's a good place to start." Gabriel's voice was rough yet soft as he added, "I ache for you, Bella."

Arabella studied his face. All flippancy had disappeared from his expression. "I know. But have you ever felt anything beyond lust, Gabriel? For any of your paramours? I don't want to be just another one of your meaningless conquests."

Gabriel's gaze grew so intense, it made Arabella's breath catch. "You're not a meaningless conquest at all. So it seems I might be falling for you." He caressed her cheek with the back of his fingers. "Just a little."

Can it be true? Or is he just saying that? Arabella searched his eyes. "You promised me you would only ever be honest."

"May God strike me down, I am." Gabriel's tone was fierce and his gaze blazed with green fire. "Tell me what I need to do so you'll accept more than my kisses. I'll do anything. Not being able to have you in all the ways that I want is killing me." He speared his fingers into the hair at the back of her neck, then laid an ardent kiss upon her lips. "You're all I think about. Dream about." His words were a desperate plea against her mouth. "I have to have you, Bella, or I'll go insane." He seized her hand and placed it against his chest. "Can you feel that? My heart thunders for you. I burn for you. It's been this way from the very start."

Arabella was shaken. "I want to take you at your word," she whispered. "To trust you. I know love takes time to grow, but perhaps . . ." She drew a shaky breath. "It would be foolish of me to demand the impossible, but if you could at least swear to be true to me for now . . . at least until you have your heir. That would help."

"It will be the first time in my life I've made such a vow. But for you, Bella, I will."

"Thank you," she whispered. "Tonight you may have more than kisses. You can have all of me."

"Thank God," Gabriel groaned. He raised her hands to

his lips and kissed each one in turn. "You won't regret this, sweetheart. I promise you that I'll do my best to make you feel cherished. I want no one else but you. And that's the truth."

Gabriel gathered her close and kissed her. His mouth was hot and demanding, and his hands were everywhere, at her throat, at her breasts, at her waist, stroking and feeding her desire. He pushed her down onto the cushions again, and this time she could feel the evidence of his own arousal pushing against her hip. The thought of having all that male hardness inside her again made her moan into his mouth, and moist heat welled between her thighs.

Gabriel began to loosen her bodice to expose her breasts. "Are you ready for me, my darling?" he murmured huskily. "Are you wet?"

"Yes," she whispered, helping him with the ties of her stays and chemise.

"Excellent." One of Gabriel's hands slid beneath the hem of her gown and traced a slow path up her calf to her lower thigh to where her silk stockings ended and bare flesh began. As he tugged at the ribbon garter, he captured one of her aching nipples between his wicked lips and began to suckle. The pleasure was so exquisite, Arabella gripped his head and moaned again . . .

And then there was a knock at the sitting room door.

Arabella gasped and Gabriel swore beneath his breath as the knocking continued, louder and more insistent.

"My lord?" It was Ryecroft. "I'm sorry to disturb you and Lady Langdale. But there's a most urgent matter that requires your attention."

"What the hell?" Gabriel pushed himself up to a sitting position. "I dismissed him. It's our wedding night, for Christ's sake."

"There must be something terribly wrong," said Arabella, pulling her chemise, stays, and bodice back into place. Apprehension and thwarted desire made her clumsy—her trembling fingers couldn't manage to do up all the laces and ribbons.

"The bloody house better be burning down, that's all I can say," grumbled Gabriel as he got to his feet, then swore again when he noticed the telltale swell at the front of his breeches. "What's going on, Ryecroft?" His voice was thunderous as he crossed the room. Tugging his shirt out to cover his groin, he then yanked the door open. "I'll have your guts for garters if it's not a dire emergency of some kind."

"My lord, I am so, so sorry." The pale-faced valet was visibly quaking. "Lord Sleat is downstairs. He apologizes for intruding but he says he must speak with you. That the matter can't wait."

"Fucking hell." Gabriel ran a hand through his hair. "Get me a robe or something, will you?"

The valet scurried off, and Gabriel turned back to face Arabella. "I'm going to have to see him, sweetheart. If it were anybody else, I'd probably tell the dog to go to hell. But MacQueen wouldn't be here unless it was important."

"I understand," she said, rising to her feet. Her bodice was back in place now. "Would you like me to come too? I don't know if I can help . . ." She faltered and blushed. "Of course, I don't want to intrude. If it's a private matter."

Gabriel frowned. "You wouldn't be intruding, Bella. Yes, do come . . ." He held out his hand. "I don't want to keep secrets from you. We'll deal with this together."

They met MacQueen in the drawing room.

"What's happened?" asked Gabriel without preamble as he entered the room, Arabella's hand still in his. The Scottish marquess was perched on the edge of a gilt-legged chair that looked as if it might crumble beneath his substantial muscular bulk. With his black eye patch, he looked more like a pirate than a marquess.

However, as always, MacQueen's manners were perfect. He rose to his feet and affected an elegant bow as soon as he saw Arabella was with Gabriel.

"My lady," he said in his rumbling baritone. His storm

cloud–gray eye held a light of concern as his attention shifted back to Gabriel. "I apologize for disturbing you both, but I thought you needed to know what's going on."

The Scot shifted uncomfortably on his feet, and the skin prickled at the back of Gabriel's neck. MacQueen had personal demons that in some ways outrivaled his own, but Gabriel had never seen his friend quite this unsettled.

"Well, out with it, man. You're making me nervous."

MacQueen's mountainous shoulders heaved as he drew a deep breath and his gaze riveted on Gabriel's. "I'm loath to be the bearer of bad tidings, especially on your wedding day, Langdale, but it would seem your uncle, Stephen Holmes-Fitzgerald, passed away early this evening."

"Oh, Gabriel, I'm so sorry," murmured Arabella. She squeezed his hand.

Grief gripped Gabriel's chest, stealing his breath. "Thank you, sweetheart. It wasn't unexpected," he said at length in a choked voice. Indeed, he had to swallow past the hard lump clogging his throat before he could continue. "I saw him yesterday and he was in a bad way."

After another moment, he dashed a hand across his eyes before focusing back on MacQueen. "How did you hear?"

"After I farewelled you here, I went to White's . . . and your cousin, Captain Holmes-Fitzgerald was there. He was well in his cups and telling anyone who would care to listen that his father had just died." MacQueen paused, his gray gaze as hard as granite. "And that he was going after your title because you're a bastard."

A muscle pulsed in Gabriel's jaw. "Also not unexpected." Christ, he needed a drink. Crossing to the oak sideboard, he sloshed a sizable amount of cognac into two glasses—one for himself and one for MacQueen. "Would you like one, Bella?"

She shook her head as she settled herself on a sofa. "No, thank you. I prefer whisky. If you have it."

"I do."

A smile split MacQueen's ruggedly handsome face. "You have good taste, Lady Langdale."

Arabella inclined her head. "I'll probably cough and

splutter when I sip it, but it reminds me of my dearly departed grandfather. He was fond of a wee dram before bed."

Once they were all armed with drinks, Gabriel claimed the space beside Arabella, and MacQueen took the gilt-legged chair again.

After draining his glass in two mouthfuls, Gabriel dragged an unsteady hand across his mouth. He caught Arabella's gaze. Her lovely face was pale and grave, but she was composed. It meant a lot that she wanted to face this crisis with him. She wasn't a fainthearted miss by any means. Which was fortunate indeed in light of the present circumstances. "I'm afraid I'm going to have to go away, Bella. Tonight in fact."

"Where to?"

"To Scotland. The inquiry agent I sent up north wasn't able to uncover any useful intelligence in Springfield. But when I saw my uncle yesterday, he said something that piqued my interest." Gabriel recounted the odd exchange to Arabella and MacQueen. "My uncle made me wonder if he'd actually been present at my parents' anvil wedding. I'm probably searching for hen's teeth, but I can't completely discount what he said. Not when there's so much at stake." He reached out and covered Arabella's hand with his.

She gave him a reassuring smile. "Of course you must go. Don't worry about me. I'll be quite fine."

He raised her hand to his lips and kissed it. "Thank you. You're far too good for a scoundrel like me, do you know that?"

She blushed and MacQueen cleared his throat. "I'll go with you. My coachman knows the Great North Road better than the back of his own hand."

"We'll travel in tandem then." Even though there was only two of them traveling, Gabriel knew that MacQueen needed his own carriage.

Plans were made to meet in an hour, and then the Scotsman took his leave.

"How long will you be gone?" Arabella asked as the door shut behind the marquess. "Will you miss the funeral?"

Gabriel grimaced. "I'm afraid I will. Not that Timothy

would let me attend anyway. As to how long I'll be gone, six or seven days at the most if we also travel at night. The roads will be in good condition this time of year." He rang for a footman to issue orders for his four-in-hand carriage to be readied and brought around. "But I'll leave you with my town coach so you can get out and about around town. And if you need to purchase anything and I don't have an existing account at the store, start one, or ask Jervis to send for my man of affairs to arrange it. I'll also leave you with a substantial sum; I've a stash of pound notes locked away in the library. I'll show you where I keep it and give you the key." Sliding a hand behind her slender neck, he drew her close and kissed the top of her head. "I'll miss you, my sweet. More than you'll know. But I have to go. All going well, I'll be back before you know it with good news."

CHAPTER 16

If you are feeling under the weather—as one is wont to do after a particularly taxing Season—perhaps consider taking a tincture of opium such as laudanum.

Whether one is afflicted with a megrim, cough, toothache, fever, or rheumatism, or simply suffers from poor sleep, it is guaranteed to improve one's well-being.

The most astute lady will always have some near to hand.

The Beau Monde Mirror: A Lady's Guide to Beauty

The Seven Dials Dispensary, Covent Garden, London

August 3, 1818

As Gabriel's town coach drew to a halt outside the Seven Dials Dispensary, Arabella exhaled a shaky sigh. In her gloved hand, she clutched a letter from Dr. Radcliff; it had come with yesterday's post to Langdale House, and was addressed quite correctly to 'The Right Honorable, The Countess of Langdale'. After all this time—five whole months in fact—he'd finally reached out to her. And Arabella didn't quite know how she felt about it.

No, that wasn't quite true. She'd considered Dr. Graham Radcliff a friend, perhaps even a kindred spirit, and if she were completely honest with herself, his neglect stung. However, when all was said and done, she must put aside her pique if she wanted her dream to come true. Thanks to Gabriel's generosity, she would have the money required to form her own charitable society. Then, once like-minded people such as Lady Chelmsford and her well-connected bluestocking friends were on board, they could establish more dispensaries for the poor and an orphanage in Edinburgh, even Glasgow. With such grand ambitions, Arabella couldn't do this on her own; a physician's professional expertise and advice were essential too.

She still needed Dr. Radcliff.

Gabriel's footman, Soames, let down the steps and helped Arabella to alight from the town coach onto the busy, dusty, litter-strewn street. It was just past noon and the summer sun beat down upon her; even though she wore a plain straw bonnet, she squinted against the glare. The clinic was located in a two-story building of dull brown brick, crammed between a shop selling secondhand items of a dubious nature and another vacant store with boarded-up windows. *The Seven Dials Dispensary* was painted in neat black lettering upon a white wooden sign hanging above the dark blue door. Through the clinic's open windows, the cries of babies along with the hubbub of adult voices reached her. A light breeze set the sign swinging and carried the odor of rotting refuse from a nearby alleyway, making Arabella wrinkle her nose.

Seven Dials was one of the poorest, most overcrowded areas in London. A slum. Indeed Arabella understood from Dr. Radcliff's letter that crime was rife here, particularly at night, so she must be careful when visiting. Even during the day, one had to take care not to become a victim of a pickpocket.

Of course, the grandness of the Earl of Langdale's town coach and the liveried servants in their powdered perukes and green satin waistcoats with brass buttons had attracted quite a bit of attention. Passersby stared openly with hard, suspicious eyes as Arabella shook out her skirts and adjusted her glasses upon her nose. A trio of painfully thin ragamuffins with dirty faces and bare feet scurried past, an emaciated dog at their heels; one of the boys poked his tongue at her before they all darted down the alley. In deference to the Londoners who lived here, Arabella had donned one of her plainest, workaday gowns of striped cotton and carried her old leather satchel, rather than a reticule, in an attempt to blend in. But it hadn't helped. It was clear she didn't belong here. However, she wouldn't be deterred.

As she crossed to the dispensary's door, a sallow-faced man in shabby clothing appeared at the entrance of the shop and leaned against the doorframe. His gaze wandered over her in a slow, insolent inspection that made the hairs stand up on the back of her neck.

Arabella was suddenly grateful that she'd brought Soames and another young strapping footman with her. If Gabriel discovered that she'd ventured into the Seven Dials slums unaccompanied, he'd be livid with her for putting herself in danger. And rightly so.

Soames accompanied her to the front door and opened it. She smiled her thanks, then passed into the crowded interior.

The stench of unwashed humanity hit Arabella instantly. It was not an unfamiliar smell given the places she'd sometimes ventured with her grandfather in Edinburgh. Considering the day was so hot, it was no wonder the room was so malodorous.

"Would you like me to come with you, my lady?" asked Soames, eyeing the front waiting room of the dispensary with distaste. There were at least thirty souls crammed into the small space, and the atmosphere was stifling. Mothers rocked crying babies in their arms or held toddlers on their hips while their other children pulled at their skirts. A few men with a variety of injuries lurked by the window: a youth cradled his badly cut hand; a middle-aged man with a bandaged foot and a makeshift walking stick sat on one of the few wooden chairs; another man nursed a bruised, swollen jaw. Arabella was instantly reminded of her grandfather's clinic, and she couldn't help but make a mental assessment of who should be seen first.

"No, I'll be fine," she said firmly and lifted the letter. "Dr. Radcliff is expecting me."

"Of course, my lady. I'll wait by the door."

"Thank you." Through the crowd, Arabella could just make out a middle-aged woman in a pinafore and cap with the look of a nursing sister about her, sitting at a wooden desk at the back of the room. By the time Arabella introduced herself and Dr. Radcliff had finished treating his current patient, she was flushed and perspiring and grateful indeed to be ushered into the quieter, cooler physician's room.

Dressed rather informally in his shirtsleeves, waistcoat, and trousers and a stained apron, Dr. Radcliff was clearly in the thick of things. Nevertheless, his voice was filled with warmth as he greeted her. "Miss Jardine . . . I mean, Lady Langdale, how wonderful it is to see you again." His brown eyes were just as kind as Arabella remembered as he bade her to sit down on a wooden chair before his scuffed deal desk. A fair amount of sunlight filtered through the lace-curtained front window, and there was also a small barred window and another door, which Arabella assumed led out to the alley at the back of the building.

"Thank you for seeing me," she said as she placed her satchel on the desk and then nervously smoothed her skirts. "I can see how busy you are."

He removed his apron and hung it on a peg between a cracked leather settee and a glass-fronted cabinet filled with an array of bottles, including Kendal's Black Drop and Godfrey's Cordial. "It's always busy," he said. "But it would be remiss of me not to see you after all this time. How are you?" He took a seat on the other side of the desk and folded his hands with their well-manicured nails on the blotter. Arabella immediately recalled the time she'd tried to capture the touch of his fingers in her hand on that long-ago rainy day at the Foundling Hospital. My goodness, how innocent she'd been back then.

Dr. Radcliff spoke again, pulling her from her memories. "I was most surprised to receive your letter informing me you'd wed. And to someone as illustrious as the Earl of Langdale."

Arabella wasn't sure if there was a sarcastic edge to his voice as he'd uttered his last pronouncement. Choosing to ignore her suspicions, she smiled. "Believe me, I was most surprised when he asked me to marry him too. I certainly didn't set out for the Continent in the hopes of finding a husband. Especially an earl."

"Well, I think your grandfather would have been most proud you've made such an excellent match. So tell me . . ." He leaned back in his chair. "What can I do for you? I hope I'm not being rude by asking if this is a purely social call, or is there something else you would like to discuss? If I recall correctly, your second to last letter—the one you sent from Paris—mentioned you wanted to speak with me about the financial considerations involved in establishing a place like this"—he waved an expansive hand—"or perhaps even a foundling hospital or orphanage."

Oh, he had received her letter but hadn't responded. At least she now knew. But it didn't really matter now that she had his full attention and he seemed interested in discussing her project. Arabella sat forward in her seat. "Yes, I would indeed. Obviously right now is not an ideal time to talk considering how many people I saw in the waiting room. So I'd be happy to come back another day or we could arrange to meet elsewhere . . ."

Dr. Radcliff grimaced. "It won't make much difference. I'm always needed a hundred different places at once. Though there's a particularly nasty ague going around at the moment that's keeping me on my toes. I'm actually running out of laudanum." He nodded toward the glass-fronted cupboard. "I usually have another nurse who assists me, but she's succumbed to the ague too."

"Oh, no. How unfortunate." The earsplitting wail of an unhappy toddler penetrated the room, and Arabella was struck with an idea. "As you know, I have nursing experience, as I used to assist my grandfather in his clinic. I would be quite happy to help you out for a few hours in exchange for the opportunity to pick your brain. Think of it as a trade. We can talk in between patients."

Dr. Radcliff frowned. "Are you certain? I mean, you are a countess now."

Arabella waved a dismissive hand. "I hardly think that

signifies. Besides, my husband is away at the moment attending to . . . to a business matter. I won't be missed. And to be perfectly frank with you, I do miss helping out with patients. I also have something special to show you." She patted her satchel. "In here, I have a new medical instrument called a *stéthoscope* that can be used to enhance auscultation. One of the physicians at L'Hôpital Necker invented it."

"Very well, Lady Langdale. We have a deal." Dr. Radcliff smiled as he stood. "I have another pinafore here so that you can protect your gown while we work."

"Wonderful." A feeling of immense satisfaction settled over Arabella as she rose too. "I'm going to enjoy being of use. Just let me tell my driver and footmen that they can collect me again in a few hours, and then you shall have my undivided attention."

Langdale House, St. James's Square, London

"I'm afraid Lady Langdale is not at home, my lord," said Jervis after Gabriel swung through the front doors of Langdale House and asked after the whereabouts of his wife.

He frowned as he passed his hat and gloves to the butler. After traveling nonstop on a wild-goose chase to Scotland and back—as he'd feared, he'd not found anything useful in Springfield—he was exhausted, dejected, and frustrated, not to mention hot and bothered. But the sight of Arabella's lovely face would no doubt restore him.

"So when will she be back?" After he'd bathed and eaten, Gabriel intended to have his wicked way with her if she was also so inclined. He still hadn't quite forgiven MacQueen for interrupting them.

A shadow of concern flickered across Jervis's face. "In a few hours I expect, my lord. Lady Langdale instructed Soames to fetch her later this afternoon . . ." He swallowed nervously, which was very out of character for Jervis. He was never rattled.

What the hell is going on? Gabriel tugged at his damnably tight cravat. "From where? Is she with one of her friends? She shouldn't be out shopping on her own. Unless she took one of the maids."

"I'm afraid she is by herself, my lord. I'm of the understanding she went to visit a medical dispensary in Seven Dials . . ."

What? Gabriel froze as alarm and fury rose in a great wave. He pinned Jervis with a white-hot glare. "What did you say? Because I really hope to God I misheard you."

To his credit, Jervis didn't look away as he repeated that Lady Langdale was currently visiting a dispensary in the slum of Seven Dials. And yes, she was on her own. "When she dismissed Soames, he was led to believe she would be assisting the dispensary's physician this afternoon. A Dr. Radcliff? She requested the town coach return at three o'clock to pick her up."

A muscle twitched in Gabriel's jaw as he fought to suppress the urge to rip out someone's jugular. Whether it was Soames's, Dr. Radcliff's, Jervis's or anyone else's for that matter, he didn't overly much care. According to the hall clock, it was half past one. "Send for the coach now," he growled. The savage menace in his tone was clear. "And summon Soames and whoever else was with her. I want to know why my staff thought it was remotely acceptable to leave their mistress in one of the most dangerous parts of London. They're bloody lucky I don't have time to horsewhip them."

Whether he horsewhipped the doctor or not remained to be seen.

The Seven Dials Dispensary, Covent Garden, London

By the time his carriage pulled up outside the dispensary, Gabriel had managed to rein in his anger to the extent that the lives of his footmen and driver weren't in any immediate danger.

Although, that might change if anything untoward had

happened to Arabella. Soames's piss-weak excuse for leaving—that Arabella had dismissed them so they wouldn't have to wait about in the hot afternoon sun—was simply not good enough, not by a long shot. He was still toying with the idea of dismissing the whole bloody lot of them for not doing their duties.

Throwing the coach door open, Gabriel leapt out without waiting for the steps to be let down. The Seven Dials Dispensary was situated on a street that was at least wider than some of the other narrow lanes and alleys that led into the cutthroat rookeries. It had been a long time since he'd ventured into the depths of this slum with his father, both of them looking for trouble just for the hell of it, so he knew exactly how dangerous this area was.

The dispensary's waiting room seethed with disgruntled adults and screaming children, and it was quite an effort to carefully push his way through the crowd to reach the back. A perspiring middle-aged woman who sat behind a desk—a nurse perhaps—looked up in surprise when he grasped the handle of the only other door; a small brass plaque proclaimed the office to be Dr. Graham Radcliff's.

"Wait, you can't go in there, sir," she cried and began to rise from her seat, but it was too late. Gabriel had pushed through into the room beyond.

"Gabriel? What are you doing here?" Arabella was standing by the office window holding a red-faced, crying baby on her hip. Behind her glasses, her eyes were owlishly wide with surprise. "I didn't think you'd be back until tomorrow."

"I've come to take you home, dear wife." Gabriel's tone brooked no argument as his gaze darted to the room's other occupants: the baby's mother, haggard beyond her young years, sat on a wooden chair with a grubby, runny-nosed toddler squirming in her lap. A trim-looking man with graying hair at his temples ceased his attempted examination of the noncompliant child.

"Lord Langdale, I presume," he said as he straightened and eyed Gabriel with annoyance. "I'm a tad busy right now if you hadn't noticed." He rumpled the toddler's matted hair.

"I'm not here to interrupt you, Doctor," Gabriel said drily as he lounged against the door. "I just have need of my wife." His gaze locked with hers across the room. "Arabella?"

Arabella blushed to the roots of her hair. She clearly understood his double entendre. "I . . . ah . . . I made an arrangement to assist Dr. Radcliff this afternoon," she said with a frown.

Gabriel cocked a brow. "An arrangement, you say?"

"Aye." Arabella transferred the squalling baby to her other hip, and it gripped one of her flyaway curls in its tiny fist. Once she'd freed herself, she added, "His nursing assistant is unwell so I offered to help. And I wanted to show him my *stéthoscope*."

"That's very admirable but I'm afraid it's time to go. I'm sure Dr. Radcliff won't mind. Will you, Doctor?"

Gabriel watched as Radcliff schooled his expression into one that approximated "professionally pleasant." "No, of course not." He nodded at a glass-fronted cabinet near Arabella. "If you wouldn't mind passing me a bottle of Godfrey's Cordial before you go. Little Tom here has a fever, but a few drops will soon have him feeling a lot better."

"Yes, certainly."

Godfrey's Cordial. Gabriel swallowed as he watched his wife take the dark bottle of opiate tincture from the cupboard and carry it over. His heart crashed against his ribs as if he'd just run a mile, and his hands began to shake.

"Are you all right, my lord?" Arabella's brow furrowed with concern as she handed the bottle to Dr. Radcliff. "If you want to step outside, I'll join you in a minute."

Gabriel's gaze fixed on the doctor's hands as he uncorked the bottle. Ravening need gripped his throat while shame and self-loathing curdled his gut.

"Gabriel?"

He drew a ragged breath and forced himself to look at Arabella. "No, I'm not all right," he whispered. And then he bolted from the room.

* * *

When Arabella stepped outside, Soames nodded in the direction of the alleyway. "He's just down there, my lady."

What on earth? Arabella rushed into the narrow, dark, filthy space and gasped with shock when she saw Gabriel doubled over, his fisted hands on his thighs. His breath came in short, hard pants.

"Gabriel . . ." she murmured. She hovered by his side, wanting to offer comfort but sensing he was in such a state of distress that he would reject her.

"Christ . . . Arabella . . ." He lifted his head and stared at her with the haunted, terrified eyes of a trapped creature. "I don't . . . I don't want you"—he sucked in another breath—"to see me like this."

"Believe me, I've seen far worse," she said quietly. And that was the truth.

He straightened abruptly and scrubbed a shaking hand down his face. His breathing, while it still sawed in and out, seemed to be slowing.

"I'm sorry," she said, and took a step closer. A sliver of guilt penetrated her heart. "I should have asked you to leave the room before I took the laudanum out of the cupboard. That was unthinking of me."

He shook his head. "It's not your fault. It's mine." He sagged against the wall, eyes closed, one booted foot propped against the dirty brickwork. His long black lashes were a sooty smudge against his ashen cheeks. "Laudanum. I swear it's devil's water." His Adam's apple convulsed, and when he spoke, his voice was low and raw. "I want it so much, I hate it. And I hate myself for being so weak. Every time I see it, the craving for it grips and tears at my insides. Sweet Jesus." He tipped his head back and pinched the bridge of his nose. "What you must think of me, Bella."

Arabella bit her lip to stop herself from crying. To see Gabriel like this made her heart weep. "I think you are a wonderful man, and I don't think any less of you because of this," she said gently. "We all have things we'd like to change about ourselves. No one is perfect." Soames appeared at the head of the alley, but she waved him away. "How long have you been battling this affliction?"

Gabriel shrugged a shoulder. "It feels like forever. But in truth, ever since I was eighteen. It was my father who introduced me to the stuff. Evil bastard."

He opened his eyes and expelled a shaky sigh. "It didn't become a fully fledged problem, though, until Waterloo. After I was shot, I took laudanum to ease the pain, especially after the wound became infected. But then I came to rely upon it more and more until I was drinking the stuff at all hours of the day and night, for no other reason than the pleasure it brought me. After I nearly stepped out in front of a carriage in Pall Mall one night, Nate, MacQueen, and Max were so horrified, they carted me off to MacQueen's remote hunting lodge on the Isle of Skye. That was almost three years ago. I've overcome the physical need for the drug, but every time I see a bottle of it . . ." He rubbed a hand across his mouth. "The hunger eats at me like nothing else. I don't think I'll ever be rid of it completely."

Arabella nodded, then reached for his clenched hand. When his fingers relaxed and curled around hers, she smiled. "I'll help in whatever way I can," she said softly. "I'm here for you."

Gabriel nodded but he didn't return her smile. The expression in his eyes was grave, perhaps even a little hard and cold as he said, "It would help if you didn't decide to visit a dispensary located in one of London's worst slums, Arabella. On your own. What, in God's name, were you thinking?"

Arabella blinked at him, astonished by his anger. "I was perfectly safe. I was with Dr. Radcliff."

"That man wouldn't stand a chance against any of the ruffians around here. Even the street urchins could best him in a fight. Come." His hand still gripping Arabella's, Gabriel tugged her toward the street and his carriage. "Let's go."

Arabella followed, but all the while, irritation bristled at his high-handedness. Was this how things were going to be? She understood Gabriel's concern, but really, he was overreacting.

Once they were in the carriage and on their way, she tugged off her glasses and slid them into the pocket of her borrowed pinafore; they were pinching the sides of her head and she could feel a megrim brewing. She'd left her gloves, bonnet, satchel, and *stéthoscope* behind in Dr. Radcliff's office, but that didn't really matter. What mattered was her husband sounded like he might be about to forbid her from visiting the Seven Dials Dispensary. And she wouldn't stand for that.

She drew a bracing breath. "Gabriel, I'm sorry you were worried about me. The last thing I want to do is upset you. But surely, you must understand that from time to time, I will need to visit poorer areas like Seven Dials. My charities will be less effective if I don't have a good understanding of what needs to be put in place—"

"Arabella, *you* need to understand that as my wife, the Countess of Langdale, you cannot venture into the worst parts of London with little to no protection." Tension was etched into every line of Gabriel's face, and his eyes blazed with strong emotion. "There's danger lurking around every corner. Even in plain sight, for that matter. Anything could happen to you. I'm happy for you to set up any number of charitable concerns, but I don't want you visiting slums like Seven Dials. I'm firmly of the opinion that you're too good for a place like that."

"Gabriel," she said softly. "I was born in a place just like that. A Glasgow slum. And years later, my grandfather discovered that my mother probably died in that same Glasgow slum after my father, a ne'er-do-well soldier, abandoned her. It breaks my heart knowing that she's likely buried in an unmarked pauper's grave somewhere. So you see, I'm not so very different from the people who live in Seven Dials."

"Oh God, Arabella, I had no idea." A sympathetic light filled Gabriel's eyes. "That's utterly tragic."

Arabella nodded as tears misted her vision. "I'm grateful my mother was able to place me in the Great Clyde Hospital and Poorhouse before she passed away. As I told you once before, I was a wee infant, only a few months old, when the hospital took me in, so I don't remember her at all. But I miss her all the same."

Gabriel's black brows descended into a puzzled frown. "You also mentioned your grandfather found you. That he was the one who came to claim you."

Arabella tightly plaited her fingers together, mustering the courage she needed to share every shameful detail about her past. So he would understand what drove her. "Yes, but it wasn't for some time. Six years in fact. You see, my grandfather didn't approve of my parents' match as he'd heard rumors my father, William Jardine, was a scoundrel of the first order—by all accounts, he was a handsome corporal but without means. My mother Mary met him at an assembly ball—his regiment was stationed in Edinburgh— and she was instantly smitten. When they eloped, he deserted his post—my grandfather later heard that William had been charged for assaulting another soldier—and they effectively disappeared. But after eight months, when William had abandoned my mother, she wrote to her sister out of desperation; she was penniless and heavily pregnant with me in Glasgow. But Aunt Flora, who's always been very devout, was so scandalized by what her sister had done—that she'd eloped and had entered into an irregular marriage rather than a church-sanctified union—she hid the letter . . . as well as the very last one Mary sent, which contained the details of my whereabouts and the scrap of her kerchief after she'd felt compelled to give me up. Flora believed my mother was a wanton and deserved to be shunned. And it was clear she didn't want to have anything to do with me."

Arabella sighed shakily. "But that's not the worst of it . . ." Apprehension gripped her heart, but she needed to tell Gabriel the most disturbing part of her mother's sad tale. She plowed on. "In her last letter, my mother confessed she'd become a prostitute and that she'd taken me to the orphanage because she feared she was unwell. She hadn't been able to find work and she'd become so desperate . . ." She swallowed to clear the ache of tears gathering in her throat. "She pleaded with Flora to ask my grandfather if she could return home, but apparently Flora was so disgusted, she completely washed her hands of her sister."

"Good God, Bella. I'm speechless." Sympathy and horror colored Gabriel's voice. "To say I'm shocked at how merciless your aunt was would be an understatement."

Gabriel's words of support gave Arabella the strength to continue. "It wasn't until years later, when I was six, that my grandfather discovered Flora had kept the letters from him. He'd forgiven my mother for eloping by then and was incensed that Flora had denied him the opportunity to reach out to his daughter, to help her when she'd needed him most. He traveled to Glasgow to claim me. And I'm so glad he did. Who knows what would have become of me otherwise."

"Yes, thank God he did." Gabriel's eyes burned with anger as he added, "And your aunt Flora is a spiteful, callous witch."

Arabella breathed a sigh of relief. "You're not upset your wife might very well be the illegitimate daughter of a prostitute? I've been too frightened to tell you."

"Of course not." Gabriel's expression softened. "My heart weeps for what happened to your mother. It makes me despise your aunt all the more."

"Thank you for being so understanding." Arabella firmed her gaze. "So you can see why supporting the poor and improving their lot in life is so important to me, Gabriel. The Great Clyde Hospital and Poorhouse was a cruel institution, and from an early age, I knew what it was like to be hungry and cold, and yes, to be unloved. If I can make things better for others in similar circumstances, I will." She lifted her chin and added in a determined voice, "And I pray that you will help me, and not stand in my way."

A muscle flickered in Gabriel's lean jaw. "By that you mean you'll disobey me and continue to visit Dr. Radcliff and that god-awful dispensary?"

"How dare you describe his clinic in that way," Arabella retorted, her voice stiff with indignation. "Dr. Radcliff is a wonderful physician with progressive ideas, and my grandfather esteemed him highly. And I have nothing but the utmost respect for him too."

"You do, do you?" Gabriel's expression had turned savage. "And you'd really defy me to keep on seeing him?"

Arabella bristled. "I don't *want* to defy you, but if you give me no choice, what else am I to do?" She attempted to soften her tone. "Surely we can reach a compromise. I could take more of your footmen with me to Seven Dials. Or I could arrange to see Dr. Radcliff at the Foundling Hospital. He's on the board."

Gabriel's nostrils flared with anger as he demanded, "Why are you so set on seeing him? How long have you been corresponding? Don't think I didn't notice that you wrote to him from Switzerland, the day after our wedding day."

Arabella gaped at him as she was struck by the oddest thought. "Are . . . are you jealous?"

Gabriel's glare was fierce. "Damn right I'm jealous. You're my wife and you're cultivating a relationship with another man."

"It's a working relationship," she fired back. "He's only a friend. And you have no reason whatsoever to distrust me."

He snorted. "Yet you kept me at arms-length for weeks before you decided to let me into your bed again. Not that we got very far before we were interrupted. I'm beginning to wonder if you've been harboring a secret tendre for this medical paragon of perfection all along."

"That's not fair. My reasons for keeping you at bay were quite clear. I didn't believe I could trust you with my heart."

The carriage drew to a halt outside Langdale House, but before the footman opened the door, Gabriel growled, "This conversation is far from over, my sweet."

"Good," huffed Arabella as she gathered up her skirts to alight. "Because I still have plenty of things left to say."

Ignoring Jervis's greeting at the front door, Gabriel

reached for Arabella's hand and all but pulled her across the entry hall. He set a rapid pace and by the time they reached her sitting room, Arabella was out of breath and flushed with exertion.

Nevertheless, she shivered when Gabriel shut the door and locked it. Tension radiated off him in waves as he turned back to face her, pinning her with a narrow-eyed, penetrating glare. "In the carriage, you didn't immediately deny that you have tender feelings for Radcliff, *my lady.*" His voice was laced with suspicion. High color flagged his cheekbones. "Why is that, I wonder?"

A fiery blush scalded Arabella's entire face as she pulled off her pinafore and dumped it onto a nearby chair.

"Stop . . . stop twisting things," she countered, holding her ground in the face of her husband's unjustified displeasure. She was still breathless, and her chest rose and fell in rapid pants. She'd done nothing wrong and had nothing to be ashamed of. She did have a girlish infatuation for the doctor once, but not anymore. "I do not care for Dr. Radcliff in that way . . . And in any case . . . I don't see why you have cause to complain." Resentment and outrage sharpened her tongue as she continued, "You're the one who's stated over and over again that you don't think you can ever be faithful to me. *I'm* not the one with a long history of mindless, indiscriminate philandering. *You* are." She punctuated each point with a slashing wave of her hand. "The night before our English wedding, when I had no idea where you were, you might very well have been with any one of your paramours. Someone like Lady Astley."

Gabriel's eyebrows shot up. "You know about her?"

Arabella batted away a loose curl that had become plastered to her hot cheek. "Apparently everyone in London knows about your affair with her, so why should it bother you that I know too?"

"You have nothing to worry about where she's concerned," Gabriel said gruffly. He loomed over her, his own chest heaving. "I never gave a fig about her."

"And according to you, you don't give a fig about me either," she snapped. "And you never will."

"That's not true. I think about you every minute of every day." Gabriel caught her about the waist, spun her around, and pushed her up against the door, trapping her there with his lean, hard body. "Don't you remember what I said to you before I left for Scotland, Bella?" Capturing her face with one large hand, his eyes seared hers. "I burn for you. I promised to be true."

He dipped his head, and his mouth grazed across her lips, then upward over her cheek to where her pulse beat frantically at her temple. "God help me." His breath was hot and ragged against her ear. "Since I've been away, all I've thought about is kissing you. Peeling the clothes from your body until you are gloriously naked." The hand at her waist slid upward to cradle her breast, and his thumb brushed over her taut, throbbing nipple. "I've dreamed about burying my face in your dew-drenched cunny, my tongue sliding through your golden thatch, licking and tasting every delicious little part of you until you scream my name. As I've lain in bed, unable to sleep, night after night, I've pictured myself thrusting into your beautiful body again and again until we both quake with pleasure." Drawing back, his blazing gaze locked with hers. "I swear I want no one else but you. Let me love you."

Arabella fisted her hands and pushed against the rock-hard wall of Gabriel's chest; her body urged her to surrender but her head said no. Her heart pounded in her ears. "But don't you see?" she whispered, her voice snagging on a sob. "The problem is, you don't love me. And I don't know if I can believe a word you say."

"Well then, perhaps you will believe this."

Before she could draw breath to protest, Gabriel claimed her mouth in a fervent, desperate, devouring kiss. His tongue plundered, lashed against hers. His hands roamed over her body, touching and stroking everywhere, her throat, her breasts, her hips. When he seized her derriere and pulled her hard against him, his steel-hard erection pressed into the softness of her belly.

And Arabella's resistance melted away like a snowflake in the summer sun. She wanted Gabriel too. Wanted his drugging kisses, wanted his touch, wanted everything he had to give, even if she couldn't have his love.

All of a sudden he dropped to his knees, his hands gripping her hips. His eyes burned with brilliant green fire as he looked up at her from beneath hooded lids. "Tell me you're wet for me, Bella."

Her throat was so tight with desire, she had to swallow before she could respond. "I am."

"Part your legs. I want to pleasure your honey-sweet quim with my mouth."

Oh, dear Lord. He hadn't been jesting before. "Are you sure?" she whispered as she moved one foot to the side.

"Of course I'm sure." He reached beneath the hem of her gown, the cotton fabric bunching as his hot hands slid slowly upward over her silk stockings to the tops of her naked thighs. "Hold your skirts. I can't wait to taste you."

Inhaling a trembling breath, Arabella complied with his request. Now that her most intimate parts were exposed to her husband's gaze, she felt vulnerable yet so excited she could barely breathe. Her pulse leapt wildly as Gabriel kissed and then touched his tongue to the bare flesh just above the ribbon garter at her knee. When he pushed his nose against her mound and inhaled her scent, his warm breath stirring her curls, she gasped. One of his long fingers traced a path along the damp seam of her sex.

"How lovely and wet you are," he crooned huskily as he gently parted her plump, swollen folds even further. "I knew you would be, sweetheart." In the next instant, his tongue darted out and the tip flickered against the tight, throbbing bud of her clitoris. She jolted and whimpered as every nerve ending was set alight. She'd never experienced such exquisite sensation.

She felt Gabriel's mouth curve in a smile against the tender skin of her thigh. "Hook your leg over my shoulder."

Now that she knew what he could do with his wicked tongue, Arabella did as he asked without hesitation. She should be ashamed to be doing such a wanton, even depraved thing, but at this very moment, she wasn't.

Her sex spread wide, Gabriel slid two fingers into her

slick entrance, thrusting gently in a maddening rhythm. Arabella moaned and leaned back against the smooth oak panels at her back; her thighs trembled and her inner muscles gripped him, drawing him deeper. There was no discomfort, only burgeoning pleasure. His mouth pressed against her clitoris and he teased the straining, oh-so-sensitive hooded peak with little nibbles and licks and sucks. His fingers plunged harder and faster, and Arabella rippled about him. She couldn't control the noises escaping her—a mixture of tiny whimpers and rapid, shallow pants. The tension inside her was building, winding tighter and tighter until she almost couldn't bear it.

When Gabriel began to suckle in earnest, his eager lips drawing hard on her pulsing, quivering flesh, she couldn't suppress a joyous cry as incandescent rapture suddenly flared to life inside her. *Yes. Oh yes, oh yes, oh yes.*

Arching against his hot, wicked mouth, his lips and tongue continued to torment her until she was shuddering violently. "Gabriel, stop. Have mercy," Arabella gasped, her fingers spearing into his silky black curls as she tried to push him away.

He groaned low in his throat. "I can't get enough of you, Bella."

"I'll fall." She clutched at his head. Indeed, her legs were so weak, she could barely stand.

"No, you won't." He bathed her sex with one last languorous lick before he relented and raised his head. "I've got you."

He surged to his feet and crowded her against the oak door, pinning her body there with his weight. Then his mouth crashed over hers and he kissed her with such ruthless, breath-robbing ardor, Arabella's head began to spin. There was a trace of muskiness on his lips and she realized it was her own essence she tasted, but rather than being repulsed, she was aroused. Even though her womb still pulsed with the aftermath of her climax, desire sparked again.

All at once, Gabriel dragged his mouth away. "Forgive me, I have to be inside you." His hoarse whisper gusted across her ear, making her shiver. "I can't wait a moment longer." He ripped off his coat, then tore open the fall of his breeches, freeing his hot, hard erection. "Raise your leg and wrap it round my hip, darling girl."

As she did so, he slid an arm beneath her bottom, lifting her so she was on tiptoe. The broad head of his manhood nudged at her entrance.

"How . . . how will this work?" Balancing on one leg was difficult, so Arabella clutched at Gabriel's wide shoulders. "You're so tall. I don't think I can do this."

"Trust me, we'll manage." Gabriel hoisted her higher as though she barely weighed a thing. "Wrap your arms and legs about me, Bella," he rasped, "and hold on tight."

With both hands clasping her delectable arse, Gabriel lifted Arabella off the ground. Need seared though him like a lightning bolt, stealing his breath and his sanity. He had to have this beautiful, passionate, remarkable woman right now or he'd die. Pressing forward, he anchored her against the door and pushed into her glorious heat and wetness with one sure thrust.

Oh, God. Gabriel groaned and buried his face in Arabella's deliciously scented neck. Lust beat hot and hard through his veins, making his cock throb in a way it never had before. She felt so fucking good, he had to hold perfectly still to stave off the overwhelming urge to come immediately. How had he managed to go without this woman for so long?

As he fought to regain control, he was aware that Arabella's breathing was short and shallow. She gripped his shoulders so tightly, he suspected she'd drawn blood even through the cambric of his shirt.

Guilt crashed through him. Christ, this was only Arabella's second time, and he was taking her roughly like a doxy on the street. "Sweetheart," he gritted out. "Are you all right?"

She feathered a kiss across his temple. "Aye, I'm absolutely fine." Her soft, warm breath caressed his ear. "It burned a little at first but now it just feels wonderful. Marvelous in fact."

As if to prove her point, her internal muscles quivered and clenched around him so tightly, Gabriel wondered if she might be about to come too. "I'm going to move now," he murmured. "I'm afraid I won't last long."

"Do what you will," she whispered and kissed him again. "I've had my pleasure. Take yours."

Gabriel didn't need any further encouragement. Gripping Arabella's hips, he began to rock his pelvis, pumping in and out of her tight, moist heat. His frenzied, desperate plunging soon had him gasping and swearing and shaking. He could feel his orgasm gathering, charging toward him like an inexorable force, tightening his muscles, making his balls contract. Arabella was almost there too. Her silken, feminine core was rhythmically squeezing him, milking him, like a tightly fisted hand.

He bit down on her neck, then groaned, "Tell me you're mine, Bella." He had no idea why he wanted to hear her utter such a thing, but he did. "Tell me," he panted. "Say it."

"I'm yours," she cried on a ragged gasp. And then she came.

Screaming his name, Arabella spasmed around his swelling, throbbing cock, and Gabriel couldn't hold back. Passion rose in a hot, hungry wave and he gave in to its pull. Shuddering, moaning, he crushed Arabella's trembling body against the door as his seed erupted inside her in long, hard, violent spurts. Pleasure flooded through him in great pulsating waves. He'd never experienced a climax so sublime. So perfect.

It was earth-shattering. Cataclysmic.

Soul changing.

"Bella." Gabriel raised his head and sought her mouth. He'd just had her, yet he still craved her taste. Her warmth. "Sweet Jesus, that was astounding."

"Yes . . ." She kissed him back, her tongue dancing with his. "I'm beginning to understand why you enjoy bed sport so much."

"This wasn't sport. This was—" *Oh, hell.* Gabriel's heart all but stopped. "Arabella . . ." He caught her drowsy gaze. "I didn't withdraw. I came inside you."

"Oh . . ." Arabella's forehead dipped into a frown. One of her hands came up to cup his jaw, but then her kiss-swollen lips twitched with a small smile. "You're not about to tell me you have the pox or the clap after all, are you?"

He appreciated her attempt at levity but he couldn't return her smile. "This is serious, Bella. I promised you I wouldn't get you with child until my title was assured. Which doesn't look likely at this stage . . ." He sighed heavily. "I neglected to tell you I didn't find anything useful in Scotland. Not a goddamned thing."

Compassion lit Arabella's hazel eyes. "Don't worry. It will be all right. Whether you are the Earl of Langdale or simply Mr. Holmes-Fitzgerald, our child will be loved and will want for nothing. That's enough for me. Nothing else matters. Nothing at all."

A strange warmth suffused Gabriel's heart, and his vision blurred with unexpected tears. "I don't deserve you," he whispered.

She smiled tenderly. "Probably not. But I think we can muddle along together, don't you?"

This time Gabriel did smile back. Resting his forehead against Arabella's, he murmured, "Yes." He'd never been more sincere in his life.

CHAPTER 17

The Season has ended and no doubt many of the
ton are repairing to their country estates.

But never fear, our intrepid editors will be sure
to keep you abreast of all the latest scandals, both
big and small, wherever and whenever they
transpire . . .

The Beau Monde Mirror: The Society Page

Langdale House, St. James's Square, London

Later that day . . .

"More wine, Bella?"

Arabella tilted her head and smiled at Gabriel,
who was currently playing servant. "Yes, please," she said,
pushing aside her plate of cheese, sliced apricots, and plump
red grapes. "But only just a little."

They were eating a light alfresco dinner on the terrace
rather than in the stuffy dining room. Behind the horse
chestnut, the evening sky was awash with glorious shades
of burnished gold, orange, and crimson. The scent of summer roses and freshly cut grass drifted past on a light
breeze.

Gabriel replenished her glass with the pale but sweet
Rhenish wine, then subsided into his seat beside her with a
satisfied sigh. Even with smudges of fatigue beneath his
eyes and in a state of elegant dishabille—he currently wore

shirtsleeves, waistcoat, snug-fitting buckskins, and boots—he was effortlessly handsome. Sprawled in his chair with his long, muscular legs stretched out before him, Arabella was suddenly filled with a wave of desire. She wondered if Gabriel would want to bed her again tonight.

Anticipation curled through her, making her more light-headed than the wine had. What they'd done this afternoon was astounding. Her husband's lovemaking—dare she call it that?—was addictive, and even if she did fall pregnant, she wouldn't regret a single thing.

She pressed her hand against the peach muslin skirts hiding her belly. No doubt Gabriel would be even more vehemently opposed to her visiting the Seven Dials Dispensary if he suspected she carried his child. They hadn't settled their differences over that particular topic, but she was reluctant to spoil the evening, so she let the subject lie.

Gabriel reached for her hand and brought it to his lips. "I must confess, I'm exhausted, Bella."

She smiled at him. "I don't doubt it. The last few weeks have been hectic indeed."

He frowned and played with her fingers. His silver rings glimmered in the warm and golden gloaming. "Yes . . . What are your plans for tomorrow? Are you seeing any of your friends?" His tone was mild, but Arabella sensed he was fishing for information about Dr. Radcliff. She still couldn't quite believe he was jealous of her perfectly innocuous relationship with the doctor. It suggested that perhaps Gabriel did care for her a little, just as he'd claimed a week ago on their second wedding day.

He was waiting for her to respond, so she thought it best to put him out of his misery. "I'm going to see Lady Chelmsford and some of her other well-connected friends who are members of the Mayfair Bluestocking Society. Charlie, Sophie, and Olivia—she's just back from Brighton—will be there too. Charlie's aunt thinks the society will be most interested to hear about my plans for establishing an orphanage in Edinburgh. Such a project will require considerable capital, so they'd like to discuss holding an event to raise funds later this year. I'd also thought about writing to Bertie to see if his father's bank, Arbuthnott and Allan, might like to be involved in supporting the cause; the head office is in Edinburgh. I don't think you'd be too happy if I spent *all* your money."

Gabriel gave a wry smile. "I have plenty, don't you worry, pet. I don't know if I ever told you, but my mother was an heiress in her own right."

"No, I didn't know that."

"Yes, her father, Walter Standish, made a fortune from mining in Yorkshire. When he passed away, my mother inherited the lot. My father already had his own fortune, so you see"—he shrugged a shoulder—"I'm practically swimming in blunt."

"Goodness. Perhaps I should start *two* orphanages."

He kissed her hand again. "Start as many as you like. As long as you don't get too busy overseeing them." His gaze dipped to her belly and she blushed. "It might be the case that you'll be busy with your own child before too long."

Arabella drew breath to say she was certain she could manage being a mother *and* doing her charity work when Jervis appeared on the terrace. "My lord, my lady." He gave each of them a deferential bow. "I apologize for the interruption but"—his gaze transferred to Gabriel—"you have a visitor."

Gabriel straightened. "Really? At this hour? Can't whoever it is come back tomorrow? It must be getting onto nine o'clock?"

"Yes it is." A strange look flitted across Jervis's face. Was that little quirk at the corner of his mouth a smile? "But I do think you'll want to see this particular person, my lord."

"Well, who is it?" Gabriel scowled at his butler. "Do you have a name? Or a card?"

"Yes, indeed." Jervis approached and offered his master a small cream card embossed with gold lettering. "She gave me this. I hope you don't mind, but I installed her in the drawing room." He nodded at the set of French doors at the other end of the terrace.

"She?" As Gabriel took it and read the name, he shrugged. "I don't know a Mrs. Caroline Renfrew." He passed Arabella the card. "Do you, Bella?"

She shook her head.

And then Gabriel's whole demeanor changed. "Her name is Caroline?" His gaze sharpened on Jervis. "Out with it, man. Who the bloody hell is this woman?"

Jervis's face split with a broad smile. "I haven't seen her for fifteen years, but I do believe it's your mother, my lord."

What? Gabriel shot to his feet. He felt as though he'd just been struck by a bolt of lightning. "You're joking."

"Indeed I'm not, my lord."

Gabriel reached for Arabella with a shaking hand and caught her fingers in his. "I can hardly believe it, Bella. This could change everything for you and me. For us."

She smiled up at him. "I pray it is indeed the case, Gabriel."

Gabriel turned his attention to the still-grinning butler. "She's in the drawing room you say?"

"Yes, my lord."

"And you're sure it's my mother?"

"Yes. I'm completely sure."

Gabriel nodded. "All right." Judging by the name printed on her calling card, it seemed she must have heard about her husband's death and remarried, but then had decided to eschew her title, the Countess of Langdale, even though it was her right to still use it. He supposed he couldn't blame her. And it probably explained why he'd had so much trouble finding her.

Nerves skittered about his gut as he snagged his coat off the back of his chair. "How do I look, Bella?" he asked as he adjusted his cravat. His pulse hammered so fast, it felt as if he'd just boxed a round at Gentleman Jackson's.

She rose to her feet. "Handsome as always."

He dragged his fingers through his hair. "Christ," he muttered. "I probably need a haircut."

Arabella laughed. "Yes, you do. But I don't think she'll

care. She's your mother, Gabriel. And she's come home to see you."

He blew out a sigh. "Yes . . ." He clasped Arabella's hand in his again. "I hope to God she can help. This affects us both equally . . . and the future of our children."

She gave his fingers a gentle squeeze. "You know how I feel about that. But yes, I hope she can help too."

Drawing a deep breath, Gabriel took Arabella's arm, and together they entered the candlelit drawing room.

As soon as he saw the attractive, dark-haired woman in a well-cut, peacock blue gown, hovering by the empty fireplace, Gabriel knew it was his mother. Felt it to his very bones.

She turned away from her examination of a Meissen figurine on the pale gray marble mantelpiece and her green eyes, so like his own, came to rest upon him. A tremulous smile played about her lips. "Gabriel?" she murmured. A pale, slender hand fluttered to the strand of pearls at her throat. "I . . ." She swallowed and lifted her chin as she seemed to collect herself. "It's so wonderful to see you. It's been so long and I'd all but given up—" She broke off as her gaze flitted to Arabella. "I hope you can forgive my incoherence and apparent rudeness for intruding at such a late hour." She inclined her head. "I trust you are Lady Langdale?"

Arabella nodded. "Yes. And you're not intruding at all, Mrs. Renfrew."

"Please, call me Caro," she said, then frowned. "Unless, of course, you think that's too familiar . . ." Her mouth twitched with a nervous smile. "This encounter is so out of the ordinary, I'm not sure if the usual rules apply."

"I don't think it's too familiar at all. And please, call me Arabella."

His mother's hesitant yet yearning gaze returned to Gabriel. His mind and his heart were caught up in such a wild tumult, he struggled to find the right words to express everything he was feeling. Indeed, his tongue seemed to be tied to the floor of his mouth. Swallowing past a lump the size of a boulder in his throat, he whispered in a voice hoarse with emotion, "Would it be all right if I call you Mother?"

Tears shimmered in the former Countess of Langdale's emerald green eyes, and she bit her lower lip to still a tiny wobble. "Of course you may," she murmured. "I would like that very much."

To hell with it. Gabriel crossed the room in a handful of ground-eating strides and caught her up in a fierce hug. He felt his mother's arms come up around his back and settle lightly on his shoulders. Then her fingers curled into the fabric of his coat as her body quaked with gentle sobs.

Gabriel pressed his own wet cheek against her smooth brown hair. The delicate scent of orange blossoms wove around him like an enchantment, transporting him back to his childhood. Joy and sorrow mingled in his breast. The bittersweet memories made his heart ache. For so long he'd resented this woman for abandoning him, but now that she was here, his anger had dissolved faster than the sugar in his coffee.

At last, when they drew apart, his mother looked up at him with slightly puffy, red eyes. "You've grown into a fine young man, Gabriel," she murmured. "I'm glad to see that you're so settled and happy."

He frowned. *Settled and happy.* Never in his life had he thought himself to be either of those things. "I suppose married life suits me," he said, and was jolted by the thought that perhaps that wasn't a lie.

"Might I have a glass of brandy?"

"Of course."

He poured one for himself, one for his mother, and a whisky for Arabella, and then he joined his wife on a damask-upholstered sofa while his mother took the adjacent bergère.

She took a delicate sip of her drink, then her intelligent green gaze met his. "I heard you were looking for me? Is that true?"

"Yes, and it's been quite a challenge to say the least," he replied. "Almost like searching for a needle in a haystack, blindfolded with my hands tied behind my back. Of course, I had no idea you'd wed and might be using a different name."

"Yes, I'm so sorry." His mother's brow creased in sympathy. "It would have made it doubly difficult to find me."

Arabella sat forward and her incisive gaze met his mother's. "So how did you hear Gabriel was trying to contact you, Caro?" she asked in that smooth, unruffled way of hers that Gabriel secretly thought of as her doctor's voice.

"A few weeks ago, I was staying in Cologny near Geneva, when one of my oldest and dearest English friends, Lady Wilfred, who's been spending the summer in Nyon, paid me a visit. She mentioned a handsome young man with jet black curls and green eyes who went by the name of Gabriel Holmes-Fitzgerald, the Earl of Langdale, was looking for me." Her attention slid to Gabriel, and a concerned frown creased her brow. "I'm sorry if she was a bit standoffish at first. My friend can be quite the lioness. I'm afraid she's heard the most frightful gossip about you, and she thought you might take after your father a bit too much. But by the end of your visit, she was convinced you were of sound character and your intentions in seeking me out were sincere."

"I'm very glad," said Gabriel. Actually, he was relieved beyond belief. He found Arabella's hand on the sofa beside him and gave it a small squeeze. He wasn't unconvinced his remarkable wife was the one who'd made all the difference when she'd so ably assisted the baroness's grandson.

"When Lady Wilfred gave me your card, I thought I must be dreaming." A luminous smile lit his mother's eyes. "I was never sure if you received any of my letters, and there have been many times when I thought I might never—" Caroline broke off and wiped a tear from her cheek. Drawing a steadying breath, she added softly, "I hope you can forgive me for turning into a watering pot."

"There's nothing to forgive," murmured Gabriel. He reached out and touched her arm. "I take it Lady Wilfred informed you that I'd returned to England?"

"Yes and that you'd recently married a lovely young

Scottish woman. So"—Caroline smiled shyly—"here I am. I couldn't wait to see you. *Both* of you."

Gabriel smiled back. "You have no idea how pleased I am that you did decide to come all this way." It didn't sound like Lady Wilfred had mentioned he needed to speak with his mother about an urgent matter. But how best to broach the messy subject of Timothy's quest for the title? As he took a sip of his brandy and contemplated what to say next, his mother began to speak again.

"It shouldn't surprise me, but I can't believe how much you've changed," she said quietly. "Of course you would have. You were a slight, thirteen-year-old boy when I last saw you. And now look at you." She smiled at him with genuine fondness in her eyes, but then a haunted look crossed her face. "You're so much like Michael. The resemblance is uncanny."

Gabriel grimaced. He wasn't sure he wanted to hear that he looked exactly like a man he'd grown to despise. "I . . . I have some sad news actually. I'm not sure if you've heard but . . . did you know Uncle Stephen passed away just recently? He had a belly canker."

She nodded and her expression grew solemn. "Yes, I did know. I saw his obituary in the *Times*. The hotel I was staying at in Calais had all the English papers. He was a good man."

"He was . . ." Gabriel's tone was acerbic as he added, "But Timothy isn't."

"Oh, really?" His mother's forehead pleated into a frown. "That's such a shame."

"It's more than a shame I'm afraid." Gabriel held his mother's gaze. "You see, Timothy wants to challenge me for the title."

His mother's eyebrows shot up. "But that's absolutely ridiculous," she exclaimed. "He doesn't have a legitimate claim whatsoever. It's yours."

"Ah, but you see, that's the crux of the matter," said Gabriel drily. "My cousin believes *I'm* illegitimate."

His mother's brows snapped together. "But you're not." Her whole body bristled with righteous indignation. "You were born within wedlock."

"But you and Father eloped, did you not? Your irregular Scots marriage may not even be deemed valid given the evidence supporting it is so scant."

His mother sat up very straight. "Well, I can assure you that we were married legally," she said vehemently. "And here in England, not just over the anvil."

Shock jolted through Gabriel, and beside him, he heard Arabella gasp. "What . . . what did you just say?" he asked, unable to hide the note of incredulity from his voice.

"It's true your father and I eloped to Scotland," his mother said with the steady gaze of someone who spoke the absolute truth, "but when we returned to Hawksfell Hall in Cumberland, my father was waiting for us. He wanted our union to be recognized by the Anglican Church, so he carted Michael off to the Archbishop of York to obtain a bishop's license. Two days later, we married quietly in the private chapel at my family's estate near Appletreewick in Yorkshire. My father also insisted that a marriage contract be drawn up, otherwise he would disinherit me. 'An anvil wedding isn't good enough for my daughter. And you shall have your own money,' he said to me. Your uncle Stephen was one of the witnesses. And my godmother."

Am I dreaming, too? Gabriel shook his head. It seemed that Uncle Stephen had spoken the truth even though he was in a laudanum-addled state. "Please don't tell me you're jesting. I couldn't bear it if you were."

His mother's expression softened. "I assure you I'm not. Our union is recorded in the parish register at St. John's in Appletreewick, and I have a copy of the marriage lines. They're with my belongings at Mivart's Hotel—that's where my husband and I are staying while we're in town. I'll make sure you have the certificate first thing in the morning. Your title and your legacy are safe, Gabriel. You and your lovely wife"—she cast a smile Arabella's way—"have nothing to worry about."

Gabriel closed his eyes and reached blindly for Arabella's hand. She curled her fingers around his, and his heart swelled. "Thank you, Mother," he said at length when he felt sufficiently in control of his voice. "Words cannot express the gratitude I feel right now." How was it that in the blink of an eye, the burden that had been weighing him down for months and months had suddenly been lifted clean away? The relief coursing through his entire body was so heady, he was almost drunk with it.

"Think nothing of it, my son," she murmured. "I'm just so pleased that after all this time I can do something for you. I want nothing but the best for you, and of course"—she directed a smile at Arabella—"my new daughter-in-law."

Gabriel ventured to ask his mother about her own marriage. "Tell me about your new husband. I take it you are happy . . ."

His mother's smile widened. "Oh, yes. I've known Colonel Renfrew—Douglas—for some time, so when he proposed a little over a year ago, I couldn't say no. He's such a noble, kindhearted man. He resigned his commission after Waterloo, and so now we're free to roam about as we please. For the most part, though, we tend to divide our time between Edinburgh and the Continent." Her forehead creased into a troubled frown. "I'd learned about Michael's passing soon after it happened via British friends. They seemed to think it was some sort of illness that took him. I was in Paris at the time. Even though we were quite estranged, the news did come as quite a shock."

"Yes, he'd been ill." Gabriel didn't want to visit the fraught subject of his father's demise right now, so he said, "Why didn't you mention in your last letter—the one you sent in September last year—that you'd remarried?"

His mother's smile was faint. "I suppose I wasn't sure how you'd react. I hoped that you'd read both of the letters I sent to you after your father passed away, but I couldn't be sure. I imagine your father threw all the others straight into the fire."

"He didn't. He kept them all. After he died, I discovered them all bundled up neatly in a locked box in his desk. But I didn't look at a single one until this April when I needed to find you." Gabriel clenched his fist on his knee. "I was so angry, I just couldn't bring myself to read them before then . . ." He thought his bitterness had dissipated, but it seemed it was still simmering just below the surface.

His mother nodded, remorse etched into every feature. "I understand, Gabriel. Honestly, I do. What I did was unforgivable . . ." Her voice cracked and she swallowed hard. Her eyes shimmered with tears as she whispered, "Leaving you was the hardest thing I've ever had to do."

Gabriel couldn't disguise the harsh, accusatory edge to his voice as long-suppressed resentment and grief surged in a great wave. "Why? Why did you? I would have done anything to go with you, but you left me with him. *Abandoned* me. You knew how bad he was. How he despised me. There were rumors you absconded with a lover . . ." He shook his head, unable to go on.

"I'm so sorry, my dear boy. I deserve your censure. And there's no easy, neat answer." Caroline dashed tears from her eyes. "I think I might need a little more brandy."

Gabriel stood abruptly. "Of course." He needed more brandy too.

Once he'd replenished everyone's glasses, he reclaimed his seat and waited for his mother to continue her tale.

"I didn't want to leave you." She began so quietly, Gabriel almost missed what she said. Her breath caught, and her every word seemed to be weighted with guilt and regret as she added, "But I just couldn't stay . . ."

A sigh shivered through her, and a flicker of sadness crossed her features. "Your father and I, we both fell head over heels in love during my very first Season. Even though my father didn't approve of Michael whatsoever—he was a known rakehell—I was so besotted, I decided to risk all to be with him. I couldn't refuse him when he proposed that we elope. But then, a few years after we were wed"—her expression grew troubled—"Michael began to change . . ."

Her gaze flitted to Arabella. "I fear I'm going to be most indelicate. I hope you can forgive me."

Arabella smiled. Compassion gentled her voice. "I'm not easily shocked, Caro. But if you would like me to leave, I will."

"No, stay, Bella." Gabriel gripped her hand. "I don't want there to be any secrets between us."

His mother's nod was imperceptible, and a tear slipped down her ashen cheek. Inhaling another shaky breath, she continued her story. "After you were born, your father began to drink and gamble more than he'd ever done before. He was always restless and constantly sought new, more exciting diversions. But when he began to bed other women, quite openly, I couldn't bear it. I was heartbroken." Her gaze slid away and she sipped her brandy as though fortifying herself for what she would disclose next. "But it was worse than that," she whispered. "Michael wanted . . ." She touched her throat and closed her eyes as a violent shudder washed through her. "He wanted me to do all kinds of shameful, wicked things too. Depraved things not only with him but with other women. And sometimes other men. He insisted I drink to excess. Take laudanum. And I was so very terrified I'd get the pox."

Bloody blazing hell. Horror seized Gabriel's heart while black, bloody anger stormed through his veins. He gripped his brandy glass so tightly, he was surprised it didn't shatter in his hand. "I had no idea," he whispered. "The filthy, evil bastard. If he were still alive, I swear to God, I'd tear him limb from limb."

"You were so young, Gabriel, and such a kind, sensitive boy. I did my best to keep everything hidden from you. I don't know if you remember, but when you were seven years old, I tried to leave with you. Thanks to my father, I had the financial means to live independently, but everything went wrong."

A memory stirred of a carriage ride in the dead of night. Angry shouts and the blinding flash of a lantern. His father's face twisted with rage and his mother's sobs. Gabriel had always thought it was a nightmare, but it seemed it wasn't. "I remember," he murmured, his voice hoarse with strain. "We left Hawksfell late one night. But Father gave chase and caught up, didn't he?"

"Yes. He was so irate . . . He threatened to . . ." Caroline closed her eyes for a moment and her lower lip quivered.

"Suffice it to say, I knew I couldn't take you with me when I left him the second time. He'd hunt us to the ends of the earth to find you, his heir. So I waited until you were thirteen and had started at Eton. I convinced myself you didn't need me anymore. That you would be all right. That your uncle Stephen would look out for you. But I knew deep down those were the lies I needed to tell myself to justify my actions. There was never another man though. I left because I had to, not to be with someone else."

Gabriel felt as though a barely knit wound in his heart had just split open, releasing a fresh rush of pain. "I remember the letter you sent, just before my first semester ended. You promised me that you would come back someday. But you never did. You didn't even say goodbye." His voice emerged as a fractured whisper. "You lied to me. You broke my heart."

There were tears streaming down his mother's cheeks now. "I'm sorry, my baby boy. I'm so, so sorry." She pressed a hand to her lips, but she couldn't contain her sob.

In that instant, Gabriel's heart nearly cracked in two. Abandoning his seat, he gathered his mother into his arms. "I forgive you, Mama. I forgive you," he said in a choked voice against her hair. "I understand why you left. If I'd known you were living through such hell, I would've insisted you leave too."

Gabriel glanced over his mother's head and could see that Arabella was openly crying as well. He gave her a shaky smile, which she returned. There was no judgment in her gaze, only compassion. He was struck all over again at how remarkable she truly was.

And he realized, for the very first time, he never, ever wanted to put her through the agony his mother had been forced to endure.

His heart might not be capable of love, but for Arabella's sake, he wanted to be a better man. For her, he would curb his libertine ways and hold to his promise to stay true.

Sometime later, when they had all sufficiently recovered, his mother took her leave, promising to bring the marriage lines to Langdale House tomorrow morning.

"Your mother is quite an extraordinary woman," Arabella said as Gabriel closed the door to her sitting room. "And beautiful too. You look just like her."

He tugged his cravat loose. "Do you think so?"

"Aye. Definitely." Arabella blushed when he removed his coat and then began to work on his waistcoat buttons. She hovered in the middle of the Aubusson rug, a garden of dusky red and yellow roses beneath her pretty, slipper-shod feet. "What are you doing?" she asked breathlessly. Her warm hazel gaze drifted over his body, and when her pink tongue darted out to moisten her lips, lust arrowed straight to his groin.

He tugged his shirt off and shot her a wicked, lopsided smile to make her blush grow deeper. "It's obvious, isn't it? I'm undressing. And then I'm going to take great pleasure in removing every single stitch from your delightful body, dear wife. Oh so slowly." He advanced toward her with unhurried, purposeful strides. He lowered his voice. "We're going to make a baby, Arabella. And if you don't have any objections, I'd like to start right now."

"I don't," she said huskily. Even though her cheeks were bright with color, she lifted her chin, challenging him. "Not if you can make me feel as wonderful as you did this afternoon."

He caught her against his naked torso, thrilled to feel her pliant body shiver in his arms as he brushed a teasing kiss over her delicious, petal-soft lips. "That, my darling Bella, is something I can guarantee, not just tonight but every night. I've decided my new mission in life is to give you so much pleasure, you'll never want to get out of bed again."

The way she fervently returned his next kiss suggested that she really didn't object at all.

CHAPTER 18

❧

The *Beau Monde Mirror* has it on good authority that there was quite a set-to at a certain gentleman's club in St. James's.

Speculation is rife, but could there be some truth to the rumor that there was a very real pretender to the Errant Earl's title?

In any case, it seems there's no love lost between Lord L. and his equally errant cousin.

The Beau Monde Mirror: The Society Page

White's, St. James's, London

August 4, 1818

Gabriel leaned back in his seat, a brown leather wing-back chair in a relatively quiet corner of White's, and sighed with contentment. What a damn fine day he was having.

He was gratified that Arabella was doing what she loved. This afternoon she'd planned to meet with Lady Chelmsford, Lady Malverne, Lady Charlotte Hastings, and Miss Olivia de Vere at the Mayfair Bluestocking Society's rooms on Park Lane to discuss her charity work while he'd spent a few hours at Gentleman Jackson's with Nate, MacQueen, and Max. And now he and his friends were enjoying a quiet tipple to celebrate the fact that his title was well and truly safe before he headed home to spend the evening with his thoroughly delectable, thoroughly willing wife.

He certainly could get used to married life if it were like this all the time.

"I still can't believe your mother turned up in the nick of time," said Nate as he waved over a footman to refill their champagne glasses. "Talk about the devil's own luck."

"Yes indeed," agreed Gabriel. "To say I'm relieved would be an understatement. I wasn't looking forward to dealing with a very public legal battle. Things were bound to get messy. My family name has been dragged through enough muck over the years. I'm also glad for Arabella's sake. Having to face such a huge scandal when the ink is barely dry on our wedding certificate wouldn't have been fair to her either."

Max smirked. "Well, that's a first for you, Langdale. Showing genuine concern for a member of the fairer sex. I'm beginning to think you pair are a love match after all."

MacQueen nodded. "Aye, I swear he talked about naught else but his wife on the way to Gretna Green and back. If he didn't have his own carriage, I would've been tempted to throttle him. No offense intended, Langdale. Your wife is a bonnie lass to be sure, but for the life of me, I don't know what she sees in you."

Gabriel raised an eyebrow. "MacQueen, believe me, I'm still trying to work out what she sees in me too."

"Have you spoken with your cousin yet, to tell him the news?" asked Nate after a tray of bacon-wrapped oysters and Scotch quail eggs arrived. "I imagine he'll be none too pleased that his plans to become the next Earl of Langdale have been well and truly quashed."

"Not yet." Gabriel reached for a Scotch egg and popped it in his mouth. After a night of vigorous bed sport, and an afternoon of boxing, he was famished. He patted his breast pocket. "I have my mother's marriage lines right here, and I was rather hoping Timothy would drop by White's this afternoon or early this evening so I could show him he hasn't a hope in Hades of staking a claim."

MacQueen gave a low whistle. "That's a bold move, Lang-dale."

Gabriel shrugged. "You know me. I rarely do things by half measures."

"Oh, we know," said Nate with a wry smile.

Talk turned to what all their plans would be for what remained of the summer; Nate was returning to his Gloucestershire estate, Deerhurst Park, with Sophie on the morrow, Max intended to spend time at his ducal estate in Devonshire, and MacQueen would remain here in London. Even though he tended to avoid Hawksfell Hall like the plague because of its isolation as well as the painful memories it evoked, Gabriel decided he might like to show it off to Arabella after all. Yes, some quiet time rusticating by the shores of Grasmere, making new memories with his lovely wife, sounded perfect.

"He's here." Max leaned forward, elbows on his pantaloon-clad thighs. "And he's seen you."

Gabriel looked up. Sure enough, Timothy had walked through the door and was smirking at him from across the club floor. Sipping his champagne, Gabriel watched his cousin saunter toward him, Timothy's arrogant sneer growing more pronounced the closer he came.

Gabriel decided there was nothing he would enjoy more than wiping that smile off the conceited prick's face.

"It won't be long before they don't let your sort in here," Timothy said as he stopped, bold as you please, in front of their small group. His pale gray eyes, with their unusual feral light and pinprick pupils, were riveted on Gabriel.

So Timothy was still taking too much opium. Gabriel couldn't say he wasn't surprised. He put down his champagne glass with studied nonchalance and got to his feet. "That's where you're wrong, I'm afraid. Ennobled bastards like me are welcome anytime. Drug-addled, second-rate scoundrels with delusions of grandeur like you . . ." He shrugged a shoulder. "Perhaps not."

"You're accusing me of being drug addled?" Timothy scoffed. "Now that's rich. Even a simpleton would know that if you're a bastard, you're not entitled to the earldom."

An audience was gathering behind Timothy, but Gabriel didn't mind if his cousin was about to receive a public set-down. A lesson in humility was well overdue.

"Oh, I might've left out I meant 'bastard' in a purely figurative sense." Gabriel pulled out his parents' marriage lines from his coat pocket and unfolded the parchment. Stepping closer, he thrust the paper under Timothy's nose. "Not only were my parents married in Scotland, they wed a few days later in England. The bishop's license was issued by none other than the Archbishop of York." Gabriel's mouth twisted with a wry smile. "I know who's well and truly rogered, and it's not me, old chap."

Timothy's face paled and his eyes widened as his gaze slid over the paper. A muscle flickered in his jaw. Beneath his bespoke Savile Row tailored clothing, his whole body vibrated with barely constrained rage.

"What, you've got nothing to say, *cuz*?" prodded Gabriel, tucking the marriage lines back into his coat.

Timothy bared his teeth and leaned forward. "Fuck you and that piece of paper," he spat. Spittle appeared at the corner of his mouth, but he didn't wipe it away. "Everyone knows your mother was a whore anyway. She might've been married to the Earl of Langdale, but I'd wager my left testicle Michael Holmes-Fitzgerald wasn't your sire."

"How dare you insult my mother." With a low, guttural growl, Gabriel launched himself at Timothy, but Max and MacQueen were at the ready and grabbed him by the shoulders, forcibly hauling him back.

"Not here," warned Max in his ear as Gabriel struggled against the implacable hold of his friends, particularly MacQueen's; the man was built like a Highland bullock. "You don't want to get banned because of this cur. He's not worth it."

Max was right. Even so, it took some effort for Gabriel to conquer the overwhelming urge to knock the living daylights out of Timothy right in the middle of White's.

"I'd suggest you get out before I call you out for impugning my mother's character." Gabriel forced the threat through clenched teeth. "Even if you won't own up to your raging opium-eating habit, you'll at least acknowledge that in the field, I'm bound to put a bullet right between your eyes before you even *think* about pulling the trigger."

Although Timothy was visibly seething, his countenance paled. Everyone knew that Gabriel Holmes-Fitzgerald was a brilliant marksman. "You think you're so much better than everyone else, Langdale. But you're not. And someday, someone is bound to put you in your place."

Glancing over his shoulder, Timothy saw at least half a dozen other club members as well as a few of the burlier members of White's staff gathering behind him. "It's all right, gentlemen. The show is over. I'm leaving."

He threw Gabriel one last baleful look, then turned on his booted heel and stalked out.

When he'd gone, Max and MacQueen released Gabriel, and he rolled his shoulders to ease the tension. "Shall we finish our champagne, my friends?" he asked as he flicked out his coattails and took his seat.

"Aye," said MacQueen, settling back in his leather chair. "Your cousin is goddamned lucky that none of us"—his steely gaze flickered between Max and Nate—"decided to call him out either."

Max helped himself to a bacon-wrapped oyster. "In any case, he's sure to get blackballed from the club after this incident."

An hour later, after they'd quaffed a second bottle of champagne, Gabriel and Nate both took their leave, pleading their wives expected them home. Shrugging off Max's and MacQueen's good-natured ribbing about how there was nothing more pitiable than a henpecked husband, they emerged onto St. James's Street. Malverne House was in the vicinity of St. James's Square so Nate and Gabriel began to amble down the busy thoroughfare together, enjoying the late afternoon sunshine. They hadn't progressed all that far when a shiny black town coach pulled alongside them and the carriage door was thrown open.

A husky but very feminine voice floated out. "Lord Langdale."

Gabriel halted in his tracks. "Lady Astley?"

From beneath the brim of his beaver hat, he squinted into the shadowy interior of the carriage. Yes, it was indeed the Countess of Astley who'd called his name.

What on earth did *she* want?

Beside him, Nate frowned. "Be careful, old chap," he murmured.

Gabriel took several steps toward the open door, and as he did so, Camilla, Lady Astley sat forward; the exotic, musky scent she used drifted out, enveloping him in a sensual cloud.

"I'm rather busy right now," he said in a low, tight voice. Salacious memories of Camilla tangled up with him in fine linen bedsheets rose unbidden in his mind, but he firmly pushed them away.

Tightly curled flaxen ringlets brushed her flushed cheeks as Camilla leaned toward him, her gloved hand outstretched. "Lord Langdale, please . . . I must talk with you." Her countenance was wan, the skin pulled tightly over her high cheekbones.

"Are you all right?" he asked.

She shook her head. "No, I'm not." Her gaze flitted to Nate, his mouth flat with suspicion, before returning to Gabriel. "Please, my lord. I beg of you. You're the only one who can help."

The beseeching, harrowed look in her blue eyes was one Gabriel had never seen once during their wild affair earlier in the year. Something was clearly wrong. But having a discussion about the matter in the street was inadvisable, if not out-and-out perilous. If Lord Astley ever found out about this meeting, the cuckolded earl would be sure to call him out.

Even worse would be Arabella's reaction. He'd promised her that he would stay true. She'd never forgive him if she thought he'd strayed.

A tear trickled down Camilla's cheek, and Gabriel swore beneath his breath. A multitude of misgivings eating at him, he sighed heavily and climbed inside the carriage. "I won't be long but you'd best go on without me," he said as he glanced back at Nate. "Safe travels to Gloucestershire." And then he pulled the door shut.

Hyde Park, Mayfair

"What a glorious afternoon," declared Charlie as she slid her arm through Arabella's. "Taking a walk with you all"— she glanced back over her shoulder at Olivia and Sophie, who were following close behind them—"is almost like old times at Mrs. Rathbone's Academy, isn't it?"

Arabella laughed. "A little. But instead of Mrs. Rathbone haranguing us for not marching briskly enough, we have a retinue of our own servants keeping pace."

A small knot of footmen in three different kinds of livery denoting the households of Langdale, Westhampton, and Malverne trailed behind their mistresses—it was quite an entourage and seemed quite ridiculous, but Arabella understood why. A countess, a viscountess, and the unwed daughter of an earl along with their heiress friend simply didn't go walking about in public places without suitable protection.

The walk had been Charlie's idea when the Mayfair Bluestocking Society's meeting about charitable endeavors drew to a close. As the society's rooms were on Park Lane, they had but to cross the road to reach Hyde Park. Lady Chelmsford, who also resided on Park Lane, had repaired to her town house, claiming her bones ached far too much, but they were all welcome to join her for a late afternoon tea after they concluded their stroll. Arabella was quite happy to do so given Gabriel was currently busy with his own friends.

She smiled to herself and her pulse quickened as she recalled everything she and Gabriel had done last night. And would probably do again tonight. She was beginning to understand why Sophie always looked so aglow.

Even though the Season had drawn to an end, the park's thoroughfares were still quite abuzz. Charlie gave Arabella a little prod in the ribs with her elbow as they wandered across the grass to avoid a curricle bowling by at a rapid pace. "Penny for your thoughts, Arabella. Does that little secret smile of yours mean what I think it means? Have you and Gabriel settled your differences?"

Arabella blushed. "Yes. We have," she whispered. "Not only that, because his title is now well and truly safe, we're going to try for a baby. I promised him an heir." She'd told Charlie, Sophie, and Olivia about Caroline Renfrew's opportune arrival before the meeting started, and naturally, they were all delighted for her and Gabriel.

Charlie gave her arm a small squeeze. "Oh, I'm so excited for you, Arabella. I'm waiting for Sophie and Nate to announce any day now that she is increasing."

They began to follow a path that wended its way toward the Serpentine. When they paused by the banks of the lake beneath the shade of a willow to watch the swans and ducks drifting past, a tiny bubble of laughter escaped Olivia.

Arabella, Sophie, and Charlie all blinked at her in surprise. Olivia was always so quiet and serious, it was most out of character for her to have a fit of the giggles. "What's so amusing, pray tell?" asked Charlie.

Even though Olivia wore a shady poke bonnet, it didn't hide her bright blush that precisely matched the fuchsia pink of her well-cut walking gown. "Oh, dear. I th-think that every time I see a b-body of water, I'm going to be reminded of sea bathing in B-Brighton."

"You went sea bathing?" exclaimed Sophie. "In one of those machines?

"Yes," Olivia said. "M-my aunt Edith wanted to try it as her physician told her it was useful for alleviating the symptoms of rheumatism."

"Aye, that's quite true," added Arabella. "My grandfather would often recommend taking the waters in Scarborough to his patients."

"What was it like?" asked Sophie, her blue eyes wide with interest. "I think I would be quite frightened to try it. I'd worry I'd slip and drown. And do those bathing machines really conceal you from the sight of others?"

"Oh yes, they do. N-no one at all can see you behind the enormous canvas awning. And the water wasn't too deep. Actually"—Olivia lowered her voice and beckoned them all closer, away from the footmen—"it was quite exhilarating. Especially when I removed the horrid flannel garment my aunt gave me to wear."

"Olivia de Vere. Don't tell me you bathed naked in public. You wicked girl," whispered Charlie in mock horror, but then she grinned. "I'm very impressed."

Olivia's mouth twitched with mirth. "It's all your fault, Charlie, for lending me those wicked memoirs about Miss Fanny Hill. They've put all sorts of naughty ideas into my head."

"They're certainly wicked," agreed Sophie with a small, knowing smile. "But most enlightening."

"Goodness gracious. I think I've missed out by not reading them," remarked Arabella.

Charlie gave her a gentle poke. "You're married to one of London's most notorious rakehells, Arabella. You of all people would *not* be missing out."

Olivia's smile faded to be replaced by the glummest expression Arabella had ever seen. "I sometimes wish I could meet a rakehell who'd fall madly in love with me," she said. "I caught a glimpse of my neighbor, Lord Sleat, earlier today as I was leaving our town house, but he didn't notice me. He was striding off somewhere or other."

"Oh, he was probably meeting up with Gabriel, Nate, and Max, the Duke of Exmoor," said Arabella. "Gabriel told me they were all going boxing and then meeting at White's."

Charlie folded her arms and tapped her chin with a finger. The sunlight reflecting off the lake made her topaz brown eyes shine like gold. "We must engineer a social occasion to get you two to meet. I'm sure Lord Sleat is just right for you, Olivia."

"I wish I possessed your optimism, Charlie," replied Olivia with a wistful sigh. "At least my c-cousin Felix is away on the C-Continent so I don't need to worry about him proposing anytime soon. There's b-bound to be an enormous to-do when I refuse him."

Arabella reached out and squeezed her arm. Olivia had been concerned for some time that her aunt and uncle may try to force her to wed their son to keep the money in the family. "If you need anything, you only have to ask."

"Yes," agreed Sophie. "If we weren't leaving for Deerhurst Park early tomorrow, I'd throw a soiree and exhort Nate to invite Lord Sleat along. And I wouldn't care if he said Hamish MacQueen is too wicked for you. It's not up to him to decide what's best for my friends."

"It's such a nuisance that the Season is over," added Charlie. "I'd ask my aunt to throw a dinner party, but I'm afraid she's accompanying me to Elmstone Hall. We leave the day after tomorrow. But perhaps we can arrange something when we're all back in town in October. I imagine your aunt and uncle won't give you permission to attend unless my aunt acts as chaperone again."

Olivia's doe brown eyes lit with a warm smile. "Yes, that's true," she said. "Even so, that sounds wonderful. October isn't that far away." She turned her soft gaze on Arabella. "Are you repairing to Gabriel's estate up north?"

"I . . . I expect so." With a mounting sense of dismay, Arabella was suddenly aware that all her friends were looking at her expectantly and she hadn't a clue how to respond. It would suggest that she and Gabriel weren't as close as she'd led them to believe. Dissembling seemed like the best option. "We've been so busy of late. You know with traveling, and the wedding. And then there was this title business and Gabriel's mother arrived . . . We haven't spoken about his . . . I mean *our* plans just yet."

"I've no doubt you will," said Charlie with a soft smile of understanding. She took Arabella's arm. "Come, let's go back to Chelmsford House for that spot of tea my aunt promised us."

Pausing on the edge of the pavement as they waited to cross Park Lane, Arabella studied the passing traffic. When a smart, black town coach rolled close by, she felt Charlie tense beside her.

"What's wrong?" she asked.

Charlie patted her arm. "Nothing at all really," she said as they crossed the road. "I just saw the Astleys' carriage and caught a glimpse of the countess through the window.

Of course you don't have anything to worry about now that you and Gabriel are growing closer."

Arabella sighed as they gained the pavement on the other side and headed toward Chelmsford House. "I really wish Lady Astley would quit town. Bumping into her could prove rather awkward. But perhaps we will be leaving soon too. I must confess, a quiet sojourn in the country sounds rather appealing. And Hawksfell Hall is bound to be lovely."

"I'm sure it is," agreed Charlie with a reassuring smile. "I believe it's on the shores of lake Grasmere. While it's not Switzerland, you'll have beautiful views all the same."

During afternoon tea, as Arabella observed Sophie's radiant happiness—especially when she talked about Nate—her own contentment dimmed.

One thing Sophie and Nate had, that she and Gabriel didn't, was love. Gabriel had promised to be faithful, but could she take him at his word? She didn't want to compare him to his father, Michael, but after Gabriel was born, he'd grown bored with Caroline. What if faithlessness ran in the family? Did an emotionally uncommitted rakehell ever really change his spots?

She trusted Gabriel wouldn't look elsewhere until after she'd given him a son. But over time, his ardor was bound to fade. Without love, what was there to bind him to her?

Nothing at all.

It was a dispiriting, even heartbreaking thought. As she listened to Lady Chelmsford chat enthusiastically about raising funds for dispensaries and orphanages and foundling homes, she thanked God she had work to fill her life. And her friends.

And perhaps one day, a child.

If only she could have her husband's love, then life would be perfect indeed.

Somewhere on the streets of London . . .

Gabriel settled into a corner of the Astleys' carriage as it moved off, and blew out a disgruntled sigh. In such close quarters, his former paramour's perfume was quite cloying, and he had to stifle the urge to throw open a window. Strange how he'd never noticed that before.

"What's wrong, Camilla?" he asked carefully as he removed his beaver hat and placed it on the velvet upholstered seat beside him. "Whatever the matter is, it sounds rather urgent."

A sigh shivered out of the countess. "Thank you for agreeing to talk with me," she said in that distinctive, sultry voice of hers that he'd once found so appealing. "And yes, it is urgent."

Gabriel cocked an eyebrow, waiting for her to elaborate. When she didn't, impatience sharpened his tone. "I don't have all day."

"I know," she said in an uncharacteristically demure tone. Attired in a dusky blue silk gown with a matching spencer and bonnet trimmed with ivory satin roses and seed pearls, she was the epitome of tonnish elegance. Yet Gabriel knew from experience that she was a voracious lover with wild tastes in the bedroom. "It's just so very good to see you."

"If this is an attempt to inveigle your way back into my bed, it won't work. I'm married now—"

"No. No it's not," she said. She entwined her gloved fingers together and sat up very straight. "You made it very clear that you do not care for me after that terrible night at Astley House. Because if you did, you would have responded to my letter."

Gabriel kept his face impassive. He wasn't about to tell her that he'd only glanced through it before throwing it into the fire. "Well, if you simply wish to berate me, you can let me out here." He raised his fist to rap on the coach's forward-facing window, but Camilla held up a hand.

"Wait, I'll get to the point," she said. There was genuine panic in her eyes. "It's about my husband, George . . and me."

Gabriel rubbed his jaw. "Yes?"

"And you . . ."

"What about me?" Irritation sparked. "I haven't seen you for months, Camilla."

"I know, I know." She closed her eyes as though gathering her thoughts. "I'm not explaining myself very well, I'm afraid."

Again Gabriel waited. The carriage rocked as they rounded a sharp corner, and he glanced out the window. They were in Mayfair, heading toward Park Lane. Christ, he hoped Arabella didn't see him. The Mayfair Bluestocking Society's rooms were close by.

When he turned his gaze back to Camilla, he discovered she was studying him. "I'll try to be more succinct," she said. "After our affair ended and I heard you left town for the Continent, I tried very hard to reconcile with my husband. For some years, we've been living separate lives. George kept a mistress and I dallied with whomever I took a fancy to. He tended to turn a blind eye as long as I was discreet, but with you, I wasn't. I was in love with you and I didn't care who knew."

Gabriel held her gaze steadily. "I never promised you love, Camilla. From my perspective, it was a purely carnal affair."

"I know that," she said crossly. "But sometimes falling in love cannot be helped. It just happens." She drew a calming breath. "Anyway, I digress. What I'm trying to say is, George and I were beginning to repair our relationship, but then you came back to town. And even though you are newly wed, and I've reassured him I'm devoted to him, he's convinced you and I have taken up again. I cannot reason with him and now . . ." She swallowed and tears glazed her eyes. "Now he's threatening to divorce me even though I've told him over and over again there's nothing between you and me any longer. I suppose I cannot blame him for not trusting me, but it really isn't fair."

Gabriel scowled, resisting the urge to be moved by her stricken expression and desperate air. "I'm sorry, but what do you expect me to do about it? Last time I met your husband, he very much wanted to kill me." In hindsight, it had been beyond foolish for him to accept Camilla's invitation to the ball at Astley House in April. He'd been reckless and too cocksure. "I doubt he'd listen to a word I say, let alone believe me."

"But can't you at least try?" Camilla pleaded. "You can swear on your honor as a gentleman that we are no more. I couldn't bear the public humiliation if George were to divorce me. It just isn't done. Aside from that, I realize I do indeed care for him. Please, Gabriel." Tears brimmed in Camilla's eyes again and overflowed. Her fulsome bottom lip quivered. "You're my only hope."

Hell. Gabriel ran a hand down his face. The niggle of guilt he'd been ignoring wormed its way to the surface of his conscience. "Very well," he said with a heavy sigh. "I'll do it. Will he be in tomorrow morning?"

"Yes. Yes he will." Camilla's whole face brightened. "Eleven o'clock is a good time. He'll be in his study, going through his accounts."

Gabriel knocked on the carriage's front window and it drew to a halt. They were on Bond Street.

"I'd appreciate it if you could ensure your husband's dueling pistols aren't loaded and that there aren't any sharp objects in the room," he said as he jumped out of the carriage onto the street.

"Of course." Camilla raised a hand in farewell. A grateful smile hovered on her lips. "Until tomorrow."

Gabriel gave a curt nod and shut the door. Putting his beaver hat on, he strode down the street in the direction of home where his beautiful, adorable, and fascinating wife waited for him. He didn't want to visit Astley House, but now that he had Arabella in his life, the sooner he permanently slammed the door on this whole sorry chapter involving Camilla, the better.

CHAPTER 19

Has the newly wedded Errant Earl taken up with a former paramour already?

There have been reports that Lord L. was seen entering the carriage of Lady A. late yesterday, not far from a well-known gentlemen's club on St. James's Street.

Once a filthy libertine always a filthy libertine, it would seem . . .

The Beau Monde Mirror: The Society Page

Langdale House, St. James's Square, London

August 5, 1818

"More hot chocolate, my lady?" asked Soames politely. "I can ask Cook to make another pot."

Arabella inclined her head. "Yes, thank you. And the morning papers if they've arrived."

"Of course, my lady. I'll check with Jervis." As the young footman bowed and quit the terrace, Arabella smiled after him.

She was enjoying a lazy breakfast in the warm August sunshine. The sky was a blazing, glorious blue, the bees buzzed about the summer roses, and a light breeze stirred the leaves of the horse chestnut. After another wonderful night spent in Gabriel's arms, she was as content as a cat who'd just lapped up a whole bowl of cream. Her husband was the most magnificent, attentive lover she could ever wish for, and this morning she refused to entertain thoughts about whether or not he would tire of her. It was useless to speculate about what-ifs. She'd given up guarding her heart long ago, so for now, she would just have to trust him or go mad.

Last night over dinner, Gabriel had also discussed traveling to Hawksfell with her in a few days' time. Arabella would miss her friends and the opportunity to put more of her charity plans into action straightaway, but as Olivia had declared yesterday, October wasn't that far off.

Of course, because they were quitting London so soon, Gabriel was inordinately busy. He'd risen early, gone riding in Hyde Park, and after returning and changing, he'd left again to attend to his business affairs before Arabella had even woken up. But to her delight, he'd placed a rose upon the pillow beside her with a small note informing her that he'd be back by early afternoon.

Arabella finished the last of her hot chocolate. She supposed she should get changed out of her simple day gown and don something smart and fashionable, as there were a number of matters she had to attend to as well. She should to speak to Mrs. Mayberry as she still hadn't secured a lady's maid. And after yesterday's meeting, she needed to write to Dr. Radcliff about a few things. The Mayfair Bluestocking Society was keen on establishing dispensaries in other areas of London such as Southwark and St. Giles, and they also wished to invite the physician to one of their meetings. And Lady Chelmsford had offered to liaise with the board members of the Foundling Hospital, but she wished to meet with Dr. Radcliff first.

Such meetings and introductions would need to wait until the autumn, but there was no time like the present to set the wheels in motion. Arabella sighed. It would be much easier to arrange everything if she could see Dr. Radcliff in person at the Seven Dials Dispensary before she left London. But because Gabriel had been so upset, she was reluctant to create discord between them when things seemed to be going so very well.

One of Gabriel's footmen had already retrieved all her belongings from the clinic the day before so she didn't even have that excuse to justify a visit.

Soames returned with the papers and hot chocolate, and after slipping on her glasses, Arabella perused the front pages of the *Times*, the *Morning Post*, and the *Morning Herald*. And then at the bottom of the pile, she saw the *Beau Monde Mirror*.

She pulled a face as she withdrew it and flicked it open. She knew Gabriel subscribed to the high-society scandal rag that purported to be a newspaper, but she tended to eschew it given the editors had dubbed her, Sophie, Olivia, and Charlie "Disreputable Debutantes" on more than one occasion.

There was bound to be something about Gabriel in here. During dinner last night, he told her all about his altercation with Timothy in White's yesterday. Curious as to what had been said about her husband, she skimmed through the newspaper until she reached the Society page.

And then her world disintegrated as one of the articles leapt out at her:

Has the newly wedded Errant Earl taken up with a former paramour already?

There have been reports that Lord L. was seen entering the carriage of Lady A. late yesterday . . .

Oh, God. Arabella's breath caught on a sob as horror lanced through her body, almost cleaving her heart in two. *Please, please, dear Lord above, let this be false. Just nasty, unfounded gossip without a speck of truth to it.*

With shaking hands, Arabella put down the newspaper and closed her eyes against a wave of hot, stinging tears.

But what if it *was* true? As much as she hated to admit it, the story about the Disreputable Debutantes' expulsion from Mrs. Rathbone's Academy three years ago had not been false at all. What if Gabriel *had* spent part of the afternoon with Lady Astley after he'd quit his club? Was he truly capable of bedding the countess and then coming home and lying with her, his wife, but a few hours later? Of making love to her all night long? Of whispering all kinds of wicked yet wonderfully sweet words in her ear until she'd begun to believe she was beautiful in his eyes?

Could he really be that two-faced and cruel?

Arabella pushed a tightly clenched fist against her mouth to stop another sob escaping.

Her husband had been a libertine. He'd admitted he possessed a large appetite for all things carnal. Lady Astley was beautiful, and by all accounts, the pair had clearly shared a grand passion. Arabella wanted to trust her husband, but how could she when he didn't love her?

Her mind reeling, Arabella rose shakily to her feet. She was torn between the desire to confront Gabriel and the impulse to run far, far away. To curl up and hide somewhere like a wounded animal that needed to lick its wounds.

One thing was clear, she wouldn't be able to sit here, waiting for him to come home. It was only ten o'clock, and he might not be back for hours. She'd learned long ago that keeping busy was best when one had been dealt a blow of such magnitude.

Brushing away her tears so the servants wouldn't see she'd been crying, Arabella quit the terrace and made her way to her room. She'd don her brand new leaf green walking gown with black frogging and then call for Gabriel's town coach to be brought around. There was no way she'd be able to concentrate on writing letters to Dr. Radcliff, so she was better off going to see him in Seven Dials instead. But she wouldn't deliberately provoke Gabriel's ire—she'd take several footmen with her, and she'd ask them to stay posted outside the dispensary the entire time she was there, which wouldn't be long. And then she'd go and visit Charlie at Hastings House in Berkeley Square. Even though her friend would be busy getting ready to leave for Gloucestershire on the morrow, she was sure to lend a sympathetic shoulder to cry on.

She rather hoped Charlie had an oilskin coat handy, as she had a storm cloud's worth of tears to shed.

Astley House, Cavendish Square, London

Drawing a deep breath, Gabriel raised his gloved hand and rapped sharply on the polished front door of Astley House. He still hadn't worked out why he was doing this for Camilla. No, that was a lie. Deep down, he supposed he felt a tiny bit sorry for her. And yes, somewhere in his heart, there was a smidgeon of reluctant guilt.

He sighed. He must be going soft at the ripe old age of eight-and-twenty.

But then another thought occurred to him, one that startled him from the top of his head to the tips of his Hessian-booted toes. Perhaps Arabella had exerted a hitherto unrecognized but nonetheless powerful influence over him. Could it be that his sweet, noble, kindhearted wife had somehow altered the very fabric of his misbegotten being so that a thread of honor now ran through him?

It was an intriguing, if not altogether perplexing notion.

He just hoped to God that Astley didn't try to put a bullet in him as soon as he set foot in the house.

After half a minute, the door opened to reveal a vaguely familiar footman who looked suitably dispassionate . . . until he took a good look at Gabriel's face; the way his eyes widened, it was clear he recalled Gabriel's brazen visits to Astley House earlier in the year.

The young man's Adam's apple bobbed nervously above his starched cravat—no doubt he'd been warned by his master not to admit the Earl of Langdale—but as he opened his mouth to speak, a pale-faced Camilla appeared behind his shoulder. "I'll look after his lordship from here, thank you, Mathers," she said quietly.

The footman blushed, and Gabriel cocked a sardonic brow as he handed over his beaver hat and gloves. The lad had clearly misinterpreted Camilla's use of the phrase *look after*. Good Lord, even the servants thought he was here to swive their mistress again. This didn't auger well for what lay ahead.

Camilla, looking for all the world like a slender wraith in a gown of filmy white muslin, ushered him through the vestibule, past the marble staircase that led up to her bedchamber, and toward the hall that would take them to her husband's study.

"Does he know I'm coming?" asked Gabriel in a low voice.

Camilla shook her head. "No, I thought he might bar you from entering the house altogether if he knew."

Wonderful. Astley would be mightily impressed when Gabriel ambushed him in his own den. He really hoped the man didn't keep his dueling pistols in his desk, or he was a dead man.

They paused before a set of polished walnut doors, and Camilla exhaled a shaky sigh. Her blue eyes were filled with apprehension. "I'm afraid he's been in a foul mood all this morning. I'm not sure why. He's barely said two words to me. But thank you for doing this." She laid a slender hand on his arm. "I do think it will help my cause immensely if you unequivocally deny we're still having an affair."

"For my sake as well as yours, I sincerely hope so," murmured Gabriel. Sending up a silent prayer to heaven that he'd soon be walking out of here and returning home to Arabella, he squared his shoulders, lifted his chin, and pushed through the door.

As soon as Lord Astley saw him, he shot to his feet. "What in the devil's name are you doing here in my house, you filthy dog?" he roared. "How dare you set foot in here?"

Gabriel hovered by the door, prepared to bolt if Astley made a move to grab a pistol or even throw a letter opener or penknife at him. Even though the man was of middling age and developing a paunch, he was in high dudgeon. No doubt he could do some damage if Gabriel wasn't ready to dodge anything headed his way. He raised his hands in a placatory gesture. "I'm just here to talk, Astley. Nothing else. It's come to my attention that you seem to be laboring under the misapprehension that your wife and I—"

"Oh, there's no misunderstanding," bit out the scarlet-faced earl. He lifted a newspaper in the air and snapped it open. "As soon as you returned to town, I suspected you were fucking my wife again. And now I read this." He jabbed his finger at the paper, and Gabriel realized with mounting horror that it was a copy of the *Beau Monde Mirror*.

"Astley, you know that paper contains nothing but utter rubbish—"

"Do you deny that you hopped into my wife's carriage yesterday afternoon? Don't try to tell me you were both off to do a spot of shopping on Bond Street." His voice dripped with sarcasm.

Camilla, who'd been quivering just outside the open door, stepped into the room. "George," she began. "It's not what you think. It's true I saw Lord Langdale yesterday, but it was only to—"

"You. Shut it," he growled. He threw the paper down on his desk, and his blistering gaze landed on Gabriel again. "And you, get out before I put a shot through your unscrupulous black heart."

Gabriel crossed his arms over his chest to indicate he wasn't budging and leveled a cool stare at the irate earl. His gut told him Astley had more bark in him than bite, but all the same, he couldn't afford to let down his guard, even for a second. "Your wife and I are not having an affair, Astley. That's what I came here to tell you."

The earl leaned forward, his hands splayed on the ox-blood red leather blotter. It was the stance of a bull ready to charge. "All evidence to the contrary," he snarled.

"Yesterday, Lady Astley entreated me to speak with you. To tell you that we *have not* picked up where we left off. That's all. Nothing else. If you hadn't heard, I'm newly married and very happily so. I wouldn't jeopardize what I have with Arabella, my wife, for the world."

Astley made a scoffing sound in his throat. "Why should I believe a word you say, Langdale?"

"Because . . ." Gabriel paused as the most astounding realization struck him. He knew exactly why, and idiot that he was, it had taken him far too long to see something that should have been blindingly obvious for days, if not weeks. Firming his gaze and his voice, he said, "Because I love my wife with my entire heart, and I would never, ever betray her. That's why. And if you don't believe me, I don't really care a jot." He stepped back toward the door, then stopped on the threshold. "And maybe, just maybe," he added over his shoulder, "if you stopped screwing other women and paid some attention to your own wife for once, perhaps you might be happy too. Good day to you."

When Gabriel reached the street, he couldn't keep the spring from his step or the grin from his face. While it was indeed fortunate that Lord Astley hadn't tried to castrate or murder him, that wasn't the main reason for the pure elation suffusing his heart and his soul.

He was in love. Undeniably, completely, not-a-doubt-in-his-mind in love.

He wanted to carve it in stone and shout it from the rooftops. From the spires of Westminster Abbey and St. Paul's and St. George's. From the Tower of London and in the halls of Parliament. He was in love with Arabella, his wife. And he couldn't wait to tell her.

The Seven Dials Dispensary, Covent Garden, London

The dispensary was far less crowded than the first time Arabella visited; there were only about a dozen patients gathered in the front room, so she didn't need to push her way through to Dr. Radcliff's assistant at the back. Dressed as she was in her couture walking gown, Arabella certainly received her fair share of curious, if not outright hostile looks. In hindsight, it had been silly of her to don attire that marked her as an outsider. But then she'd also arrived in a grand town coach with the Langdale coat of arms emblazoned on the door, and Soames, in his emerald satin waistcoat, black livery jacket with gold frogging, and a powdered peruke, stood out like a sore thumb as he waited by the front door.

The assistant indicated Arabella should take a seat as Dr. Radcliff was presently busy with a patient. As she waited, the pain of Gabriel's apparent betrayal throbbed like a deep wound inside her. She wanted to remain impartial rather than assume the worst of her husband, but the old, familiar voice in her head that whispered she was far too plain and practical and dull to hold Gabriel's interest kept intruding into her thoughts.

To try to distract herself, she began to examine the waiting room's other occupants. There were several young mothers with children on their hips or clinging to their skirts. An older woman with a bruised, swollen eye sat near the door, and a man nursing his arm in a makeshift sling slouched by the front window. A tall man in a long dark coat and a felt hat pulled low over his brow pushed past Soames and limped across the room to claim a vacant seat in the far corner.

Arabella frowned when she noticed he wore breeches of a decent quality and superior cut rather than workaday trousers, and his top boots were highly polished rather than dusty and scuffed. *How odd.* As her wary gaze sought his face— the wide brim of his hat cast his features into shadow—she sensed rather than saw the man was staring directly at her. Indeed, his regard was so intense, his manner completely still yet somehow agitated, the hairs on the back of her neck began to rise. She was about to attract Soames's attention when the assistant called her name.

Chiding herself for being fanciful, Arabella gathered up her reticule and followed the woman into the dispensary's treatment room.

"Lady Langdale, I did not expect to see you so soon," said Dr. Radcliff as soon as she walked through the door. He smiled as he gestured toward a slender woman standing to one side of his desk. "You remember Miss Helen Reid, don't you? She was the matron at the Foundling Hospital."

Arabella blinked in surprise. "Oh, yes. Yes I do," she said as the dark-haired woman dipped a small curtsy. "Good morning to you, Miss Reid. I take it you no longer work at the hospital?"

"No, I don't, Lady Langdale," she replied, and a bright blush pinkened her cheeks. "When Dr. Radcliff opened the dispensary and asked if I would like to work alongside him, I couldn't refuse. He's such a wonderful doctor."

"Miss Reid and I are engaged," said Dr. Radcliff as he cast Miss Reid a fond look. "We are to be married at the end of the month."

"Oh, how lovely. Congratulations to you both," said Arabella with a heartfelt smile. Perhaps Dr. Radcliff had harbored a tendre for the attractive nurse all along. That would certainly explain why he hadn't corresponded with her while she was away. "I'm very happy for you," she added. And she genuinely was.

"Now, what can I do for you today, my lady?" Dr. Radcliff gestured to the wooden chair that still sat in front of the desk. "Last time we met, you were telling me all about your marvelous philanthropic ventures. I was discussing them with Helen the other day"—he turned to smile at his *fiancée*—"wasn't I?"

"Oh, yes indeed," agreed Miss Reid. She took a seat upon the nearby leather sofa, and Dr. Radcliff sat behind his desk. "I'd love to hear about your ideas to establish more dispensaries like this. And perhaps a well-funded orphanage up north too?"

"All going well, those plans will come to fruition." Arabella sat carefully and removed her bonnet and gloves. She was grateful that Dr. Radcliff hadn't brought up Gabriel's intrusion and rather abrupt departure when he'd visited two days ago. She didn't really want to discuss anything to do with her husband right now lest she burst into tears. "Since my last visit, Dr. Radcliff, I've met with the Marchioness of Chelmsford and the Mayfair Bluestocking Society, and things are moving along quite nicely. In fact, Lady Chelmsford wanted me to—"

The door behind her burst open and then slammed shut, and Arabella jumped like a startled rabbit. At the very same moment, Miss Reid gasped and Dr. Radcliff leapt to his feet so abruptly, his chair toppled over. Good heavens, had Gabriel decided to interrupt a second time?

"Now see here—" began Dr. Radcliff, but as Arabella turned in her seat to see what was going on, a strong masculine arm snaked about her body and roughly yanked her out of the chair.

Oh, God. It wasn't Gabriel. It was the strange man she'd observed in the waiting room. Arabella sucked in a lungful of air to scream, but the man's hand clamped over her mouth as he hauled her up against his body. Cold terror sliced through her, freezing her blood as something hard and metallic was jammed against her temple. Was that the muzzle of a pistol?

Judging by the horrified expressions on the faces of Dr. Radcliff and Miss Reid, it was indeed.

A timid knock came at the door, and the voice of Dr. Radcliff's assistant filtered through the wood. "Doctor? Is everything all right? I had to assist a patient for a moment, and then I heard the door slam."

"Tell her everything is fine and to go about her business," growled the stranger. "Then lock the door and throw the key out that window behind the desk."

Dr. Radcliff, as white as a sheet, nodded. "It's all right, Mrs. Fraser," he called out. "A draft blew the door shut, that's all." After he locked them in, he directed his attention back to Arabella's captor. "What do you want?" he asked in a low, urgent voice. "If it's money—"

"Shut the fuck up, or Lady Langdale gets a bullet in the brain."

He knows who I am? Arabella's mind felt sluggish. Everything was sharply in focus yet didn't seem quite real. Surely any moment she'd wake up. This had to be a nightmare.

The man's breath drove in and out in hot, rapid gusts against her ear. With a jolt of surprise, Arabella realized that beneath the pungent odor of male sweat, he smelled of money and refinement. His shirt was freshly laundered, his cravat starched, and his soap had sandalwood and citrus notes. Even though his tone had been harsh and his words coarse, his speech marked him as someone from the upper classes. What on earth did he want with her? If only he'd take his hand away from her mouth, surely she could reason with him. Make him see sense. Find out what he needed.

While every fiber of her being urged her to struggle against him and scream for help, to call out to Soames and Gabriel's other footmen, she didn't. With a gun pressed to her head, to do so would be foolhardy indeed. She didn't want to inflame the situation further.

Dr. Radcliff was speaking again. "Tell me what to do." His hands were raised in a placatory gesture. "Whatever's wrong, I'm sure I can help. Just let Lady Langdale g—"

"I said shut it." The man began dragging Arabella toward the second door at the back of the room. "Where does that lead?"

Dr. Radcliff swallowed. "To an alleyway. But it's locked."

"Well, fucking unlock it," the stranger snapped. "You." Miss Reid started so violently, the man had clearly addressed her. "Do you have a key?"

When she nodded, he barked, "Then open it. Now." The pistol's muzzle jabbed into Arabella's temple again, and she whimpered against the smothering crush of the man's fingers. She clutched at his sleeve but his tight grip didn't ease up, even for a second.

Dr. Radcliff gave a curt nod, and Miss Reid retrieved a key from the desk drawer. But as she started forward, Dr. Radcliff grasped her arm. "I'll do it."

"No, you bloody well won't," hissed the man. "Step back."

The doctor immediately released Miss Reid and she hurried over to the door. With shaking fingers, she pushed the key in the lock and turned it.

"Open it and then lock the door behind us. I'll be listening. So don't you dare try anything."

Arabella's knees were like jelly, and there didn't seem to be enough air in her lungs as she was forced into the dark, narrow laneway.

And then Miss Reid shut the door and the key scraped in the lock.

Oh, God. She was all alone with an armed madman in a deserted back alley. And she still had no idea what he wanted. Was he trying to kidnap her to extort money from Gabriel? Did Gabriel have an enemy she didn't know about?

Before she could think on it further, her captor slammed her hard up against the rough bricks. Her cheek scraped the wall as he released her mouth.

"Now, my lady, you're going to walk briskly to the end

of the alley. I'll be behind you the whole way." The man's voice was harsh in her ear. "You're not going to scream and you're not going to plead with me or ask questions. And you're not going to run. Because if you do, I'm going to put a bullet between your shoulder blades. Do I make myself clear?"

The man grasped her head so tightly, Arabella couldn't nod. But she managed a fractured whisper. "Aye."

"Good." The man's large hand remained on her neck in an uncompromising, bruising grip. "Walk."

With no other option left open to her, that's exactly what Arabella did. The alley wasn't long; she could see a brightly lit main street up ahead. Other people. Perhaps when they got to the end, she could make a run for it. Scream. It might be her only chance to escape. Bow Street and the Runners' office weren't that far away. Maybe Dr. Radcliff was in the process of sending for help already. Soames could be looking for her right this minute.

She had no idea where Gabriel was. If he'd taken up with Lady Astley again, would he even care she'd been kidnapped?

Tears stung Arabella's eyes, and she pushed the horrible thought away. Speculating about her husband's fidelity, or lack thereof, would prove fruitless in this situation. She needed to keep her wits about her, not let terror or despair take over.

All of a sudden, her captor pushed her sideways into another, far narrower alley. "In here."

What? No! Arabella stumbled over a pile of rubbish, and her shoulder connected painfully with the sharp brick corner of one of the buildings. She cried out, but the stranger was relentless, driving her on before forcing her down another passageway, then up a short flight of stairs. And then all at once she found herself in a dismal, squalid courtyard. Decrepit lodging houses towered above them, their open doors and broken windows staring at her like dark, impassive eyes. Sagging lines of washing hung overhead like limp, ragged flags, and the air was fetid with the smell of human waste and garbage. A small group of street urchins barreled past, ducking down the passage from which she'd just emerged.

"Remember, if you scream, you're a dead woman," the man ground out. He forcibly marched her across the court-yard toward another dark alley.

No doubt, a man gripping a woman about the neck wasn't an unusual sight around here, so no one—not the drunken man sprawled in a doorway, nor the old woman lugging a bucket of water, nor the adolescent girl throwing slops from a window—called out or tried to intervene.

Panic and anguish rose up in a great wave, clogging Arabella's throat. No one was going to help her, and her chances of escape were diminishing by the second. She had to do something. All at once she twisted her body and made a break for it.

Behind her, the man swore but she'd barely made it five steps before he tackled her; her glasses went flying as he sent her sprawling, face-first, onto the filthy ground.

She tried to kick out, to crawl away, but then his weight was upon her and he grunted, "Bitch." Pain sliced through her head, and then her world turned black.

CHAPTER 20

Word about town is that a certain countess—who recently wedded London's most Errant Earl—has become a champion of the poor, and that the Seven Dials Dispensary is her charity of choice. Why else would a coach bearing the earl's crest and his liveried staff be seen in the vicinity of this establishment on more than one occasion? Unless something else is going on . . . Lady L. does possess her own disreputable reputation after all. Our intrepid reporters will be sure to keep an eye out for any further developments.

The Beau Monde Mirror: The Society Page

Langdale House, St. James's Square, London

"What do you mean, *someone* has taken my wife? That a gun was held to her head?" Gabriel roared at an ashen-faced Soames. "Where did this happen? When?"

He'd barely crossed the threshold at Langdale House when the footman had greeted him with the news that something unbelievably terrible had happened. That Arabella was missing.

Kidnapped.

To his credit Soames didn't shrink away from Gabriel's fulminating glare. "Two hours ago, my lord, and I believe it might have been your cousin, Captain Holmes-Fitzgerald, who took her," he replied. "I caught a glimpse of him when he entered the Seven Dials Dispensary, but I didn't realize he was up to no good until—"

"You took my wife into Seven Dials again? What were you thinking?" Gabriel clenched his fists so he wouldn't wrap his hands around the footman's throat to throttle him.

"I'm sorry, my lord, but she asked—"

Gabriel made a chopping motion with his hand. "I don't want to hear your pitiful excuses. What else can you tell me? And it had better be helpful."

"Yes, my lord. Dr. Radcliff summoned the Bow Street Runners as soon as he was able. Lady Langdale was in the treatment room, talking to the doctor, when your cousin burst in and forced her to leave via a back entrance. Radcliff reported her captor held a gun to her head and threatened to shoot her unless she complied. But I believe the Runners are scouring the streets of Seven Dials and Covent Garden as we speak. There should be someone here to apprise you of the situation shortly."

"I should bloody well hope so." His stomach churning with fear and wild anger, Gabriel strode across the vestibule in the direction of the library, where he kept his dueling pistols locked away in a cabinet. "And make yourself useful. Send for Lord Sleat and the Duke of Exmoor," he barked. The more men he had on hand that he could trust implicitly, the better.

Once Gabriel had gained the library, he poured himself a cognac and tossed it back in one savage gulp. *Christ.* He wiped a shaking hand over his mouth.

How could this have happened?

Arabella, the first woman he'd ever fallen in love with— the woman he loved beyond all reason—was in dire danger.

Timothy must have gone mad. What did he have to gain by doing something as insane as this?

Revenge. Because I thwarted him. Because I taunted him and publicly humiliated him.

The answer sat more uncomfortably in Gabriel's gut than the cognac.

One thing was certain: Timothy was a dead man. To think of him putting a gun to Arabella's head, of frightening her, of hurting her in any way, it made him want to smash his cousin's head in. To tear him to pieces, slowly. To gut him with a blunt, rusty butter knife.

He'd just loaded his pistols when MacQueen and Max arrived. He poured them and himself another glass of cognac, then explained what was going on.

His friends were both grim-faced when he finished.

"Whatever you need us to do, we will," said Max.

"Aye," agreed MacQueen.

"Just help me find her." Gabriel tucked a pistol into the back of his breeches. Taking a deep breath, he looked them both in the eye. "Because I love her."

Somewhere in Seven Dials . . .

When Arabella came to, she had no idea where she was for several seconds. Lying facedown on a hard, dusty floor, she turned her throbbing head to the side and then groaned. A heavy fog clouded her mind, and her mouth felt odd, as though it were packed full of dry sawdust. And then she stiffened and her heart hurtled against her ribs as everything came back to her with terrifying clarity.

Oh, God. The man at the dispensary. The gun at her head. She'd tried to run but he'd knocked her down, and she had the vague, dreamlike recollection that at some point, he'd forced her to drink something bitter and foul. Laudanum perhaps.

No wonder she felt so cloth headed. She was drugged and gagged and bound up like a trussed goose on Christmas morn. Her arms were tied so tightly behind her back, her shoulders felt as though they'd been wrenched from their sockets. Her ankles were lashed together too. Indeed her bonds were so tight, she was certain her circulation had been cut off; she couldn't feel her toes.

Icy terror trickled through her veins, making her shiver, and nausea swelled. Cold sweat prickled along the length of her spine. Was her kidnapper still with her? She still had no idea who he was or what he wanted.

If she had any hope of surviving this ordeal, she couldn't give in to the panic careening through her body. Or the pull of the laudanum. Even now, it tugged at her consciousness making her groggy as a drunkard. Forcing her heavy eyelids open, Arabella tried to take stock of her surroundings.

The room she was in was dimly lit, and from her position on the floor, all she could see was a warped, scuffed skirting board, a cracked plaster wall, and, if she tilted her head upward, the chipped sill of a curtainless window with a broken glass pane. A glimpse of dark, gunmetal gray sky.

Somewhere in the distance, thunder grumbled. And there were voices. A woman's raucous cackle. The high wailing cry of a baby. A man swearing. A door slammed.

A barrage of questions skittered through her mind. Was she still in Seven Dials? How long had she been missing? The weather had changed, so perhaps several hours had passed. If that were the case, the Bow Street Runners might already be searching for her. Surely Dr. Radcliff had sent for help by now. He would have informed Gabriel as well.

Gabriel. Unbidden tears of despair flooded Arabella's eyes. Was he worried about her and looking for her too? She didn't want to believe the article in the *Beau Monde Mirror*

But what if *was* true?

Arabella forced herself to take slow, even breaths around the gag. *Stop it. You can only deal with one mess at a time.*

A noise behind her—a scrape like a leather shoe on the wooden floor—made Arabella start. Her breath froze in her lungs as she listened, ears straining for another sound.

"So you're awake are you, Lady Langdale?" The stranger hauled her up into a sitting position so quickly, Arabella's head swam and she had to fight another wave of nausea. She slumped against the wall, eyes closed, her head pounding her breath coming in short, shallow gasps around the gag and through her nose.

When she opened her eyes, it was to discover her captor was squatting close by, watching her . . . and she sucked in a startled breath. He'd removed his hat, and in the gray light filtering through the window, she could at last see his face.

His wide mouth lifted at one corner as he smirked. "You know who I am, *my lady*?"

Ignoring the pain in her head, she nodded. *Yes.*

Although the stranger's eyes were a pale icy gray rather than vivid green, there was no doubt in her mind that he was related to Gabriel. His hair was a riot of dark brown curls, and beneath his derisive expression, he was handsome with a bone structure similar to her husband's: she could see it in the lines of his strong jaw, his slashing brows, and high cheekbones. There was even a dimple in his lean cheek.

This man had to be Timothy Holmes-Fitzgerald.

But what did he want with her?

As if reading her thoughts, he said, "My cousin has something I need, so I'm going to arrange a trade. Don't worry"— he reached out and touched her face, almost tenderly—"one way or another, this will soon be over."

He stood abruptly and walked a few steps past the end of a bare, narrow cot to the other side of the small, ramshackle room. Snatching up a dark bottle from a scarred packing crate by the closed doorway, he took a swig, then leaned back against the dirty wall, scratching his jaw.

Was he quaffing Kendal's Black Drop like water?

Fear churned in Arabella's belly. She'd thought Timothy's pupils were constricted by the light coming through the window, but now she realized he was more than a little affected by the opium in his veins. That would explain his jerky movements, the slight tremble in his hands as he raised the bottle to take another large sip. And perhaps even this insane course of action he'd set in motion.

Had the laudanum made him go mad? Her grandfather had personally observed that too much of the drug could have a negative effect on a person's state of mind as well as the body. Over time, a patient who used opiates regularly could become irritable and anxious, have changeable moods and irrational thoughts, and unpredictable behavior.

Thunder rumbled again, closer this time, and Arabella shivered.

Timothy said he was going to "trade" her. Had he demanded a ransom from Gabriel? Did he need money? Or was kidnapping her merely an act of revenge because Gabriel had foiled his plans to usurp the earldom?

If only Timothy would remove this blasted gag, then she could ask him.

Arabella's gaze flitted to the other side of the room where a concertina screen stood, draped with a ragged-looking gown and chemise. Out of the corner of her eye, she thought she'd detected a slight movement behind the screen's threadbare fabric panels. A shifting of the shadows. And then came a feeble wail. Was that the infant she'd heard earlier?

Timothy shot a dark scowl at whoever was behind the screen. "I thought I told you to keep that baby quiet," he growled. "I certainly paid you enough. And where's your other brat, by the way? I'm going to need him shortly."

Arabella's heart sped up. Dear Lord above. Someone else *was* in the room. Someone who might help her if she could just attract his or her attention. But when Timothy turned his gaze back to Arabella, his next words dashed her hopes entirely.

"It's amazing what a few half crowns will buy you these days. A desperate whore's silence and a bottle of Kendal's Black Drop." He lifted the laudanum and took another slug. "If I had the time, and I didn't think she had the pox, I'd probably get a fuck out of her too."

The Seven Dials Dispensary, Covent Garden, London

Where, in God's name, was Arabella?

Gabriel stood in the treatment room of the Seven Dials Dispensary, staring out of the front window into the busy street, at the local folk rushing by as they sought cover before the storm hit. Even though dusk was still a few hours away, the afternoon had grown as dark as night as ominous black clouds rolled in over London. It wouldn't be long before the heavens opened.

The weather matched Gabriel's mood perfectly, savage and thunderous while his gut roiled with worry. Ever though a small team of Bow Street Runners, Dr. Radcliff, Max, and MacQueen had been helping him to scour the streets and back alleys and question the local inhabitants of Seven Dials for hours, it seemed that Timothy and Arabella had vanished without a trace.

But then, his cousin could just have easily bundled Arabella into a carriage, which meant they weren't in Seven Dials or the Covent Garden area at all. Indeed, they could be anywhere by now.

Behind him, he could hear Max and MacQueen talking in low voices to Sergeant Watkins, an officer of the Bow Street Runners, as they studied a map of the area, marking off which streets they'd covered, and planning where they should search next. Runners had already determined that Timothy quit his Russell Square residence about nine o'clock this morning—the butler reported his master had taken a hackney coach rather than calling for his own carriage—and he hadn't returned. He also appeared to have taken one of his Manton dueling pistols from its box.

Resting his forearm against the window frame, Gabriel closed his eyes for a moment and tried not to give in to the despair burning through his veins. He still had no idea what his cousin wanted. What he hoped to achieve by taking Arabella.

Revenge . . . The word held more menace than the thunder rolling toward Seven Dials. It was the only thing that made sense.

If his dog of a cousin harmed one single hair on his wife's precious head . . . Gabriel clenched his fist so tightly, his knuckles cracked.

Strangely, he was so focused on finding Arabella, he'd almost forgotten the glass-fronted cupboard to his left contained bottles of laudanum. For the first time in his adult life, he could honestly say he didn't want the vile stuff.

He only wanted Arabella.

"Langdale?"

Gabriel turned at the sound of his name. It was MacQueen, and there was a note of excitement in his friend's voice which immediately sparked his interest. "What is it?"

The Scotsman crossed the room in half a dozen long strides. "Miss Reid, Radcliff's nurse, just noticed this on the floor in the waiting room." He held out a folded sheet of grubby paper. "It looks like someone pushed it under the front door. Your name's written on it."

"I take it that whoever delivered it is long gone?" said Max.

MacQueen nodded. "Aye. It would seem so."

Gabriel took the proffered sheet—a crumpled playbill—and read aloud the message that had been scrawled on the back in lead pencil.

Cuz,

>   *No doubt you want your wife back and I'm prepared to make an exchange. I want your parents' English wedding lines. That's it. Simple as that.*
>   *Someone will collect you at six o'clock sharp from the Seven Dials Dispensary and bring you, and you alone, to the place where we'll make the exchange. If I see a Runner or any one of your cronies follow, you'll never see your Lady Langdale again.*
>   *On that you have my word.*

>   *T.*

Gabriel ran a shaking hand down his face. Thank God, Arabella was still alive. But even so, terror gripped his heart. It was already half past five.

He lifted his gaze to his friends, Sergeant Watkins, and Radcliff.

"I have only half an hour to retrieve the marriage lines from Langdale House. Perhaps not even that. It's less than a mile between here and St. James's Square, but the streets will be jammed with traffic at this time of day."

Sergeant Watkins grimaced. "And it will take at least ten minutes to summon a mounted officer."

Max stepped forward. "I'll go. You know I'm the fastest

runner out of the three of us." He threw off his jacket and loosened his neckcloth. "I'll be back in twenty minutes."

Gabriel wasn't about to argue with him, not when Arabella's life was at stake. And it was true, the Duke of Exmoor could sprint like the devil with all the hounds of hell at his heels. "Ask Jervis to help you retrieve the lines," Gabriel called after him; Max was already heading for the door. "The certificate is in the top drawer of my desk in the library."

"Done."

"Are you sure you want to do this?" asked MacQueen as soon as Max had disappeared. "Give in to your cousin's demand?"

"What choice do I have? Nothing matters more to me than Arabella. Nothing." Gabriel shrugged. "Besides, unless the bastard intends to burn down the church in Appletreewick and York Minster Cathedral to destroy any and all evidence of my parents' union, it won't do him any good. He's clearly not thinking straight, and I'm not willing to risk Arabella's life by trying to reason with a drug-deluded madman." He cocked a brow. "After my stint on Skye, you of all people should know that won't work."

MacQueen nodded. "Do you want the Runners to be involved?" he said in a low voice so Watkins wouldn't overhear.

Gabriel glanced at the officer who was currently talking to Dr. Radcliff. "What would be the point? I don't trust them not to mess things up. It's a perfectly simple trade. I give Timothy what he wants, and then I'll have Arabella back safe and sound."

And then I'll hunt him down and kill him, but no one need know about that right now. However, judging by the knowing look in MacQueen's eye as the Scot clapped him on the back, Gabriel suspected his friend knew exactly what he intended.

CHAPTER 21

Is this the most sensational on-dit ever to grace the pages of the *Beau Monde Mirror*?

According to a reliable source from Bow Street, the Countess of Langdale was kidnapped from the Seven Dials Dispensary!

The Beau Monde Mirror

The Seven Dials Dispensary, Covent Garden, London

The wait was interminable, and Gabriel was certain all his pacing had begun to wear a track in the wooden floor. However, true to his word, Max was back within the allotted time frame. As he burst through the front door of the dispensary, the storm broke.

"I trust . . . this is what you need?" said Max, wiping the sweat from his brow with his shirtsleeve as he handed over the certificate.

Gabriel unfolded the piece of parchment to check it, then nodded. "Yes. Thank you, my friend." He tucked the lines into the breast pocket of his coat. Glancing out the window at the rain lashing the streets of Seven Dials, he grimaced. "This bloody storm is going to make things interesting."

"Aye," agreed MacQueen. The light within the dispensary had dimmed, and Radcliff's assistant, Miss Reid, was presently lighting several lamps to ward off the gloom. "I wonder who the 'someone' is that your cousin will send."

"I have no clue," said Gabriel. "I only hope that Timothy isn't playing me for a fool, because if he is . . ." He shook his head as a wave of rage crashed over him.

"I'm sure you've considered this might be a trap to get rid of you," said Max. "That he might be luring you into some dark rookery before setting a mob of hired footpads onto you."

"Yes, which is why I'll get you and MacQueen to shadow me." Sergeant Watkins had already agreed to stay out of the way. His bright red Runner weskit would make him stick out like a dog's bollocks.

"Of course." The duke squeezed his shoulder. "You know we'll always have your back."

Thunder reverberated overhead and lightning briefly illuminated the room. Indeed, the rolling boom was so loud, Gabriel almost missed the knock on the back door of the dispensary.

"Well, this is it," he said grimly, checking the pistol at his back was still securely wedged into his breeches. Mac-Queen had his second pistol, and Gabriel was pretty certain Max had at least a knife secreted somewhere on his person. "Wish me luck, gents."

As soon as he pulled open the back door of the dispensary, he was greeted by a sharp slap of cold rain in the face. Swiping the water out of his eyes, he squinted into the dark alley, confused that he couldn't see anyone at first. And then he felt a tug on the hem of his coat. A drenched urchin, his hair plastered to his skull, stared up at him with eyes that were too big for his painfully thin face. He couldn't have been more than five or six years old.

"This way, guv."

The boy darted off down the rapidly flooding alleyway, and Gabriel sprinted after him. He couldn't afford to lose him in the bowels of Seven Dials.

They'd barely gone twenty yards when the urchin ducked abruptly to the right; it was as though he'd disappeared into thin air. Gabriel skidded to a halt so quickly, he nearly ended up on his arse in the filthy mud.

Where the hell had the scamp gone?

Christ, there was another narrow alley running between two buildings, piled with sodden, stinking rubbish. Gabriel had to turn his shoulders to squeeze into the space. None of them had thought to look down here; they'd assumed the passage was a dead end. He trusted MacQueen and Max were watching and would follow suit.

Narrowing his eyes against the sting of the rain, Gabriel saw the boy dart off to the right again. When he turned the corner in pursuit, he was faced with a short flight of stairs that led into a small courtyard surrounded by derelict lodging houses.

The urchin scampered across the yard and paused in a black yawning doorway. He held up a small hand. "Wait 'ere, guv. I'll be back in a tick."

Chest heaving, heart hammering, Gabriel drew to a halt. Was Arabella here somewhere? Had she really been this close to him all this time?

Pushing his sodden hair out of his eyes, Gabriel scanned the dark windows and the openings to other stairwells. Frustration pounded through his veins. So much rain sluiced off the roofs of the surrounding buildings, it was impossible to make out a goddamned thing.

At least he didn't appear to be in any immediate danger of being set upon by a band of thugs in Timothy's employ.

Thunder cracked overhead and lightning flashed, blinding him momentarily. When he could see again, he noticed the urchin was back, beckoning him forward toward the doorway.

When he was only a few yards away, the boy held up his hand again. "Mr. Timothy says you have somefink of 'is. You're to give it to me."

Gabriel shook his head. "Not until I know he's going to give back something of mine first." Raising his voice above the din of bucketing rain, Gabriel shouted, "Where is she, Timothy? You shan't have what you want until I see she's all right."

The boy glanced back up the steep, narrow staircase as if seeking direction from someone just out of sight. Was Timothy up there? With Arabella?

God, Arabella.

Anger, fear, and hope seared through Gabriel's body, tightening every muscle, sharpening his senses. He slid his hand behind his back, beneath his sodden coat, and wrapped his fingers around the smooth, walnut handle of his perfectly balanced Manton pistol.

Just one shot, straight between the eyes, and it would all be over for his dear cuz.

He wouldn't miss. He never did.

The barefoot urchin descended a few more steps, and then behind him, Gabriel caught a glimpse of bright green skirts and elegant slipper-shod feet beneath the dirt-smeared hem.

Arabella. Thank God.

"Gabriel?" Almost drowned out by the steady drumming of the rain, Arabella's soft Scots burr was little more than a faint, hollow echo as it drifted down the stairs. "I'm here . . . with your cousin. I'm all right, but he . . . he has a pistol."

Fear and unspeakable tenderness gathering in his throat, Gabriel had to swallow before he could summon a voice that was passably steady. "I know, Bella. Everything will be fine. You'll be with me soon."

"Good God, cuz, I don't have time for this." There was no mistaking Timothy's sneering tone. "Did you bring the marriage lines or what?"

"Wait! Gabriel, no. Don't you dare give them up for me." The alarm was clear in Arabella's voice. "You need them."

"Not as much as I need you, Bella."

"Oh, please," jeered Timothy. "Enough of this sentimental claptrap. I think I'd rather put a bullet in my own brain than listen to you two carry on a minute longer."

"If you'd be so obliged, it would save me the trouble." Gabriel tightened his grip on his pistol. Damn Timothy to the hottest pit of Hades. He was using Arabella and the crumbling brickwork above the doorway as a shield.

"So how is this going to work, Timothy?" he called up the stairs. "I've got the certificate right here in my breast pocket."

"Give the lines to the boy. When I've seen they're real and you haven't tried to dupe me, you can have your wife back."

"Let Arabella come farther down the stairs first."

"You think I'm stupid? Not on your life, cuz."

Fucking hell. Gabriel swiped a hand across his eyes to clear his vision. It seemed he had little choice. "All right then. Let's do this."

As Gabriel beckoned the boy forward, he risked edging a few steps closer to the door. He could now see Arabella's legs from the midthigh down. But Timothy, sniveling coward that he was, was wedged firmly behind her on the narrow landing.

He couldn't get a clear shot. The risk of hitting Arabella was too great.

The urchin approached, small hand out, and Gabriel passed him the folded document.

Dear God, let Arabella come through this unscathed. Nothing else matters.

As the boy dashed back into the stairwell and scurried up to Timothy, Gabriel withdrew his pistol and crept forward. Now was his chance.

Anger hardening his resolve and steadying his hand, he took up a position on one side of the doorway. If Timothy was distracted, even for a moment . . .

He was about to peer around the doorjamb when Timothy called out, "Thank you very much, cuz. You can have your baggage back."

And then Arabella screamed.

Oh, God. Timothy had pushed her and now she was falling, tumbling headlong down the steep wooden staircase.

With her hands still tied behind her back, Arabella had no way to break her fall. Her shoulder and then her side slammed painfully into one step, then another as she tried to roll sideways . . . and then all of a sudden Gabriel was there, catching her. Saving her from certain death.

"Arabella." Sprawled across the stairs, Gabriel lashed her hard against his strong body, her chest to his, cushioning her, slowing her forward momentum. "Oh, sweet Jesus Christ."

Panting, he buried his face in her hair. "I thought I was going to lose you."

"You . . . you haven't." Arabella closed her eyes and breathed in Gabriel's comforting, wholly masculine scent. She couldn't quite catch her breath, and her head, ribs, and shoulder hurt, but she would be all right. Gabriel had come for her, and given the way he was cradling her and raining kisses over the side of her forehead and cheek, she knew that he cared. That's all she needed for now.

"Langdale. I heard your wife scream. Can I help?" The Duke of Exmoor's deep, cultured voice drifted up the staircase.

Gabriel lifted his head. "Do you have that knife of yours handy, Max?"

"Of course."

The duke sliced through the bonds at her wrists, and then Arabella moaned as she rolled her stiff shoulders forward and the circulation began to return.

"My poor darling," murmured Gabriel. "Can you sit?"

Arabella nodded. "I . . . I think so."

"Good." Gabriel carefully eased her into a sitting position. His strong arm stayed around her shoulders, steadying her. And then his hand came up to cradle her face. "Let me look at you, my love."

My love?

Did Gabriel really just say that? Before Arabella could think on the significance of such a thing, he was turning her head gently this way, then that. Beneath his sodden black curls, his brow plunged into a deep frown. Arabella suspected her cheek was bruised and scraped from her earlier fall in the courtyard. When he felt the back of her head and encountered a particularly sore spot, she winced. The blow Timothy had dealt her when he knocked her out had left a rather sizable egg on her crown.

"I could kill my cousin for this," Gabriel muttered. Judging by the cold anger in his voice and the fire in his eyes, Arabella believed him.

The duke cleared his throat. "MacQueen was watching the building from the other side, so if Timothy tries to cu and run via another entrance, he's sure to give chase."

"Excellent." Gabriel brushed such a whisper-soft kis across Arabella's forehead, her heart fluttered. "Let's ge you back to the dispensary so Radcliff can examine you. His mouth tipped into a warm smile. "I have it on goo authority he's a very skilled physician."

Bemused by her husband's gentle—dare she think i loving?—demeanor, Arabella felt as if she were in a daz as Gabriel helped her to her feet and then down the remain der of the stairs. The laudanum in her system was undoubt edly making her feel slightly dizzy, and she was gratefu Gabriel was holding on to her tightly. It was almost as if h didn't want to let her go.

She wanted to ask him about Lady Astley, but consider ing Max was also waiting in the shelter of the stairwel now didn't seem like quite the right time.

The handsome duke gave her an encouraging smile. "I'r most pleased to see you've emerged relatively unscathe from your encounter with Gabriel's cousin, my lady. Yo gave your husband quite a scare. In fact, I've never seen hir so beside himself with worry. But if you'll both excus me"—the duke gave Gabriel a light clap on the back—" might dash off to see how MacQueen is doing. I'm loath t let him have all the fun."

"Go right ahead," said Gabriel. "I think I can manag things from here."

After Max took his leave and ducked out into the rai Arabella chanced a glance up at her husband. Even thoug her vision was a little blurry, she could see he was lookin at her with such tender regard in his eyes, she was begir ning to wonder if the laudanum or even a bump to her hea was making her hallucinate.

But then Max said Gabriel had been beside himself wit worry . . . And he'd also willingly given up his parent marriage certificate for her, potentially risking his entir inheritance . . .

"We should go too," Gabriel murmured. "I want the doctor to check this bump on your head. But I'm afraid you're about to get soaked." He grimaced at the sky. "At least the storm is beginning to ease a little."

"Yes . . ." Arabella drew a deep breath. "Gabriel . . . I wanted to ask—"

She got no further as her husband swept her off her feet. "What are you doing?" she gasped as he strode into the rain and across the muddy, litter-strewn courtyard.

"Carrying you back to the dispensary. There's no way that I'm letting you walk through this cesspit. And besides"—he pressed a kiss to her temple—"I like having you in my arms."

Arabella sighed and rested her head against Gabriel's wide shoulder. Even though the rain was icy and her head and body ached, for the moment she was content to go along with what her husband wanted. When they gained the alley behind the dispensary, the rain had almost stopped. A group of children had emerged and begun to squeal and laugh as they splashed about in the filthy puddles down the other end of the laneway.

"Look, there's a rainbow," Arabella murmured. "Above the rooftops over there."

"Yes . . ." Gabriel paused and smiled. Then his gaze caught hers. "I interrupted you before. You said you wanted to ask me something."

Gathering her courage, Arabella licked her dry lips and drew a deep breath. "Did you really mean it when you said that you need me . . . even more than your parents' marriage lines?" she whispered, searching his face. She really wanted to know.

Gabriel's forehead dipped into a frown. "Of course I did. You mean the world to me, Bella. Everything."

Oh, how she wished that were true. Arabella suddenly felt as if she were teetering on the edge of a very significant moment. She was terrified yet hopeful. Expectant yet guarded. Her heart pounded wildly in her ears.

Gabriel set her gently on her feet but he didn't let her go.

Of their own accord, Arabella's hands slid to his chest, and through his wet shirt, she could feel the heat of his body the reassuring thud of his heart.

"Do you still see that rainbow?" he murmured. His moss green eyes were as soft as velvet.

She nodded. It arched over his left shoulder and the distant spire of a church. "Yes . . ."

He brushed a damp, tangled curl away from her cheek "When I first proposed to you, Arabella, by the shores o Lake Geneva, my heart did possess tender feelings. The were a bright, beautiful glimmer deep in my chest, but like the rainbow we saw that same afternoon, I thought the would be just as insubstantial and impermanent. That, ove time, they would weaken and wane. But I was so very wrong What I feel for you isn't transient at all. But dolt that I am, wasn't until today that I realized my regard, my affection, m desire, indeed, all of my feelings for you are so strong, the blaze as steadily and fiercely as the summer sun. They wil never fade away. They will never be extinguished."

"What are you trying to tell me, Gabriel?" she whis pered past a throat tight with longing. "I need to hear yo say it."

"Don't you see?" His large hands cradled her face, an his thumbs caressed her cheeks with breath-stealing ten derness. His adoring gaze trapped hers. "I love you, Ara bella. With my entire heart. It belongs to you, and yo alone, forever and always."

Could it be true? Did Gabriel really love her? Arabell so wanted to believe her husband, but she had to ask hin one last thing. "And what of Lady Astley?"

He frowned. "What of her?"

"In today's *Beau Monde Mirror*, there was a report sta ing that you'd been with the countess yesterday afternoor I didn't want to think the worst of you . . . but you tw shared such a great passion . . ."

"Ah, yes . . . I heard about that . . ." A shadow crosse Gabriel's face, but he held her gaze steadily. "It's true I me with her. But we only had the briefest of conversations. Sh asked me to speak with her husband. To deny we were hav ing another affair because he was threatening to divorce her. So that's what I did. This morning, I told Lord Astley that I couldn't possibly have taken up with his wife again because I'm deeply in love with *my* wife and I would never, ever betray her. And that's the truth of the matter, Bella. Indeed, I rushed back to Langdale House to tell you just that, that I love you, but then I learned you'd been kidnapped. And I've never been more terrified in my life."

Arabella reached up and touched his handsome face with trembling fingers. She believed him. No, it was more than that. In her heart of hearts, she trusted him. "Well, I'm here now, safe and sound in your arms," she whispered.

"Yes . . . but the question is, how do you feel about me, Bella?" he murmured huskily. "For the longest time, I thought you might care for me . . . But of course, total ass that I am, I've given you cause to doubt me, over and over again—"

"Shh." Arabella placed a finger against his lips. The naked yearning in her husband's eyes was too much for her to bear. It was cruel to make him wait a moment longer, especially when the words she'd always wanted to say danced on the tip of her tongue. "I don't just care for you, Gabriel, you silly, adorable, complicated, utterly divine man. I'm madly, completely, head over heels in love with you, and I think I have been since the moment I first saw you in that dark, cold dungeon in Switzerland."

Gabriel picked her up and spun her around three times before backing her against the brick wall of the dispensary, caging her in with his body and his arms. "I've never been so filled with joy," he whispered, capturing her face with one gentle hand. "With you by my side, there will always be light in my life, Arabella." And then he kissed her with such fierce yet reverent ardor, Arabella's heart swelled with incandescent happiness too.

EPILOGUE

❦

And gazing in thy face as toward a star,
    Laid on thy lap, his eyes to thee upturn,
    Feeding on thy sweet cheek! while thy lips are
    With lava kisses melting while they burn,
    Showered on his eyelids, brow, and mouth, as
from an urn!

Lord Byron, "Childe Harold's Pilgrimage"

Hawksfell Hall, Cumberland, England

August 20, 1818

Sketchbook in hand and a thoughtful frown creasing h[is]
brow, Gabriel lounged naked among a pile of soft-as-a
cloud pillows in his massive four-poster bed in Hawksfell[']
opulent master suite. Although, lucky man that he was, [it]
wasn't just his bedchamber anymore. It was Arabella's too[.]
Sometimes he had to remind himself that this idyllic exi[s]-
tence with his wife wasn't just a dream.

"I need your opinion, Bella," he called out. The shadow[s]
were growing long, and Arabella was dillydallying in th[e]
sitting room next door. "I want to begin painting your po[r]-
trait tomorrow, and for the life of me, I cannot decide whic[h]
pose I like better. You're just too lovely."

"You know I'm a wee bit busy at the moment, so tippin[g]
the butterboat over me will get you nowhere, my lord," Arabella called back.

"Hmmm, it did this afternoon," he rejoined. "Quite spectacularly, if I recall."

"Ha, if I agree, your head is bound to swell. And I think it's quite inflated enough already."

Gabriel smirked. It wasn't his head that was in danger of swelling at the moment.

Flipping over the page of his sketchbook, he smiled as he studied one of the drawings he'd rendered earlier today. He'd rowed Arabella across Grasmere to the tiny island that was part of the Hawksfell estate, and there, beneath the shade of a weeping willow, he'd spread a blanket and made slow, sweet love to her. As he'd kissed and caressed her, and progressively laid her bare, he'd cataloged in teasing whispers against her satiny skin everything he adored about her exquisite body and fair face.

When she was flushed and sated with pleasure, he then convinced Arabella to remain gloriously naked so he could sketch her, his very own beautiful, golden-haired water nymph.

One particular pose kept catching his eye. Arabella lay with her back arched and her arms thrown elegantly above her head, her curls cascading about her face like a tousled golden waterfall. He traced a fingertip along the line of one of her slender legs. The swell of one perfectly round and plump breast. *Yes, perhaps this one . . .*

Gabriel reached for the glass of claret on his oak bedside table and took a swig. Thank God Arabella's bruises had almost faded and that she hadn't sustained any serious injuries. Unlike Timothy . . .

After his cousin had emerged from an entrance on the other side of the derelict lodging house, MacQueen had given chase through the rain-wet streets of Covent Garden. Apparently the Scot caught up to Timothy, snagging the back of his coat, but as Timothy twisted and jerked away, he slipped on the road and his forward momentum sent him sprawling across a busy thoroughfare, directly into the path of an oncoming coach. He was killed instantly.

Gabriel felt not one iota of sorrow or sympathy for his cousin. The dog tormented and abused Arabella and almost killed her by throwing her down the stairs. Fate or God or the devil himself might have robbed him of the chance to mete out his own justice to his despicable cousin, but in the end, Timothy had received his just deserts. As far as he was concerned, if Timothy was now roasting in some fiery pit of hell, that was even better.

"Bella?" Beyond the green velvet bed hangings and the wide casement window, Gabriel could see that dusk was melting into night. The sky above the gently sloping wooded hills on the far shore of Grasmere was awash with hues of rose and deep lilac and dusky blue. A full moon was rising just behind the branches of an ancient oak on Hawksfell's grounds. "You're taking far too long, my love."

She laughed. "I'll be there directly, you impatient man. I'm just finishing my letter to Charlie."

"You said that half an hour ago when you were finishing your letter to Sophie. Or was that Olivia?"

"I've written to them all. Lady Chelmsford too. And your mother."

God's teeth. Gabriel cast aside his sketchbook. "If you don't come soon, my sweet but exasperating wife, I'll have to march in there, throw you over my shoulder, and carry you to bed." *And then I might tie you up with silk rope.* Gabriel's cock twitched. Now there was a thought. They hadn't tried that yet. Perhaps he'd add a blindfold to the mix too . .

Another laugh. Soft and throaty that sent another bolt of lust straight to Gabriel's groin. "If you stop nagging," she said, "you shall have a reward."

Reward? Gabriel grinned. "I like the sound of that."

"Oh, you will."

Arabella put down her swan feather quill, sprinkled sand across the last page of her letter to Charlie, and smiled to herself. She'd send this off tomorrow with all the others, a neat pile of carefully folded letters sat on the edge of the dark green leather blotter of the escritoire. As she'd just told Gabriel, there was one each for Sophie, Olivia, his mother and the Marchioness of Chelmsford.

Arabella was particularly looking forward to working again with Lady Chelmsford and her Mayfair bluestockings under the banner of the Mayfair Trust when she returned to London in October. Indeed, the plans for fund-raising and securing the support of other wealthy patrons for her charitable causes were well afoot; in the autumn there would be a series of subscription balls and *musicales* and even an art show to raise money for three more medical dispensaries in London, and of course, her greatest dream, a well-funded and properly staffed orphanage in Edinburgh. Gabriel's mother, Caro, had also expressed interest in courting the favor of the Arbuthnotts and other well connected gentry and philanthropic-minded members of the ton who resided in Edinburgh. Apparently she was also quite well acquainted with Eleanor Kerr's sister, Lady Cheviot. Arabella had smiled to herself when she'd learned that. She'd never gain Aunt Flora's respect or affection, but at least her aunt could no longer dismiss her as a nobody and a disgrace to the family.

Aside from attending to her charity work, Arabella was also working diligently to uphold her promise to her husband—to provide him with an heir. Her mouth twitched with a smile as she closed the lid of the elegant rosewood escritoire. *Working diligently.* It was certainly no hard task to make love with one's breathtakingly handsome, attentive, and adoring husband, if not once, then at least several times a day. She was fast becoming addicted to pleasure.

For years and years, she'd always thought she was too plain and practical and not made for love at all. But oh, how wrong she'd been.

Whenever she was in Gabriel's arms, she felt like Aphrodite.

Putting aside her glasses, Arabella picked up a branch of candles, then padded across the sitting room through to her dressing room.

Gabriel called out again, "What are you doing now, love?"

"Getting your reward ready. I promise I won't be long."

Arabella put down the candelabra and threw off her gown and undergarments. She still didn't have a lady's maid. But at times like this, she rather liked not having the prying eyes of servants around. She liked the freedom of being able to do as she pleased, without judgment.

Although she rather hoped she'd please Gabriel shortly too.

When she entered their bedchamber, candelabra in hand, Gabriel scowled at her from the bed like a petulant boy. "You're wearing far too many clothes," he said as his gaze roamed over her tightly cinched robe of rich amber silk.

Arabella laughed as she placed the branch of candles on an oak side table. "You're incorrigible."

Beneath half-mast lids, his green eyes glimmered with desire. "Wicked too. If you only knew what I was thinking, you'd be most shocked, my Lady Langdale." As he spoke, the richly embroidered silk counterpane slipped, and it was abundantly clear in which direction his thoughts ran; the linen sheet barely concealed his arousal.

"Yes, you are wicked *and* incorrigible," she agreed as she approached his side of the bed, drinking in the sight of his lean, ridged torso and the swell of hard pectoral muscles. "It's a good thing I love you for being both." She reached for the sash of her robe. "Are you ready, my lord?"

He gave her a lazy, lopsided smile that belied the sharp, hungry look in his eyes. "You know I am."

She tugged the knot at her waist undone and slid off her robe, and her husband's mouth stretched into a wider, thoroughly lascivious grin.

"Ah . . ." he murmured. His burning gaze traced over her naked legs and gaping décolletage before returning to her face. "Are you certain that's not one of my shirts?"

Unable to resist teasing him a little more, Arabella ignored his question and pointed at the bed. "Show me these sketches. Oh, bother, I forgot my glass—" She began to turn away, but faster than a striking hawk, Gabriel's hand shot out and grasped her wrist.

"They can wait till later," he growled as he threw off the sheet and pulled her onto the bed. "This wicked libertine wants to thoroughly pleasure his wife."

He claimed her mouth in a demanding, ravishing kiss, his tongue plundering as his hands commanded her body.

He urged her to straddle him, then through the cambric of his shirt, his large hands cupped her breasts, stroking and kneading her flesh, driving her wild.

"God I love you," he groaned against her lips. Then he dipped his head. Covering one of her nipples with his hot mouth, he suckled it through the fine fabric. When he transferred his attention to the other breast, nipping and sucking, Arabella clutched at his wide shoulders. Shimmering, pulsating desire was unfurling deep inside her. Between her thighs, she was slippery with need.

"I want you inside me," she whispered against his stubble-clad cheek. She rocked her hips against his hard, heavy length in an attempt to ease her own torment and urge him to take action.

"Soon." Gabriel reached for the hem of his shirt. "I like this very much," he pulled the garment up and over her head so she was completely naked, "but this is even better."

Gabriel returned to pleasuring her bare breasts, and within moments, Arabella was mewling and writhing in a frenzy of thwarted lust. "Please, Gabriel," she moaned, biting his shoulder, then kissing his jaw. "Take me. Let me ride you."

"Very well, my wanton, wicked, demanding wife." He kissed her, his tongue stroking deeply before he leaned back a little. "Do with me what you will. I'm all yours."

"Aye. You can be sure that I will." Arabella grasped his shaft with one hand, and after raising herself up, slid the velvet-smooth head of his manhood through her damp folds until it nudged her dew-slick entrance. Then, slowly but surely, she lowered herself onto his pulsating, rock-hard length.

"Oh . . ." Arabella moaned her delight at the same moment Gabriel hissed with pleasure.

"Sweet Jesus, you feel good," he groaned against her throat, the drift of his hot breath making her shiver. One hand came up to grip her nape beneath her tangled, tumbling hair. "So tight, so wet . . ." He kissed her mouth. "So perfect." Drawing back a little, his gaze bore into hers. "Love me, Bella."

She cradled his jaw with tender fingers. "Always."

Arabella set up a slow, gentle, rocking rhythm at first, her sheath gripping her husband's shaft in the most intimate of caresses. But it wasn't long before the hunger for more took over. The pace of their coupling increased as both of them chased after bliss. Gabriel captured her about the waist and thrust his powerful hips, while Arabella frantically plunged up and down on his hammering cock. The velvet night was filled with her desperate pants and Gabriel's guttural groans.

This perfect union, this shared intimacy, this spiraling wild pleasure, this was all she'd ever want or ever need. And she knew that to be true for Gabriel too.

Soon the exquisite friction of Gabriel's driving thrusts sent Arabella over the edge into the waiting arms of ecstasy. Clutching his shoulders, she shuddered and sobbed his name. Gabriel pumped into her once, then twice more, and with an exultant cry, he fell into pleasure too.

Burying his hands in her hair, Gabriel leaned his forehead against hers. At length, when his breathing slowed, he drew back. His eyes shone with tears and adoration as he whispered, "I love you. And this . . ." He reached for Arabella's hand and placed it on his chest where his heart beat steady and true. "This will be yours even when the stars no longer burn and the sun ceases to shine."

Unable to speak, her own heart brimming with untold happiness and boundless love, Arabella's lips trembled in a smile. Because there wasn't a doubt in her mind that her husband spoke the absolute truth.

TURN THE PAGE FOR A LOOK AT
AMY ROSE BENNETT'S NEXT BOOK . . .

HOW TO CATCH A SINFUL MARQUESS

DUE OUT IN FALL 2020.

Town might be quiet at the moment, but the *Beau Monde Mirror* will endeavor to keep our readership abreast of all the latest tonnish on-dits.

If there's a scandal brewing—an illicit affair, an elopement, or someone high in the instep puts a foot wrong—you can be sure we'll let the proverbial cat out of the bag first.

The Beau Monde Mirror: The Society Page

16 Grosvenor Square, Mayfair

September 14, 1818

If it weren't for Lady Charlotte Hastings's troublesome tortoiseshell cat, Olivia de Vere would not be in such a mortifying predicament right now.

Of course, if Charlie were actually here at this very moment (as opposed to being miles away at her father's country estate in Gloucestershire) she would surely tell Olivia that her current situation—straddling the six-foot-high, ivy-clad wall adjoining the Marquess of Sleat's back garden as she made a futile attempt to coax said cat from the branches of a towering beech tree—was an "opportunity," not a disaster waiting to happen.

Olivia shot a quick glance at the back of her guardians' rather grand town house. Or, to be more precise, *her* town house, considering the rent was drawn from her very own inheritance money, currently held "in trust." When she ascertained that no one was watching her, she permitted herself a tiny sigh of relief. If Uncle Reginald or Aunt Edith caught her committing such an indecorous act, or her cousins Prudence and Patience, or even worse, her warden-cum-lady's maid, Bagshaw . . . Olivia shuddered. There would be the devil to pay, that much was certain.

Ever since she'd been expelled from Mrs. Rathbone's Academy for Young Ladies of Good Character three years ago for decidedly unladylike conduct—along with the other three members of the Society for Enlightened Young Women, Sophie, Arabella, and Charlie—she'd been mired in disgrace and labeled a social pariah. A "disreputable debutante," according to scurrilous gossip rags like the *Beau Monde Mirror*.

She really couldn't afford to court disaster again.

But it seemed that's exactly what she was doing.

Her gaze flitted to Lord Sleat's town house. Now, if the forbidding yet altogether fascinating marquess happened to discover what she was up to . . . Olivia shivered again. While she longed to make the man's acquaintance, this was *not* a prudent way to go about it by any means.

As Lord Sleat was a good friend of Lord Malverne—Sophie's husband and Charlie's older brother—Olivia had it on good authority that the Scottish marquess was considered to be a very eligible bachelor indeed. Of course, Lord Sleat also had a well-earned reputation for being one of London's worst rakehells. A serial seducer of women.

However, Olivia was certain the marquess wouldn't even spare her a passing glance at this particular moment in time. With her skirts and petticoats rucked up about her knees, her silk stockings torn and smeared with something mucky and green—moss, perhaps—she looked an absolute fright. Not only that, what she was doing certainly bordered on trespassing.

If Lord Sleat *did* see her, he'd be well within his rights to summon the Bow Street Runners.

But what could she do? She absolutely had to rescue her dear friend's beloved pet. If Peridot fell or escaped into the mews . . . Visions of the cat darting between carriages and horses' hooves or being stalked by a lascivious tomcat filled Olivia's mind, and her whole body trembled like the dark green leaves above her head.

Despite her edict to the servants that Peridot should not be let out unless accompanied, the cat had somehow slipped into the garden on her own. When Olivia looked up from the pages of *Northanger Abbey*—she'd been reading in her bedchamber after dinner—and spied Peridot leaping from the wall into the tree, her heart had taken flight like a panicked bird.

And now here she was, her heart still fluttering wildly, her belly tumbling with fear, and her head spinning with dizziness whenever she looked down. How inconvenient that she'd belatedly discovered she was terrified of heights. She huffed out a breath to blow a stray lock of hair away from her face. She daren't let go of the brick wall, lest she fall. She'd already lost one of her shoes; in the process of clambering onto her precarious perch, her pink silk slipper had slid off her foot and landed in a dense, rather prickly looking bank of rosebushes guarding the perimeter of Lord Sleat's garden.

On her side of the wall, the stone bench she'd climbed upon looked far away indeed. And part of the ivy-choked latticework she'd used as a makeshift ladder had already cracked ominously beneath her weight. But she really couldn't afford to panic about how she'd get down. First of all, she had to reach that blasted cat, and quickly. The light was fading fast, and it wouldn't be long before her presence was missed.

Olivia drew a bracing breath. "P-P-Peridot." Her stammer was little more than a ragged whisper. "Here, p-puss, puss. There's a good k-kitty now." Knees trembling, heart pounding, she forced herself to inch forward along the wall so she could peer up into the beech canopy.

There. Directly above her on a sturdy branch, but just out of reach, sat Peridot, her black, white, and tan fur barely visible in the shadows. The cat's fluffy tail twitched when Olivia called her again. A disdainful gesture if she'd ever seen one.

Little minx. If Olivia survived this foolhardy escapade, she was going to pack Peridot into her basket and send her back to Berkeley Square posthaste. Let the Hastings House staff deal with their young mistress's cat. Charlie meant well when she'd suggested in her last letter that Olivia might like to look after Peridot for a few weeks until Charlie returned to London in the first week of October. On the surface, her reasoning was sound: a pet would provide Olivia with congenial company and affection, as well as being a source of amusement—three things that were sorely lacking in her life.

Ignoring the scrape of the brickwork along the tender flesh of her inner thighs, Olivia crept forward again. And then the hem of her muslin gown snagged on something, and she winced at the sound of fabric tearing.

Damn, damn, and double damn again.

How on earth was she going to explain the damage to Bagshaw? She'd be sure to tattle to Aunt Edith, who'd tell Uncle Reginald.

And then she'd be punished.

But at least Peridot will be safe—

"Ahem."

The low, unmistakable sound of an adult male clearing his throat made Olivia simultaneously jump and squeak with fright.

Oh, no. No, no, no. Her heart plummeting like a dislodged stone, Olivia's gaze whipped down to meet that of a man. But not just any man.

It was the Marquess of Sleat. The very object of her girlish infatuation.

The subject of all her silly, romantical dreams.

In the flesh.

And what flesh it was. Well over six feet of muscular, broad-shouldered, square-jawed man glowered up at her.

Her grip tightened on the wall. Her pulse stuttered and heat flared in her cheeks. Mortified didn't even begin to describe how she felt.

Horrified would be closer to the mark. Definitely shaken and utterly speechless.

She'd never seen Lord Sleat this close up before. Indeed, she'd only ever glimpsed him at a distance as he quit his town house before striding off down Grosvenor Square or climbing into his coach. And there'd been that one occasion when he'd lounged on the stone-flagged terrace overlooking this very garden. In the summer gloaming, she'd spied the glowing tip of his cheroot cigar and the flash of amber liquid—perhaps whisky—as the light of the setting sun glanced off his raised glass.

Charlie had once described him as being the epitome of a Highland warrior crossed with a pirate. As Olivia continued to gawp in awkward dismay at the marquess, she decided her friend's assessment was quite accurate. A thick sweep of sable hair falling across his brow partially obscured a jagged scar and the black leather patch covering his left eye socket. His other eye, the iris a dark storm-cloud gray, pinned her with a hard, distinctly sardonic stare.

"Two thoughts spring to mind." Lord Sleat's baritone voice and Scot's burr coalesced into a rich deep rumble that Olivia swore she could feel vibrate through her body like a roll of distant thunder. "First of all, what the devil are you doing? And secondly, how the hell did a wee lassie like you get up there?"

One dark eyebrow arched as he waited for Olivia to respond, and for a moment, she wondered if she'd misjudged the marquess's mood; she swore she glimpsed a quicksilver flash of humor in his gaze.

Amused or not, she still had to answer. She swallowed to moisten her dry-as-a-desert mouth. To undo the knots from her perpetually tangled tongue. "I . . . I . . . I . . . I . . ." She screwed her eyes shut as she attempted to wrestle a coherent sentence loose. "I . . . My f-f-friend's c-cat is . . ." Lifting a trembling hand, she pointed at the branches overhead. "Peri . . . P-Peridot . . ." Her mouth twisted with frustration. "Sh-Sh-She's s-s-stuck . . . She's stuck up there."

As Lord Sleat crossed his arms over his wide chest, the fabric of his navy blue jacket pulled tight across the impressive swell of bunched bicep muscles beneath. "You're trying to rescue your friend's cat." Judging by his flat tone and skeptical frown, the marquess clearly doubted the veracity of her statement.

Nevertheless, Olivia nodded. "Y-yes."

He took several steps closer to the wall and his gaze shifted to the beech tree. "Are you sure she's stuck?" He squinted up into the gently waving branches. "It's been my experience that cats can generally look after them—"

At that precise moment, Peridot elegantly sprang from her leafy hidey-hole onto the wall. With another contemptuous flick of her tail, she then leapt to the ground, landing right beside Lord Sleat's shiny black Hessians.

Olivia's jaw dropped. She'd never seen a cat perform such a daring feat with such alacrity. She suddenly felt like the biggest fool in Christendom.

To make matters worse, Peridot began to purr and blatantly rub her body all over the marquess's boots. Her tail twined between his legs, as though she was claiming possession of the man.

Charlie's cat wasn't a little minx at all. She was a brazen minx.

Lord Sleat bent low and scooped Peridot into his arms. The cat's purring grew louder, and when the marquess stroked her beneath the chin with one long finger, she closed her bright green eyes and rubbed her fluffy cheek against his paisley satin waistcoat as if she were in the throes of ecstasy.

Good Lord, what a hussy of a cat.

As Olivia scowled down at Peridot, Lord Sleat spoke. "Well, all's well that ends well it would seem . . . except for the fact that you are still stuck on my wall, Miss . . ." He cocked an eyebrow again.

Olivia drew a steadying breath in order to control her stammer. It wasn't usually this pronounced. However, the stress of trying to retrieve Peridot, combined with her newly discovered fear of heights, and coming face-to-face with an overwhelmingly masculine marquess whom she'd been secretly daydreaming about for several months—all of these things were wreaking havoc on her equilibrium. Not to mention the fact that Lord Sleat's attention had drifted to her bared lower leg and slipperless foot. It seemed Peridot wasn't the only one being brazen. But Lord Sleat was a rake after all.

Her face aflame, Olivia at last summoned her voice. "Oh-Oliv-liv . . ."

"Lavinia?" supplied Lord Sleat as his gaze met hers again.

Olivia only just suppressed a sigh. She supposed the marquess was only trying to be helpful by supplying the rest of her name . . . even if he'd got it wrong.

But what was the point in trying to correct him or providing her surname so he could address her as Miss de Vere, as decorum dictated? Despite the fact they were neighbors, it was highly unlikely that she'd ever have such a close and personal encounter with this man again. Not unless her martinet of an uncle and her equally exacting aunt could be persuaded to let her attend any ton social events.

Charlie, Sophie, and Arabella might try to matchmake when they all returned to town next month, but Olivia suspected it would all come to naught. So, she simply smiled and nodded her agreement. Lavinia would do.

"Well, Miss Lavinia," continued the marquess. A crooked smile tugged at the corner of his wide mouth. "Would you like me to help you down?"

This time, Olivia did manage to find her voice. "Oh, yes, p-please, Lord Sleat. I'd be m-most grateful."

He promptly deposited Peridot on the lawn. "You know who I am?" he said as he straightened and pushed his way into the evil-looking rosebushes bordering the wall. His snug-fitting buckskin breeches and Hessians clearly provided his legs with adequate protection, as he seemed oblivious to the thorns.

Olivia nodded. "Of course, my lord. D-doesn't everyone in London know you?"

He flashed a wolfish grin as he reached toward her. His large hands settled about her waist, holding her steady. "It seems my reputation precedes me, Miss Lavinia. Now, if you'd be so kind as to swing your other leg over to this side. That's it. And hold onto my shoulders. Ready? Because here we go."

Before Olivia could even draw another breath, the mar
quess's grip tightened on her middle and she suddenly
found herself suspended in the air. In the next instant, he
made a deft turn and lowered her to the ground in a long,
slow, effortless slide, her body grazing the length of his.
She was acutely aware of his body's heat. Its granite-like
hardness. The power of his arms and the shifting contour
of his mountainous shoulders beneath her hands. By the
time her feet touched the grass, she was more than a little
breathless and her pulse was racing so fast, she felt giddy.

To combat the wave of dizziness, she closed her eyes,
her hands lingering about the marquess's neck. Given that
his hands remained about her waist, he didn't seem in any
hurry to relinquish his hold either.

Thick silky hair brushed the backs of her fingers. His
distinctive masculine scent—a potent mix of leather, musk,
and exotic spices—teased her senses and for one mad mo
ment, she contemplated pressing her face against his shirt
front, just so she could get closer to him.

No wonder Peridot had looked so beatific in his arms.
He smelled divine.

"Are you all right, Miss Lavinia?" Lord Sleat's voice
was no longer a gruff rumble, but low and soft like a lion's
gentle purr.

Olivia forced herself to open her eyes and take a step
back. How fanciful she was becoming. Not to mention
shameless. She might already have a sullied reputation in the
eyes of her family and polite society, but she really shouldn't
risk making it worse. "Y-yes. I'm quite f-fine," she stam
mered. Her cheeks bloomed with heat as she realized the
marquess might think she'd actually swooned in his arms.

Lord Sleat frowned down at her. "Not quite, lass," he
said, plucking her pink slipper from a nearby rosebush.
Then, before she knew what he was about, he knelt down
on the grass and, like the prince in a fairy tale, he slid her
slipper onto her foot. His touch seemed to sear through the
silk of her stocking to the flesh beneath, making her shiver
with awareness. Looking up at her, his mouth curved in

ecidedly rakish smile as he relinquished her ankle. "Now everything's just right."

Olivia swallowed and her blush deepened. "Th-thank ou." Was the marquess deliberately trying to make her woon again? Because if he was, he was very close to succeeding.

She really should go.

Something tugged the back of her muslin gown and when she glanced down, it was to discover Peridot had ounced on the torn flounce trailing from her hem. Naughty uss. She picked up the cat and bobbed a quick curtsy. "My ord, I thank you again for your . . . for your assistance. But 's time P-Peridot and I bid you adieu."

He inclined his head. "Of course." He gestured toward he terrace and the open French doors. The shadows had engthened, and candles and lamps glowed warmly in the egant drawing room beyond. "Let me escort you out."

Olivia froze. "Oh." She shook her head. "I d-don't ink . . . Is there by any ch-chance another way? A gate ading to the m-mews? I don't mean to cause offense, but s you are a b-bachelor, and I am . . ."—she lifted her hin—"and I am unchaperoned, it m-might invite unwanted ttention if I leave via your front door." Good Lord, if her unt and uncle's priggish butler, Mr. Finch, caught sight of er leaving Sleat House, she'd be done for.

Lord Sleat nodded. "Ah yes, you are absolutely right. A iscreet exit would be wise. Come." He began walking to-ard the end of the garden with long, sure strides, and Olivia ad to rush to keep up. "Let me show you something."

He stopped before a narrow gap in a waist-high box-ood hedge. Ivy cascaded over the top of the wall like a imbling, verdant waterfall. "See here." With a sweep of is arm, Lord Sleat roughly pushed aside the heavy green urtain. "There's actually a secret gate connecting these wo gardens, but it hasn't been used in years."

Peering into the shadowed recess, Olivia blinked in sur-rise. "My goodness." Sure enough, a small door of weath-red gray wood had been neatly concealed in the brickwork.

Ivy, moss, and lichen had crept their way over the paneling and the ornate, wrought-iron hinges were rusted with age.

Lord Sleat tugged at some of the ivy tendrils curling around the bolt. "I believe one of my wicked forebears had it installed so that he and his mistress—who resided next door—could conduct their clandestine affair more easily." Lord Sleat flashed a grin over his shoulder. "Shocking, I know. Especially considering the lady in question was married."

Oh.

The marquess jostled the bolt, and with a begrudging, wince-inducing grate, it slid back. Then, after delivering a small kick with his booted foot, he pushed the gate open on protesting hinges.

"There we are," Lord Sleat said with a gentlemanly bow. "I trust this serves your needs."

"Yes, it d-does. Most adequately." Transferring Peridot to one arm, Olivia held her torn skirt with her other hand and dipped into another small curtsy. "Thank you again, my lord. For everything."

"The pleasure has been all mine, I assure you." He caught her hand and brushed a kiss over the back of her fingers, making Olivia blush to the roots of her hair. "And just in case you ever need to rescue Peridot again," he said, winking, "I'll leave the gate unlocked."

Olivia inclined her head. "You're too kind."

He laughed and mischief glinted in his eye. "You wouldn't say that if you really knew me, lass." Leaning closer, he added in a seductive, velvet-soft voice, "I'm afraid wickedness runs in the family, so you'd best leave before a sinful scoundrel like me is tempted to ruin more than just your reputation. Farewell, my lovely Lavinia."

Goodness. She couldn't quite believe a man like Lord Sleat was flirting with tangle-tongued, quiet-as-a-church-mouse Olivia de Vere. She muttered a stammered farewell in return, then ducked through the small gateway and the curtain of ivy on the other side. When she emerged into the garden, she heard the door scrape shut. And her heart fell

t the thought that she might never see her mysterious marquess again.

With a heavy sigh, she rounded a small knot of rosebushes and made her way back to the house with Peridot in
her arms. No, she wouldn't let disappointment weigh her
down. Because even if Bagshaw tore strips off her, and her
aunt and uncle locked her away in her room for the next
week, she would not regret a single thing.

She'd finally met Lord Sleat and he was everything she'd
imagined him to be—ruggedly handsome and roguish, yet
essentially a gentleman. A small smile played at the corner
of her mouth. The memory of their fleeting yet thoroughly
stimulating encounter would sustain her for many a long,
lonely night to come, of that she was certain.

However, all her pleasant musings about Lord Sleat fled
when she gained the upper gallery leading to the bedcham-
bers. To avoid her aunt, uncle, and cousins, she'd given the
drawing room and the library a wide berth. Indeed, she
didn't encounter anyone besides a pair of housemaids lighting the last of the upstairs lamps . . . until she reached her
room.

No sooner had she turned the brass handle than another
door a bit farther along clicked open. And then a voice she
dreaded and loathed in equal measure floated down the hall
like a malevolent spirit.

"O-liv-liv-livia . . ." The singsong taunt and the mocking
tone were all too familiar. "How are you, my sweet little
c-c-cuz?"

Damn, blast, and drat. Olivia opened her bedroom door
and pushed Peridot inside before turning around to face her
cousin, Felix de Vere. The veritable bane of her existence.

The man her aunt and uncle wanted her to marry to keep
her fortune within the de Vere family forever.

When pigs fly. Tamping down her dislike and dismay as
best she could, Olivia pasted a neutral expression on her
face as she forced herself to meet Felix's frost blue gaze. He
swaggered toward her in his perfectly tailored ton buck
attire—purchased with her inheritance money, no doubt—

then propped a shoulder against the beveled oak doorjamb. He was so close—crowding her in, attempting to intimidat her—she could smell the brandy on his breath. See th glints of gold in his evening beard.

For a man who was five-and-twenty, he was as imma ture as a playground bully. Not to mention as vain as peacock.

"You-you've returned f-from abroad," she stated a smoothly as she could. Considering her pulse was skitte ing around like a panicked field mouse about to be set upo by a weasel, she was surprised she could make her mout work at all.

He smirked as he tossed a thick wave of tawny hair ou of his eyes. "Clearly. But you haven't answered my ques tion." His insolent gaze traveled down her body and then h laughed. "Good God, Livvie, you look like you've bee tupped. Torn skirts. Flushed cheeks. Disheveled hair." T emphasize his point, he plucked an ivy leaf from the top her head and crushed it between his long fingers befor dropping it on the Turkish runner. "What have you bee up to?"

Olivia's face grew hotter. Despite her best efforts to loo him in the eye, her gaze slipped to his elaborately style ivory cravat. "If you m-must know, I was rescuing m friend's c-cat from a tree. In the back g-garden."

"Rescuing a cat?" he scoffed, crossing one booted ankl over the other. "You must be joking."

Olivia lifted her chin. "Of course I'm n-not. It belong to Lady Charlotte Hastings, Lord Westhampton's daught and the Marchioness of Chelmsford's n-niece. She's awa at the moment and—"

Felix raised his hand. "Enough. I don't care who owns or why you're looking after it. Just make sure it doesn't g under my feet or I'll snap its scrawny neck." He clicked h fingers with a loud snap. "Like that." Leaning closer, h lowered his voice. "You know I will, c-c-cuz."

Olivia swallowed and her hands curled into fists. Sh didn't doubt him for a minute. She'd seen Felix kick Unc Reginald's hunting dogs when he'd thought no one wa looking. Cruelty ran through his veins, of that she was certain. "You really are de-de-de—"

Before she could complete the word despicable, he gave a snort of laughter and chucked her under the chin. "Delightful. Yes, I know. Goodnight, c-c-cuz. Dream of me, won't you?" He dipped his head and whispered in her ear. "Now that I'm back, you know it won't be long until you're mine."

With that, he pushed away from the door and strolled back down the hall, humming an indistinct but jaunty tune.

Alone in her room, Olivia gently scooped Peridot off the damask-covered window seat and into her lap.

"Don't worry, puss. I won't let Felix hurt you," she murmured. The cat purred as Olivia ran her fingers through her soft-as-silk fur. Tears of despair burned her eyes.

What on earth was she going to do?

Aunt Edith and Uncle Reginald had been dropping not-so-subtle hints for at least a year that the day would come when she would have to marry, and that the natural choice—actually, the only real choice she had for a husband—was Felix. Who else would want to marry a wicked hussy who'd been caught red-handed smoking cigars and swilling spirits while poring over shockingly lewd books and pictures at a young ladies' academy?

After Olivia had been expelled from Mrs. Rathbone's school, and the scandal had spread far and wide, her aunt and uncle had been so appalled and ashamed of her that she'd been denied any sort of real Season for three years running. And so had Prudence and Patience, much to their unrelenting chagrin.

Olivia sensed their resentment every time she walked into the room. The way they excluded her from conversations. Openly sniggered whenever she tripped over her words, which was often. She'd been relegated to the role of "poor, put-upon companion," at the beck and call of her cousins and her aunt to perform the most menial, mundane tasks. Always overlooked, and frequently banished from their company when they grew tired of her presence.

Even then there was little reprieve given that she also

had to contend with the constant scrutiny of the dour and pernickety Miss Agnes Bagshaw. While she'd ostensibly been employed as a lady's maid for Patience and Prudence, the woman seemed to spend an inordinate amount of time monitoring Olivia's activities and snitching to Aunt Edith if she happened to "step out-of-bounds." Ruining a gown, as she'd just done, would be enough to ensure that she was confined to her room for at least a day with only the simplest of fare for meals.

There were times when Olivia felt as though the lowliest maid in her uncle and aunt's household was afforded more respect and consideration. Things would have been so different if her parents were still alive . . .

Unbidden tears welled in Olivia's eyes. They'd both been killed in a terrible carriage accident five years ago and she missed their loving presence keenly. Indeed, it was a constant ache in her heart. She hated thinking about that day and all the might-have-beens. It hurt far too much.

Besides, dwelling on the past wouldn't help her now.

Olivia emitted a despondent sigh and put Peridot aside. She really should change out of her torn gown and into her night rail. And then she'd attempt to remove the stains from her silk stockings before Bagshaw discovered the damage. She hadn't any salt, but with any luck, soap, warm water and a small soft brush would do the trick.

Settling on the low chair before her cherrywood dressing table, Olivia took down her hair. She couldn't bear her melancholy reflection in the looking glass, so she dropped her gaze to the small pile of pins growing in front of her.

Things could be worse, she told herself. At least she had real friends in the world who did care for her. Unfortunately, the number of occasions she'd been allowed to socialize with Charlie, Sophie, and Arabella since the academy incident had been few and far between. A mere handful of rare, treasured moments that she held safe in her heart like all the precious mementos in her keepsake box.

A small, sad smile curved her lips. Perhaps she should keep a section of the torn flounce as a special reminder of her encounter with Lord Sleat. She'd much rather marry a noble, kindhearted man like him.

A vivid memory of a glowing Sophie and her handsome, besotted bridegroom, Lord Malverne, suddenly entered her mind's eye. In June, Lady Chelmsford had persuaded Aunt Edith and Uncle Reginald to let Olivia attend Sophie's wedding at Lord Malverne's lovely country estate in Gloucestershire. Lady Chelmsford, who'd acted as her chaperone, had promised to procure Almack's vouchers for Prudence and Patience next Season if her aunt and uncle agreed to the arrangement. It had been the perfect enticement; Aunt Edith hadn't been able to resist.

Sadly, Lord Sleat hadn't been at the wedding. Or Arabella; she'd been in Switzerland, where she'd met and married Gabriel, Lord Langdale. By all accounts, both she and Lord Langdale were deliriously in love. Just like Sophie and her adoring viscount.

Olivia began to ruthlessly braid her brown hair. It would not be like that with Felix. He despised her, and it was abundantly clear he only wanted her for one thing—her fortune. Marriage to him would be intolerable. But it had been easy to brush it all aside—his odious presence and her aunt and uncle's insidious hints—when Felix had been away at university, and more recently when he'd embarked on a Grand Tour of the Continent this summer.

But now he was back . . . Olivia shuddered and gazed at her own reflection, her pale face pinched with worry, her dark eyes solemn. No one should have to marry against his or her will.

But what if Uncle Reginald and Aunt Edith do try to force you to marry Felix, Olivia de Vere? What will you do then?

The terrifying answer was: she really had no idea.